New Beg

The Birdie

CW00523579

Alison Craig is an award-winning radio and TV presenter from Scotland. She was a presenter on *The One Show* and hosted many other programmes on BBC and independent radio and TV when a health issue stopped her in her tracks.

Since then, she has concentrated on writing the result of which is *New Beginnings at The Birdie and Bramble*, her first novel.

Alison's married and lives with her husband David and sausage dog Charlie in Edinburgh. She has one grown-up son Louis, who can found in his own flat or in Alison's fridge inhaling the contents.

Twitter: @Alisonsdiary
Instagram: @Alisonsdiary
Facebook.com/Alisonsdiary

Also by Alison Craig

Blue Skies at The Birdie and Bramble
Snowdrops at The Birdie and Bramble

New Beginnings at
The Birdie and Bramble

Alison Craig

First published in Great Britain in 2021 by Orion Dash,
an imprint of The Orion Publishing Group Ltd.,
Carmelite House, 50 Victoria Embankment,
London EC4Y 0DZ

An Hachette UK Company

1 3 5 7 9 10 8 6 4 2

Copyright © Alison Craig 2021

The moral right of Alison Craig to be identified as
the author of this work has been asserted in accordance
with the Copyright, Designs and Patents Act of 1988.

All rights reserved. No part of this publication may be
reproduced, stored in a retrieval system, or transmitted
in any form or by any means, electronic, mechanical,
photocopying, recording, or otherwise, without the
prior permission of both the copyright owner and the
above publisher of this book.

All the characters in this book are fictitious, and any resemblance
to actual persons, living or dead, is purely coincidental.

A CIP catalogue record for this book is
available from the British Library.

ISBN (Mass Market Paperback): 978 1 3987 0919 5
ISBN (eBook): 978 1 4091 9554 2

Typeset at The Spartan Press Ltd,
Lymington, Hants

www.orionbooks.co.uk

To David Howie Scott, with love and thanks.

Chapter 1

Half asleep, hair damp and out of control, I'm speed walking to the tube, like millions of other Londoners, on my way to work. Well when I say Londoner, I'm actually from Scotland but I've been down here nearly three years so I like to think I'm getting the hang of it.

For instance, when I get on the tube at Clapham South I go the wrong way. Intentionally. I know it sounds like I'm off my head but the fact is, if I go to the end of the line I can get a seat so when the train heads back into London I'm all set. By the time it stops at Clapham South I'm all tucked in, reading my book and watching as a few brave contortionists snake, twist and push their way into the jammed carriage. To be honest it's hell, which is why over time I have developed the Top Five Golden Rules for Tube Travel for visiting friends and family.

They are as follows:

Rule 1.
  Avoid eye contact. Don't speak to people. Don't say good morning. And for God's sake don't smile. Or you will be regarded as an alien or end up with a stalker.
Rule 2.
  Carry reading material. A Kindle, a copy of *Metro*, the back of a packet of fags, anything rather than catch the eye of the staring man.

Rule 3.

There is always a staring man. There is one on every tube, and at rush hour I suspect, every carriage, and Sod's Law you will end up opposite or next to him; so eyes down at all times, especially if you've ignored my advice in Rule 2.

Rule 4.

Download an app to keep you calm. This means if the train stops, for instance, under the River Thames on the ancient Northern Line, it will stop you hyperventilating as you imagine the millions of tons of water pressing down on you, in the dark tunnel you are now trapped in. This will also reduce the possibility that you will grasp the arm of the alarmed woman next to you and burst out crying. So all you have to do is calmly pop in your earbuds, close your eyes and do some deep-breathing exercises.

Rule 5.

Never travel back on the tube if you've had a skinful late at night, as the odds are you will fall asleep and end up travelling back and forth on the underground all night or until such time as you wake up at a random stop and/or are murdered.

I learnt all of the above through personal experience, apart from the last one. And just to clarify, I have fallen asleep for hours on the tube but I have not been murdered. Obviously.

So I reckon I've almost cracked the whole tube thing although as usual, despite leaving over an hour for my journey this particular morning, I was late. Again.

Arriving to the raised eyebrow of my nemesis and boss Felicity, I gave her a cheery smile, which she ignored, so I speedily made for my desk. Plopping my bag down I spotted a major ladder in my tights, from the ankle right up past my knee.

'Bollocks,' I muttered.

'And bollocks to you too,' said a grinning Marcus, passing my desk at that exact moment.

I felt my face redden and smiled back. He winked and walked on. Company policy was no relationships within the office.

'Don't shit on your own doorstep,' was how it had been delicately put during induction.

I had no intention of doing any such thing.

Until Marcus. We had been seeing each other for nine and a half months. Well more than seeing to be honest.

The moment we met, the equivalent of the Disney fireworks went off in my nether regions and I could not get enough of him. He appeared to feel the same way and so we ignored company policy, launching headlong into a very physical relationship. Half the fun was the furtive looks and secret assignations, regularly emerging from the boardroom, staff kitchen, a lift jammed between floors, an empty office, one after the other, flushed. The quest to remain undetected became our raison d'être – it was thrilling. Part of our elaborate dance was that we virtually ignored each other when there was anyone else in the room, which was how I was fairly sure we had avoided detection thus far.

It wasn't easy. One reason being the aforementioned nemesis and pain in the arse Felicity.

Felicity and I had started at Go Radio on the same day as graduate marketing trainees three years ago and being fellow newbies, I naively thought we'd be allies. But it was clear from day one she was ruthlessly ambitious, as I watched her ingratiating herself with the powers that be in a laughably obvious fashion, giggling and carrying on like a helium-filled pony. Amused, I watched from a distance then was astounded when about a year ago she stomped over to my desk on her vertiginous wedges and announced she was being promoted to Marketing Executive so would now be my boss. She said it with humour but the way she licked her lips I just knew she was going to relish her new-found power. And she did, bossing me around, undermining my contributions at marketing meetings and just yesterday when I tried to talk to her, she actually held her hand up in front of my face indicating I should shut up until she was ready to hear what I had to say. I was spitting feathers.

The one thing that made working in the same office bearable was Marcus. She had no idea we were involved and she bloody loved him. As he was an advertising salesman she had no direct dealings with him but she would jump at the chance to talk to him and whenever he was on our floor, her eyes followed him like a vulture. He was well aware of the power he held over her and of what a bitch she was to me, so we would exchange knowing glances, just before he flashed his superstar grin in her direction, which always elicited an almost Tourette's-like whinny of appreciation. This morning was no exception.

'God, Marcus is looking particularly hot this morning,' she mooned, letting her guard down momentarily as he disappeared out of sight.

'Is he? I didn't notice,' I said, stifling a grin, head down and fiddling about in my bottom drawer and retrieving the spare pair of tights I kept for such emergencies.

So the morning began very much like any other really.

Loads of emails needing attention, regular coffee machine trips to catch up on the latest chat and a brief interlude in the stationery cupboard with Marcus, which came to a very abrupt end as Felicity marched in unannounced. Without missing a beat, Marcus deliberately knocked over a box of pens causing enough of a distraction for me to leave as he crouched down to gather them all up. Felicity dropped to her knees willingly to help.

Holding back a snort of laughter, I wandered back to my desk, feeling more than a little hot under the collar when I felt my mobile phone, on silent, buzzing in my pocket.

Personal mobiles were frowned upon during hours of business but everyone pretty much ignored that policy too.

Glancing down at the screen I recognised the prefix as St Andrews, my home town in Scotland. Although I didn't recognise the actual number, I decided to pick up.

'Maddy?' said a familiar voice.

'Yes?'

'Hello, dear. It's Uncle Ted.'

My gut plunged. My dad's oldest and dearest friend never phoned me. Ever.

'I'm afraid I've got some bad news, dear. It's your dad.'

Silence.

'Maddy?'

I didn't need to hear the actual words – gut instinct and worst fears took over – but hear the words I did.

'There is no easy way to say this, darling. I'm so sorry to have to tell you – he died this morning.'

With those words, my world shifted on its axis.

As I was unable to speak, Uncle Ted picked up the slack. 'We were playing golf, and he just keeled over on the eighteenth green. It was instant. It was as if someone flicked a switch.' He clicked his fingers. 'Out he went, just like that. He sank his putt to win the hole and he just dropped there and then. He knew nothing about it.'

'Oh God, what a shock ... Are you all right? When did it happen?'

'Just after ten this morning.'

I looked at the clock; it was just before twelve.

'Who was with him?'

'The usual Monday foursome: me, Fraser and Stevie.'

His brother-in-law and his best friends in the world, friends since the day they started school together some sixty-five years earlier.

'Are they OK?'

'Well, obviously everyone's very upset as you can imagine but never mind us, it's you we're worried about.'

Numb. Speechless. In shock. Poor Ted didn't know what else to say. Hours seemed to pass. Finally he broke the silence. 'OK, darling. You need time to take this all in, so I'll leave you to collect your thoughts. Phone me back when you can.'

Felicity, give her credit, instantly understood something was very wrong and chose not to admonish me for using my personal mobile. Instead she watched me silently.

Marcus wandered past and, though he looked concerned, was apparently unwilling to acknowledge me in public, so with a quizzical look he ambled past.

Like an automaton I blurted it out: 'My father's dead,' and burst into tears, after which Felicity took over. She demanded someone make me a cup of hot sweet tea, ordered a contract taxi to take me back to my flat, told the driver to wait whilst I collected my belongings and then to drop me off at King's Cross Station. I hugged her tightly, feeling her stiffen under my grip, and thanked her profusely as she bundled me into the cab.

The journey north was something I usually relished but not today. I texted Ted to let him know what train I was on and then, avoiding the eye of the woman opposite me who looked like she wanted to chat, laid my head against the window. I watched inner-city London slide past until the light changed as the train snaked up the east coast revealing the North Sea and green open countryside. I was on my way home to Scotland. My heart had never felt so heavy.

My last conversation with Dad had been Saturday, 7.30 p.m. The only person who ever used the landline was Dad, so when it rang I answered it with a breezy 'Hi, Dad!'

'Hello, darling!' his voice boomed warmly down the line. 'How are you doing?'

'Great thanks.'

'Lovely, I was just …' BZZZZZZZ. The front door intercom cut through our conversation.

'Oh Dad, sorry – that's the buzzer. It's Marcus in an Uber. He wasn't due for another ten minutes. I'm sorr—'

BZZZZZZ. I cringed with irritation. He was so impatient. 'Och don't you worry – off you go,' Dad said.

'I'll give you a shout tomorrow night …'

'OK, darlin', now off you go and enjoy yourself!'

'Thanks, Dad. Lots of love,' I'd chirped and without hearing his response replaced the receiver, rushing off without another thought.

Of course Saturday night with Marcus had gone into the wee small hours, which ruined Sunday morning, and by the time we crawled out of bed, brunch with friends was on the cards. Still feeling delicate, after that we sloped off to the cinema and by the time I got back to the flat it was far too late to phone Dad and, being honest, it hadn't even crossed my mind.

Hot tears welled; my chest tightened.

At any point on Sunday night I could have picked up the phone and called Dad. But I didn't. Having had such a heavy weekend, once I got back from the cinema I had run a bath and lain there, eating four slices of toasted cheese. After that I felt so gross I took root on the sofa to watch a couple of episodes of *Game of Thrones* and, prodding my podgy boozy tummy and feeling remorse for my lack of self-control, the last thing I wanted to do was talk to anyone. If that was all, I could have lived with it but, my heart beat quickened, as I lay there beached on the couch staring at the screen, the landline rang.

I knew it was Dad – the only one who uses my landline. I knew it was him and yet there I lay like a slob, looking at the phone ringing and thinking, 'Bugger it, I'll phone him tomorrow. I'm too tired.' Slightly irritated as the ringing obscured the dialogue, I pressed pause on the TV and har-rumphed and lay there listening as it clicked onto answer and his gruff warm tones radiated round the room, 'Hi Maddy, it's just Dad. No message, just phoning to say hello. Hello!' He chuckled as he replaced the receiver.

Phoning to say hello, and goodbye, as it turned out.

My gut twisted. I was finding it hard to breathe.

Christ, when was the last time I had spoken to him prop-erly? The horror of not being able to actually pinpoint that moment was too much to cope with. Had I really taken him for granted that much?

We saw each other at Christmas. Well when I say see, I arrived on Christmas Eve about 6 p.m., jumped in the shower and was off to the pub with Sarah and some of my old school friends at speed. An annual tradition that despite being twenty-nine was still adhered to. Dad knew that only too well. Every year I did it. So he knew I wouldn't get back in until after closing time, and would be so hungover on Christmas Day I could barely speak as he cooked the whole Christmas lunch for the two of us. No pre-packed bung it in the oven stuff here. No no no. A free-range turkey, bread sauce, home-grown Brussels, mini butcher's chipolatas wrapped in smoked local bacon, and his gravy, a thing of beauty having been reduced and cooked over many days.

Hours of preparation and all eaten in a matter of moments as we sat companionably opposite one another with skew-whiff paper hats on our heads. When Dad made a move to clear up afterwards I predictably said, 'Don't, Dad, I'll sort it all out later,' but as soon as I sat on the couch I fell into a Brussels-sprout-hangover-fuelled sleep.

When I awoke he was sound asleep, Norton recliner fully extended, snoring his head off, crass Xmas TV blaring, which I switched off, leaving him be, kissing him on the forehead and padding off to bed. In the morning when I got up he'd done all the clearing up. He always did.

The tradition then was a huge pot of tea and some yellow peril, as he called it – French toast to anyone else. But Dad had called it yellow peril since his Scout days, so I did too. After consuming slabs of sopping eggy bread, fried in gener-ous doads of butter, drizzled with maple syrup, it was time for a head-clearing walk along the beach. Both wrapped up against the biting wind with scarves, hats and long insulated coats, we battled the elements and laughed loudly as Dad's wee dog Frank ran in and out of waves, chasing gulls. With rosy cheeks and cleared heads we came home, put the kettle on and took root on the couch to watch Boxing Day TV.

With a twist in my gut I realised I couldn't even recall what we spoke about. Nothing important. Nothing mean-ingful. Nothing that would leave him with the impression that I loved the very bones of him. The huge spade-like hands, twinkly blue eyes, his big undulating hooter – the family hooter, which he told me as a child I would likely grow into when I was about twenty-five. Twenty-nine now and it hadn't come to pass, and despite knowing this was one of his silly stories, I still gave my face a good look in the mirror of a morning to see if it had started growing. His huge bendy thumb that he said made him one of the best guitar players in St Andrews and his shock of red hair, which he preferred to describe as spun gold. His thick head of hair had remained red as his friends over time became bald and sparsely thatched. He told them gleefully this was revenge for having been the brunt of every ginger joke on the planet since he was born. His way of telling a story: halfway through he would start laughing himself and be quite hysterical by the time he got to the punchline, which was irrelevant by then as everyone else was laughing uncontrollably too.

No, none of that. Nothing groundbreaking. Meaningful. Heartfelt. Just a meal. A snooze, a hangover, a walk, a laugh. Not the most auspicious way to say goodbye to your beloved father. But how could I have known? How could he have known? How could anyone ever know?

My first regret. And it was a biggie.

I'd planned to go up at Easter but then a chance came up to go on a last-minute skiing holiday with Marcus and when I phoned to suss him out, to see if he would be pissed off if I changed my plans, he said, 'Maddy, don't be daft. Go for God's sake, go! And if you don't, I will!' As I knew he would.

Dad taught me to ski in the mountains of Scotland when I was just five years of age, instilling in me not just a love of the mountains but a lifelong passion for the sport. We would take off early on a Saturday or Sunday morning for the two-hour drive to the slopes, with a packed lunch that would be eaten before we got halfway there. Neither of us able to resist the home-made Scotch eggs Dad rolled in foil warm from the oven before we left. Once parked, we would rug up in multiple layers of ski gear in the back of the car before spending the whole day on the slopes. From the tentative sliding on the nursery slopes to his undisguised pride as I skied for the school. He loved it as much as I did, and I knew when I told him about the last-minute opportunity that when he said 'go for it' he meant it, so off I went without a care in the world. A feeling, for the life of me, I cannot remember now.

I bought and wrote him a postcard and didn't get it together to buy a stamp so that was dog-eared and stained in the bottom of my handbag when I flew home a week later. Then I was straight back to work and, well, life just took over. The months came and went and here we were just a few weeks later and ... tears welled up.

Not now. Now was neither the time nor the place.

My gut twisted as I screwed my eyes shut, trying to retain control.

Five and a half hours later I arrived in Leuchars and right on cue there was Auntie Faye, deep concern etched on her face, scanning the faces of the emerging passengers streaming past her. Her eyes lit up when she saw me and just as quickly turned into limpid pools, filled with tears.

'Och, Maddy, I am so so sorry,' she whispered into my hair as she engulfed me. Now it felt real. Now the stone that had lain in the pit of my stomach since hearing the news rolled up, nearly choking me. Dropping my bag, I surrendered to the comfort and warmth of this lovely woman who had been more of a mother to me than anyone. With my legs like water, Faye ushered me gently to the car and, grinding the gears in her ancient rusty Volvo, drove us back to the farm just a few minutes' drive away where Uncle Ted stood anxiously in the doorway looking out for us.

'Darling,' he said, opening the car door and helping me out. 'Come here.' He embraced me strongly. 'Now, come on in, I think we could all do with a drink.'

Uncle Ted's measures were well known to knock you into next week, which on this occasion was perfect.

I was shown through to the posh lounge, a sign of how remarkable a day this was. The 'entertaining lounge'. The 'always ready to receive visitors' room. Lovely but formal, and immaculately kept. I had never actually been a guest in here, my role whilst growing up generally being to pass round crisps and nuts to any friends they were entertaining before rushing off to the TV lounge to watch rubbish, drink lemonade and eat crisps. I sat upright and managed to retain a façade of maturity and control as Faye fussed about producing bowls of nuts and crisps in an attempt to absorb the eye-poppingly strong gin I now held.

'Now,' said Ted as he settled into his chair and picked bits of imaginary fluff off his trouser leg, 'I don't want you to worry about a thing. We will take care of all the arrangements, Maddy.' His eyes met mine. 'You get to our age and sadly we know the drill.' I looked back at him as he glanced at Faye who nodded sagely. He continued, 'Some time ago Joe asked me to take care of his affairs. You know what he was like. A place for everything and everything in its place. Obviously with your mum not being around and you being the only child...'

I swallowed, unable to think of anything to say. Faye reached for her gin as he continued, 'So... basically... you are the only beneficiary of the will.'

'Ted! It's a bit soon for all of this isn't it?' Faye admonished, putting her gin down with a clunk, registering the look on my face.

'Oh sorry, dear,' Ted said, suitably cowed and turning back to her, and then to me. 'I just wanted you to know you're going to be... OK.'

None of this had even crossed my mind. I didn't want

anything. Any things. I didn't want anyone, just Dad. I wanted to bury my face into the shoulder of his scratchy holey jumper with the vaguely doggy smell, as it stretched over his seven-pack, as he affectionately called his tummy, as he sat at the kitchen table tying fishing flies and listening to *Gardeners' Question Time*. And to kiss his whiskery cheek.

'Oh right...'

By 'OK' of course he meant the restaurant.

'The restaurant,' confirmed Ted interrupting my reverie, 'and Frank of course.'

Frank the dog. I had completely forgotten about him.

What on earth would I do with him in London? Dad's little hairy wingman as he called him. It was all completely overwhelming. I had no idea what to do or say. I drained my glass rather too quickly and put it down with a wobbly hand. I was completely worn out.

Now it was Faye's turn. 'Maddy, you must stay here for as long as you like. It's been a terrible day, a terrible shock. You need time to come to terms with what's happened... to adjust... so make yourself at home here. For as long as you like.'

I knew she meant every word, which on this day of feeling so lost and alone and with no idea what to do or say, helped.

'Thanks, Auntie Faye – that's so kind of you, but you know I really feel I need to get on with things. I need to keep moving and get home – no matter how hard it is.'

The truth was I was on the brink of losing it at any second and if I didn't keep going I would have little choice but to give in to the overwhelming urge to take to my bed and never emerge. One step at a time. I had to keep going. I heard Dad's voice in my head. *'The show must go on.'*

'OK, darling, of course. One of us will drive you over

13

tomorrow, whenever you're ready. But for now it's been a long day and if you don't mind me saying – you look absolutely puggled.'

Tears sprang into my eyes as I nodded and hauled myself out of the chair. I silently hugged each of them before thanking them in a strangulated voice. After trudging upstairs to bed, I crawled under the covers, fully clothed, and cried myself to sleep.

The worst day of my life was over.

Chapter 2

By 5 a.m. I was up drinking tea. Faye appeared about 7 a.m. in the old quilted M&S dressing gown I remembered from when I used to stay with them as a child. Finding me fully clothed and staring out over the fields to St Andrews, she instinctively knew I wanted to get going. No point in postponing the inevitable. 'Let me have a quick cup of tea, write a note for Ted and I'll drive you home,' she said, patting my shoulder, not waiting for an answer.

Home.

Pulling up outside 125 North Street, my eyes filled with tears. Dad's world. The restaurant, The Birdie & Bramble, was the place Dad could be found night and day, unless he was on the golf course. He lived above the shop, as he called it, in the flat upstairs and had done since before I was born. This was his place.

His home. His life. His golf clubs stacked in the shed out the back, his brother-in-law Fraser's butcher's shop right across the road. The flat was where he would lay down his weary head but he liked to be amongst the bustle and nonsense that revolved around the restaurant and the golf club.

We pulled up outside the restaurant just after 7.30 a.m. The Birdie & Bramble. The faded exterior bringing a myriad of emotions to the fore. I looked at the frontage as the car ground to a halt. 'Thanks, Faye. Do you mind? I think I want to do this on my own,' I warbled.

'Of course, dear. If you're sure?' she said, turning and giving me a huge hug. 'Right then...' Her voice faltered. 'I'll phone you later to see how you're getting on...' she hesitated '...if you're sure?'

I nodded, choked. 'I am. Thanks. You've been brilliant... and I don't know what I'd do without you,' I said into her shoulder, hugging her back tightly.

We broke apart, both struggling to retain control. 'OK, darling, let's talk later,' she said with fake breeziness as I pinged off my seatbelt, howked my bag through the gap between the seats and got out of the car.

As she drove away I saw Faye's shoulders going. We were both in bits. Taking a deep breath I straightened myself up and squared up to the front of the restaurant.

The keys to Dad's flat were burning a hole in my pocket, which would have to wait. There is no way I could face that. It was too soon. Step by step. The Birdie & Bramble first. A glance at my phone confirmed it was too early to get the keys from the lawyer so I had no option but to face Uncle Fraser, Dad's brother-in-law. He was up at the crack every morning to open up his butcher's shop directly across the road, where we had always kept a set of spare keys. I knew as soon as I saw Uncle Fraser this nightmare would be even more real. I had no choice. It had to be done. I took a deep breath.

The old bell jangled as I opened the door. And there he was, Uncle Fraser in his blue and white butcher's apron, ruddy-faced, in the same position I had seen him a thousand times. Looking up from the job in hand, his face fell instantly from the robust pudgy-cheeked butcher's grin he kept for his customers to one of great concern. He rushed round from his side of the counter. After wiping his hands on his apron he encompassed me in his great oxters, squeezing hard.

'Och, Maddy. I canna believe it. We're all just ... devastated. It's just bloody awful ... I'm so sorry ... really ... Your dad ... well ...' He coughed, struggling to retain control. 'He was a great man ...' His voice rose an octave. 'Like the brother I never had ...'

Unable to speak, I nodded into his shoulder. Eyes over-flowing, I clung on to him. He signalled one of the juniors and clearing his throat managed to say, 'Go and get the spare keys for The Birdie & Bramble, Jono.' Wordlessly the boy scuttled off. Uncle Fraser held me at arm's length, gripping my shoulders and looking directly at me.

'Now, Maddy, do you want me to come over the road with you?'

'Doh,' I snottered.

He squeezed my shoulder harder, then released me and fished about in his pocket. He produced a scrunched-up hanky, which I took gratefully. 'OK.' He nodded. 'But if you change your mind, or you want anything at all ... we ... well we are family and we are all in it together.' He gestured with his arm round the shop, reddening. 'I didn't know whether to open or not – I didn't know what to do but I couldn't just sit at home and think about ... you know ... I have to keep busy ... It's not that I didn't love the very bones of the man,' he said as the boy stepped back into the room and handed him a battered white envelope, which he passed to me. I glanced down and saw *Joe's keys* written in my father's hand on the front. The boulder lurched up my gut.

'I understand, Uncle Fraser, really. Really. Thanks,' I managed to blurt out. 'I just ... I don't ...'

'Shoosht, dear ...' He embraced me once more, and after coughing, added in a cheerier tone, 'Now would you like a cup of coffee or a bacon roll before ...?' He left the words unsaid.

I shook my head. 'No thanks ... em ...'

'Look, Maddy, there is no right or wrong way of doing this,' he said, sounding more like himself, 'just your way, so on you go, but remember we are just here across the road ...'

Our eyes locked and I smiled. He understood. I mouthed 'thanks' and as the bell jangled, announcing his first customer of the day, I slipped out.

As I crossed the road, The Birdie & Bramble looked exactly the same. The picture window with moniker scrawled in faded gold italics across the centre. Obscuring the restaurant within, a heavy faded curtain. Stuck to the window was a hastily written sign that simply read, 'Closed'. Recognising my own twelve-year-old scrawl, my gut lurched at this stopgap fix, which Dad had never quite got round to changing. Not one for frills and graces my dad.

To the right of the picture window an ornate metal gate led to a narrow stone exterior corridor and heavy oak door. My hands shook as I unlocked the padlock on the gate and approached the door. It was an ancient thing, far older than the building itself, one of Dad's 'finds'. A vast door he'd procured from an auction somewhere, which he was told had come from St Andrews Castle itself. Dad thought it would give The Birdie & Bramble the look of somewhere that had been there forever. 'It was a bargain – I couldn't resist it!' A bargain indeed. Well it was until he had to pay for it to be cut down to fit the aperture of the front door of the restaurant. That had cost more than the door, which took a great deal of time and stour. But he was right; it looked great and the very patina of the wood gave the sense of history and solidity he had been after.

It had its practical uses and was often left open during the summer evenings allowing light, air and the fizzing atmosphere of St Andrews to bubble in. Students, locals, golfers and tourists wandering the streets, talking, laughing, the cacophony of the small town always alive with a beating heart between May and September. Of course the winters in Scotland were long and that very same door insulated the restaurant, keeping it cosy and inviting, shutting out the wild weather and biting wind that so often battered the east coast of Scotland.

Taking a deep breath, feeling the familiar knots and ridges under my hand, I stepped inside and slowly closed the door behind me. The only sound was the tick-tock of the clock. The room was dark and quiet – although only closed for two days, it felt utterly cold and empty.

This business was my dear dad's life, but it hit me hard that I hadn't actually been present for some years other than to pop my head round the door to let him know where I was off to, drop something off, pick something up, or wave a hasty goodbye as I ran off somewhere – so engaged was I in my own world. Hectic school days and long carefree holidays had merged seamlessly into university, graduation and finally work. Where had the time gone?

I had worked in The Birdie & Bramble from the moment I could stand, washing dishes, peeling potatoes, setting tables, and when my childhood clumsiness subsided sufficiently, I was let loose serving tables, then when I hit eighteen manning the bar, but never to the exclusion of my life. Dad believed wholeheartedly that I should fully enjoy my freedom and young years and he loved nothing better than seeing me bowl out of the door to join in with whatever shenanigans the other kids and I cooked up. Being an only child himself, he understood friends were incredibly important and he was determined I should be enjoying myself until the realities of life as an adult inevitably kicked in.

Dad loved the restaurant and worked hard day and night

to ensure its success but if I needed or wanted him to be anywhere then that is where he would be. School plays, parents' evenings, Brownie badge-awarding ceremonies – he was an enthusiastic and dedicated father. I always knew I came first and as result I loved The Birdie & Bramble too. It was huge part of my life and only now did I realise how much I had taken for granted that Dad and it would always be there.

The alternative hadn't crossed my mind or if it had, I had quashed it quickly. After graduating I was back in St Andrews working at The Birdie & Bramble as I applied for what seemed like countless marketing jobs all over the country, until finally I was offered a real job at Go Radio. Dad was as thrilled as I was, taking me for a celebratory meal at The Peat Inn, a Michelin-starred restaurant down the coast. And then I was off to my new life in London with my father's blessing, feeling loved, secure, with a spring in my step and without a backward glance.

Things hadn't changed at all in The Birdie & Bramble, the chairs still draped in the rather over-ornate slipcovers Dad had proudly ordered from Jenners in Edinburgh when I was no more than twelve. Ditto the monogrammed carpet, which had been commissioned in the 1980s when business was booming. Glancing at the familiar mishmash of framed photographs adorning the walls, including opening day, with Mum and Dad standing and grinning proudly, my heart crumbled.

A series of three photos caught my eye: the first of the massive castle door far too big for its intended position. The second was of my four-year-old self being used to illustrate how big it actually was and how small I was. And then me standing proudly beside it, pointing as it was cut to fit the doorway where it still stood after all these years. There was a veritable rogues' gallery adorning the walls and Dad smiled out from many of them. His celebrity squares, he called them, as every golfer who had ever been into the restaurant had been captured for posterity. A mixed bag of faded Kodak prints, out-of-focus disc camera, instant cameras, and more recently digital photographs, which had amazingly escaped the memory card on his phone and been printed.

There was a convoluted story behind each photo. Dad's heroes. I felt sick as I recalled the last time Dad had launched into one of the dozens of tales in his repertoire and I had rolled my eyes at the assembled crowd insinuating 'oh God not again' as I had heard them a hundred times before. Which of course I had. What I would do to hear one of them now.

The main back wall of the dining room was a shrine to the golfers who had been through the doors of the restaurant over the years, from his hero Jack Nicklaus to the remarkable trousers of Payne Stewart, and the Latin good looks of Seve Ballesteros. In its heyday the great and the good of the golf world had all been to The Birdie & Bramble. My heart ached as I surveyed the images of well-known golfers adorning the wall, all smiling and being held tightly round their shoulders by my red-haired big-nosed father, beaming beside them in his golf club V-neck.

My father's favourite photograph was of himself, on the eighteenth green with Jack Nicklaus minutes after he won the Open in 1978. Nicklaus had eaten at The Birdie & Bramble the day before the competition started and recognising a passionate fellow golfer in Dad, the two men had enjoyed a long and entertaining conversation about the game. The evening ended with Nicklaus promising him a ticket to the final day if he got through and true to his word, that is exactly what he did. Which explains the pride of his life: the photo of himself, shoulder to shoulder with

Nicklaus and the trophy. Although Jack had just won The British Golf Open, it was Dad who looked like he might burst with happiness.

Since that momentous day Nicklaus made a point of coming back every year he was in the town without fail until he retired, believing superstitiously that without The Birdie & Bramble he would never have won the Open Championship.

Next to the golfers are photos of other celebs, including Sean Connery, Michael Douglas, Clint Eastwood, Catherine Zeta-Jones, Hugh Grant and Bill Clinton. Scrutinising the photos for the first time in years it dawned on me the dateline of all this glamour and fun petered out in the early nineties, underlining harshly that the halcyon days of The Birdie & Bramble were long gone. Such sadness I had never imagined as a sob erupted from me and instinctively I made my way behind the bar to grab a napkin to stem the effusive tears now rolling down my face.

The tears stopped as they had started – a rollercoaster of emotion. I looked at my phone. Good God it was almost two o'clock! Hours had passed, which was confirmed by my belly rumbling, indicating I must be hungry and yet there was no way I could eat a single thing.

Drawing back the heavy damask curtains from the front window cast some natural light into the room whilst revealing the murky windows, further evidence things had slipped. Once upon a time Dad would have cleaned them inside and out with a bucket of water and vinegar and a handful of balled-up newspaper. A technique I had introduced to friends in London as they poured scorn on my 'Scottish Highland nonsense'. They'd laughed only to acquiesce when the sparkling clean windows revealed it worked like a dream.

Motes of dust hung in the shafts of light, showing each

table was set and ready for a busy service. Red tablecloths, the same faded damask as the curtain, red cotton napkins, rolled up to the left of each placemat, held in place by a crude dark wooden napkin ring. Rectangular green place-mats bordered with a gold scroll, three sets of cutlery at each setting and two glasses, one for wine and one for water. In the centre of each table a small lavender pottery vase with a single plastic rose. A time capsule.

A stack of A4 laminated menus lay in a bundle on the bar counter next to a stainless steel tray holding sets of stainless steel salt and pepper shakers.

The oval bar had a thick undulating wooden top, smoothed from years of use, tucked into a corner. It was so out of fashion it was back in. But this was the real McCoy and despite its not insubstantial age, very tidy and on first impressions scrupulously clean. It was agony not to see my father behind it.

Standing behind the bar I noticed a saucer with slices of lemon sitting on the stainless steel draining board. Next to the small round sink was an ice bucket full of water, thawed ice cubes, as if someone had abandoned it a moment or two beforehand. On top of the bar a stainless steel egg cup full of cocktail sticks, each with a wooden olive decoration at one end ready for the 'wee snacks' Dad always served with his spectacularly good gins.

The dark oak dresser was overpopulated with yet more framed photos. Above the bar hung two plastic orange pendant lights and behind it three bowed shelves held rows and rows of different shaped and sized glasses – all gleaming, clean, lined up ready for use. It may be old-fashioned but it was still deeply loved and cared for.

The arch behind the bar that led through to the kit-chen was reminiscent of a set from an eighties sitcom. The silence was deafening. From dawn to dusk there was activity. Deliveries, preparation, paperwork – Dad more often than not in the thick of it 'directing traffic'. Checking his orders, the food, the fridge, the plan, the bookings, whilst exchanging banter with whoever popped in and out: the kitchen porter, front-of-house staff, delivery men, a customer or a meandering tourist who had wandered in inadvertently looking for the loo. The place had always felt – I struggled for the right word – ah yes that was it – gulp – alive.

The kitchen was his pride and joy, and despite myself I smiled as my eye settled on the stove, the only nod to the new millennium. An eight-burner gas stove where originally a baby Belling would have looked quite in keeping. The new stove was Dad's one concession to the professional kitchen, as everything else was from another era altogether. 'A real bobby-dazzler,' he was fond of telling everyone proudly once he had reluctantly consigned his ancient antique range to the scrapyard. Dougie the chef was horrified and had used it as if it were an electric baby Belling, afraid of its impressive capabilities in relation to his own very underwhelming ones.

Ironically the purchase of this 'bobby-dazzler' had had the opposite effect on the business than that which was intended. Output went down and quality was inconsistent, especially as Dougie had developed an ever-increasing love of the drink.

A sea of light blue Formica covered all the cupboard doors in the kitchen. The original stone floor undulated slightly, hinting at its great age. It was scrubbed clean – not one crumb was visible. No plates, glasses, utensils or cutlery were on show. Everything was in its place. I confess to being impressed as he was not the tidiest man in Europe and it must have taken some doing.

On the kitchen wall was a cork noticeboard on which

24

was pinned a piece of foolscap paper: the weekly rota. Again in Dad's writing.

Joe, as he called himself for the purpose of the rota, was written in for five days and nights of the week. Sundays The Birdie & Bramble was open – 'the golf course is shut so of course we are open!' Mondays they were closed and he golfed every Monday. Twice.

St Andrews, on the east coast of Scotland, an hour north of Edinburgh and a mere hour and a half from Glasgow – Scotland's biggest cities – is recognised as the home of golf. A charming seaside town of twenty thousand. People come from all over the world to play on any one of the amazing courses that surround the area. The jewel in the crown of world golf being the eighteen-hole course where many believed the game itself was invented: St Andrews Old Course.

After years of playing every other course in the area until he could do so with his eyes shut, five years ago Dad had become a member of The Royal and Ancient – a lifetime ambition and his proudest achievement – a member of the oldest golf club in the world and he loved it. He loved every blade of grass, every rule and restriction. Every moment spent playing on the course was the joy of his life and when he wasn't playing on it he was talking about it. After each round he would relive every shot with his friends in the clubhouse. Even in the winter months when the weather was appalling, he would wrap himself up in a selection of garish sweaters, waterproofs, a woolly bobble hat with only the family hooter visible to the untrained eye and march round the course with his golf bag slung over his shoulder. Never happier.

'It's just the namby-pambies who need a caddy,' he'd expound to anyone who'd listen. 'The whole point of golf is, it's great exercise. No point in getting some other bugger to carry your clubs.' Of course, despite his forthright opinions he was well known and liked by all, including the St Andrews caddies, and in the high season when they were short-staffed he'd been known to help them out on occasion, by carrying a visitor's clubs when they were caught short.

Occasionally the wild Scottish weather defeated even him, which is when he could be found watching golf on TV. On video (yes he still had a VHS player), on Sky or on DVD. He knew every golfer, past and present. He knew their caddies, their stories and never tired of his subject. Always clad in a pair of smart trousers and his R&A V-neck sweater so he could be off to the course at a moment's notice. The only time I remember him looking disappointed in me (albeit briefly) was when I washed his soft green cashmere R&A V-neck sweater in the washing machine and it shrank so much it would have been tight fit on Barbie. My bottom lip was going when I took it through to show him, holding it between my thumb and forefinger. Initially his face crumpled too, until looking at the tiny wee jumper we both became quite hysterical with laughter. It had become a long-running joke.

The golf club and the game were his life. And ultimately his death. There was a part of me that acknowledged, even at this most acute point of grief, that if he was to going to go, going on the golf course he loved most, doing what he loved most with his best friends in the world around him, was surely the best way possible. It was us, the ones left behind, who were reeling and stunned, trying to grasp what had happened.

Turning my attention back to the rota, I recognised Dougie the chef's name. He had been there for as long as I could remember. William was on almost as many shifts as him. There were a few other names I didn't recognise: Mouse and Torbeck. I wondered if they knew.

If they had been told.

They would be worried for their jobs. Wondering what was going to happen. They were not alone. I had absolutely no idea.

The phone sat on the bar, flashing eight messages.

Suddenly I felt overwhelmed by the day, the loss, by the feeling that everything was going on as it ever did and yet I felt utterly changed. Nothing would ever be the same. I was a girl without a dad. My dad.

I slumped in the nearest chair, put my head in my hands and closed my eyes. Everything in this place emanated the very essence of Dad. I could hear his voice, see his cheery grin, imagine a bellow of laughter, hear him whistling George Formby songs as he pottered around behind the bar. His Groucho Marx impression.

As the feeling of despair sank in, suddenly there was a light knock on the front door and it opened slowly. A head appeared round it with a tentative 'Hello?'

Oh God, company was the last thing I felt like.

'Maddy?'

I nodded uncertainly, wiping tears from my eyes. Standing up, I realised it was Dad's right-hand man, William, immaculate in a freshly laundered blue and white striped shirt. He walked over to me and gave me a hug.

'I am so sorry for your loss ... Joe was ... well just a lovely, lovely man,' he said with such affection and warmth my eyes filled with tears again, as did his. His voice breaking, he battled on in a forced cheery tone: 'Listen, I don't want to disturb you. I'll leave you to it. I just wanted to give you my number.' He handed me a Post-it note with a number hastily scribbled on it. I glanced at it, unable to speak.

'Right, that's me, I'm off,' he said, walking towards the door.

As he opened it to leave I heard a plaintive 'wait' escaping from my mouth. 'Please stay. I'm sorry. I didn't mean to be rude but I didn't expect anyone and...' I ran out of puff again.

He stopped in his tracks, his hands going to his face. 'Oh God don't even think about it. I can't imagine what you're going through and I was surprised to be honest. I didn't think you'd be up so soon ... so I was just popping in to check everything was OK and I saw the lights.' He paused. 'Listen, I know we've only met in passing but he told me so much about you, I feel like I know you.'

'Really?' I couldn't help myself.

'Oh yes,' he went on. 'He thought you were the bee's knees.'

I smiled, recognising one of Dad's expressions immediately. 'Oh he did?' My bottom lip wobbled.

'Yes. He did.' Seeing my expression and tears flooding back he deftly changed the subject, stepping back into the room and towards me.

'You look like you could murder a cup of tea,' he said.

'Yes...' I hesitated. 'Or maybe something stronger?'

'Okey-doke,' he said, upping his pace and walking towards the bar. 'Me too. What do you fancy?'

'A large gin and tonic.'

He grinned. 'Leave it to me.'

William slid behind the bar and plucked two cut-glass crystal goblets from a shelf before deftly slicing some fresh lemon. He disappeared briefly to the kitchen for some ice, plopped three cubes into each glass, ran a slice of cut lemon round the lip before dropping it into the glass and free-poured a generous measure of gin into each. After flipping the top off two wee bottles of tonic, he poured them in and with the final flourish of a swizzle stick passed one over to me.

'Wow, you've got the knack haven't you?' I said after sampling the sparkling, icy cold gin with a kick. 'That's a great gin!'

He grinned. 'I had a great teacher.' He raised his glass. 'To Joe.'

We clinked glasses.

Sitting in companionable silence for a few moments, the warm trickle of gin thawed the feeling of the curling stone in my gut, helping to relax me a little. I ventured a wobbly smile.

'Thanks,' I mumbled.

'So how long are you up for?' asked William.

'I'm not exactly sure. I reckon a week or two at most. Just enough time to get all his affairs in order.'

I'd said words for real about my own father. My dad. Daddy. The one with the great big strong hands and sparkly blue eyes. '*His affairs in order.*' He had gone. He was not here. I would never see him again. My throat constricted, the weight in my gut was back, and despite gritting my teeth and holding my breath, it rolled up slowly to my solar plexus and then it felt like a balloon inflating. It was impossible to swallow it down again as it erupted in the form of a great racking sob.

The floodgates were open. William gently patted my hand and then I had no choice but to give in. Instinctively he put his arm round me whilst I rocked back and forth and unexpurgated grief took hold.

I seemed to be weeping and wailing for an age but dear William stayed put, patting my back, and when finally I let out an enormous sigh, signalling the latest bout of upset had come to an end, I was hugely embarrassed so retreated slightly from his arms. 'I'm so sorry,' I snuffled, taking the napkin he offered and blowing my nose into it. 'I'm not much of a crier, but I'm making up for it now. I can't control it – it just starts and then … Oh God look at your shirt!' Mortified, I spotted his no longer immaculate shirt with a wet sodden left shoulder, mascara and dodgy-looking body fluids on it.

'Don't you worry about this old thing,' he said, pooh-poohing his soiled clothing. 'Better an empty house than a bad lodger,' he said gently. Old thing, my foot. It looked like a Savile Row tailor had just pressed it ten minutes ago, which made me warm to him all the more. 'Now listen, Maddy, I think we should get out of here. It's been a long day. I'm going to take you back to my place.'

Oh God here we go. I knew he was too good to be true. Noticing my hesitation he went on.

'Oh aye, I should probably mention I am spoken for and when we get home you'll meet the lovely Noel. He's my long-suffering partner who will be waiting for me right now … probably wondering where I've got to as I said I'd be ten minutes, tops. Listen, I'll give him a quick call and ask him to set one more place for dinner, then we can lock up here and head off. You shouldn't be on your own. Not tonight.'

'Oh I don't want to impose, really. I'm not much company …'

He cut me off. 'It doesn't matter … I am!' He snickered at his own joke and despite the grimmest of all grim situations I found myself smiling and gratefully accepting.

'Thanks, William, that would be lovely.'

So as William ran about locking up and making sure everything was in its place – including washing and drying the two crystal goblets, buffing them to gleaming and return-ing them to their rightful place – I splashed my face with cold water and tried to get my great puffy red eyes under control. All the while I reiterated in my head on a loop: '*The show must go on.*'

Chapter 3

William and Noel lived less than one hundred metres from the restaurant on the adjacent street in the smallest chocolate-box terraced stone house.

'Here we are,' William said, opening the front door, stepping aside and ushering me in first. Blasting in from the cold darkening day right into the heart of their cosy welcoming sitting room felt wonderful. My cheeks warmed instantly, thanks to a crackling fire roaring in the grate. The hearth was framed by two worn squashy chairs and on the corner of the overstuffed sofa opposite the fire on a threadbare woollen blanket lay a very sleepy wee dog. As William heaved the heavy wooden door closed behind us, the dog opened a lazy eye and half-heartedly wagged his rough wee red tail.

'Frank!' I squawked. Recognising my voice, the dog's eyebrows shot up as he burst from his lethargic curl into an Exocet missile. A hairy wee sausage dog, no more than eight inches high and twice as long as any dog that height deserved to be, he was wagging his tail with such fervour, whimpering and jumping up and down like a tiny kangaroo trying to reach me, demonstrating utter joy, as I bent down to greet him.

'Well well, would you look at that! He's really missed you. He's been so quiet, he won't eat, won't wag, won't even go out for a walk since …' William hesitated.

My eyes brimmed with tears. 'I know how he feels,' I mumbled, bending down and scooping the hairy wee sausage up, causing him to squirm with happiness as I held him up and inhaled the very essence of him.

As always he smelled of the seaside: salty, windswept, gritty with sand. He felt like home, I thought, burying my face in his coat.

'Why hello there,' said the extraordinarily handsome man who had just wandered into the room. 'You must be Maddy.'

'Yes,' I said, plopping the dog down. 'It's lovely to meet you ... and you must be ...' Mortified I couldn't recall his name.

Taking control of the situation, he continued, 'Noel. Yes indeed I am ... and lovely to meet you too ... Now, I've made up the spare room as I wasn't sure what your plans are.'

Good God. I hadn't even thought that far ahead. I thought I'd stay at Dad's flat, but now I was here, the reality of leaving this warm welcoming home to go back to The Birdie & Bramble and upstairs to Dad's empty flat was too upsetting to contemplate. An alternative was more than welcome but I had just met these two lovely men and I didn't want to impose so felt I should at least try to object.

'Are you sure? I don't want to put you out?'

'Positive,' said Noel, 'it won't put us out at all – it's lovely to meet you and anyway—' he turned his superstar grin on the dog '—it doesn't look like Frank will let you out of his sight even if you wanted to.'

'Yes, you have made the wee man's day,' added William, arriving back in the room with what to the untrained eye looked suspiciously like another of his delicious gins.

'Come on, Maddy, you grab this; I'll grab your bag and I'll show you up to your room. You can freshen up and then I'll make us all something to eat.'

'There is nothing that won't wait 'til tomorrow,' added Noel gently.

'Well if you're sure? It's so very kind of you.' Tears burned behind my eyes.

'Of course we're sure,' added William, changing gear. 'And now, madam, this way please,' he said with a flourish, ushering me up a tiny undulating stone staircase that led straight from the living room to an equally petite landing. I felt like Alice in Wonderland. Opening the door revealed the most perfect little room just big enough for a brass-knobbed double bed immaculately made up with crisp white linen, a surfeit of plumped pillows, a bedside table with a gingham-checked reading lamp already switched on, a pile of *Elle Decor* magazines, a vase of new daffodils and a white seersucker dressing gown draped over the bed. 'The bathroom's right next door.' He indicated another door. 'It's a sliding door as we're so short of space. Noel and I sleep downstairs so this is for the exclusive use of you and ...' There was sudden WHUMP! as Frank who clearly wasn't going to let me out of his sight, jumped onto the bed via a small footstool. 'His nibs!'

'Thanks, William. Really, I don't know what to say.'

'Don't say a thing. It's the least we can do,' he said, giving me a squeeze before shutting the door gently behind him as he left.

I fell onto the sumptuous bed like a stone and as the duvet puffed round me, Frank tramped over the mountain of bedding. Looking into his eyes I saw his expression mirrored my own – one of loss and confusion. 'Come on, you,' I said, patting the bed next to me. 'You and me, we'll stick together.' Following instructions, Frank turned round and round punching the duvet with his wee fat paws and making his nest beside me as I went on more to myself than him. 'We'll be OK ... won't we?' And then abandoning his nest the wee dog spooned into me. Snaking my arm round him I let out an enormous sigh and the tears came.

Chapter 4

As I opened my eyes the next morning for a glorious moment, I forgot where I was. And why.

Reality snapped back all too quickly when I found myself on top of the bed fully clothed, for the second night in a row. I must have gone out like a light the second my head hit the pillow.

Launching onto my elbows I looked round. A warm dent on the bed next to me suggested Frank had been there 'til recently. On the floor my bag sat abandoned, unopened. I stood and opened the curtains, revealing fluffy white clouds moving quickly across a blue, blue sky. I had no idea what time it was. My phone was dead so I tiptoed into the dinky bathroom next door where folded fluffy white towels sat on a small wooden chair at the end of a clawfoot bath. A small basket packed with luxurious botanical products sat on the window ledge where someone had propped a note.

'Taken Frank round the block ... relax make yourself at home ... lots of hot water ... enjoy a bath. I'll be back to make breakfast. W x'

Unable to work out what on earth to do next, I took the path of least resistance and followed instructions, running a hot bubbly bath. Lying underwater, floating and listening to my breathing, feeling weightless, I wished I could stay there forever. After a lovely long soak I found a hairdryer in the bedroom and blasted my hair before making an attempt to rebuild my devastated-looking face. I felt more like myself on the outside, but still knotted and clenched on the inside. At least I smelled nice. I checked the mirror and tried in vain to tame my scraggle of hair, which as usual after being newly washed looked as though I had been electrocuted.

'Right,' I said to my reflection, 'you are your father's daughter so you will get up and despite looking like the Wild Woman of Wongo, you will get on with it.'

Fixing my face into a smiling formation, I slicked on some lip gloss and padded downstairs.

I heard the words 'Mind your head!' the split second before my forehead walloped into the low-hanging doorjamb.

'Ouch!'

'Oh God you poor thing,' said Noel. 'We always give people the "mind your head" lecture when they arrive in Lilliput but we just didn't get a chance last night, Maddy. I am so sorry.'

'It's OK,' I said, rubbing the throbbing spot where it had chubbed me.

'Rub this on it – it really it works,' ordered Noel, rushing over with a butter dish.

I looked at him, unable to tell if he was pulling my leg or not.

'Really,' he said as he scooped some up on his finger and gently dabbed it on the rapidly emerging egg. 'Now, if I promise not to rub any more condiments on you, can I tempt you through to the kitchen for a nice cup of tea?'

Sitting down I watched as Noel made a pot of tea. What a handsome man, I thought, but before I could scrutinise him too closely the door flew open and Frank tore in followed by William.

'Good morning!' He grinned as I lifted the sandy wee sausage dog onto my knee for a good-morning snuggle.

'He wouldn't leave your side this morning until I bribed him with a biscuit.' He laughed. 'He is so happy to have you home.'

The boys dismissed my apologies for missing supper the night before as they bustled about and William made breakfast.

Noel was distracted as I drank my tea. He texted, sipped his coffee and scribbled a few notes in a leather-bound note-book. He wore immaculate dark jeans, a crisp white shirt, buttoned up to the top and a beautiful silk print tie. His belt and shoes matched perfectly. He definitely moisturised. He looked a million dollars. Suddenly he stopped and smiled at me, staring. 'Sorry,' he said, 'busy day ahead.'

'No no, on you go,' I said, embarrassed to be caught scrutinising him. Hefting up the enormous mug of tea William had placed in front of me and taking a sip, I took in my surroundings.

The oversized farmhouse table took up almost all of the floor space. The kitchen itself was tiny, charming, with freestanding units built round an Aga, which was belting out heat. It was toasty. Frank jumped down, padded over to his basket in front of the stove and fell asleep. William and Noel deftly stepped over his snoring form. Business as usual. Having eaten nothing at all since the previous morning – and that had been a hastily grabbed banana from Auntie Faye – I practically inhaled the delicious cooked breakfast that was placed in front of me. Two poached eggs, warm buttered wholemeal toast, crispy bacon, divine butcher's sausages, a large grilled buttery mushroom and a slow-cooked tomato with a sprig of rosemary on it. Every morsel slipped down a treat.

'Mmmmmmmmm,' was all I managed to say as I sat back and wiped my mouth on the chequered linen napkin. 'I swear, that is one of the best breakfasts I have ever had.'

William reddened. 'Ooh away you go,' he said, leaping up to fill the teapot with more hot water, clearly thinking I was exaggerating, which I wasn't.

'No! Really!'

'Well that's very kind, Maddy. It was your dad who taught me everything,' said William. 'He was a genius behind that stove.'

Words failed me. The natural bonhomie halted as the reason I was in this place drove home once again. My bottom lip wobbled as I recalled the long-talked-of plan to learn all the 'tricks of the trade' from Dad, which I had never taken the time to do, not that I didn't want to, I just … well … there didn't seem to be the right time … and now … Tears stung behind my eyes. Well now it was too late.

Dad's culinary expertise I had completely taken for granted. When I was growing up he'd effortlessly whipped up delicious snacks whilst chatting on about this and that. I loved being asked round to my school friends for tea where I chomped into Bird's Eye fish fingers and potato waffles or Heinz beans and bacon burgers because they was a novelty for me. At the age of ten I rather enjoyed the tinned fast food experience and most certainly did not appreciate how damn lucky I was having my own personal chef. It took a surfeit of fish fingers and oven chips at friends' houses to realise everyone's dad didn't cook the way mine did.

Every day after school I'd head to The Birdie & Bramble where Dad would cook whilst I told him about my day, and then we would eat tea together before I went upstairs to the flat and he opened the doors for evening service.

We simply ate what was in season.

In the summer months, there were scallops the size of golf balls in their shells with a crumb or two of Stornoway black pudding, fresh langoustines sautéed in garlic butter with a handful of fresh green salad leaves picked from the garden and dressed with a simple French dressing. 'Never gild the lily,' Dad would say, as he put his latest creation down in front of my ten-year-old self with the same aplomb he would save for the Queen – were she ever to come to The Birdie & Bramble.

Between May and September, with the door of the restaurant wide open, our tea was often interrupted by friends calling out as they went on their way. 'Aye aye, Joe'; 'Och look at you two – two peas in a pod' and other familiar words filtering through as we chatted through our respective days.

Summer nights were magical in St Andrews. The bright skies and light nights – and on one of the longest days: 23rd June, Dad's birthday, it barely got dark at all. The freedom that living in such a close community gave us was wonderful. After wolfing my tea and getting any homework out of the way as quickly as possible, I'd spill out onto the street, gathering up whoever else was out to play, on the way to the Mercat Cross, our meeting place, before running down to the vast sandy beach only a hundred metres away.

If the tide was out we'd take bandy nets and scour the rock pools, paddling and hauling our treasure back home in small plastic buckets. Crabs and rockfish released back into the water would dart off at speed amongst sea anemones and razor clams. On these balmy evenings we stayed out to within seconds of our agreed home time before, sandy-toed and heart-happy, quietly we would troop back for bedtime. A cold drink, a nightly resistance to having a bath and then finally capitulating, jammies on, scrubbed clean, rosy-cheeked, I'd clamber into my big quilted bed and lie peeping through the gap in the curtains at the sky, still blue, the birds still singing amidst the lazy fading sounds of a summer evening in the streets below. The feeling of wanting to be grown up pervaded, wanting to be part of whatever was going on outside or downstairs as the low murmur of voices would burst into gales of laughter before settling once again. These rhythms and sounds I fell asleep to each night.

Much as I adored summer, I loved winter all the more.

The pay-off for our balmy long evenings of idyllic beach-combing were the short dark days of winter. Chill icy wind was common on the east coast. It could be dark by 4 p.m. so we spent these months swaddling ourselves in coats, scarves, hats and gloves, and wore reflective armbands handed out by the school to keep us safe by punctuating the wet dark-ness as cars slid past. Arriving home in winter, pushing into the heart of The Birdie & Bramble was wonderful. With the wood-burning stove lit to warm the restaurant for the evening, I'd sit toes curled under me in the one easy chair, thawing my hands on the hearth, enjoying hot chocolate and a buttered crumpet as Dad bustled in and out talking, cooking.

Winter food was part of the joy too – slow-cooked cas-seroles, rich unctuous meaty sauces mopped up by chunks of home-made bread, buttered kale and cabbage. A hearty fish pie, creamy caper peppered sauce with mounds of but-tery mashed potato topping. Every night there was a pud. An apple crumble, junket, crème caramel. After tea I would do my homework as The Birdie & Bramble prepared for evening service. Though an only child the comings and goings of folk in and out all the time felt like a big family, with everyone involved in the business, and I felt more at home in The Birdie & Bramble than in my home itself.

This was our routine every night except Sunday when Dad would hand over the reins to Dougie, the sous chef, choosing instead to cook a full roast dinner for the two of us, and various waifs and strays, upstairs in the flat. My favourite night of the week. The next day, Monday, The Birdie & Bramble was closed and I would be up and off early, dropped in for the breakfast club at school as Dad headed to the course to begin his thirty-six holes of golf.

After I went to uni he announced he wanted to spend less time in the kitchen and more time on the golf course, so bit by bit he brought Dougie on board, giving him more and more responsibility.

Dougie had been there as long as I could remember. Dad took him on aged sixteen as a part-time kitchen porter in the year The Birdie & Bramble opened and with a complete lack of ambition or drive, Dougie never left. Over time he became involved in the food preparation and eventually starters and sweets.

He was a decent enough cook so when Dad wanted more time to play golf and enjoy himself, he simply asked Dougie to step up to the plate.

It worked well for them both. Dougie got more money and Dad more time to spend on the golf course. Dad ate all his meals at the restaurant, but recently had been happier front of house, socialising, chatting and enjoying a far less stressful environment. It made sense – after all, he was nearly seventy by then.

The thought of him standing back, slowing down, making plans for the future of the business, pragmatically accepting he was not as young as he used to be, made sense but made my heart ache. I had been so damn busy with my own life I had paid very little attention to how much my father's life had changed.

William, noticing my trembling lip, said, 'Your dad kept up the tradition of a great Sunday Roast. He'd often ask his friends — ourselves included — round for a slap-up meal.'

'It was the highlight of our week!' added Noel, giving me a gentle smile before putting his dishes in the dishwasher and heading off to finish getting ready for work. William settled into the chair next to me, topping up our mugs of tea. 'I ended up learning loads about cooking from your dad at The Birdie, and I absolutely love it.'

'God Bless him,' Noel called. 'I've never had it so good.'

Another pang.

Seismic shifts in my father's life and I knew nothing about them.

'Oh God.' It suddenly dawned on me. 'Does Dougie know what's happened?'

'Aye. He doesn't have a phone so I tracked him down at The Rum & Lash — the pub, his second home.' He looked at me for reassurance. 'I wanted to let him know before the jungle drums got to him. He was gutted as you can imagine and by all accounts has been on a bender to end all benders ever since.'

'Poor guy — he won't know what the hell's going on but thanks for doing that, William. I know I couldn't face it — not yet.'

Just then, Noel reappeared. 'I'm going to be late. I have to run,' he said, landing a gentle kiss on the top of William's head and squeezing my shoulder as he negotiated the various obstacles on his way through the wee kitchen. He stopped briefly to look me in the eye.

'Maddy. You are welcome to stay as long as you like … as is that cheeky crater.' He laughed, pointing at Frank, who opened an eye proving he was listening to every word.

'Thanks, Noel, you are a doll,' I said, nudging the dog

gently with my foot as he closed his eyes and gave a dramatic sigh.

'You're welcome,' he shouted as he disappeared out the door.

'What a lovely man,' I said to William.

'Yes. Everyone prefers him to me,' he joked.

He had such a twinkle in his eye, I giggled.

'Right, come on, let's get this lot sorted.' William galvanised me into action. 'Then we can take his nibs out for a proper walk on the beach, blow away the cobwebs and make a plan.'

With a full tummy, and a very empty heart, I helped tidy up and then we wrapped ourselves up and took Frank to the beach.

A wild and windy day, clouds rushing overhead, we walked the one hundred metres to the beach to find the tide was well out and the West Sands looked wonderful. An endless, golden slick of sand looking north as far as the eye could see.

Walking side by side and taking it in turns to throw the stick for Frank, I felt so comfortable with this lovely man I felt no need whatsoever to fill the silence with polite conversation. Companionable silence.

We walked for a good half hour before heading back towards the town, the profile of the building in the distance, St Andrews tower, marking the boundary.

'Fancy a coffee?' asked William as we neared the town.

He was a mind reader to boot. 'God, yes please.'

'OK, come on then, let's head to the restaurant and I'll demonstrate my barista skills and ...'

He was cut short as my phone rang. As I glanced down, a picture of Brad Pitt flashed up. Marcus had put that in as his profile pic, thinking it was highly amusing. 'It's my boyfriend.'

'OK, I'll leave you to it,' said William, discreetly clipping

Frank back on the lead and heading off in the direction of The Birdie & Bramble.

'Mads babe. How are you? God I'm so sorry. It all happened so fast. One minute you were there, the next gone. I had no idea what was going on. I tried phoning about a hundred times last night but couldn't get you.' He stopped babbling and slowed down. He exhaled. 'So how are you?' he repeated.

'I just can't quite believe it,' I managed, chin wobbling, tears flooding my eyes.

'God. I know, I am so, so sorry. I wish there was something I could do. Is there anything I can do?'

'No thanks. Nothing really. My Uncle Ted is taking care of things but when I find out when the funeral is, will you try and come?'

'Yeh babe, of course.'

'Thanks. That would mean such a lot. Really.'

'OK, as soon as you know, text me the details and let's have a proper chat tonight, yeh?'

The noise of phones and the busy office behind him made it clear this was not a good time. 'Listen I have to go.'

'OK. And Marcus?'

The line went dead.

'Thanks,' I said to no-one.

So I conceded I may have misjudged his reaction when I got the bad news. Sudden guilt flooded over me, that for even one moment I thought the reason he didn't show any emotion or sympathy publicly was protecting his position at work in light of our illicit romance. Of course when it came to such a life-changing event, all bets were off and obviously he did care or he wouldn't have phoned and said he would come up to the funeral to support me. I had underestimated him and would make up for it when I got the chance. Feeling a little lighter, I slid my phone back into my pocket just as it rang again.

'Morning, darling.' This time it was a very gruff-sounding Uncle Ted.

'Hi.'

'How are you doing?' But before I could answer he went on, 'Sorry, Maddy, stupid bloody question. Right.' He coughed. 'Faye and I sat up late last night, made a few calls and we wanted to tell you—'

I heard Faye in the background saying: 'Ask! Ask! Not tell!'

Ted, flustered, rephrased it. 'Yes, yes, sorry of course – I mean we wanted to *ask* you, how do you feel about Thursday? Is that too early for the funeral?'

'This Thursday?'

'Well yes.'

'You mean *tomorrow*?'

'Em.' Cough. 'Yes … gosh … yes well … I suppose I do.'

Of course it was inevitable but it was surreal and I didn't know what on earth to say. I was shocked.

'Maddy? If you think it's too soon it's no problem. Why don't we leave it for now?'

My throat seemed to close. 'Oh … well …' In tandem my nose blocked magically. 'I'm afraid I have no idea … I just know he wouldn't want a …' My voice trailed off, tears spilling down my cheeks.

'Fuss,' Ted finished, reading my mind.

'Fuss,' I repeated. 'Yes.'

'To be honest these things normally take a lot longer – ten days to two weeks – but Stevie the Slab is taking care of everything and as you know it's not what you know, it's who you know round here. Anyway, he's managed to move things around so if you wanted to get it done sooner rather than later you can.'

God. I had barely had time to come to terms with the fact my dear dad was no longer here and the thought of him being put in the ground was horrific. On the other hand the alternative of him being somewhere – I had a flashback to too many detective shows – in a cold room, covered in a sheet, all alone, was worse.

'Maddy, are you still there, dear?' Faye said gently, having commandeered the phone.

'Yes … sorry I was just thinking …'

'It was too soon – sorry, darling, we were just trying to help. We just …'

'No, you're right,' I blurted.

Faye continued, 'I mean Joe lived his whole life in St Andrews and you know what the jungle drums are like – everyone will know by now … good news travels fast, and bad news faster …'

She was making sense. Dad was a home bird. His life was St Andrews and on the odd occasion he had been winkled out of the place on a holiday, he couldn't wait to get back. 'I could ask William to put a note in the window of the restaurant so customers and suppliers know.'

'We already asked Ewan. He said he'll put something in the paper tomorrow.' She added, 'All we need to know is are you sure?'

'Yes,' I said.

'OK, I'll leave you to it. Here's Ted.' And she gave him the phone.

'OK, Maddy … I'll take care of that. Now have you thought: do you want a private do or are all friends welcome?'

That was easy. 'Friends. He lived for his friends.' And realising the significance of that oft-used phrase, I juddered to a halt, unable to continue. A sob choked out.

'OK, darling, leave it with me. I'll call you later with the details, OK?'

I nodded, cutting the call off as grief took hold and the realisation of what was happening hit home hard.

Taking a detour to clear my head, I texted Marcus the details, adding that I understood if he couldn't make it as it was incredibly short notice to fly up from London.

I arrived at The Birdie & Bramble about half an hour later.

William looked up as I entered.

'There you are!'

Taking a seat, I told him the news. 'The funeral's to-morrow.'

'Gosh.' His eyebrows shot up. 'That's fast.'

'I know – do you think it's too soon? You see Dad's friend Stevie the Slab is the undertaker so he's pulled out all the stops.'

William nodded. 'I know Stevie – he's in here a lot – and no I don't think it's too soon. A funeral is an awful thing to face but people say the sooner it's over ...' he hesitated '...the better.'

We sat in silence for a moment.

'Anyway how are you doing?' I asked, keen for a distraction.

'Good. I'm just steeling myself to deal with this,' he said, plopping down an A4 diary, a weighty tome, bursting at the seams with bits of paper, receipts, newspaper cutting scraps, lists, and notes flapping out of almost every page.

'Bloody hell. I thought you said you were a minimalist,' I joshed.

'Yes, I am and as you know your dad was a maximalist. His kitchen was a finely tuned operation with some help from myself but the one area I was not allowed to tinker about with was this—' he patted the book affectionately

'—this was his bible. No-one could get it off him for love nor money. This holds his life, business and bookings – so one of us had better get to grips with the contents because goodness knows what lurks inside.'

I must have looked a little scared.

'Oh God, don't tell me it's a family failing. Is it? A deep fear of paperwork and organisation?'

I grinned. 'Well ... Dad was admittedly terrible at these things but I have news for you – I'm worse.'

William groaned. 'Oh God, out of the frying pan into the ...'

'Well if you can't stand the heat get out of the kitchen,' I batted back.

'Touché. OK, leave this with me. You go and put the kettle on – we're going to need coffee ... and lots of it.'

'Deal,' I said, disappearing into the kitchen fast before he changed his mind.

Coffee freshly brewed, I sat down beside William who was staring at the book, still steeling himself to deal with it.

He flipped a few pages as I looked over his shoulder. Every Monday he had GOLF written in big bold letters. In addition, next week there was a: Golf Outing with the Boys to North Berwick.

Really the only things in the book were his golfing commitments and a few scrawled bookings.

My heart twisted.

'So are these really the only bookings?'

'Well yes, this has always been very much a "turn up and you'll always get a table" sort of place.'

I looked at him. 'So no-one ever booked?'

'Locals? No and well ... visitors just sort of found us, I suppose. The concierges would phone occasionally from the hotels but that was just to check we had space and we always did.'

I continued flipping through the pages and found a few random dates and bookings, all with names and most without numbers. What a system.

I read out a few of the names. William nodded. 'Yes, I know them all I think, all regulars.'

Heartsore for the lack of any system, the sort of thing I had the skills to help with, I thought guiltily. Hell I'd studied marketing at university and yet had failed to apply any of my hungrily gained knowledge to make even one small inroad to help Dad in – what was becoming clearer by the minute – a failing business.

'It's not your fault, Maddy,' said William the mind reader, slipping the book back in front of himself as if removing it from my eyeline would help the searing guilt of being a bad daughter.

'I...'

'No, not I...This was your dad's business, his life, his way of doing things and he loved it. You know that – he was what he was.'

I nodded. He was right. Dad would no more have discussed his business with me than fly in the air. It was just the way of him. He led his life and just wanted to give me the confidence and freedom to lead mine.

'Now there's no point in us both poring over this—' he tapped the book '—why don't you take the messages off the answering machine in the kitchen and I'll crack on with this.'

Dad was a self-confessed Luddite when it came to anything technological. No website. No online bookings. Just a fairly basic answerphone and ye olde paper bookings book.

One weekend about three years ago I had started a

Facebook page but as Dad didn't have a computer it had been largely ignored. The world of social media was one he didn't care to engage with. 'I prefer actual living breathing people, not fichering about on the bloody internet,' he stated firmly anytime I had raised the topic. Subject closed.

So the answerphone that sat on shelf in the kitchen was still the nadir of technology as far as The Birdie & Bramble went, and when I pressed play the first thing I heard was my hesitant twelve-year-old voice reading slowly.

'Hello! You are through to The Birdie & Bramble – we can't take your call just now. Please leave a message after the bleep, I mean beep.'

I pressed stop, took a deep breath, blew my nose and wiped away the latest bath of fat tears. It seemed nothing about this process was going to be easy. That twelve-year-old voice, a carefree me with no concept of time, life and the inevitable changes the future would bring. After a seriously strong coffee that William had correctly predicted would be required, a few minutes later I tried again. Pen and paper at the ready, I wrote as quickly as I could.

There were eight messages, two offering condolences, a few hang-ups, one selling PPI, one booking, someone looking for confirmation of Dad's attendance at a golf match and then I heard William making a strangulated noise, so I pressed STOP and ran through to the dining room.

'What is it?'

He slid the book over to me.

'Look,' he said.

All I could see was yet another blank page.

'Not that,' he said. 'This.' And he handed me a scrap of lined paper. On it was a barely legible scrawl, a handwritten receipt in Dad's writing.

'*Wedding. Sherry Gosling. Lovely woman! Deposit paid 200 pounds. Budget for the day two grand!*'

'So when is it? Maybe it's already been? If not, we'll have to get in touch, explain the situation and help her find somewhere else.'

'Turn it over,' he said, looking worryingly white, pointing at the paper in my hand.

'Twenty-two, five,' I said, reading it out loud, as my brain failed to compute what I was actually seeing.

'That's ...' He paused as I blinked at him, my mouth opening and shutting, gawping. 'Saturday,' he stated in a much higher voice than I had heard him use before. He stood up, strode over to the bar, grabbed a bottle of whisky and poured us a generous dram each.

'Oh. My. God. This Saturday?' The penny dropped.

'Yes! This Saturday!'

'Well obviously we can't do it,' I said matter-of-factly.

'Quite.'

'What will we do?'

'Hide?'

As far as I was concerned this was the perfect solution but before I could make my way under the floorboards, he added, 'I'm joking, Maddy – it's quite simple really – we can't let them down.'

I looked at him. 'Are you insane?'

'Possibly,' he said, draining his glass.

'It's in three days,' I said, draining mine.

'In catering that's a lifetime,' he said in a shrill tone, hysteria just below the surface. He poured another dram.

I snorted with laughter and held out my glass for a refill. 'It is ...' he insisted.

The smile was off my face now. 'William. There is no way we could get it together that fast; plus, it seems almost ...' I

51

searched for the right word, '…disrespectful … and wrong … and don't forget another wee issue – the chef's gone AWOL. You said yourself Dougie is on a major bender.'

His face dropped. It was the first time I had seen him anything other than positive.

'There must be more than just that scrap of paper?' I pressed, pointing at the rest of the papers and cuttings that lay in the askew pile.

'Not that I can see,' he said, flicking back and forward through the book hunting for any other clues. 'What about on the answer machine?'

'Well not as far as I've heard … but I stopped it before the end …' I stood up. 'Let's have a listen.' And the two of us marched into the kitchen. Pencil poised, I pressed play.

'Joe. Gordon Ferguson here – will be in on Tuesday for early supper with the boys – it's Jean's birthday – hoping you could do us a wee cake for a surprise. You know my number so give me a shout when you get this.'

William nodded. 'I'll take care of that.'

Beep. There was a delay of a few seconds and fully expecting a robotic automated sales call, I was ready to press next when we heard it.

'Hey, Joe – it's Sherry here – Sherry Gosling – the blushing bride.' A lovely warm American voice giggled. 'I'm just checking in to say we're all on schedule this end, flying in overnight Thursday direct from JFK to Edinburgh. I'm picking up my dress on Friday and then will be arriving late Friday night, staying at The Old Course Hotel ready for the big day on Saturday. I can't believe it's finally here,' she gushed. 'Our numbers have dropped by two – so we are now at thirty-eight but other than that we are good to go. So will be there at 2 p.m. sharp Saturday. Call me if there are any problems – otherwise see you then!' There was a pause.

'Make sure the sun is shining!' She laughed and then there was a click as she hung up.

William and I looked at each other. She sounded lovely. Giddy with excitement, as any bride should be. Thirty-eight people and by the sounds of things, some if not all coming all the way from America. Holy shit.

'Holy shit,' I confirmed.

'Yes quite,' said William. 'OK.' I could tell he was fighting to control the hysteria that lurked just below the surface. 'We have no choice. We're not letting her down, and realistically between the two of us...'

He looked at me for reassurance. I shook my head vigorously.

'OK, don't panic,' he countered, resting his hand on my arm, trying to quell my urge to run for the hills. 'Let's get a hold of Dougie and get him back in to help. If you're confident to scrub up and help out front then the two of us can handle that side of things.'

He sounded so confident I almost believed him.

'And what about this place?' I said, assessing the dark and empty restaurant.

'We'll spruce it up a bit.'

I guffawed. 'Spruce it up a bit? Do they have napalm in St Andrews?'

'It's not that bad. Admittedly it is a bit sad and dark today but for good reason. I'll phone Mouse, our part-timer; she's about to graduate from art school and by the time we've waved our magic wand over it, it will be fabulous. We'll just have to do our best and make it a day to remember. A last hurrah for this lovely woman and her wedding and for us so we can remember The Birdie & Bramble as a busy buzzing restaurant rather than this.' He waved his arm around.

I nodded. Of course. He was right. We couldn't let them

down, not at this late stage, and I knew Dad would have gone all out to make it a brilliant day.

William looked at me, egging me on. 'Come on, Maddy, you know what Joe would have said.'

Like a tap tears filled my eyes again. 'The show must go on,' we said in unison.

'Exactly – so let's do it – for him.'

Demonstrating diminishing sanity, against my better judgement and belief we could pull it off, much to my surprise I agreed.

First things first, we had to try and find Dougie, the pissed chef, and appeal to his better nature to come back and help us out one last time. I assumed this would be William's job until he piped up. 'Will you have a word with him?'

My eyebrows shot up. 'Me? Why?'

'Well he loved your dad and he's never been that keen on me.'

'I couldn't imagine anyone not being keen on you. Why?'

'He's old-school and when I arrived he was quite defensive about any changes I suggested – no matter how small – so I just think our best shot is if you try to talk him round.'

'OK,' I concurred. 'I'll do my best. Where do you think he is?'

'The Rum & Lash.'

'Oh. Can't I phone him?'

'He hasn't he got a mobile.'

'Oh. OK then, I'd better get cracking ... What time is it?'

'They're open from 8 a.m. 'til yon time – they'll be open,' he said, sensing correctly I was looking for any excuse not to go. But I could tell by the look in his eyes I wasn't getting off that lightly.

'OK.' I stood up and put my coat on. 'I'm off. I'll report back as soon as I can.'

'Thanks, Maddy. And good luck!' he shouted as the door shut behind me.

Chapter 5

It was a blue-sky day but cold as hell and as I stood in the corridor outside, the chill took my breath away. The icy east coast wind whipped in, freezing my nose and my hands as I stuffed them into my pockets. Pulling my full-length duvet coat tight round me, Frank at my heels, I clipped his lead on and was ready to stride out when I realised I had no idea where I was going.

William laughed when I re-entered the restaurant.

'I wondered how long it would take you to realise … it's not one of your trendy student-type pubs.' He handed me a hastily drawn map on a Post-it. 'If you head down to the harbour, you'll see it on the left-hand side, usually with some grey-faced codger outside having a fag.'

It was the first time I'd walked through the town since arriving. I took in the familiar streets, houses, shops and people. Despite everyone being wrapped up against the elements, myself included, we recognised one another. Some nodded, others smiled and two or three stopped to offer their condolences. I had forgotten what a real community felt like. I had been living a very insular life in London until I met Marcus.

The first year I in lived in London, I shared a big house in Clapham with four others but the days of communal living and sharing fridges predictably lost their charm, so two years ago I moved in with Keira, a sports journalist who was away more often than not. After the novelty of my own space wore off, though I never admitted it, I felt quite lonely. Sometimes shop assistants or tellers in the supermarket were the only people I spoke to in person between Friday night and Monday morning.

I never confessed this to anyone, especially Dad. He would have been absolutely horrified to think of me killing time with box sets and wandering round shops until Monday morning came round. Of course I knew people at work, but our socialising was done during the week. On Friday everyone beetled off to whatever area they lived in and stayed there until Monday rolled round. When Marcus and I met, part of the attraction was the novelty of having someone to share my weekends with. Having someone to crawl onto the sofa with and snuggle up to meant weekends were ... well weekends again. Simple things.

Coming home to St Andrews underlined how much my life had changed.

Battling the elements, I was just about to pass a woman with her head down, wrestling a double buggy, when I realised it was Sarah – my oldest and bestest school friend. I felt awful. I hadn't been in touch.

'Sarah!' I exclaimed as we came up level on the pavement.

'Maddy! Hi! What a lovely surprise.' And then her face fell, as she remembered. 'Oh God, I am so so sorry. I heard just now about your dad – what a shock,' she said.

'I know. I'm so sorry, I should have phoned you but ...'

'Maddy! Don't be daft. You know where we are and please, if there is anything we can do, even if you just fancy a cup of tea, a G and T and a howl, come round any time day or night ...' She smiled up at me, a look of concern etched on her face.

I smiled back. She knew me so well I didn't need to pretend anything.

'Thanks, Sarah. I really appreciate that ...'

'Mummy!' came a plaintive cry from within the water-proofed buggy.

'Ah no rest for the wicked.' She grinned, crouching down and saying in a gentle voice, 'Shoosht, darling, we're almost there,' before turning back to me. 'I meant what I said ... any time.'

We said our farewells and I continued my journey to find the drunken chef.

The sea was dark and churning up angrily. The wind blew straight into my face as I leant hard into it to retain a vertical position. Like a slap in the face, invigorating, pinpricks of rain stung my face and within minutes I saw The Rum & Lash. Despite the weather, as William had said the frontage was non-existent but the clue I was heading in the right direction was a wee guy in a kagoul. He was huddled in the doorway and smoking a cigarette.

So keen was I get in out of the squall, I pushed the Public Bar door firmly just as someone was pulling it from the other side to come out, so I more or less fell into the place with Frank. Like a rammel of bricks, I thought, feeling my cheeks flare red, as I dropped Frank's lead and busied myself smoothing down my ridiculously knotted hair and unravelled the scarf, which was in danger of strangling me. Composure marginally regained, I unzipped my sodden coat and looking up realised that despite it being only 11.30 a.m. the place was busy. Three or four men sat at the bar nursing their drinks; a few others were dotted around the tables. I was the only woman in the place.

Approaching the bar, I tried to look nonchalant whilst

ordering a lime and soda. The barman eyed me as he poured the drink.

'You're Joe's girl.'

I was out of practice with being in this close community. I had forgotten there was no escape. Dad had spent his entire life within five miles of this very spot and relished the fact he knew virtually everyone, as they did him. It was one of the reasons I had left St Andrews as soon as I could. How could you rage against the machine and spread your wings in a place where everyone knew your father, your father's father and your business.

The barman continued, seeing the expression on my face, which had fallen, all pretence of confidence gone. 'Och, hen,' he said, his face softening, 'we're all so sorry to hear about your dad.'

There was a low rumble of consensus from the others.

I smiled and acknowledged his sentiment with a nod, unable to trust myself to speak. He understood.

'Well, Joe and I go back a long way,' he said with conviction, 'so this one's on the house. Are you sure you wouldn't like something a little stronger?'

'Oh no,' I blurted rather too quickly and noticing a flicker of disappointment cross his face thought better of it. 'Actually, yes, that would be lovely thanks.'

He gave a satisfied nod. 'A wee dram it is then.'

After putting two tumblers on the counter he carefully selected a bottle from the back of the bar. He twisted the top off and free-poured two generous measures.

'The Mortlach. Joe's favourite,' he stated.

Silently we raised our glasses, as one of the other men, overhearing our chat, stood up rather unsteadily and gave a toast.

'Fa's like us? Damn few. And they're a' deid.'

The barman looked at me and rolled his eyes. 'He means well.'

I snorted. You couldn't make it up, I thought, as the man settled back on his stool and continued staring into space.

We clanked our glasses together. 'To Joe,' he said as we both swallowed them in a oner.

A warm feeling spread across my belly and I felt my shoulders relax just enough to realise I'd been so clenched they had been up somewhere round my ears.

Suddenly I felt stronger, braver – hell, like my father's daughter.

'Thank you,' I said, smiling at the barman. 'I'm looking for Dougie.'

'The chef?'

'Aye.'

'That's him.' He indicated the man who had just made the toast.

I looked again. Shocked. I hadn't even recognised him. The man I had known since I was a girl was a wiry chatterbox with a jaunty gait and a twinkle in his eye. The person I saw now was a sad, defeated old man. The barman continued, 'Aye ... he's taken it hard.' Recognising my expression, he added, 'You'll no' get much sense out of him. He's been in here day and night since ...' he hesitated '...well you know.'

I nodded and made my way over to Dougie, who sat at a small round copper dimpled table. He had developed, as Dad would have described it, a very expensive nose and was nursing what looked like a pint.

'Dougie?' I asked.

He looked up, jaundiced eyes unfocused.

'Mind if I join you?' I pulled up a stool and sat down.

'Mmmm,' was all he managed.

'It's Maddy,' I said, slowly watching as his eyes rolled back towards me, showing a vague flicker of recognition. I gave him another clue. 'Maddy, Joe's girl.' At this, a light seemed to go on behind his rheumy eyes and he reached out and clasped my hand.

'Och, Maddy ...' He shook his head. 'Maddy pet ... Joe's lassie ...' Tears filled his eyes. 'I loved that man ... He was a ... true ... gent. And,' he added, voice trembling and tightening his grip, 'the bestest friend I ever had and ...' He lost focus for a moment before snapping back and leaning in closer. 'I'll tell you something.' To punctuate the importance of this next revelation, he released my hand and grabbed my forearm with surprising strength. 'He was that proud of you ... telling us about how well you were doing in that London. Och ...' His eyes dropped down to the pint again and his spark dimmed. He slumped back releasing my arm. 'It's the end of an era.'

I nodded. He seemed to have run out of steam. We sat in silence for a moment.

'The thing is, Dougie, I want to talk to you. I was hoping you could help me out ...'

'Anything, pet, anything,' he said, reaching for his pint and draining it with one hand whilst waving at the barman with his other hand, indicating another one was required.

'William and I have been in, going through all the stuff, and we've managed to cancel all the bookings except one.'

Dougie's unfocused expression did its best to stay with me.

'It's a wedding party.'

Still no reaction.

'It's this Saturday.'

He took a slurp of his new pint as he nodded to the barman who had just delivered it. 'The thing is, Dougie, we've got to do it. They've paid a deposit and they're coming all the way from America. If these people turn up and the place is shut, it will be the worst instead of the best day of their lives. I couldn't bear that. We just can't let them down.'

Dougie's eyes swivelled to my face, trying to focus. 'This Saturday?'

'Yes.'

'Then what?'

'Then ...' I looked at him directly. 'I don't know.'

'Right,' he said, staring at the table, taking out a pouch of tobacco and rolling himself a wee tabby, putting it to his lips, and lighting it.

'OK, Dougie, but this weekend – this one last time ... please ... you know what Dad would have said?'

Dougie gave a worryingly wheezy guffaw as he removed some stray fronds of tobacco from his nicotine-stained lip. 'Aye, the show must go on.'

I smiled at him. 'Well?'

'Well ... write it all down on here.' He proffered a sodden beer mat. 'Then I won't forget.'

I was not getting a good feeling about this at all.

'OK, Dougie ... well how about I phone you?'

'I don't have a phone.'

'A mobile?' I asked.

'Any phone.'

And before I could continue, before I could get any sense out of him, his head lolled back and he let out a low rumbling snort, leaving me face-to-face with his scrawny purple Adam's apple. I looked up to find the barman watching.

'Ah that's him,' said the barman. 'He's been here since yon time.' He glanced at the clock. 'It's about now he keels over for an hour or so and then when he comes round he'll just keep on drinking – he's afa' man.' He shook his head sadly. 'Lost.'

Well I am nothing if not a trier. So yanking a pen and

a piece of paper from my jacket pocket I jotted down the details:

'Wedding. The Birdie & Bramble 2 p.m. Saturday.' I rolled it up and left it poking out of the pocket on his shirt. Then I primed the barman to draw his attention to it when he came round.

Emerging from the dark, boozy atmosphere of the pub, the chill north-east wind instantly rendered the effect of the whisky null and void as I hiked back up to the High Street and The Birdie & Bramble to report back to William. 'Aw shit.'

'Why?'

'He is seriously back on the booze. He's been off it for nearly four years.'

'Oh shit.' I could see his point.

'OK, Maddy. Tell me exactly what happened.'

So I did, confessing he was virtually unconscious when I left.

'Shit. Hardly a contract of employment then.'

'No. Fair point. Shit,' I concurred. 'OK then, it's on to Plan B?' I looked at him. 'Do we have a plan B?'

William laughed but not in a very amused way. 'Well not yet.' Fiddling about in his ream of papers, he selected a few bits, plucking them out and putting them down on the table. 'Looking at Joe's rather brief notes I have to say from what I've gleaned, it's all fairly straightforward. Well when I say straightforward, it is if you have a chef!'

'What about you?'

His left eye twitched. 'Me?' He prodded himself in the chest with his index finger.

'Yes, William. You. I wasn't joking when I told you that breakfast we had this morning was the best I've ever had. You are a seriously talented cook.'

'Cook, maybe. But chef?'

'Well, what's the difference? And as you said it's a total one-off and, you never know, Dougie might rally. So I suggest we make our plan, get it all ordered up and then if Dougie turns up well and good and if not? Well the wedding breakfast goes ahead. Belt and braces.'

'Maddy, when they booked a wedding "breakfast", I don't think they meant actual breakfast – cocoa pops, poached eggs and haggis.' William was clearly unconvinced.

'How hard can it be?'

He looked at me. 'OK, you do it.'

I felt the blood drain from my face. 'Oh God not me!'

He eyed me suspiciously.

'I can't do it. I used to dabble but honestly I haven't cooked properly for years.'

William tilted his head, trying to gauge if I was joking.

I confirmed I wasn't. 'But I can follow instructions and I will be your willing slave.'

He glanced at me.

'And I do make an outstanding margarita.'

His face broke into a grin. 'Well in that case …'

'So how about it? Let's get everything prepped assuming Dougie will turn up and if not then, well, we'll just have to give it our best shot. One last hurrah for The Birdie & Bramble – as a mark of respect for Dad. He would never let anyone down, especially on the biggest day of their—'

But before I could finish William capitulated. 'OK OK, for God's sake stop!'

'Does that mean you'll do it?'

'Of course I will – to be honest you had me at last hurrah.'

I jumped up and hugged him hard.

'Maddy Campbell, you've got a hug like an all-in wrestler – bloody hell!'

And so we settled down side by side at the table, the bookings book open between us, trying to decipher what Dad might have had in mind.

The sum total of our investigations was they had requested 'Scottish food' and that was about it.

We agreed to make it as simple as possible.

William wrote frantically and I watched him scribble, score out and look up, his forehead ridged, eyes ablaze, as I topped up his tea and sat in wonder as he pulled it together.

'OK,' he said decisively. 'Scottish seafood is the best in the world. I'll get on to Davy the Fish. He'll give us credit and order up the goodies for Friday afternoon. That means I can cook it up late on Friday night then first thing on Saturday, we can put it out on platters. It will give us a head start.'

'Yes brilliant! It will taste great – it''ll look fab too.' Egging him on, I continued, 'So if we are going cold buffet, how about Uncle Fraser's rib of beef – it's legendary. I will sort that out with him, so all you need to do is ...'

'Cook it?' He looked at me, his eyes beginning to crinkle at the edges with what almost resembled a smile.

'Well yes,' I agreed, 'but that could be made earlier too and then served cold with home-made horseradish sauce, mountains of fresh buttered kale and a new potato salad. It'll be just like a Sunday lunch but posher ...'

'And bigger ...' he added, chewing the end of his pencil and rereading the notes.

Another refill of coffee and we talked through the possibilities. Within thirty minutes the menu we settled on was simple but delicious.

Champagne and canapés.

Seafood platter, home-made mayonnaise, warm brown bread and unsalted butter served with chilled French Chablis.

Cold roast rib of Scottish beef, fresh green salad, potato

salad. Home-made horseradish sauce. A hefty red wine was earmarked for this.

Scottish cheeseboard and oatcakes.

'Actually that sounds manageable,' William said slowly, still referring to his list.

'It sounds delicious!' I enthused.

'Oh of course we'll need a sweet,' he went on.

'I'll make Thelma's Hazelnut Cake – it was the first thing Dad ever taught me to make. I love it so much that when I was feeling a bit homesick in London, I would whip one up and eat the lot in one sitting, so tick that box.'

Thelma's Hazelnut Cake – The Birdie & Bramble's unique dessert – was a family recipe from my Grandma Thel, which had brought many a mere mortal to their knees with hazelnut meringue, seasonal fruit and whipped cream.

'What about the wine and champagne stuff?' I asked.

We looked at each other. 'Noel,' we said out loud at the same time and laughed.

My tummy was churning, a mix of nerves and excitement.

'Can we really pull this off?' I put my hand on his sleeve and looked at him seriously.

'Yes, Madeline Campbell, we bloody well can – or if not, we'll go down in a blaze of glory!' he announced, pushing his chair back and standing up. 'But there's not a moment to spare – let's get cracking, madam. Now first things first. I'll contact the suppliers and order up the food; you head to Fraser's and get some bacon rolls. I'll make a vat of coffee and after we have scoffed that lot we'll be ready for anything.'

Galvanised into action, I shot off across the road, grateful for this mayhem that would distract me from the fact that in less than twenty-four hours I would be burying my father.

By the end of the afternoon, orders were in. Noel – once he got over the initial shock – had agreed to help with anything as well as selecting and ordering the wine, and Mouse – the part-timer – had texted back to say she was free too.

As I emerged from the restaurant, adrenalin high, my phone buzzed.

'You don't get a signal in the restaurant?' said William as I howked it out of my pocket.

It was Marcus.

'Hey, babe, how are you doing?'

'Well you know...'

'Sure. Well I wanted to let you now I've swung it so I am on the red-eye tomorrow morning but I'll have to be back tomorrow night and back in the office on Friday.'

'God that's so fantastic. I am so happy you're coming up. Thank you so much. Is there no way you can stay?' That last bit came out sounding a little desperate.

'Sorry, Mads, I really can't – you know what it's like at work.'

That sinking feeling – I really wanted to see him, to have some human contact, to feel his support. But he was coming up; hell it was going to have to do. I rallied. He was doing his best. 'That's great, Marcus. Thank you. I really do appreciate it. Now can I help sort a lift out for you from Edinburgh?'

'No, don't worry, love, you've got enough on your plate. Give me the details and I'll be there.'

Chapter 6

St Andrews is a coastal town. Chocolate-box wee Victorian houses cheek by jowl line the streets. The university is world-famous as is the derelict St Andrews Castle, the Rule tower – a mighty 156 steps to climb but the view as you get your breath back would take it away again: a panoramic view of the town and the North Sea and West Sands stretching miles into the distance. Since 1214 the tower has stood watching over the happenings, the comings, goings, the hatches, matches and dispatches of the townspeople – and this was just another day.

For me it was not just another day – it was the day I was burying my father. I woke at five. Sleep was not forthcoming so after quietly rising and showering I wrapped up against the elements. With Frank under one arm and my wellies clasped in my hand, I tiptoed downstairs and straight out the front door.

These streets I had walked a thousand times and yet today everything looked unfamiliar. Not a soul to be seen, the pavements black, slicked with rain. Muted lights glowed from within thick-walled stone houses as people stirred before waking to just another day.

Turning from the High Street towards the sea, I buried my face deeper into my swaddling as the bracing air whipped round me. My hair blew back and coat buttons strained as I stomped on apace. Slippery cobbled streets led me down towards the harbour. Carefully I tested each footstep as I went. Churning waves smashed over the harbour wall, sending spatters of salt water into my face. The overwhelming power of the sea always held me in awe but today it only served to remind me how transient our time here was and how life, however hard it feels, goes on.

Seagulls screeched above, swooping and wheeling, foraging for food. The bravest amongst them sat defiantly on the harbour wall, almost prehistoric in size. The less brave perched nonchalantly on bollards, their glassy yellow eyes watching as I passed. Hitchcock's *The Birds* always came into my head at this point – no soundtrack, just Tippi Hedren or in this case Frank and I, surrounded by powerful birds, staring eyes, loud squawks, pointy beaks and an attitude that would make Ray Winstone look quite cuddly. *When Seagulls Go Bad: The Sequel.* We wouldn't stand a chance.

Luckily they had already eaten and the rubbery footsteps of my galoshes coupled with Frank's tick tick tick continued. He was enjoying a rare freedom off the lead, padding along the pier past small brightly painted fishing boats that bobbed as the tide ebbed. A handful of fishermen checked their nets, oblivious to our passing amidst the clanking of bells, creaking of ropes and mooring chains. Inhaling the dry salty smell of the nets, I stepped over lobster creels, the worn and tufted blue-roped cages with wooden-planked bottoms piled up for inspection for holes before being mended and hoisted back into the grey churning sea and dropped for the day's quota.

I was making my way to the worn stone steps at the far end of the pier, carved into the outside of the harbour wall over a hundred years ago for fisherman to haul their catches onto or collect supplies for their lightly tethered boats. As we sat on the top step, I noticed the wind had dropped off and a barely perceptible mist settled onto my hair and skin.

Frank nudged my arm, tucking in for warmth, so I held him close. The ever-present gulls offered a real spectacle now, wheeling and diving, circling, hunting before plunging into the sea. Snatching their prey, the fish often still thrashing in the grip of predatory beaks as they were gulped down, the birds rising up straight away to start the process again. Here in this place I felt a deep sense of peace. Of contentment. Acceptance. The circle of life.

Tempting as it was to sit for hours rather than face the day that awaited, I glanced at my mobile and saw it was already 7.30 a.m. In less than two hours I had to bury my father.

Dad had never been a religious man and it transpired that his friends had all agreed many years before what each one of them wanted when their time came. He had planned everything to a tee and Ted relayed and made sure it was just what he wanted. It was to be a celebration of life and the bar was to be open. No black ties, no Bible readings, just an open mic for a few stories from a few friends, a few drams and two pieces of music – his favourites.

The golf club said yes to Fraser when he asked about holding it in The Club Room, less than 300 metres from the restaurant and Fraser's shop.

William and Noel offered to walk me round but I felt my place was with Uncle Fraser, and so I arrived at his cottage early and rapped on the door.

The door opened immediately and I found myself staring straight into the face of my cousin Hamish.

'Hamish! Oh my God. You're back!'

His knotted hair and baggy yoga trousers suggested he'd arrived thirty seconds ago.

'Aye I was on my way back from Thailand, and the minute I landed I got the news so I jumped straight on the overnight bus. I'm so sorry, Maddy.' He squeezed me hard. 'I'm so glad I made it. I would never miss saying goodbye to my favourite uncle.'

A sob escaped as we both said in unison 'only uncle' and then he held me tight again. It was so good to see him.

Fraser broke the moment with a cheery: 'Right, come on, you two – we have places to go and people to see and you're not going in those trousers, my boy. Go and get changed. We're leaving with or without you in ten minutes flat!'

Hamish and I released each other. My cousin rolled his eyes at his dad and tore off to get changed, appearing five minutes later in a suit he must have bought at a charity shop in the nineties. It was far too small. His wrists and their numerous frayed wristbands dangled out from the end of the too short arms, and his sockless feet were visible from the too short legs. I didn't care what he looked like; he was here and that was all that mattered, though I could see Fraser fighting the urge to say something. It was neither the time nor the place so silently we left the house for the short walk to the golf club. As we turned the corner, the famous clubhouse dominating our view, Fraser took my arm exclaiming, 'Well now, Maddy, would you look at that – a mark of the man indeed – the golf club flag is flying at half mast.'

'Well well well,' said Auntie Margaret, 'I've never seen that before.'

I smiled as tears filled my eyes. A detail I would never have noticed and yet one I knew would have made my dear dad burst with pride.

As we got closer we saw a number of people gathering, greeting each other sombrely and filing in.

'Looks like a good turnout,' Hamish remarked.

'Oh aye. Joe was a well-kent and well-loved face – they'll come from miles around.'

I confess I thought Fraser was exaggerating in his default

setting as a caring and supportive uncle and brother-in-law, but on entering the clubhouse the low murmur of voices became increasingly loud until some would have said an unseemly loud noise surrounded us. My grip tightened on Fraser's arm as he stopped briefly before we joined the throng. He put his great big hand over mine and squeezed.

'Come on, lass. Let's get this over with. Now, are you ready?'

I nodded, unable to find my voice.

A large carpeted room was set out with rows and rows of chairs. A makeshift stage at the front held a lectern and a small reading light. Golfing shields illustrating the history of this club adorned the walls and the music that was playing was as far from a hymn as you could imagine. It was 'Leaning on A Lamp Post' by George Formby – an absolute favourite of Dad's and one he would sing at the drop of a hat, given half the chance. There was no resemblance whatsoever to the austere atmosphere of organised religion. Dad would have approved.

As we entered the room the low buzz petered out, the crowd settling. Everyone took their seats as Fraser led me to the front where we took our places sandwiched between Auntie Margaret and my cousin Hamish. Uncle Ted and Auntie Faye flanked us on one side, William and Noel on the other. I felt supported and grateful to have such lovely people around me. Prior to this moment I had decided I might say a few words but when it came to the bit I just couldn't do it, so Ewan Blair, the editor of the local paper and long-term friend of Dad, stood up and did a wonderful eulogy. Full of laughs, a brief history, and some outrageous tales of his shenanigans over the years.

I couldn't be specific about any of it other than the two songs. Firstly 'Ae Fond Kiss' by Eddi Reader – a Robert

Burns song, which even on the best of days could reduce me to a sobbing wreck. This had a similar effect on the assembled throng and just as the strains of that trailed off, our tears of sadness merged into tears of mirth as 'Our Glens' by Scotland The What? began, which everyone, thanks to the overhead projector, joined in.

Uncle Fraser, tears swimming in his eyes, instinctively clapped when the song stopped and as he realised what he had done went bright red by which time his cue was picked up by the others, starting with slight hesitation and building to a crescendo of clapping and cheering, which continued for several minutes, as my hands stung and tears rolled down my cheeks. Such a joyful outpouring of affection for my dear old dad raised the rafters and naturally reduced me to a blubbering wreck whilst at the same time filled my heart to overflowing.

At just the right moment, Uncle Ted took to the front of the room and announced, 'Right, you lot, the bar is open and as our dear friend was aye first to the bar – today is no exception – the first round's on Joe.'

It was over. I slipped my arm through Uncle Fraser's as we filed out towards the bar. He put his arm round me. 'Your dad wouldn't want any tears or long faces so let's just go straight to the bar and get a drink,' he said, taking control. I nodded.

Heading in that direction we stopped briefly to say hello to one or two people and by the time we got to it, there was already a huddle. At one end of the bar Dougie huddled over a pint and a nip, and to my surprise next to him was Marcus. It was the first time I had seen him, and when he spotted me he held out his arms. I automatically walked over and allowed myself to be wrapped in his embrace for a moment – warm, human contact, my eyes tightly shut, relishing the moment. I would have preferred to stay right there but reluctantly I released my grip and accepted the large whisky Fraser handed me.

Before I even had a chance to introduce them, Marcus faded into the background as Fraser stood by my side, supporting me as a seemingly endless stream of people came to pay their respects. I got a mighty comforting hug from Sarah and some other old school friends who had come along. Some of the folk I knew, some I didn't, some I recognised, some I didn't, some hugged me hard, others shook my hand, but without exception the feeling I got from every single one of them was the deep affection they had for Dad. Of course I knew he was a special man but I was hugely touched when I realised how many other people recognised and shared that opinion.

One whisky, two whiskies. I had no idea how much time passed as Fraser introduced me to all comers. I did my best to take on board who was who, when I noticed a vaguely familiar man making his way through the crowd towards me. Broad in the beam, in a garish three-piece tweed, agitatedly he checked his straggly comb-over as he approached. He's nervous, I thought, putting my hand out to introduce myself, but instead of shaking it he thrust an envelope into it.

'Thank you,' I said as he reddened, grunted, and then turned and blustered away through the crowd as fast as he could, without a backward glance.

'How odd,' I said. 'Remind me, who was that?'

'The Laird,' Fraser said in a voice that betrayed he was not a fan. 'Barclay MacPherson.'

'Well it was nice of him to come and pay his respects. He didn't need to,' I said, automatically defending this stranger.

Fraser opened his mouth to respond but before he could

elaborate, Hattie Cordiner, the local drama queen, pushed in, and a cloud of overpowering perfume engulfed me.

'Och, Madeline. Your dad.' She craned her neck, bringing her face ever closer, not a respecter of personal space, I thought, as her powdery fizzog brushed my cheek and she bared her lipstick-covered teeth. 'Whit a lovely lovely man he wiz.'

I nodded but before I could get a word in, her smoke-and-whisky-soaked breath washed over me. 'He had a glad eye for me once, you know, when we were kids.' Her claw-like grip tightened on my arm as her watery eyes tried to focus on mine. 'Oh yes, if I had my time again,' she sighed.

'Och, Hattie, away you go,' said Fraser shooing her away. 'You've had a skinful – don't be upsetting Maddy with your nonsense.'

Her mouth set in a tight line, she backed off. 'It's probably time we made a move. Once the drink's in it's wits out,' Fraser said, looking at Hattie's wobbly retreat.

I nodded. I had not had a moment to think. I had no idea what time it was. I was bone-tired. I just wanted to go home. I turned to the bar but couldn't see Marcus.

'Have you seen Marcus – the man who was here earlier?' I asked Fraser.

'No,' he said, craning his neck and scanning the room.

I did my best to hide my disappointment. 'OK, I should say goodbye to … everyone,' I muttered with no enthusiasm whatsoever.

'Don't worry about that, dear, people understand. Come on, we'll just slip out.'

The relief I felt at his words was huge and so I let him lead me towards the door, nodding but not engaging with the stragglers, and then we were outside in the cold, quiet, dark evening.

'A dram back at our place?' he asked. I did my best to smile.

'No thanks, Fraser, I'm absolutely done in.'

'No problem. Me too. Where are you staying?'

'With William and Noel.'

'OK, come on then I'll walk you back. It's been a long day.'

The boys perfectly judging the situation as ever had left a note, a flask of soup and some sandwiches, instinctively knowing I would want to be alone. Slumping onto the sofa I checked my phone.

Text: *'Hope you are OK. So sorry didn't get to say goodbye. Had to get the last flight back so slipped out. Will call tomorrow. M xx'*

Heavy-limbed, I climbed the stairs to my room, closed the door and howled into my pillow, until I fell asleep.

Chapter 7

The following morning was surreal. The alarm was set for 6 a.m. but I was awake some time before it went off. Lying there cosy, snuggled up in my duvet, Frank's gentle snoring punctuating the peace, back in St Andrews. If I dwelled on the events of the previous day and its seismic significance, I would simply roll over and stay there for, well, possibly forever, but thankfully there was the small matter of a wedding to prepare for and such a distraction could not have been more welcome.

We had just over twenty-four hours to get The Birdie & Bramble shipshape. It was a big ask but William and I were determined to do our best for the bride and groom, whoever they were. This was The Birdie & Bramble's last hurrah and our chance to make it a day to remember for the rest of their lives – and ours – hopefully for all the right reasons.

A brusque knock at the door interrupted my pep talk to myself.

'Cup of tea?' said a very perky-sounding William, swinging his head round the door.

'Yes please,' I said, shuffling up to a seated position, plumping up my pillows before taking the big steaming mug of tea from his outstretched hand.

'Are you OK?' he asked in a gentler tone, perching on the bottom of the bed.

I nodded.

'Sure?' he persisted, his eyebrows aloft and giving me a direct look.

'Yes,' I said, sounding a lot more confident than I felt.

'Good because I don't mean to be insensitive but we have a helluva lot to do and I think the earlier we get stuck in, the better.'

'Yes, boss.'

'OK, breakfast in five.' He grinned and with that he leapt up and was off back downstairs at speed.

After a couple of big sips of the strong sweet tea, I peeled the duvet back and had a brief snuggle with Frank who was still sound asleep, curled up in a ball, next to where my legs had just been. Sensing movement, he opened one lazy eye.

'You've got ten minutes longer in bed, you wee hairball, then we are off – we've got a wedding to organise!'

Opening the door of The Birdie & Bramble, all our bluff and bluster stopped. It was sobering to see the deflated, dark, unloved-looking restaurant in the cold light of day. Could we really pull this off?

'Oh, William,' I said, my bowels loosening at what we had taken on. 'Can we really throw a wedding here? It just looks so...'

'Yes, we bloody well can.' He cut me off, refusing to engage in my doubting tone. 'I have a list.'

'Oh that's OK then,' I said sarcastically, 'we can relax now.'

He squeezed my arm. 'Relax? No. But be confident you are in the hands of a bossy control freak who will not rest 'til it's done? Yes.'

Despite my misgivings I returned his grin as he updated me on progress so far. William, it seemed, had been up most of the night too but he'd had a more constructive time.

'I phoned Mouse last night. She's coming in this morning.

She's great – she helps out in the kitchen and she's graduating from art school this summer so she's bound to have some ideas of how to dress the place up.'

'Great.'

'Unfortunately the usual part-timers are students and they're all on exam leave or holiday.'

'Well if we need anyone else, my cousin Hamish is back. He's been working in bars and restaurants for the past two years all over the world. I'm sure he'll help us out.'

'Sounds good – I'll leave that to you,' he said, putting my initials by that particular item on the elongating list.

'Right!' he said, pushing his chair back and standing up. 'We need to start clearing this restaurant and making it look fresh and inviting – how do you feel about doing that?'

'As a lapsed domestic goddess – deliriously excited,' I retorted and seeing a slightly crestfallen look, jollied him along. 'I am ready, willing and able to get started. What about you?'

'Well if you're happy to sign for any deliveries, I'm just going to nip over to have a word with Uncle Fraser about the beef,' he said, putting his jacket back on and heading for the door.

'Oh God you're not leaving me here are you?' I said, panic rising.

'Mouse will be here any minute – you can manage 'til then,' he said so convincingly I almost believed him as I marched into the kitchen and grabbed a pair of marigolds to get stuck into the cleaning. But before I had even snapped them on, I heard the front door open again.

'Coooeeee!!!' A high voice pierced the quiet.

Gloves on, I walked back into the dining room and found this high falsetto squeak rather incongruously had come from a girl completely clad in black. Long black hair hung like curtains over her shoulders. She had white face,

79

heavy black eye make-up, black fingerless gloves revealing black-nail-varnished fingernails, a baggy dress and big heavy Doc Marten boots – yes, they were black too. Her lipstick, although black, was all the more noticeable for the multiple piercings she had running from the corner of her top lip, almost joining in the middle. Her ears and her nose were similarly bejewelled. The 'Oh!' that escaped from my lips before I reined myself in gave away my surprise. 'Mouse?'

'Yes,' said the sweetest lilting voice I had ever heard. Such mellifluous tones emanating from this stalwart-looking goth!

'I know, I know,' she countered, 'it's not my real name – my real name is Dorcas – but when I was in primary 2, some bright spark thought I sounded exactly like Minnie Mouse so I got lumbered with the nickname Mouse from that day to this. Everyone, including my parents, assumed my voice would change as I grew up—' she prodded her tummy '—and out.' She grinned, causing her multiple piercings to clink along her top lip. 'But the voice and thus the name has stuck ever since.'

She laughed a surprisingly deep laugh before returning three octaves higher to say, as she took a step forward, 'You must be Maddy. I'm so sorry I didn't make it along to say goodbye to Joe yesterday – I loved that man like a…' She hesitated.

'Father?' I filled the pause.

'Yes.' She looked crestfallen. 'I'm sorry, that was a daft thing to say.'

'No it wasn't. I'm just so happy to know Dad had such lovely people around him.' She blushed, shifting from boot to boot. 'And I can't tell you what a relief it is to know you're here to help me and William.'

'My pleasure,' she said, revealing behind her black lipstick, meticulous even white teeth. 'So, what do you want me to do?'

I looked at her, brain in neutral.

'OK, I vote we start with a cup of tea,' she said, taking control. And so we did.

Like a white witch, I thought, as I watched her capably bustling round. It was apparent she knew The Birdie & Bramble like the back of her hand. Within a minute or two, as I walked round like a rabbit caught in headlights not quite sure where to start, she produced a tray with a teapot, two cups, saucers and even a wee jug of milk and, I kid you not, a doily-covered plate with half a dozen Hobnobs on it. Setting it down in the dining room, I thought: externally a goth – internally Mary Poppins/Berry.

'I'll pour,' she said, channelling Berry and going about her business. Sipping my hot sweet tea, as ever it seemed to make everything seem better. I started the ball rolling.

'William told me you were a bit of a whizz with decor and the like. I was really hoping we can turn this—' I waved my arm at the dark, uninspiring room behind me '—into a beautiful setting for a wedding by the end of today.'

She laughed.

I didn't.

She looked at me, her smile falling away as it dawned on her. 'Oh my God, you're serious?'

I grinned.

'Shit,' she said, 'then we'd better get cracking.'

'OK, give me my instructions,' I said, digging into my bag for paper and a pen. 'Oh I completely forgot about this,' I said, grabbing the envelope the Laird had handed me at the funeral, which I had hastily stuffed into my vast cavern of a bag. 'It was thoughtful of him to give me a card,' I murmured more to myself than anyone else.

'Who?' Mouse had no idea what I was talking about.

'Barclay MacPherson, the Laird. Yesterday he came along to pay his respects and gave me this,' I said, waving a rather utilitarian brown envelope in front of her. Quite different to the usual creamy embossed envelope associated with sympathy cards and handwritten letters, I thought briefly as I fished out the contents. To my surprise it was not in fact a card at all.

I read the address at the top out loud.

'Fitzpatrick and Gordon, Solicitors.' I didn't get a good feeling.

'What the?' said Mouse, standing up and boldly reading over my shoulder as I continued.

By Hand.

This notice is served by Sir Barclay MacPherson to repossess the residential flat located in 125/2 North Street. The tenancy agreement between the proprietor, Sir James B. MacPherson, and the tenant, Mr Joe Campbell recently deceased, is now null and void.

In 28 days' time the property reverts back to the possession of Mr Barclay MacPherson and his heirs in perpetuity.

In recognition of the circumstances of the termination of this agreement therefore the property must be vacated and returned to the estate in good and proper condition by the agreed date.

Yours sincerely, on behalf of Sir Barclay MacPherson

And there was an illegible scrawl.

Shocked, I slumped back in my chair as William pushed the front door open with his backside, barrelling in backwards and clutching a crate of beer.

'Uncle Fraser is a complete star – he has a beautiful well-hung rib of beef in the cold store for us and a few other ...' He stopped mid sentence, clocking my expression. 'Maddy, what is it? You look awful.'

Sick to the pit of my stomach, I handed him the letter.

'The bastard,' said Mouse under her breath.

William read the contents.

'Oh. My. God.' His expression was incredulous.

'He can't do this! Can he?' I demanded, anger flaring.

'Well I have no idea but whether he can or not, but what a shitty thing to do the day after your father's funeral.'

'The day of the funeral,' I whispered, 'he gave it to me at the funeral.'

William's eyes popped. 'What a heartless bastard.'

My heart thudded hard, tears burned behind my eyes, I couldn't breathe …

My life was falling apart. The flat above The Birdie & Bramble was the only home I had ever known. The place as a newborn Mum and Dad had taken me back to, the last place I could remember my lovely mum, of her stroking my hair, singing to me, her perfume, her smile. Happy hectic days with Dad in the midst of it, in his element, juggling family life with his business below. The soundtrack to my life, the constant low rumble of a busy restaurant, muffled voices punctuated with bursts of laughter. When I left to go to uni, I left from here and about year after that, when my dearest Grandma Catherine passed away, Dad talked about moving to Archie and Catherine's Estate cottage, as long term it would be better to be on one floor as he got older. There was also a bit of outside space for Frank. But when push came to shove Dad stayed put, above the restaurant, saying it was better to be in town, close to the business and his beloved golf course after all. I had all but forgotten it was rented. The idea of having to leave it was too much … It was too soon, I couldn't think clearly. I couldn't think at all. I was upset and confused. I had forgotten how to breathe. I looked at William, who was pacing as Mouse stood back and munched a Hobnob, watching.

William halted his pacing and broke the silence. 'The Laird is completely out of order. Always has been. He's been sniffing around trying get your dad out for years.'

'I had no idea,' I mumbled, falling even further into despair. 'Dad never said a word.'

'OK. Listen, we need to calm down and think logically about this before we all plunge into the depths of depression. First things first, Maddy, you need good legal advice. Your dad's lawyer?'

'Gerald Collins.'

'OK, you need to speak to him. Do you have his number?'

'Em … I …' I felt disconnected as if I was floating, looking down on myself. 'I … no … not offhand no …'

'Right I'll google him, and phone and tell him what's happened – it might be all bluff and bluster. The Laird is a bully and a chancer and there's no point in worrying about it 'til it's happened.'

'Well it has happened.'

'No it hasn't. This is a letter. That's all – and we're not going down without a fight.'

William went off to call Gerald and made me an appointment to see him at five o'clock that afternoon. As if I didn't have enough to deal with, I thought, thanking him whilst wanting to roll into a ball and stay there.

Bless William, he was full of encouragement. I loved him for being so gung-ho! I knew he was taking on the role of the optimist amidst the devastation that surrounded him but the alternative at this point was unthinkable – defeat, no wedding, no last hurrah, no nothing. My head felt like it might burst as I looked round the restaurant – dark, lifeless, a wedding in less than twenty-four hours and we were chefless in St Andrews. Mouse stroked her lip piercings, staring at the

84

floor, and even William, despite his speech to the contrary, looked momentarily lost.

A groaning dark wave of pessimism hit me. For heaven's sake. What on earth were we thinking? What a ridiculous idea. There is no way we could do a wedding in a day. These things take months – hell in some cases years – to organise. And the state of the place! Sure, it was fine for old friends and customers but beneath the bonhomie of The Birdie & Bramble lay a rather shabby little room in need of some serious TLC.

A torsion deep in my gut stopped me in my tracks. I looked at the door. With all my heart I willed this to be a bad dream and for Dad, clad in his ubiquitous golfing V-neck, to breeze in and take control. To look after the business, to give Barclay MacPherson what for ... to look after me. Even William, who I now knew was a force of nature, had a look of deep concern on his face as he watched me carefully.

'I'm sorry, I just don't know if I can do this ...' My voice quavered.

'I know, I know,' he said, his tone softer, pulling up a chair and sitting down opposite me, taking each of my hands in his. 'It's shit,' he stated.

I looked at him – I hadn't been expecting that.

'You're in shock,' he went on. 'Of course you are. You've just lost your lovely dad. And as if that wasn't bad enough, suddenly you've to deal with all this stuff, 500 miles from where you live and work. And you are now mother to that hairy baby.' He nodded to the doorway where Frank stood, his sausage dog eyebrows knitted in concern. Mouse nodded, staring at the table. 'Maddy, you're in this situation through no fault of your own. The fact you chose to honour the booking for this wedding was a brave decision – not an easy one – but little as I know you, you're so like your dad honestly it didn't surprise me at all. Gumption. That's what your dad called it.'

I managed a watery smile.

'Then to cap it all, bloody Barclay MacPherson sticks the boot in. The man is a great big blustering arse and has made it clear for all the time I've been here that all he wants to do is get your dad out of the flat and The Birdie & Bramble.'

'Why The Birdie & Bramble?'

William hesitated. Surely to God there was not more bad news.

'Go on,' I ordered.

'OK, well it's not The Birdie & Bramble business as such but the building it's in.'

I felt sick to the pit of my stomach.

'I'm afraid he owns the bricks and mortar of the restaurant too.'

My heart sank further. It was over. This was too much. I hadn't realised MacPherson owned the whole building.

'But,' he went on in a higher, more encouraging tone, 'until the lease on The Birdie & Bramble runs out, or is sold, he can't touch it. I would put money on the fact he is counting on you being so upset about him repossessing the flat that you'll just want to clear out of St Andrews altogether, thus handing him the opportunity to get the flat and the restaurant building back in a oner, which is what he's been trying to do for years.'

'Why did he hate Dad so much? Why does he hate me?'

'Maddy, as bad as this sounds, it's not personal. As I said, the man is an arse. He inherited the estate from his father Sir James B MacPherson a few years ago and has systemically run it into the ground. He's a gambler and a womaniser and is in debt up to his arse. Your grandpa and grandma's cottage was the last one on the estate still to have a tenant in it and the minute Grandma Catherine passed away he took that back too.'

The penny dropped.

'Is that why Dad didn't move in there?'

William looked down.

'Tell me the truth, William,' I ordered.

He lifted his head. 'Yes, I'm sorry to say. At the time Joe thought there was no point in worrying you with all the ancient politics of what was going on up here when you were so far away ...'

My eyes swam with tears. So that was why he had stayed in the flat, despite getting Frank. His white lie to me, which I had swallowed without question. He had been trying to protect me as he always did from anything unsavoury over which he had no control. It all made sense now. Why hadn't I quizzed him more about it? He had spoken of having outside space, somewhere for the wee dog to run about, a bit of peace and quiet. Jesus. So wrapped up in my own life I hadn't given it much, if any, thought at all. I wasn't much of daughter was I?

William continued, 'Of course Barclay sold the cottage for a pretty penny and as much as I hate to say it, the precedent has been set and cruel as it is, he may well be perfectly within his rights to do the same with your flat upstairs. The timing and the way he's done it underlines he's nothing but a heartless selfish buffoon, but it is his to sell.'

Mustering anything to say amongst this continuing litany of horror was too much.

William's tone brightened. 'The good thing is, the lease on this business is yours now ... so you're the boss.'

I looked at him aghast. It hadn't crossed my mind.

'Look, whatever you decide to do with the restaurant,

there is bugger all he can do about it. And if you give up now – if you roll over and capitulate – then he wins.'

I was so tired. I just wanted to close my eyes, rest my head on the table and sleep. Sleep until this was all over. All sorted. I was lost. I had no idea what to do.

'I just don't know if I can do this ...' I said, not even looking at him, my face buried in my arms, cheeks wet with tears. He gripped my arms with both his hands.

'Maddy, you're not alone. I'm here to support you.'

'Me too,' piped up Mouse.

I lifted my head.

'And so is Noel,' William continued. 'We're all in this together. And this may well be the hardest thing you ever have to do but, and I don't know whether this is comfort or a threat—' he lightened his tone '—but we will be right by your side.'

He held out a hanky, which I grabbed gratefully and after an enormous blow, I focused on him and the undisguised affection in his expression. I had known this man for fewer than three days and yet I felt like I had known him all my life. My instinct told me to trust him implicitly. Dad had. And I could see how much he loved Dad; plus every word he said seemed to make perfect sense. I had no arguments. I had no ideas. I was numb. I had no feelings or ability to think at all. Our eyes locked. He ventured, 'So, Maddy, what do you say? Let's get this show on the road, pull out the stops and put on the best wedding St Andrews has ever seen.'

Despite the dark deep feeling of swimming through mud, I felt a kernel of anger fizzing in my belly, which sparked at the thought of Barclay MacPherson. How dare he? Who the hell did he think he was dealing with? After all, I am Joe Campbell's daughter, I thought, as I excused myself. William and Mouse watched silently as I disappeared into the toilet.

I filled the basin with cold water and splashed my face, slowly and then faster and faster until the defeatist Maddy was washed away – at least on the surface – and a refreshed and determined, angry woman emerged. Smoothing down my rumpled water-splashed clothes, grabbing handfuls of my ridiculously curly hair and tying it up with the spare elastic band I always keep round my wrist, I grappled in my jeans pocket and applied a little Bobbi Brown lipstick – an instant pick-me-up for a pasty, puffy face before taking a deep breath and marching back into the restaurant.

William and Mouse were still in the same positions. Suspended animation, watching and waiting.

'OK. Let's kick his arse! I'm in!' I said with real conviction.

'Yippee!' said Mouse, barrelling over to me and punching my arm, then apologising, as Frank barked his approval and William smiled broadly and came over and slung his arm round my shoulders.

Standing side by side, staring at the stour that surrounded us, all bravado gone, I smiled at him and audibly gulped.

William took the lead. 'Yes, quite. OK, let's calm down and get this into perspective. This is a one-off. We simply don't have time to gut this place. All we need to do is make it look the part for tomorrow. The more we move things around, the more we will find to do, so I vote we leave it as it is, and dress what we have, distracting from the other bits with the clever use of...' He looked at Mouse. 'Well actually I have no idea – I need to concentrate on the food so it's over to you, Mouse.'

She took a deep breath. 'OK, I need a pad of paper and a pen—' and then turning to me '—and a cup of strong black coffee.' I looked at her. 'Please,' she added, divesting herself of her bossy persona.

William looked momentarily dazed.

'You were dealing with the small matter of the food?' I nudged.

'Ah yes.' He nodded, looking worryingly vague.

'OK, William, food. Mouse, I'll leave you to get on with the plan and I will tackle this,' I said, waving my hand vaguely at the mess surrounding us.

Twenty minutes later after googling, sketching and crinkling up her forehead in concentration, Mouse stood up, her face breaking into a smile. 'OK, Houston.' She grinned, lip rattling. 'We have lift-off.'

I was in no state to make a decision so was happy to be ordered around and so was up ladders, in cupboards, painting, washing, laughing, crying, eating, chopping, helping William wrestle the deliveries of lobster and langoustines into the kitchen and heaving vast pots of stock onto the stove to cook and prepare the fish for tomorrow and then suddenly it was 4.50 p.m.

William piped up. 'You're seeing your lawyer in ten minutes, Maddy – you better get going.'

A cursory glance in a downward direction revealed a mud, paint and food-spattered ensemble. Boots scuffed, hands red raw from washing a million things. Dashing into the loo to do some damage limitation I was dismayed to see that from the neck up it wasn't much better. The hair was well out of control, face red, make-up long gone. Just as well Gerald had known me since I was child or he would call security, I thought, digging into the pile of coats and jackets and retrieving mine before putting it on and running out the door.

'Wish me luck!' I shouted.

'LUCK!' was all I heard as the door closed behind me.

Chapter 8

Climbing the worn stone steps to Gerald's office brought me back. Dad never employed childcare of any sort and so if he had a meeting I would simply go with him. Gerald was a sweetie pie and would always let sit me down behind his desk so I could twirl round on the plush leather chair and draw on headed notepaper with a ballpoint pen as the two men talked business. The office was the same. The desk, huge, dark oak with a scratched, faded green leather top. Gerald – with less hair but still impeccably dressed in a three-piece suit with buttoned-up waistcoat and neatly tied tie, though a little stooped – smiled gently and rose when I knocked on his door and entered the room.

'Maddy, come in and sit down.'

I did. To be on the other side of the desk and on my own was quite daunting, which is why Gerald came round to my side of the desk and took the seat next to me.

'It was a good turnout yesterday,' he said, referring to the funeral.

'Yes,' I agreed, amazed it had been just one day ago. Such a lot had happened since then.

'How are you doing?' he asked in sombre tones.

'Oh, you know.'

'Yes. Quite.'

'Sorry I'm in such a state. There's been a lot going on.' I gesticulated at my shabby ensemble.

'No no, dear. Not to worry.'

A momentarily silence.

'Thanks for seeing me at such short notice. There's such a lot to do and think about and to be honest I got such a bloody shock when Barclay MacPherson handed me this letter.' I dug it out of my bag. 'Can he really repossess Dad's flat?' I asked.

'Let me have a read,' he said, taking the letter from my outstretched hand.

Gerald plopped some pince-nez on his nose, head tilted to the side and scratched his chin as he read through it. 'Well yes, Maddy, I'm afraid so. This is a standard lease, and it seems Joe, your father, was a sitting tenant and the Laird the owner and landlord. There is no denying MacPherson has behaved appallingly, but in Scots law he is completely within his rights to give notice.'

That took the wind out of my sales.

'How long do I have?'

'Well it was dated two days ago so—' he scrutinised the letter again '—you have twenty-six days to vacate. Are you staying in the flat?'

I shook my head. 'No, I've been staying with William and Noel. I've not even been into the flat to be honest. I haven't been able to face it. Not yet.' He nodded looking down. 'Perfectly understandable.'

'What I didn't realise until yesterday is that Barclay MacPherson owns the restaurant too,' I went on.

'No, Maddy, strictly speaking *you* own the restaurant business; he owns the property.'

'So he is my evil landlord.'

A smile passed over his face. 'Yes indeed he is, but have a look at this,' he said, shuffling through the papers in the buff folder open in front of him, before selecting a document and passing it over.

'Drawn up in 1977, it's an agreement between Sir James B MacPherson and your father.'

'Sir James B MacPherson – that's the Laird's father, right?'

'Yes, Barclay's father, now deceased. A well-respected man in his day and a great pal of your grandfather Archie.'

'OK, but what's this got to do with The Birdie & Bramble?'

'Well, have a read,' he said, sliding the paper over for me.

Date: May 21st 1977

James B MacPherson proprietor of 125/1 North Street, St Andrews, hereby states that the operating company, aka The Birdie & Bramble, shall be the tenant for such time as The Birdie & Bramble is trading. There will be no rent.

'No rent? That's not normal is it?' I said, looking up.

'No, it is not,' Gerald said, tapping the letter in front of me. 'Read on.'

I read it out loud: '*Let it be noted that the proprietor offered the tenant Mr Joseph Campbell the opportunity to buy the premises for an undisclosed sum, but Mr Campbell declined.*'

'How strange. Why on earth would he refuse?'

'Well maybe he couldn't raise the cash to buy it.'

'Yes I suppose … but I would have thought he could have found it from somewhere.'

Gerald nodded, looking puzzled. 'It's hard to imagine what the circumstances were. We could speculate forever but we just have to look at the legally binding facts as we understand them now, which are, as Sir James B MacPherson's heir, Barclay MacPherson, now owns both your dad's flat and the building The Birdie & Bramble is in. The bad news is he is perfectly within his rights to repossess the flat – but as long as The Birdie & Bramble is trading, he can't touch the building it is in, or you. So the agreement stands.'

I visibly sagged; the thought of having anything to do with this awful man was repellent.

'And what about the lease?'

'The lease is yours.'

'So I own the lease and he owns the premises? But I don't need to pay him a penny in rent?'

He nodded.

'Can I sell the lease?'

'Yes.' He looked up at me. 'Would you consider selling?'

'Gosh I don't know. Well, yes, maybe. Why?'

'I received this, this morning,' he said, passing over another letter, which I sped-read.

It was an offer to buy The Birdie & Bramble from Barclay MacPherson.

My blood boiled. 'Well! He doesn't waste any time does he? How much is the offer for?'

'Ten thousand pounds.'

'What a bloody cheek! No way.'

'Maddy, it's probably more than it's worth, you know.'

'That may well be,' I said, blood pounding in my ears, 'but I don't care – it's the principle of the thing. I would never sell to that bastard. I would rather starve,' I growled.

Gerald smiled. 'Like father like daughter,' he said, which I rather liked. 'I've been here before, you know. He tried to buy the lease for The Birdie & Bramble from your father many times.'

'Oh he did, did he?'

'Yes he did, but Joe would never consider it. That was a matter of principle too. Barclay and your dad had no time for one another. Ironic really as their fathers before them were the best of friends. Your grandfather Archie was Sir James's ghillie.'

God I hadn't thought about that story in years.

I knew that Sir James MacPherson – always known as the Laird in our house – had saved Grandpa's life. No-one really knew what happened on that fateful night but both men were changed forever. They had been out on the hill, stalking a wounded deer and something catastrophic happened and Grandpa's spinal cord was severed. It was a miracle he survived at all. His broken body was transported to hospital in Edinburgh where he remained for nearly a year.

As was the way with men of that generation, it was a non-subject and he would never be drawn on what happened. All he would say about the matter was the Laird saved his life.

The Laird, his dearest friend, visited him regularly and when he was finally released from hospital, it was Sir James himself who drove him back to the estate to the ghillie's cottage. Grandpa spent the rest of his life in a wheelchair. He didn't make old bones. Grandpa died when Dad was barely a teenager but Grandma Catherine remained in the cottage until the day she died just a few years ago. Which was when Dad had planned to move in – until, as I had just discovered, the Laird sold that from under him too.

Dad had always talked about Sir James with great affection. I vaguely remembered the presence of a charming elderly man, always dressed to the nines, always smiling, but I had been so young and distracted and, guilt now washed over me, I had never really asked.

Gerald filled me in. 'Your dad was just a nipper at the time of the accident and with Archie incapacitated and your gran Catherine working full-time as housekeeper, Sir James took your dad under his wing. He taught him everything he knew about the land, the art of being a ghillie, fishing, shooting, tracking. Basically he treated him the same way he did his own son, Barclay.

'Of course your dad was a lovely lad, eager to learn and as you know he loved the outdoors and all that came with it, like your grandpa Archie before him and of course like Sir James. Barclay, on the other hand, had no affinity with the land and made no secret of the fact he was deeply jealous of your dad and the affection Sir James had for him.

'Barclay couldn't wait to get away from St Andrews so when he left school with a couple of average O levels to his name, he went into the City to make his fortune.'

'And did he?'

Gerald rolled his eyes. 'No. Far from it, I'm afraid. It was the seventies and the family name and title got him into some firm or other as a futures broker. He was always a gambler and so gambled with other people's money – and lost it. So before long he ended up back here with his tail between his legs, much to his annoyance ... and of course he had no job. Sir James was under no illusions and knew his son was a liability, but he loved him nonetheless and did his best to support him.'

I nodded. It was a familiar story the world over. Blood is thicker than water. Unconditional love.

Gerald stood up and poured himself a dram. 'Want one?' he asked.

I shook my head. 'No thanks. Carry on.'

'In all fairness he did settle down for a while, met his wife, Patricia, a lovely woman.' He topped up his drink. 'That seemed to calm him down for a bit. They had a family too, but it didn't last. She left with the child and then Barclay reverted to his old ways, spending money like water, coming up with scheme after scheme ...' He shook his head.

'Like what?'

'God I can't remember now ... let me think. Oh yes, he invested in an Irish truffle farm, a vineyard in Greece.'

'Do you get wine from Greece?'

'Yes, but not much of it's drinkable.'

'So not exactly the man with the Midas Touch.'

'No. Quite. Locally they called him the liquidator. But from Sir James's point of view I suppose all these schemes kept him occupied and out of trouble, well on the surface anyway.'

'But that was all years ago and I still don't understand why he's still got it in for Dad – or me now I suppose.'

'Well your dad was a straight hitter, an honest, hard-working, respected man. Simple. And the one thing he focused on, the restaurant, he made a success – success that has eluded Barclay no matter what he has tried ... I mean he has failed to sustain any business or personal relationships – the man was, and it seems still is, a total buffoon.'

I couldn't help but smile. Gerald was not a man to talk ill of anyone, which underlined what a pillock the current Laird must be. He went on.

'Of course Joe being Joe, he rose above it and tried to build bridges over the years but Barclay just wouldn't have it. He was so jealous. Then when Sir James passed away, Barclay made it abundantly clear that any past history shared was just that, in the past.'

'Gosh that was harsh.'

'Indeed. But this rivalry had been going on since they were kids so finally Joe decided Barclay was never going to change and it was time to move on. Sir James's will provided for his widow – Lady MacPherson, Barclay's mother – and of course Barclay as their only child inherited everything else, at that time a healthy property portfolio plus a substantial sum of money, which over the past eight years he has systemically spent.'

'So I presume that's why he sold Granny's cottage when she passed away and Dad didn't get a chance to move there?'

Gerald nodded sagely.

'God. What a nasty bit of work,' I surmised.

'Yes, I would say that sums him up.'

'So where do we go from here?' I asked.

'Well Barclay owns the three flats above The Birdie & Bramble including your dad's. In fact he owns the whole building and from what I can glean, it's the only asset he hasn't pissed up against the wall yet. His father was no fool and knew him well enough, which is why he put this in place to protect your dad.' Gerald flapped the paper in front of me. 'It says here in black and white as long as The Birdie & Bramble is trading you can stay put.'

Buoyed up, I rallied. 'OK, so for now The Birdie & Bramble is safe – but what about the flat?'

He looked down, reddening. 'Yes, well I wish I could give you some better news on that but I'm afraid it's his to do with what he will.'

It was a lot to take in, the sum of which was the unavoidable truth: I had to go back to my childhood home, to empty and say goodbye. The mere thought of it filled me with dread.

'Actually, Maddy, whilst you're here, I know it's early days but I have a copy of Joe's will if you would like to see it.'

'Oh gosh, yes, I hadn't thought about it to be honest.'

'Well the good news is, it's very straightforward. Basically everything he owns is yours. No stocks and shares or anything of that ilk. His bank manager has been made aware of the situation and will be signing the contents of the account over to you and will be in touch directly and that's about it, to be honest. No complicated codicils or issues to deal with.'

Gosh, a whole life tied up just like that. Neatly wrapped up and over. It was unutterably sad.

Gerald gave me a copy of the document. 'I will go back to MacPherson's lot and tell them you are not interested in selling the lease. And I suggest you obtain an official valuation of the business so you know where you are.' I must have looked blank. 'I can organise that for you. We share the building with a surveyor, a guy called Paul Sandiman – he knows his stuff,' he went on.

'Thanks, Gerald,' I said, pulling myself up to a standing position and feeling rather weak and pathetic. 'I appreciate all your help with everything.'

'No problem, Maddy, just sorry it has to be done at all. He was a good friend and he'll be missed.'

Exiting Gerald's office, my head was positively spinning. Grief, anger and helplessness consumed me as I acknowledged that the one man who I always turned to for advice on any of life's challenges was gone and the desperately sad feeling of being utterly alone was visceral.

I needed some fresh air so nipped back to the boys' house to collect Frank for a walk. I was mulling over the intricacies of the conversation I'd just had with Gerald when Frank slipped his lead, made a break for freedom and ran straight into the fish and chip shop. Legging it in to scoop him up, the smell of hot fresh food curled up my nose and I suddenly realised I was absolutely starving.

'Hey, Frank,' said the young lad behind the counter to the sausage. 'The usual?'

And then seeing me, he remembered, he was Dad's dog. And Dad was no longer here.

He reddened. 'Och am sorry,' he said. 'Your dad aye came in with Frank for a chip and a news when they were passing – I just…' He hesitated, not wanting to say forgot.

'Don't worry,' I said in a falsely cheery tone. 'I understand.' Then clocking freshly battered fish in the display counter in front of me, I tapped the glass. 'They look good. Can I have a haddock supper please.'

'Right ho,' he said, grateful to busy himself selecting, salting, wrapping and handing over a hot, vinegary parcel.

Fish supper in hand, I wandered round the corner to the bench overlooking the beach that Dad and I often sat on, to watch the sunset and scoff our fresh battered haddock and real chip-shop chips. Frank jumped up and sat next to me, leaning in as I unwrapped my supper. Plucking a chip free, I set it down in front of him. He nosed it, gauging the heat. Watching him, I smiled and sat back.

It was hard to take on board how much had happened in the past few days, I thought, when a hand suddenly appeared over my shoulder and stole one of my chips.

'Hey!' I shouted, turning swiftly to find Hamish, grinning from ear to ear.

'Mmmmm those chips are the business. Budge up,' he said, sitting down next to me and plucking another one from the wrapper.

I smiled at him. 'Help yourself.'

We sat in companionable silence for a minute or two.

'How you doing, Cuz?' he said, nudging me with his head.

'Aw you know, fair to completely shit.'

'Yeh.'

We sat in silence for a moment munching the chips, sharing the fish. I told him about my meeting with Gerald.

He shook his head. 'God, Maddy, as if this isn't hard enough… Barclay really is a Class-A shit.'

I smiled at him. 'That's being unfair to shits.'

He grinned back at me as I scrunched up the fish and chip wrapper.

'Can you bung this in the bin for me?' I asked, nodding at the bucket at his end of the bench.

'Well I have bugger all else to do,' he said.

'Any ideas what you're going to do next?'

'Nope. I have literally been round the world – twice – and as U2 said, "I still haven't found what I'm looking for." One thing though, I keep coming back here and the older I get, I suspect I'm going to have to accept St Andrews and I are meant to be together.'

Looking over the West Sands at the glistening water and the huge sky, I felt a vague pang of inevitability too; grief could do that to a person.

'What about you?' he asked.

'I'm a London girl now and much as I love St Andrews, I've got a lot of living to do before I rock up here.'

'I get that. And how is London?'

'I love it. It's amazing – the shops, theatre, all the sights, the clubs – it's a real buzz.'

'Not for me, big-city life,' he said.

'So what *is* for you, Hamish? I've lost track to be honest... How long have you been on the road?'

'Yeh, I sort of lost track of myself to be honest... It's been over four years.'

'Do you think you might stay this time?'

'I really don't know. Dad really wants me to join the family firm, be the butcher in waiting. "Meaty my son Hamish".'

I laughed at his appalling joke.

'But can you see me in the striped apron with a link of

101

sausages round my neck standing behind that counter for the rest of my natural life? I had plans …'

'Anything would be an improvement on those trousers you were wearing the other day.'

'I got those in Thailand!' he objected.

'Not those, the suit trousers,' I laughed.

He guffawed. 'Yes it may be time for that natty little number to go back to the charity shop where I bought it for an interview after I left uni.'

'Well you got the job!'

I smiled. Hamish was as bright as anyone I had ever met, graduating with a first in Geology and duly snapped up by a huge oil company. He lasted eight months until he was so 'ethically conflicted' that in a rather dramatic turn of events he resigned, joined Greenpeace and chained himself to one of his previous employer's oil rigs, which was great PR for Greenpeace but hardly a promotional tool for future employers.

I'd give him a job any day.

Which reminded me. 'I don't suppose you fancy a few hours' work tomorrow? We are up to our arses in it—'

'Oh yeh, Dad told me you were having a wedding at The Birdie & Bramble! Are you off your head?'

'Yes, clearly.'

He smiled. 'Well it's a family failing so count me in.'

A wave of relief swept over me. 'Thanks, Cuz,' I said, knocking into him.

'What time do you want me?'

'Oh I'm not sure.' And then I had a thought. 'Actually what are you doing now?'

'I'll check my schedule,' he said, looking at the back of his hand. 'No, as I suspected, absolutely nothing – why?'

'Come with me,' I said.

We walked round the corner to The Birdie & Bramble. The lights were still on.

It was locked. After knocking tentatively on the door, I heard a very high voice.

'Hello? Who is it?'

'It's me! Let me in.'

The Birdie & Bramble door slowly opened and in we walked.

The place was transformed. It was like walking onto a film set, a fairy cavern, a twinkling dream. Gawping, I looked round. 'Mouse!' I gasped. Hamish, hands in his pockets, walked in behind me, head upturned. He twirled round and round, his various beads jangling, fixated by the installation of lights and jangles Mouse had constructed as if on invisible thread right across the ceiling. It was startling.

'Whoa, this is incredible,' he said, agog.

'Mouse!' I walked over and embraced her. 'You are amazing! How on earth?' I asked.

'I mean really amazing,' Hamish went on.

'Oh sorry, Mouse, this is Hamish, my cousin,' I said. 'Hamish, this is Mouse.'

Hamish dragged his eyes down from the ceiling and turned his attention to Mouse with a huge beaming smile, his eyes sparkling.

'So lovely to meet you, you talented amazing woman,' he enthused, hugging her.

From beneath Mouse's make-up I detected heat as he released her. 'Thanks,' she said sweetly, clearly chuffed to bits, looking down at the floor.

There was a loud knock at the door, which broke the spell.

'Right you lot – it's late! Come on, come on, have

you not got homes to go to?' said William in a ridiculous policeman-style voice.

I glanced at my watch – my God it was almost eight and it was going to be a long long day tomorrow.

Once William was dragged in to admire Mouse's work – bless him he was rather tearful – we gathered our bits and pieces, said our hasty goodbyes and arranged to meet back at The Birdie & Bramble at 7.30 a.m.

'See you then,' said Hamish.

'Are you sure, Hamish?' I said, assuming he was going to pitch up later in the day.

'I most certainly am. Got to support my old cousin,' he said – talking to me, but looking at Mouse, who coyly flicked her gaze up to him from under her fringe and, lip rattling, grinned back.

This was going to be interesting.

Chapter 9

Of course when the alarm went off the following morning, I felt like I had been asleep about fifty-three seconds.
Never a morning girl. Ever. From a scruffy-kneed tomboy,
to a grumpy, slumped teenager to the universally recognised
student sloth, I just loved my bed. It had caused any number
of dramas over the years but hard as I tried, I'd simply never
grown out of it. Even now as a supposed 'professional' in
London, I literally left it to the last possible second to roll
out of bed, arriving a minute or two either side of nine.

No. I was never happier than when horizontal so the
shock of the 6.25 a.m. alarm on this particular morning was
not to be underestimated. By 6.30 a.m. I was in the shower,
6.45 in the kitchen side by side with an equally monosyllabic
William whose expression told me being up at this time was
as alien to him as it was to me.

'Well. Today's the day,' he said, putting a perfectly steamed
cup of coffee with a kick like a horse in front of me. Being
an angel he offered to take Frank to the beach as I woke
up properly and by seven I was on my way round to The
Birdie & Bramble, wet hair scrunched up into a tight knot
on top of my head with not a scrap of make-up on to take
the deliveries.

As I happily opened the doors in the cold morning light,
the restaurant still looked so much better than it had before,
and I had no time to get maudlin because William was less

than five minutes behind me. He arrived dressed impeccably in chef's whites perfectly shaved, after-shaved and groomed. I must ask him how he does that, I thought, glancing at my scuffed Ugg boots and shapeless T-shirt. But before I got the chance there was a knock at the door.

'Delivery!' shouted a voice, as four cases of wine were plonked on the floor and suddenly we were off.

Seconds later there was a rap on the front window.

It was Mouse. 'Give me a hand in with this lot will you?' she said, opening the door wide, dragging in what looked like the Forest of Birse, great jutting branches and ferns, green leaves, wild jaggy thistles, roses, clematis, poppies, leaves of all shapes and sizes, shiny, matt, tiny, tropical, and a roll of twine for her ambitious plan of creating a magical arrangement of wild flowers and weeds.

'God there is a lot of it,' I said, assessing the quantity of foliage.

'Isn't it great?' she enthused, divesting herself of her floor-length black coat, her synapses obviously snapping.

Before I got the chance to help her, Hamish appeared round the door.

'Morning!' He grinned. 'Can I give you a hand with that?' he asked Mouse.

'Yes please,' she cooed and she busied herself with instructing Hamish on her plans for the hanging gardens of Babylon.

I checked with William if there was anything I could do to help him. He just shook his head from amongst the vast pile of stuff in the kitchen.

So I was off to the charity shops. We had over fifty candles. I had to source as many receptacles as possible for them to burn in safely: saucers, jam jars, candelabras, candlesticks and to find flat white bed sheets as tablecloths. Our budget was tiny and I was up for a challenge.

I got back to the restaurant with my swag less than two hours later and Mouse and Hamish had been working hard. The foliage was twisted and turned round the room. Amongst it all twinkling fairy lights entwined through everything flickered on and off in the dimly lit room.

Mouse took control of the candles, fixing them to the base of numerous holders, plopping them here and there, turning something pedestrian on its head and arranging themes to give off a magical intimate light perfect for distracting from the scraggy-looking floorboards. I lit a fragrant candle – a very expensive one from Jo Malone. I'd had it for years and never burnt it – it just seemed too good to burn; but needs must and the wafting aroma of fig combined with the flowers created a natural deliciously heady scent and hopefully disguised the musty carpet aroma.

Next job. Set the tables.

The long plastic buffet table we'd found folded up in the back shed had seen better days but with a good scrub, the correct size book shoring up its wobbly leg and a king-size white sheet over it, you would never guess what lurked underneath. It looked perfect and felt strong. Which was vital as this was where all the delicious things William had been preparing would be displayed. As I stood back to admire my handiwork, Mouse began to work her magic round the perimeter of the table with garlands of variegated ivy, tiny white gypsophila flowers threaded through it, sewn in place with invisible thread round the edge, giving a beautiful border for the platters of food when they arrived.

After some trial and error we had found enough tables of the same height – give or take a centimetre here and there, to create a dining table long and wide enough for the whole party. Each place was marked with a posy of heather and lavender tied with brown gardening twine and of course as we had no idea who the guests were or what their names were, there was no table plan.

The chairs, a mismatched bunch, had been sifted through to find ones that had no velour and amazingly were barely noticeable once overshadowed by the rest of the efforts made in the room. Mouse also instructed Hamish to tie a gold helium balloon to the back of each one, giving a wondrous air of fun and glamour when you entered the room.

Things were coming together.

The smells coming from the kitchen were delicious and occasionally I dared to swing my head round to see how things were going.

'Fine thanks. Just fine. Almost there ...'

He had been saying that since we'd arrived three hours before so I didn't press him for further detail or pull his leg as it was clear he was a man with a mission. The stove was covered in bubbling pots, every surface covered in clubs of greenery.

Having seen my father in the same situation for so many years, I knew the calm exterior was a ruse, as the throbbing vein at his temple, his pink face and damp upper lip confirmed. It was nearly midday and so far we were on schedule, I thought smugly; in fact, we were ahead so I got out the checklist again for the hundredth time and read out loud.

'Tablecloths? Check.

'Cutlery? Check.

'Glasses? Check.

'Napkins? Check.'

'Well not check actually, white linen,' joked Hamish. We all giggled, Mouse rather excessively, I noted.

Flowers – check check check: we were engulfed in blooms and greenery.

'Cake?' Silence.

'Shit! A cake! We haven't got a cake!' I squawked.

'Don't panic,' said William, his temple upping its throb, clearly panicking. 'Run round to Arbuckles, explain the situation and see what they can do. We've still got—' he looked at his watch '—just under two hours. And, Maddy, grab us some fresh bread whilst you're at it.'

After grabbing my jacket off the peg I ran out onto the street and, head turning right and left, realised I didn't know where on earth I was going.

'Arbuckles, Arbuckles – right!' I said out loud before tearing off in what I was fairly sure was the right direction.

'Aye aye, Maddy!' shouted Uncle Fraser from outside the shop as I sped past him.

'Sorry, Fraser, I'll explain later ... byeeeee,' I screeched, turning the corner onto North Street.

Arbuckles was a St Andrews institution. Even before I arrived, the aroma of freshly baked bread and cakes curled up my nostrils. The front door was closed tight – it was still too early for customers – so I rapped firmly on the door with a sense of purpose.

My poor heart thumped overtime as I tried again and just as I bent down to shout through the letterbox, the door opened and much to my horror I was addressing the groin of a very large white-clad floury-faced man.

God what a cringe, I thought, standing up fast and tall as I could.

'Hi, I'm Maddy from The Birdie & Bramble. We have a wedding on today and I know it's short notice; in fact,' I stuttered, 'it's no notice at all really, but I need a cake, a wedding cake. Anything will do – small, big. I was just wondering ...' I looked into the poor man's alarmed face as I exhaled and asked simply: 'Help?'

'Whoa, lassie, slow down,' said the flour-covered man

wiping his hands on a dishcloth. 'Come on in now ... and tell me all about it again ... this time in English.' His tone was amused and gentle.

My imminent danger of heart failure diminished slightly as I smiled up at this man mountain and before I could start, he interjected.

'We met yesterday, dear, at the funeral.'

'Oh God, I'm so sorry, I ...'

'Don't you worry ... there were so many folk there. I know who you are and of course we'll help you out.'

My heart twisted. Dad.

'We'll get something sorted and drop it round to you by ...' He looked at his watch. 'What time?'

'They're arriving at two.'

His eyebrows shot up but bless him he just said, 'OK, by 1.45 you'll have your cake.'

Instinctively I hugged him and, thanking him profusely as I backed out of the bakery, felt distinctly lighter – so much so I didn't break into a run. I actually walked back towards the restaurant.

I nipped into Uncle Fraser's shop on my way past to explain my bizarre behaviour earlier. The butcher shop's bell announced my arrival. Fraser broke into a smile when he saw me.

'Och look here it's Usain Bolt,' he said to the guy he was talking to, who turned round with a quizzical look on his face.

'This is my niece, Maddy,' he said.

'Oh hello,' I said, looking up at him properly. He was the most spectacular man I had seen in a long time and I was horrified to recognise the twist I now felt was definitely not one of grief. No, it was altogether lower and though it had been a while, if I was not very much mistaken it was cavewoman animal lust. Pure and simple. Happily Uncle Fraser was rattling on as my face burned.

'Look at the state of you, lassie!'

I looked down. The hug I had impulsively bestowed on the giant baker had covered me and my clothes in floury dust.

My eyes met Fraser's and we both grinned.

The stranger I had barely acknowledged grinned too.

'Hi.' He stepped towards me holding his hand out. 'I'm Jack.'

'Hello,' I said rather formally as my throat constricted. Good Lord he had the darkest eyes I had ever seen. Were they in fact eyes or just vast, deep, endless black pools. I looked away. My mind went blank. I had to leave.

'Right I'm off,' I said. 'I really have to go – nice to meet you,' I shouted over my shoulder as I opened the door to go.

'Ahem,' coughed Fraser. 'Usain, did you come in for a reason?'

'Oh yeh sorry, to say sorry I ran past you earlier but I was on my way to Arbuckles when we realised we didn't have a wedding cake for the wedding.'

'And did Rory sort you out?'

'At Arbuckles? Yes. What a lovely man.'

'He is indeed.'

'Great, well, I better fly!'

'God she's flying now!' Fraser twinkled, turning back to Jack as I flew out the door. 'Now where were we …?'

The Birdie & Bramble was a hive of activity.

'I'm back!' I shouted rather obviously, running into the kitchen to deliver the good news. 'Cake's sorted.'

'God, Maddy, you are your father's daughter – indefatigable.'

'What does that mean?'

'I have no idea – now take this,' he said, handing me a large pink still-warm lobster. 'Pop that in the space in the middle of that plate over there.' Turning round, my jaw dropped. Before I'd left, confusion and disarray had reigned; now it was as if someone had waved a magic wand. Cluttered surfaces were cleared and on the kitchen worktop sat a series of white bone china platters. The largest one had a lobster-shaped gap in it, which I filled with the crustacean I now held. There were six lobsters in all, displayed like rays of sun round a huge Cromarty crab, which took centre stage. Piled up in between and round the edges of the dish were langoustines, mussels, cockles, razor clams, crayfish.

'OK stand back,' he ordered, clutching a large bowl full of baby salad leaves and herbs with which he dressed the plate, adding some edible flowers, a few strands of fresh salty samphire and chunks of lemon. It was a triumph. It was breathtaking.

'Wow!' was all I could manage. 'Let me get a photo.'

'Well pronto then. There's no time to dilly-dally,' said William.

Grabbing my iPhone I took a quick shot as he ordered, 'Come on, I need help carrying this through. It weighs a ton.' So the two of us very carefully lifted it into position in the centre of the buffet table. In the short time I had been away, William had performed a miracle and there in front of us was displayed all manner of delicious dishes. A plate of slow-roasted red peppers virtually caramelised, strewn with fresh basil, chopped sweet tomatoes, anchovies, olive oil and garlic. A huge wooden bowl held a classic new potato salad, cut through with gherkins and red onion tossed in home-made mayonnaise. Ramekins of sauces: Marie Rose, hollandaise, garlic butter. A wee plate held curls of butter next to which was a basket filled to the brim with home-made Melba toast, the smell of which wafted up deliciously. Next to that was a chunky wooden chopping board on which was space for the French sticks I was holding, still warm from Arbuckles.

'That smell is going round my heart like a hairy worm,' Mouse piped up, hovering over this Hanoverian feast and inhaling all the smells.

To the right of the platter was a smaller plate, which held wafer-thin, sliced wild smoked salmon, almost transparent in its delicacy.

And as if that wasn't enough, to top it off, the carpaccio of beef, shavings of Parmesan, rocket and a drizzle of olive oil that was so olivey I could have drunk it in a glass. Eyes wide, words failed me.

During my absence Mouse had also been hard at work.

Between the platters and dotted round the room were jam jars of varying sizes filled with wild flowers. By each plate of food she had propped a brown cardboard label on which someone – I'm assuming her – had written in the most beautiful calligraphy what each dish was.

'Mouse, you have played a blinder,' I enthused.

'I couldn't have done it without Hamish,' she gushed, looking at my suddenly bashful cousin.

Aye, aye, I thought...

To the right of the main centrepiece sat a silver platter of ice and above that an empty plate on legs.

Seeing my puzzlement William said, 'Oysters. I will put them out the second they arrive – they have to be last-minute.'

'OK,' I said, eyes glittering, my throat tight with emotion. If only ... 'William, I don't know what to say,' I said as a great wave of emotion rolled up from the pit of my stomach and just about strangled me as it headed out of my mouth, when suddenly the door flew open.

'OK OK, now where do you want this?' said the voice behind the cake that had just entered the room.

'Oh my days!' said William as the grinning face of Rory the baker popped round the side of edifice he was carrying. It was huge.

'I can't believe you've done this for us,' I warbled, feeling a rush of affection for the big man in front of us with a big heart.

'Well we were restricted as to what we could do in an hour or two. It's basically a posh Victoria Sponge,' he said, 'but you can't beat a classic with a bit of imagination.' That was an understatement.

There were three tiers of delicious fresh sponge. The sweet aroma mingled with the other wonderful foodie smells. Each layer balanced on four columns of about five inches high, and each layer was split in the middle, overfilled with whipped cream and mixed through were fresh local rasps. On the top was a simple dusting of icing sugar. It was understated yet extravagant and smelled utterly divine.

'Wow,' gasped Mouse as she came and clocked the cake. 'I know what we need,' she shouted, turning and running outside again.

'I always have that effect on wimmin,' the baker grinned. 'So where do you want her?' he asked William, teetering slightly.

'Here, let me give you a hand!' I said as William guided us to the round table in the corner, which had looked rather sad and unadorned amidst the twirls and swirls of wedding paraphernalia that surrounded it.

Once the cake was safely in its place, Rory's shoulders dropped, he exhaled and stood back.

'Aye …' he said, rubbing his chin and admiring his handi-work, 'that should do the job.'

'Here!' Mouse rushed back in, triumphantly walking over and placing three fresh roses, one pale peach, one lemon and one cream on the top tier of the cake with a flourish. 'The finishing touch.'

It was perfect.

'If this was my cake I would be the happiest girl in the world.' I beamed at the baker who despite his floury face could be seen reddening underneath.

'Right I'm off!' he said, then taking a second he noticed the rest of the place and beamed broadly. 'Well, well, well, Maddy. This place looks—' he struggled to find the right word '—just super. Your dad would be so proud of you.' And before I had time to well up, the door opened and a small round man with a shiny bald head, in a light blue, tight-fitting suit came rushing in. 'We're here!'

Chapter 10

The next seven hours went in a flash.

William snapped to attention as the flurry of guests arrived, opening champagne and filling a tray of flutes that were waiting to be handed to each guest as they entered, elated and excited from the ceremony. Hamish welcomed them in, taking their coats.

I stood smiling like a goon until William whispered, 'You might want to get changed,' and looking down I realised I was still in my floury jeans and rumpled T-shirt.

Running into the kitchen and out into the garden, I stepped out of my clothes into the black skirt and white shirt I had laid out some hours earlier, thinking I would have time to do my hair and put on some make-up before it all started. Naive fool. Wrenching my hair down and round into a ponytail I stood up, applied a slick of lipstick and, standing tall, walked out into the restaurant. Today I was my father's daughter.

The bride was beautiful, arriving amidst a flurry of confetti arm in arm with two women. She wore a simple elegant cream dress, which stopped just above her ankle and much to my surprise bare feet, with fresh flowers entwined through her shiny black hair.

One of her companions was dressed in a green floaty dress that shimmered as she moved, the other in an impeccably cut white linen trouser suit.

As they entered the room, the shiny-blue-suited man coughed. The woman in the green dress stepped to one side and announced:

'Ladies and gentlemen, the bride and bride!' as the blue-suited man clapped his hands in glee as the throng surrounded them, hugging, clapping and clinking glasses.

And somehow – don't ask me how – we did it.

Seven hours later, after profuse thank yous, I'm sorry hugs, cards being swapped and photos being taken firstly of the wedding party, then of us, then all of us a great knot of madness in front of the restaurant, finally they began to wander off on foot. Drunk with tiredness, we watched them wandering lazily along the narrow street, trailing streamers, flowers tucked behind ears, clutching gift-wrapped boxes, wraps, linking arms and walking two or three abreast, the tinkle of their laughter fading into the St Andrews night air.

Girls held shoes in their hands – sore feet released from unaccustomed heels, ties were loosened, shirts untucked, faces flushed, shoestring straps slipped off shoulders, men's jackets slung over arms or gallantly draped over shoulders of partners, men carrying – and in one case wearing – their wives' hastily discarded hats.

Juan Sylvester had been the first to arrive and last to leave, his blue suit still shining pristinely as he weaved his way across the deserted cobbled street, rushing to join the others having spent quite some time shaking William's hand repeatedly whilst gabbling, 'Gracias, thanking you. Danke,' with emotion threatening to overtake him any second. When he finally left, still perfectly attired and coiffed, the only indication he had been at the crux of eight hours of dedicated celebrating was the imprint of heavy lipsticked lips just above his eyebrows in the centre of his shiny pate.

I smiled, imagining his horror when next admiring his reflection and discovering this very amusing imperfection.

William and I stood in the doorway silently watching the guests wend their way home, reaching the Mercat Cross, where the road split into four, embracing, planting kisses on cheeks, breaking into smaller groups and two even walking backwards, waving and blowing kisses to one another, reluctant for the day to end until, scattered asunder, they were gone.

'Well?' I said.

William's tired face turned to me. 'Well? How do you think it went?'

'OK.'

'OK?' he repeated loudly, my understated response designed to goad him had clearly done its job. Unable to keep a straight face a moment longer, my face burst into a huge cheesy grin. Realising he had been had, he nodded and smiled.

'William, it was a complete triumph! It made Elton John's Tarts and Tiaras party look rather dull,' I stated, turning and marching into the restaurant, 'and I for one would like to propose a toast.'

William, sensing fun was afoot, deftly overtook me, grabbed a recently opened and abandoned bottle of champagne from an ice bucket and held it aloft as I presented two flutes, which he filled to the top in style.

Face-to-face we clinked glasses.

'To new friends,' I said simply.

'To absent friends,' Mouse added, accepting another glass of bubbly from Hamish who had taken off his apron and joined us all.

'To Dad,' I said.

'To Joe,' added Hamish.

With the relief of the day being over and having eaten virtually nothing all day, the champagne did its work very quickly. I surveyed the scene. The tablecloth covered in scrunched-up napkins, foliage that had broken free from its hastily tied fixings, half-empty smeared glasses of all shapes and sizes, ice buckets full of upturned bottles, a blue glass jug of water ironically full, a few still-burning candle nubs. The hastily ironed tablecloth aka bed sheet from the charity shop now peppered with crumbs and spatters of red wine. All that was left of the monumental feast laid out lovingly on the buffet table was a token crust of bread, a few broken crackers and a warm pat of butter, lumpen. Virtually every morsel had disappeared.

'That is what you call evidence of a great party,' William said, reading my mind.

'I can't believe it's over.' Tiredness and champagne suddenly making me tearful, my bottom lip trembled.

'And that cake! It caused a sensation!' said Hamish, lifting the mood, indicating the four jam-and-cream-smeared tiers still in place but now minus the cake.

'I know! I can't believe they ate the lot!'

'The humble Victoria Sponge wins the day.'

'You are too modest, William – your food caused a sensation too.'

'Aye and listening to the oohs and aahs as they licked their fingers and sucked the lobster shells – if you'd recorded that you could have sold it to a porn director.'

'Mouse!' I said in mock horror as we all laughed loudly.

William was typically modest. 'I'm just happy they liked it.'

'They loved it, William. They really did. God I was worrying they were going to adopt you and take you back to America with them.'

He spluttered out a mouthful of champagne. 'Well that woman with the lips had a glad eye for you,' he retorted.

'Eric Morecambe you mean?' I said. 'Red hair, big specs and the loudest laugh I've ever heard.'

'Yes,' Hamish laughed. 'I knew she reminded me of someone.'

'Well whoever she is, she is a woman of impeccable taste, make no mistake,' Mouse said, draining her glass.

We grinned, settling into our own thoughts for a moment. Collectively exhausted.

'Well done, Maddy. You pulled it off.' William exhaled.

'No.' I looked in turn at William, Mouse and Hamish. '*We* did.' We cooried into a group hug.

'Yes,' he beamed back. 'We bloody well did!'

Chapter 11

The euphoria was short-lived. The next day it was back to London. I had to, I was working on Monday and there was no reason not to. We had achieved what we had set out to do.

That wasn't how it felt as William and Noel drove me to St Andrews Station with the dog lying on the back seat beside me, pressing against my leg. Frank instinctively knew I was going and had tried to get into my holdall as I packed. I stroked his wee body, hoping he could tell I loved him dearly.

'Are you sure you're OK if I leave Frank?' My eyes brimmed with tears.

'Yes of course, we love that wee hairball as much as you do – and don't worry, I promise if he's pining I will drive him down to London and deliver him personally.'

'I just couldn't face going back to Dad's flat yet – I have twenty-eight days – well twenty-one now to clear it. But...' my chin wobbled '...not yet...'

Noel reached into the back and patted my hand. Words were unnecessary.

We pulled into the station car park, and as usual had cut it fine so there was no time for a protracted farewell. We hugged and I felt flustered as the boys flipped my bag and me onto the train with just moments to spare, before the guard blew the whistle and I was on my way.

I watched until the boys and an indignant Frank – who

had turned his face away and was firmly tucked under William's arm – were out of sight and then I just gave in and let go. I was wrung out and had no more energy. Any pretence of control was over. I slumped in my seat, crossed my arms, laid my head down on the tiny table in front of me and sobbed. I had no idea when I would be back, and each mile the train travelled I felt a physical pull, as if I were leaving part of my broken heart behind. When I eventually raised my blocked nose and puffy eyes up and watched the scenery of my childhood recede, I wondered if I would ever feel whole again.

London was hot and clammy, the contrast in temperature always a surprise; only 500 miles apart but different worlds. Marcus had texted to say he wouldn't be at the station to meet me after all but would try and pop round later. Though disappointed not to see a familiar face in the mayhem of King's Cross Station on a Sunday evening, at least it meant he wouldn't have to witness my pink piggy swollen eyes – the result of the waves of upset that rolled over me as I relived the extraordinary events of the past seven days. On the upside it was one way to ensure no-one sat next to me on the train. There is no sane human who would choose to sit beside a snottering almost thirty-year-old woman with a sodden hanky in one hand and a bottle of water in the other.

Dragging my holdall upstairs to the flat, I fell in the door, gagging for a cup of tea. The fridge was empty with only a trickle of sour milk on offer. Binning the tea idea I poured myself a glass of warm wine and picked up the letters from the doormat.

Mostly junk mail, a postcard from Keira my flatmate who was in States covering the tennis, a credit card statement and one official-looking envelope. Flipping it over I read: *Paul Sandiman Surveyor.* I gulped. It was the valuation of the lease of the business. My mouth suddenly dry, I slugged another mouthful of wine and opened it.

The contents of the letter were as follows:

Value is in the building not the lease – As I suspected.

Lease has fifteen years to run – good.

Goodwill – had tailed off, considerably hard to quantify.

The only value would be in the business, which looking at the figures in the cold light of day were pitiful. How Dad had even managed to keep the business going on was a mystery. He had been running at loss for over three years.

Add the need for a complete refurb and the value of the lease came to a paltry £17,500.

Well at least now I know where I stand, I thought, my heart squeezing with sadness. My sweet dad's life and business distilled down to a few pounds, shillings and pence.

I needed time to mull it over and could hardly keep my eyes open, so flipping the immersion on I unpacked then ran myself a deep bath with a slick of lavender oil, which I hoped would still my mind and help me sleep.

As I lay up to my neck in the hot steamy water, inhaling for four, exhaling for five, practising breathing, I heard the click of the front door.

'Babe? Are you here?'

Marcus. I rolled my eyes. I had forgotten I had given him a key hastily at Dad's funeral so he could keep an eye on the flat. I really wasn't in the mood to see anyone. Especially someone who had clearly had a few sherbets.

'I'm in the bath,' I said quietly, hoping he would take the hint.

After a clatter from the kitchen and the sound of the fridge door slamming, the bathroom door opened slowly. 'I've just got myself a kebab – want some?' Was he serious?

I wasn't breathing at all now but holding my breath with annoyance.

'No thanks,' I said as levelly as I could through clenched teeth.

'K,' he said, sloping off. Seconds later the TV flipped on and the noise of a rowdy football match filled the silence.

I lay as long as my nerves could take it until all calmness and relaxation gone, I put on my dressing gown and padded through.

And there he was, TV blaring, kebab on the coffee table still in its wrapper, a can of lager open and lying on the couch, head slumped back, mouth open, snoring. Marcus. Drunk.

Had it been any other day I would have flicked the telly off, shoved him, told him he was snoring and that he should go to bed; but tonight I just wanted to be on my own.

I was deeply hurt he had chosen to go out partying rather than meet me off the train after the most awful week of my life. Now I just wanted him to leave. Knowing the routine, as we had been through this so many times before, I would wake him, he would say he wasn't asleep and then fall back into a snorting slumber. I would leave him for a while until his snoring got so loud I would go through less patiently and thump his shoulder and tell him to go to bed. He would grovel and joke until I would relent and then on we would go.

But not this time. I just left him where he was, hoping he woke up with a cricked neck to add to his impending hangover, and retired to the bedroom. Of course there was no way I could sleep. I was furious with him for being such a heartless, selfish prat. Exhausted by recent events and experiencing a gut-clenching sadness, which I could not imagine ever leaving me, I lay for what felt like hours until eventually I must have fallen into a fitful sleep.

I dreamt of William, cakes, Dad, Uncle Fraser, Hamish, cakes, The Birdie & Bramble, the Marx Brothers playing at The Rum & Lash, of deep deep blue eyes, of Noel, Mouse, green shimmering dresses, Uncle Ted, Auntie Faye and I was very much in the bosom of my family so was quite disorientated when nudged awake by someone touching my shoulder.

'Babe?'

Coming round I half opened my eyes.

'You awake?'

'No,' I answered, turning round away from him and assuming the foetal position.

'I'm so sorry,' he said, gently nuzzling the back of my neck.

I sniffed.

'So so sorry, Mads,' he reiterated as he snaked his arms round me, and despite my determination to remain aloof and apart, the close contact of another human being was just what I wanted. The familiar warmth of his body slid into the bed behind me and he held me close, stroking my hair and whispering sorry over and over with beery breath. I turned towards him and we kissed, and I felt myself surrender to his touch. I needed to forget, to feel wanted, even if just for a while.

Afterwards we slept and when the alarm went off, it took me a few seconds to establish where I was and what was going on.

London.

Work.

I looked at the clock – late.

Removing Marcus's arm from round my waist I jumped up, determined not to be late on my first morning back, not to give the satisfaction of 'the look'. I was showered, dressed and slugging a black coffee when Marcus appeared in my dressing gown, hair on end, at the kitchen door.

'All right babe?' he asked.

'You not working today?'

'Yeh, but I'm going straight to an appointment and I made it for half ten. Why don't you stay?' he said, kissing my neck, intent on distracting me, but I knew I had to go. Pushing him away, I kissed him gently and turned to go.

'See you tonight, yeh?' he asked, sounding quite needy and unlike himself.

'OK,' I said, my antennae twitching. 'I've got to run.'

Work felt like I had never been away. A few tilted heads, and words of condolence, a couple of sympathy cards, an email inbox overflowing, a list of appointments made in my absence I had to attend and the phone ringing constantly, it made the day pass in a flash.

I had no time to think about anything until back on the tube at the end of the day. Squeezed into the packed train, I held the overhead strap, as rolling and lurching, the tube trundled under the streets of London. Impossible to see anything other than dozens of heads in front and behind me. I was literally sardined between a woman with a grizzling toddler in her arms whose snotty nose was in danger of dripping onto my coat, and an expensive-suited man who insisted on trying to read his *Standard* holding it aloft in front of his face, which was two centimetres from mine. At least I didn't have to avoid eye contact, being so close to the Sports pages. The relief of getting off the tube and up to street level, with its marginally cleaner air, was immense. Jostling through the myriad of other people all going somewhere as fast as they could, I couldn't help but wonder. What on earth was I doing here?

Hugely enthusiastic of anything I chose to do, Dad had been on the face of it very supportive when I announced my move to London, but I could tell by the look in his eye he wished I had chosen to be somewhere closer to him. Somewhere in Scotland or at least somewhere that didn't have more than eight million other people in it too. Not a word of negativity ever. Keen to visit me, he waited until I was settled and then the second I suggested he might like to come down, he jumped at the chance, happy to stay on an ancient sofa bed in a shared house. Seeing him in an urban setting made me love him all the more. His concession to being in a city was to wear his ancient tweed jacket, the rest of him still clad as though he had just come in off the golf course after eighteen holes.

His eyes were wide with wonder as I showed him the sights of London and his natural curiosity led him to ignore the convention of city life of keeping yourself to yourself and instead he spoke to all sorts of people, asking questions and smiling a good morning as they passed. The majority of people stared back ignoring him; a few rewarded him with a reciprocal smile. He was like a huge child. It was the first time I felt I was the grown-up, a very unsettling feeling.

Once on the tube, his eyes wide, he was unable to stop himself.

'Holy tamole, Maddy, is it always this busy?'

'Huh usually it's a lot worse – I never get a seat!' I laughed. 'This is Sunday afternoon so it's the quietest time to travel.'

He grimaced. 'God I feel like I'm in *Journey to the Centre of the Earth*, starring Doug McLure,' he joshed. 'Can you no' get the bus?'

'Yeah but it would take about two hours,' I said.

'Oh OK, fair enough,' he said and that was the end of it. We were on our way to see *42nd Street* and afterwards, high on the music and atmosphere of the theatre, we tried to recreate some of the dance moves on the way to Piccadilly Station and just as we neared the tube station, he announced he was treating us to a taxi home. I think if I'd said OK, he would have flagged one down and told it to take us to St Andrews.

'If you're tired of London, you're tired of life,' I'd declared regularly, though ducking and jostling my way back to the flat today, even I conceded that might have been cooked up by the Greater London Tourist Board.

I stopped to buy milk and a ready meal. Dad would be horrified at my lack of culinary motivation these days. I slowly climbed the stairs to my flat and, turning the key in the door, I was taken aback to be face-to-face with Marcus, dishcloth tucked into the belt of his jeans in an apron-like formation. He led me into the lounge where he had set up the tiny circular table at the end of the galley kitchen for two. I smiled as he took my coat, before he turned me round and gave me a long hug.

'Maddy, I am so sorry. I'm a shit boyfriend,' he whispered into my hair. 'I don't know why you put up with me. I was just a drunken twat last night.'

I nuzzled closer to him, inhaling his scent. He always smelled so good. 'Apology accepted, if you pour me a drink and tell me what that wonderful smell is.'

'Me,' he joked.

I smiled. 'Coming from the kitchen.'

'Oh that!' he smiled back. 'Just a little something I flopped up. It'll be ready in ten so you go and freshen up. I'll pour you a glass of wine whilst I slave over the hot stove.'

And so a perfectly nice evening began. He was attentive and funny, affectionate and self-deprecating. This was the Marcus who had turned my head the first time I met him, almost ten months ago. He was full of remorse for failing to meet me off the train and of course I forgave him. Being with him was such a relief – it was easy. We knew each other so well and I acknowledged that, despite the odd hiccough, we rubbed along together very well indeed.

I smiled over at him as I finished the final mouthful of my Angel Delight. Out of the blue he announced, 'I was thinking we should go away this weekend.'

'Oh!' I was quite taken aback. 'Why?'

'Why?' He grabbed his chest with both hands. 'To spend some time together … with you, my love. It's been a while and … well I thought it might cheer you up a bit.'

I thawed further. He had hidden depths, this man. 'Aw, Marcus, that's a lovely idea. Anywhere in particular?'

'How about Brighton?' he said.

I loved Brighton with it's myriad of shops, the beach and lively atmosphere of a young creative community giving it a natural edge.

'I think that's a lovely idea!' I raised a glass and grinned. 'Here's to Brighton!' We clinked glasses. When we finished our wine he insisted on clearing the table as he settled me down on the couch with a brandy.

There was a kernel of doubt in the pit of my stomach as I listened to him humming and clattering through the dishes in the sink. Don't get me wrong, this was all very nice, but there was no escaping the fact – very out of character indeed.

I didn't have to wait long to find out why.

He joined me on the couch with a box of Maltesers, my favourites.

'So anyway,' he said, snuggling in and sliding his arm along the back of the couch, stroking and tugging my hair gently.

Here we go, I thought.

'Trevor and Keith.'

I remained silent. His two idiotic friends. I could suddenly smell a monstrous rat.

'So – have they run away together?'

He laughed too loudly and too long. This could be worse than I thought. 'No no, no, I was just going to say, then I remembered you're not that interested that … well amazingly they have managed to get tickets for the World Cup.'

Be still my beating heart.

'Oh,' I said as disinterested in football as anyone alive could be, which he knew only too well. The prickle of doubt rose. You could cut the atmosphere with a knife.

'You see, the thing is …' he went on tentatively, now brushing non-existent crumbs off the knee of my jeans. 'Keith can't go.'

'Uha.' Here we go.

'And … well … Trev's asked if I might think about taking the other ticket.' At this point his tone changed from considered and tentative to overexcited child. He couldn't help himself. 'The thing is, Mads, it's an amazing opportunity. I mean you can't get tickets for love nor money so …'

I held up my hand, stopping him mid flow. I really couldn't be bothered with silly games. Despite my natural aversion to football, his childish enthusiasm was quite endearing.

I asked him outright, 'OK, cut to the chase. When is it?'

'It's at the end of July.' He gulped. 'The 26th.' He paused as the penny dropped.

I turned to face him, no longer finding this endearing on any level. 'The 26th of July – you mean when we're on holiday in Majorca.'

'Well yes, that's the thing. We are. Well we were … well are … so that's what I wanted to talk to you about,' he said, twirling my hair round in his hand and gently tugging it.

Usually I loved him playing with my hair but this time it made me want to punch him.

I sat up. 'Yes?' I pushed him to say it. He dropped my hair and turned round to face me. How could he? Today of all days. Selfish, thoughtless. I held on tight to my emotion, willing tears not to come. Not now.

'Well we would lose our deposits but I would pay you back for yours and...' Fury rose as my heart yammered against my chest. I couldn't believe what I was hearing.

This new Marcus, this caring, catering, affectionate man was an illusion. It was the same old Marcus, the same manipulative, football-obsessed oaf just trying to get his own way.

'Oh that's OK then,' I said and for a beat he actually registered relief before realising I was being sarcastic and then, give him his due, he did have the grace to look a little afraid. As well he might.

'And,' I went on in a low controlled voice, which took all my strength, 'where is this life-changing football match taking place that you are pulling out of our holiday to see?'

'Valencia,' he said, his voice cracking, a nervous smile cracking his face.

'I think you should go,' I said in a low voice.

'Maddy...?' he whined.

'I mean it, Marcus, I want you to go.'

'To Valencia?' he asked like a stray dog waiting to be kicked.

'No. To hell.'

He didn't argue. He knew once my mind was set that was it, and he also knew that a low, controlled voice was indicative of fury, plain and simple.

What he failed to realise was it had nothing to do with football, or holidays or deposits, or him or us, it was simply to do with me. I was lost. Rootless. I missed my dad. I didn't like my job. I wasn't sure I liked London anymore, and despite his flaws and obsession with football, when all was said and done, I had been pretty sure I loved Marcus. But in three minutes flat he had illustrated pretty starkly that he didn't love me. If the boot was on the other foot, I wouldn't dream of doing such a thing. Leaving him high and dry to go off with my friend to the other side of the world to watch ... well anything actually.

I had always thought of football as the other woman and as far as I could tell, he had just chucked me for her. I was too angry and upset to deal with this. Standing up, he put his jacket on and tried one more time.

'Maddy?'

I turned away, willing the tears not to spill over now. I didn't want him to see me crying.

I heard the door close quietly behind him.

Chapter 12

I sat up most of the night trying to work out what to do.

Barclay MacPherson had offered to buy The Birdie & Bramble for a pittance – a vile, heartless man who had made it his business to destroy Dad. This option was definitely the path of least resistance but I just couldn't bring myself to do it. I kept reliving the moment that perspiring butterball had handed the letter to me at my father's wake. The thought of him gloating and getting what he wanted was untenable.

The alternative, of course, was to sell it someone else – but who? And how much would I get? I couldn't give a hoot about the cash; all I wanted was my dad and I was never going to have him again.

I'd been fighting the urge to phone William and Noel. I wanted to hear their voices, get the chat from the town, ask how Frank was, but I also didn't want to end up bleating down the phone. Blubbering was never far below the surface at the moment. I didn't want them worrying about me – they had their own lives to get on with. I had only known them about a week. It was ridiculous to put so much emphasis on this relationship – intense as it had been. So I resisted phoning. I did send a card to say thanks for everything and enclosed a small deer antler chew for Frank in the hope it would go some way to making up for leaving him behind.

Sarah, bless her, had been in touch daily by text or email just checking in to see how I was. I'd been remiss not getting back to her but she knew me well enough to realise it was because I was struggling, not because I didn't want to speak to her. I didn't want to speak to anyone; my energy was completely taken up just keeping my head above water.

Since I had sent Marcus home on Tuesday night he had sent so many WhatsApps I had lost count. I was upset, emotional and exhausted. Avoiding him at work was easy – we had spent our entire relationship acting out a charade of being disinterested colleagues. The only time I responded I asked him to leave the key to my flat in my desk at work. He only had it by default anyway. He did as I asked. Opening the envelope he had left on my desk with my key in it, I dropped another notch down the miserable scale. Had I overreacted? I mean he wasn't a bad guy, he just didn't understand what had happened to me, and in all honesty I didn't either. I was reeling so how could I expect him to understand?

Thursday morning I finally got to the office about 9.30 having spent an hour on the Northern Line on a faulty train, my calm app preventing any potential freak-out.

Flying in the door, looking like a burst mattress, I got the evil eye from Felicity as my phone buzzed. Not in the mood for any of her nonsense, I brazenly took it out of my pocket and seeing three missed calls from William, I dialled the message service. This must be serious. It was short and sweet.

'Phone me! Now!!'

My heart yammered in my chest. What now?

Please God everyone is OK. Rushing to my desk, dropping everything, I could see Felicity blatantly eavesdropping but I didn't give a monkeys, I called William back immediately.

'Maddy!' He sounded so happy to hear from me, my face

broke into a rare smile. Thank God he sounded fine. More than fine actually. 'How are you?'

'Great,' I lied. 'How about you?'

'Great!' he replied, clearly telling the truth.

'I just got three missed calls? I thought something awful must have happened.'

He laughed. 'No. No, far from it. I popped into the restaurant this morning to check everything was as it should be and I found over a dozen messages on the answerphone. People wanting to book a table.'

'What?'

'I know!'

'Why?'

'Well,' he continued, getting into his stride, 'it seems they'd all read all about The Birdie & Bramble and wanted to make sure they got a table.'

'What? Read about it? Where?'

'Well, this is the thing – apparently one of the guests at the wedding is a food blogger.'

'Oh really?' I said, feeling rather underwhelmed. There were millions of blogs out there and most had between one and no readers at all. In fact in my experience as a marketer they were usually freeloaders intent in getting something for nothing so William's news put me neither up nor down.

But his tone was still registering excitement. 'So she's written all about the wedding.'

'And have you seen it?'

'Yes I bloody have – that's why I'm phoning you, you dough ball. Are you online now?'

'Yes,' I said, grabbing my mouse and wiggling it, galvanising the screen into action.

'OK, have a look – it's foodgloriousfood.com'

Typing it into Google, I confess I was wondering what on

135

earth all the stramash was about. In a second, a site flashed up in front of me with a huge picture of The Birdie & Bramble and the headline 'Scotland's Best Kept Secret – The Birdie & Bramble'.

'Oh my God, are you sure this is a blog? It looks so professional!'

'Carry on!' screeched William down the phone.

'OK.' I sat up, suddenly awake. 'I've got it up in front of me.'

'Read it read it read it, Maddy. I'm dying here!'

So I did.

'Spirited off to Scotland for my best friend's wedding, I was totally unaware of the foodie delights that awaited. With Scotland's cliché reputation for deep-frying everything from pizza to Mars Bars, my expectations were low arriving in St Andrews, a small town on the east coast.

This charming town, known worldwide as the home of golf, has the oldest university in the world, beaches the length and breadth of the best California can offer and the most delicious food I have tasted in my long and food-obsessed life. That is not a misprint. You know me, no matter where I eat or who I'm with, the gloves are always off. There is no point in blowing smoke up anyone's ass.

Quaint, vintage, heartfelt, charming, organic, fresh, local, mouthwatering, sweet, succulent, a banquet of such unctuous delights the best way to let you share this marvellous experience is by looking at these:

The words were illustrated with about twelve photos of … well everything. Even the scratchy old piano and the yellow-tinged photo of Sean Connery … I gazed at the screen, salivating. 'Wow, the food does look amazing.'

'I couldn't have written a more glowing report myself,' William's voice boomed down the line. 'So do you think a lot of people read her blog then?' he asked.

'OK let's have a look …' I said, ignoring Felicity who was visibly twitching to know what was going on. I clicked through to Twitter. 'One point two million followers on Twitter.'

'Shit! That sounds like a lot!'

'Em, yes and—' my fingers tripped over the keyboard again, clicking here and there '—AND – brace yourself!'

'What, what?'

'She has over two point three million followers on Instagram. And one more click to her Facebook page – over 800K likes on Facebook.'

'So … then … like … potentially thousands and thousands of people have read it?' Even technophobic William noted the significance of these statistics.

'Well I suppose so … yes!' I said, linking through to other articles by the same woman.

The sophisticated bright red bob, red lips and huge specs flashed up in front me.

'Oh my God.'

'What? WHAT?' screeched William.

'It's Eric Morecambe!' I shouted, ignoring Felicity who was visibly quivering with frustration that she had no idea what was going on. 'The one at the wedding we called Eric Morecambe – remember? Huge specs, glow-in-the-dark hair?'

'The one I gave my carpaccio of beef recipe to,' said William knowingly.

'Exactly. Well her name is Molly Gosling. She writes for *The New Yorker* and … *Time Magazine*!' As I continued scrolling, the magnitude of the coverage began to dawn on me. 'Holy shit, this woman is practically a bloody household name in America.'

'Molly Gosling – I have heard of her! I never put two and

two together. Sherry Gosling – Molly Gosling. She is the bride's sister. Holy shit!'

Felicity coughed, eyes aloft, warning that Adam, our boss, was hovering. Clearly seeing me happy and animated for the first time in a long time, he suspected it had nothing to do with my job.

I wheezed into the phone, 'I'll call you back . . .' and changing my tone to formal continued, 'Yes. Good. That's excellent. Thanks for your call. I will get back to you as soon as I can.'

As I replaced the receiver, I heard William's voice in the background. 'You can't, Maddy, I . . .'

Click.

I couldn't help but smile as I clicked onto another page and tried to look bored and disengaged, melding back into the crowd, not wanting to draw any more attention to myself.

I waited until my lunch hour to call him back.

By this time he had calmed down but only slightly.

'The phone is ringing off the hook!' he exclaimed and on cue it rang again.

'Look why don't we FaceTime tonight,' I said. 'I'm under the cosh at work and I need to see my hairy wee pal—'

'And Frank.' He laughed.

'OK, I had better go, speak later.'

Arriving back to the empty flat, the relief of knowing Marcus no longer had a key was huge. After kicking off my shoes, I made myself a cup of soup, opened up my Pret sandwich, and sat down to FaceTime the boys at seven.

Noel's face immediately came into view. 'You're too close,' I said as his nose took up most of the screen. 'You're scaring me.'

He sat back. I could see William, who was sitting next to him with Frank on his lap.

'Frank!' I shouted.

The dog's ears pricked up and he looked alert but confused.

'Frank!' I said again in a softer voice, and his wee fat face came straight up to the screen, so close I felt like I could touch the wet black nose.

God I missed him so much.

After a ridiculous conversation during which I shouted 'biscuits', 'walkies' and whispered sweet nothings in his ear he jumped down, having had enough as clearly there were no biscuits or walks on offer and it was just a ruse, which gave us mere humans a chance to talk.

'I've had a brainstorm,' William burst out.

'Oh dear,' I said.

'The phone literally has not stopped all day. Countless people all looking to book tables.'

'And?' I asked.

'Well I took them,' he said, slightly hesitantly.

'WHAT?' I said. 'Why on earth would you do that?'

'Well, wait 'til I explain.' And he did. 'Some woman had phoned to book a table for the end of July.'

'End of July? She's keen. That's ages away.'

'I know, that's what I said but she reminded me: it's the Open this year in St Andrews.'

'The what?'

'The British Golf Open.'

'Oh of course,' I said, melancholy washing over me. The Open was the absolute highlight of Dad's life. The world's biggest golf competition and all the folderol that surrounded it came to St Andrews every five years or so. The thought he would miss it was too sad. Tears spilled down my cheeks.

'Don't cry, Maddy, please just listen.' I looked at him through watery eyes, stuffing my Pret napkin up my nose and mopping my tears as he went on. 'I have had the most fabulous idea! And I know you are going to absolutely love it or want to kill me.'

'OK,' I blubbed. 'Let's hear it.'

He took a deep breath. 'OK, as we have just established, it's the Open in St Andrews in the third week of July. Which—' he referred to his notes '—gives us nearly six weeks to build up to the busiest two weeks in years.'

Noel sat back, stroking Frank, listening carefully and watching William, who was now on his feet pacing.

'The thing is . . .' he turned, looking at me down the camera '. . . it's a licence to print money. You said yourself you just got a piss-poor valuation on the lease and so I propose we run the business as hard as we can until the end of the Open to at least get it back into profit; then you'll get a far better valuation – which means if you sell it, or when you sell it, you'd being doing yourself and Joe proud. If luck's on our side then you may even have a wee nest egg for the future.'

It was so left field it took me a few moments to compute what he'd just said. He took his seat next to William, eyes wide, waiting for a reaction.

As I considered it, for my own clarity I had to say it out loud. 'So if I've got this right, William, you are talking about six weeks of hard labour, day and night, to drag The Birdie & Bramble up by the bootstraps to what we hope might be profit . . .'

'Yes,' he said.

'And are you seriously prepared to give it the commitment it needs?'

'Yes I am.'

'And what about you, Noel? What do you think?'

'He agrees,' said William.

'Noel?' I said. He nodded. 'Really?'

'Yes really,' he confirmed.

It only took me a few seconds to consider. 'In that case I think it's bloody genius!' I exclaimed.

'Really!?' William jumped up, thrilled.

'Yes really!' I said, smiling as if at an overexcited child!

'So are you up for it?' he said.

'ME?' I started.

'Yes you! Of course you! We can't do it without you. You're the boss and you are The Birdie & Bramble.'

'I thought you meant you. You and Mouse and Noel – but me?'

'Yes you! Noel's got his shop, which will also be stowed out with all the tourists. It's his best time of year and there's no way Mouse and I can do it alone. Or would want to do it alone! Of course you!'

Wow. Well that was a shock. 'Me? But, William, I have my job here, my life …'

'Maddy, it's not forever,' he interjected. 'You could get time off for good behaviour and well … just have an elongated holiday really.'

I laughed. Some holiday. He made it sound so simple. So straightforward. And as I looked at him, his hands balled up into fists, the expression of anticipation on his face, a warm affection for this madman filled me from head to toe. Without any further discussion, to my surprise I heard myself saying yes.

I felt a little guilty as he danced round the kitchen with Frank in his arms; after all, my decision was not entirely altruistic. The idea of doing something sharp and shocking to Marcus – the way he had to me – was rather appealing.

Surely now I'd be able to see if he really cared for me at all. I'd had an overwhelming urge to run away and this gave me a legitimate excuse. So that's exactly what I would do.

Chapter 13

The timing was perfect. I was mooning about achieving nothing. I just couldn't settle. I felt a little uncomfortable about my motivation for my knee-jerk reaction saying 'yes!' quite so quickly as the truth was, in light of recent events, I needed to think long and hard about Marcus, about us. If there was in fact an 'us' at all. I just couldn't whip up any enthusiasm for anything at the moment. I needed to do something, and whether this would effect change for the good or bad I had no idea.

There were a few practicalities to take care of. My flatmate Keira counted on my rent to pay her mortgage. I wasn't sure how she would take my news. I couldn't afford to keep paying it whilst I was up North and I wondered if she would consider subletting to help me cover the costs. I decided to come clean, write her an email once I found out whether I could surmount the major stumbling block. My job. Or more to the point Adam, my boss. I was fairly sure he would just bin me when I asked for a six-week sabbatical to sort myself out effective immediately. Jobs were hard to find, especially ones in the media world, and deep down I really did love my job, putting my recent lack of enthusiasm down to recent events rather than the job itself.

His reaction.

'Maddy,' he said, 'when you first started here I could see

the fire in your belly and it has been noted that you've lost that killer instinct.'

God is that what it was?

'A break is just what you need. I did think you came back to work rather quickly after your father's death.' Tears welled quickly, proving his point. 'So it sounds to me like you need to recharge your batteries and work out what it is you want out of life.'

My eyes must have given the game away – I was amazed he was so understanding.

'I've seen this before,' he said cryptically. 'You are not the first, nor will you be the last.'

Speechless I looked at him.

'It's a hard thing to do to come and ask me for time to sort yourself out. You have my blessing. Go.'

Leaving his office practically genuflecting, I realised I had misjudged this man completely and rather than using this as an excuse to bin me, he had shown that underneath that cool businesslike exterior was a human being with a warm heart after all.

When Felicity heard my plan she was supportive, I suspect because I had effectively stepped out of the race, which she had effectively already won. So she helped me gather my bits and pieces together, listened carefully as I handed over ongoing projects with assurance that if any problems arose she could contact me any time.

As I tidied my desk, I felt a great weight lift and I was more than surprised when leaving at the end of the week, Felicity commented, 'Well, you've certainly cheered up.' I realised I was actually humming and I emerged onto Nightingale Square experiencing a long-forgotten lightness in my step.

Packing the flat didn't take long. I had accumulated

very few personal belongings. Most of my stour was work-orientated clothes and happily I wasn't going to need those for a while, so I stuffed them into a huge empty suitcase that lived in the back of the hall cupboard and left it there. I squished everything else into two huge holdalls. One with normal clothes and the other with gadgets, cosmetics and books. Casting an eye over the place, I thought it looked rather pathetic and impersonal compared with the familiarity of everything in St Andrews. A wave of homesickness hit me, if that were possible now I no longer had a home.

Marcus insisted on driving me to the train. I'd kept him at arm's length for the past few days but was softening towards him, suspecting I might have overreacted to his ham-fisted way of trying to postpone our holiday; after all, my perspective had left the building. Plus, with two huge bags to lug all the way from Clapham to King's Cross, it would be rude not to.

The buzzer went. I opened the door and heard footsteps loping up the stairs two by two. Marcus came rushing in and grabbed the bags.

'Traffic's hellish, Maddy, we better get going if you're going to catch this train.'

It was a mark of the importance of the day that he had taken the time and effort to drive from his flat in North London all the way down to Clapham and now back north to King's Cross Station to help me on my way.

After forcing the last of my stuff into my bag and zipping it up, I closed the door behind me without a backward glance, dropped the key through the letterbox and we were off.

It took an age to drive to the station. Marcus kept his wits about him as other road users cut us up, whizzed up behind us, and mounted pavements, determined to get where they were going faster than us, which meant thankfully the conversation was virtually non-existent. The constipated roads brought on lots of fist-waving and swearing so we were clenched from head to toe as King's Cross hove into view.

Of course there was no space to stop, so Marcus double-parked, jumped out, handed me my bags, and amidst the impatient honking of the man in the car behind gave me a brief hug and an even briefer kiss. 'Call me when you get there,' he shouted as he turned and loped back into the car, waving at the irate driver behind him. He closed the door and with a grind of gears was off.

I think we both had an inkling this was a line in the sand. Make or break. I had no idea which way it would go.

This time the journey north was spent making lists.

There was so much to think about. My brain felt like it might explode.

First things first, I emailed Keira the extraordinary events of the past few days – she was still in the US so I let her know I had sloped off back to Scotland. She came straight back and was, as ever, optimistic and enthusiastic, saying she would Airbnb the flat until I came back so I could relax, not pay rent and neither of us would be out of pocket. Thank God. I was on unpaid leave and I hadn't really addressed the money issues yet. The main issue being I didn't have any.

I had emailed Gordon Ferguson, Dad's bank manager at the Royal Bank in St Andrews, and was seeing him tomorrow. He was top of my list. I needed to secure some cash to tide me and the business over. If he said no, I had no idea what I would do. Blocking that out, I emailed Hamish asking him to keep his folks up to date with the news – and Mouse if he saw her, which if my hunch was right he probably already had, several times.

I had an open invitation to stay with the boys for as long as I liked but Dad's expression 'relatives like fish go off after three days' rang in my ears; I didn't want to overstay my welcome and I needed my own space, but I just could not face going back to the flat, the mere thought of it choked me. So I googled places to rent in the area, which were frankly extortionate at this time of year and doubly so because of the Open. People drove from Edinburgh and Glasgow to attend the Open so I put a note up on Facebook asking if anyone had a room to rent and then I sat back. Surely something would turn up.

Then I wrote a list.

A list of things that needed to be tackled before we could open our doors.

Get money. Bank. Clean. Paint. Rearrange. Menu. Suppliers. Marketing. Staff. Social media. Oh my God. There was so much to think about – my heart rate accelerated to near panic-attack status as I put down my third coffee of the day. What on earth was I doing?

'Breathe,' I said out loud to myself, trying not to hyperventilate. I closed my laptop and sat back in the seat. Head swimming, I closed my eyes for a moment and focused on the rattle of the train. Within minutes my heart had returned to near normal and the heat in the carriage helped me drift off. The next thing I knew the guard was shaking me gently to say we were approaching Leuchers Station.

William had texted saying he would collect me so I had only a minute to try some damage limitation to elevate my low-key travelling look to something less homeless itinerant and more shambolic confused woman. Fishing about in my bag I found my lip salve, face wipes and bobble to tie my hair back. I had long since given up carrying a brush or any implement that claimed to be able to get through the hair that grew out of my head. It was thick, curly and too long. Over the years I had experimented with all the hairstyles that came and went and found if it was any shorter than my shoulder, it stuck out in all directions and was even more uncontrollable. If it was long, at least the weight helped gravity direct it downwards. Since I was young enough to remember I'd spent far too much of my time wrestling with it, trying to keep it at bay. Pulling and twisting, I scrunched it into the hairband and then set about wiping my face.

The 10X mirror Keira had bought me for a laugh damn near gave me a heart attack. Aargh. Whilst sleeping, the mascara had moved from eyes to cheeks, which were streaked black leaving my small pink eyes naked. Ratty rat, I thought, scrubbing my face with the wipe until my skin was pink. The alleged waterproof mascara hadn't stayed on my eyelashes, I noted, but was now stuck fast on my cheeks. As I gave up scrubbing, I sat back and looked to my left where I noticed a girl, about my age, talking on the phone.

'Yes, Mum. Yes, Mum. Yes … I will … Uha … Yeh.' She caught my eye, smiled and rolled her eyes up, a universal gesture that meant – parents eh?

I nodded and averted my watery eyes. Oh for the opportunity to be talked at by Dad on one of his sanctimonious rants or reliving hole by hole the game of golf he had just enjoyed. I cringed as I pictured myself, phone trapped between my ear and shoulder, only half listening, making appropriate noises periodically so he knew I was still there, as I prepared something to eat or wrote and sent emails at the same time. How many times had I rolled my eyes and willed him to be quiet and stop mithering on and on? What I would do now to hear his voice, full stop.

I hadn't even managed to get a slick of lip salve on by the

time the train arrived and the moment it ground to a halt, William climbed into the carriage, claiming me with a big hug and grabbing my bags.

A venison stew, mashed potatoes and a great big glass of red wine was waiting for me and the three of us just sat smiling across the table at each other in the candlelight, as slowly we realised the magnitude of what we had committed to do.

Noel announced he'd had a brainstorm too. We looked at him – I wasn't sure I could take any more.

'You haven't been to the shop yet,' he said, 'it's actually quite like this place. It's in a wee house just round the corner on College Street. It's got a postage-stamp garden and a wee bothy in it.' I let him continue. 'We've not got round to doing anything with the bothy yet but I had a good look at it today and think it's just about fix-uppable as a little place for you to stay. If you like it.'

'Gosh! Really?'

'Yes. It means you get your own space, and you don't need to commit to a lease or anything official. You can just stop there until ...'

'That is so good of you,' I gushed.

The thought of being far away from these two lovely men, who were rapidly beginning to feel like my new family, was too much and I had already stated clearly I didn't want to impose on them by staying under the same roof. It sounded perfect.

'Come and have a look tomorrow and see what you think. No pressure if it's not for you.'

'Thanks.'

'Now, William,' he said in his bossy Captain von Trapp voice, 'I for one am having an early night as we have a lot to do tomorrow,' he said pointedly.

'OK, well I've been sitting on my backside all day so if you don't mind I'm just going to stretch my legs and take Frank round the block,' I said, launching my stiff aching bod into an upright position.

The boys sensed I wanted to be alone and as I zipped up my jacket and wrestled the dreaded hair into a beanie, they said their goodnights and gave me a key.

The street was empty, my footsteps and the tick tick tick of Frank's toes the only sound. The air was cold; glancing up I saw the sky black as coal, a sugaring of stars twinkling down. Walking through the town towards the beach, as the houses receded it seemed as if the sky became bigger, the stars brighter and as I stood, hands in pockets gazing up, I was surprised how many of the constellations I remembered. Orion's Belt, The Plough, The North Star, Venus. It was hard to recall the last time I'd taken a moment to look at the night sky. Light pollution in London had robbed me of this glorious sight, the Milky Way in its infinite glory a sweep of what looked like a wisp of cloud, in fact a myriad of galaxies beyond.

When I was a child Dad had woken me one night and before I was aware of what was happening, carried me downstairs, told me to keep my eyes closed, no peeping and took me round to this very spot when he told me to open my eyes. The Aurora Borealis. The Northern Lights. Shooting shafts of magical purples, greens, pinks flashed across the sky, his wonder as fresh as my own. Watching until the streamers of glittery reddish-greenish light slowed and dissolved, we wandered hand in hand back to the flat, silent. Sometimes words were not enough. It felt like yesterday.

Chapter 14

Early the next morning we were outside Turnbull's hardware shop to buy mops, buckets, cleaning stuff and rubber gloves.

Within an hour it dawned on us we were going to need a skip. We sat down, both feeling rather overwhelmed.

'OK, let's do this logically.'

'Mine's a large gin,' joked William.

Assessing the task, we decided the kitchen looked like the lesser of two evils.

It was a compact working kitchen and most things were still in use and everything was, despite its age, immaculate.

It was the main dining room that presented the real challenge.

The front door and the small copper dimpled bar in the corner were the only parts of the room that were not overpopulated with clutter.

Maximalism.

In addition to the necessary tables and chairs, there was a Welsh dresser, a honky-tonk piano, a wood-burning stove, a knobbly dark-wood standard lamp with squint dark red shade, which Dad used to read the collection of sheet music stacked higgledy-piggledy on top of the piano when he felt the urge to play, and a huge G-plan shelving unit along the entire length of one of the walls.

There was no time like the present and with a deep breath, I heaved a large drawer open in the gothic-looking oak dresser, which sat next to the bar. Oh my God – tablecloths laundered, folded and unused for years.

William rootled through them.

'Well, what do you think? Staying or going?' I asked.

'Going – we have to launder them and that costs money,' said William, picking up an armful and whumping them onto the bar, releasing a thick cloud of dust.

'They are everywhere,' I said as I wheeched another cloth off the table closest to me. 'Actually this table is quite nice, I think it's real wood.'

'Nice,' William agreed, marching bullfighter-like up to the next table and whipping the cloth off it with a flourish. 'Tada!'

'Yuk, that's a horror,' I laughed, prodding its light blue chipped Formica top.

'Hmmn, agreed, it's not quite as gorgeous,' said William, slapping a Post-it note on it saying 'AUCTION'.

'OK,' I said, reaching for the cloth of yet another table and whipping it off, which revealed more solid wood. 'Ooh look at this one … and look at those legs!'

The front door opened and in came Noel, impeccably turned out as usual.

'That's an Edwardian table with turned wooden leg and,' he said, looking more carefully, 'worth a few bob that.'

'Oh and you'd know all about a well-turned leg, Noel,' William laughed.

And then there were three.

Noel's expertise as an antique dealer was priceless. He could tell if something was worth a couple of quid or was better chucked out. And so the three of us set about revealing the treasure that lay hidden under the tablecloths. Seven of the twelve tables were keepers, made of knotted, solid wood.

Noel and William dragged the ragbag of others outside,

stacking them up in preparation for recycling or the auction, giving us more space to work.

'Righty-ho, chairs next, let's have a look at these,' said Noel, on a roll and enjoying himself.

Like the tables, the chairs were a similar mix of styles and materials. Some hanging together by a thread, others more robust – plastic, Formica, wood, a few classic shapes, some were even office chairs by the look of them, but what they all had in common was they were in need of a bit of TLC.

'These Bentwoods are good. The original Parisian bistro chair,' said Noel, rubbing the dust from the seat of one with a cloth and stroking the bent curved wooden back.

'Thank you, Fiona Bruce,' said William.

'Are they usable?' I asked.

'Oh yes, some with a bit of work, but most of these will scrub up very well indeed. There are a few rogue nails and dodgy-looking seats...'

'These I presume are going out,' I said, pointing at some hideous velour seats. 'Sorry, Maddy, no – but these are Ercol ladder-back chairs and once they're recovered they will look great.'

The bigger pieces of furniture didn't fare so well under the expert eye. Specifically the Welsh dresser.

'Repro,' said Noel and noticing my crestfallen face added, 'Sorry.'

'It's been here as long as I have,' I said, nostalgically stroking it, and emotions running high, I excused myself and went outside for a breath of fresh air. William followed me out. We both leaned against the wall.

'Sorry, Maddy, this must be so difficult for you. Are you sure you can handle it?'

I turned and saw his face full of concern, bless him.

It was too late to turn back now.

153

'Yes, sorry about that, I'm just tired. I am sure I can cope. I promise.'

He smiled and put his arm round me. 'If we move the dresser and some of these chairs out I reckon we can fit at least another two or three extra tables in, which is about another twelve people.'

The restaurateur's gene tingled in me. 'Well when you put it like that – it's a no-brainer.'

So that afternoon with some help from Jono the butcher's boy, the huge groaning heavy wooden dresser was dragged out onto the street, adding to the now impressive pile of stuff to be collected by the local auction house.

With the remaining chairs and tables stacked up, the room already looked so much bigger. There were only two major things left. One, the monogrammed fitted carpet, which Dad had commissioned in the late seventies when times were good. A dark red background with a golden bird motif repeating like a fleur-de-lis. In some areas threadbare, in others still a deep pile.

'This must have cost a fortune,' said Noel diplomatically.

'Dad's pride and joy in the day, but it's older than I am,' I said, prodding an edge of the carpet with the toe of my boot. 'I'll be sad to see it go but—' I drew myself up to full height '—let's get this thing rolled up and chucked out.' William smiled. 'Phew I was worried you'd want to hang onto that.'

'No! If you looked at it under a microscope you might find some extinct species on there.'

He laughed as we started to untack it from one end and roll.

The carpet came up easily, revealing perfectly serviceable floorboards underneath.

'Ooh, William, what do you think?'

He grinned. 'Well, my little carpet bagger, I think we have just saved ourselves a small fortune!'

Motes of dust hung thick in the air.

'Get that door open before we asphyxiate,' said William, propping up the carpet.

I did as I was told and he and Noel lugged it out onto the pavement.

'Looks like you're going to need a skip,' shouted Fraser from across the road. William and I looked at each other.

'There's one on its way!' I confirmed, looking round at the now vast amount of tat we had ejected.

'You're blocking the pavement – move along there,' someone barked. Assuming it was a joke, I turned round only to come face-to-face with Barclay MacPherson himself, slamming the door of a very battered-looking four-wheel drive.

Momentarily speechless, William turned on the charm. 'Everything is in hand – it will be cleared this afternoon.'

Barclay harrumphed. 'I bloody hope so,' and made a show of having to walk off the pavement to avoid the pile of junk. Glancing at it, his interest piqued. 'What are you doing anyway?' he asked.

'It's none of your business,' I snapped.

'Actually, as the owner of these premises, it is my business.'

Which rather took the wind out of my sails.

William stepped in, taking the high ground and smiling. 'Well we're freshening things up a bit before we reopen.'

Barclay's face gave him away, registering surprise.

'Reopen?' He snorted. 'I don't know why you're bothering. Seems to me you're flogging a dead horse there.'

Fury snapped me from slack-jawed to evil-tongued in a heartbeat.

'Hang on a minute, if it's a dead horse then why did *you* offer to buy it?' I snapped.

'Well I own the building and I have plans for it. As for my offer? Thought I would put you out of your misery. It's the best one you're going to get. You could say I did it out of the goodness of my heart.' He bared his teeth in an insincere smile.

'Huh! That's ironic, seeing as repossessing my dad's flat before he was cold in the ground would suggest you don't actually have a heart,' I snapped.

I sensed William cringing, not having seen this side of me before and, noting the colour of his face, I knew it was not the way he would have handled the situation.

'I realise this will all go over your head, dear, but the fact is, business is business, a lesson you would be advised to learn sooner rather than later,' Barclay said, smearing his hand over his sweaty-looking pate, and glaring.

Being face-to-face with this revolting bully, I was incandescent and beginning to shake when thank God William stepped in front of me.

'I can assure you this mess will be out of your way within the hour.'

'Well see that it is,' he grumped, opening the door and stomping upstairs to preen and strut round his beloved building.

Speechless and stunned, I was far from finished with him, and as my faculties snapped back into action, I took a step towards his receding back.

William put his hand on my arm.

'I have an overwhelming urge to kick his fat arse. I have never been spoken to like that.'

William looked at me as if I had lost my mind. 'OK well,

let's take a second … think, Maddy … it may not be the best way forward, assaulting the landlord.'

'Well when you put it like that I s'pose.'

'Look he's not worth it,' William said gently, defusing my fury enough for me to bow my head and take a deep breath. 'Come on!' he said, hooking his arm through mine, guiding me back inside.

Now there was only one item left in the room. The small upright piano. 'It's staying,' I said, standing in front of it protectively. Dad had been a keen and enthusiastic piano player, more enthusiastic on a Saturday night than a Monday morning admittedly, but there had been wonderful nights spent round that piano. 'I know it takes up space but let's leave it here for just now – it feels like he might come in at any moment, sit down and play it.' My chin began wobbling. 'Everything is changing and…' I held my hand up as William was about to launch into his spiel. 'I know it has to, but I really want Dad to recognise it as being the same place.'

William gave me a hug.

So it was settled.

Half an hour later, thank God, the skip arrived so we were as good as our word, thus dispelling any objections the Laird might have. And we filled it fast with all sorts.

The crockery was in a shocking state so out it went.

The cutlery was a mismatched array of stuff. Some of which was beautiful silver we wrapped for auction, and we agreed to splash out on some practical catering-grade dishwasher-proof stuff to replace it.

Ancient napkins and napkin rings, small scratched stainless steel salt and peppers, mustard pots, egg cups and sundae dishes were all put in the recycle pile. Woven breadbaskets mostly clogged up with breadcrumbs and dust were binned. The glasses included beautiful crystal whereas others had been collected with vouchers from the Shell garage in the seventies. A few were engraved with crass jokes or in faded gold letters brand names of long-defunct beers. We decided to keep the crystal and the good-quality clear glasses but all monograms, labels, brands and garage voucher glasses were into the charity pile.

After a while we got into a rhythm, knowing instinctively what we should keep and what we should hurl. It wasn't until we began to divest the walls of their treasure that it all became too much. Paintings, photos, cartoons of all sizes and shapes, a very dusty set of antlers on which every point held a different hat, most of which I could visualise Dad in. A straw boater as he sang 'There's an old mill by the stream, Nellie Dean', a top hat for his *My Fair Lady* favourite 'Get me to the church on time', a Scottish bonnet for 'Ae fond kiss', Jack Nicklaus's baseball cap from the year he won the Open.

Thick with dust we took each hat down until the antlers on their wooden plinth revealed a small plaque underneath it: 'Sean. A Royal Stag. Loch Carron 1963'. I ached, realising the story of Sean the stag hadn't been told for such a long time the details were already fading in my memory. There was a long chain twisted round the topmost point, which I couldn't reach. Climbing onto a table, William lifted the antlers down amidst a flurry of dust, and placed them on the floor, where I set about untangling the chain, as William wondered at the colour of the wall underneath the plinth, which must have been hanging in the same spot since the day they opened. Nicotine and years of wear had turned it from ruby red to faded pink.

The chain from the top point of the antlers finally un-knotted, I stood back. The walls were now completely empty – it was so sad, the chips and knocks over the years laid bare.

We lugged all this stuff, bar the antlers, which wouldn't fit no matter how we tried, into the back of William's car having decided it was best I sift through it all in my own time, deciding what to keep.

Just before 5 p.m. the auction van turned up and examining the mound of stuff on the pavement, after some humming and hawing, one of them declared, 'No. We'll no' fit a' that in there.'

Undaunted, William told me to keep them talking as he disappeared inside, producing two mugs of sweet tea and a couple of chunks of his Rocky Road. It had the desired effect as they visibly perked up and spent the next thirty minutes manoeuvring and squishing everything in, before doffing their caps, gratefully accepting £20 for a pint and heading off. Grinding the gears, the groaning old van, heavy and low on its wheelbase, crunched off down the road. Another item crossed off the list.

Apart from watching Laurel and Hardy filling the van and our run-in with the Laird, the only moment we had stopped was for a hot sausage roll courtesy of Uncle Fraser, who sent Jono the butcher's boy over with them at lunchtime, along with a polystyrene cup of home-made soup.

Just as I was wondering if I had the energy to put one foot in front of the other, Noel's smiling face appeared round the door.

'Good Lord, are you two still at it? I thought you would have retired to the pub hours ago. Listen, I'm on my way down to the beach with Frank. Why don't I pop in and collect you on the way back? I've got a casserole in the oven and by the look of you two, you've done more than enough for one day.'

A quick glance at my mobile confirmed it was nearly seven o'clock. We had been in there nearly twelve hours.

'God that sounds perfect. I'm starving.' My tummy rumbled in agreement, the sausage roll a dim and instant memory.

'Yeh me too,' William agreed. 'And we've got all day tomorrow to look forward to!'

The following morning Torbeck the painter arrived at 8 a.m. on the dot.

He grinned. 'Now, what you want me to do?'

'The walls, wash them, strip them only if you have to, and paint them white. Ceiling walls, skirting, the lot.'

'Okey-dokey,' he said, marching off to retrieve his ladders from the roof of his van and get cracking.

With the main restaurant now being painted, it was up to William and I to tackle the kitchen, which on the surface proved much easier than I thought.

A few cracked and chipped platters, a sieve that looked like it may have been used on the *Lusitania*, some old plastic glasses, empty stacked-up ice cream containers and unlabelled jars of things.

Drawers, cupboards, shelves, equipment, knives, serving platters, paperwork, food, tins of food, the fridge, walk-in larder, sinks, stoves, ovens, grills, extractors – it was packed to the gunnels with stuff.

'Oh my God,' was all I managed after opening just one drawer, rammed to the hilt with rubber bands, golf balls, golf tees, receipts, order pads, pencils, business cards, postcards, SIM cards, a small first-aid kit, paper clips and fluff. Perhaps my initial assessment was a bit optimistic; this was going to take an age.

William looked over at me, his face all soft. 'Maddy, you look done in.'

I felt it. The physical exertions I could handle, but the

emotional toll of rooting through and seeing before me my entire family history had yet again reduced me to tears.

'Well I always find, when it comes to things like this,' he illustrated by scooping up a handful of random things from another drawer, 'it's often easier to let someone else troll through it all.'

'Like who?'

'Well. Like me,' he said gently. 'I loved your Dad dearly but I've been surrounded by this stuff for so long the minutiae of it doesn't really bother me. I'm a born minimalist and I find it quite easy to see the wood from the trees.'

'Really?' Eyes brimming with tears, I felt my spirits lift slightly at thought of a get-out clause.

'Yes really. Now come on, it's cold in here, the paint fumes are strong as hell, so why don't you head home, put the fire on and chill out? Just leave this lot to me.'

I didn't need to be talked into it. I was done in.

I squeezed him tight, thanking him profusely, increasingly impressed with his mind-reading skills.

The division of labour meant huge progress was made during the afternoon.

Torbeck was a fast worker and as I left, he was painting enthusiastically, singing along to his battery-operated radio in a hilariously tuneless way. William was up to his oxters in stuff as I headed back to the cottage lugging two huge IKEA bags full of old framed photos and pictures.

The angel who is Noel had set the fire. Putting a match to it, I marvelled how quickly it took the chill off the place and a warm glow filled the room. After making myself a mug of coffee I felt stronger again and so settled down cross-legged in front of the fire – with Frank lying on the rug snoring beside me – and began sorting through the boxes of pictures and other bits and pieces. The frames were a mixed bag:

brass, silver, wood of varying colours and textures, plastic, velvet, gold and silver. To assess each picture equally, I eased each photograph from its frame and laid them out on the floor in front of me.

By the time Noel arrived back at lunchtime I had quite a collection. Of course he focused on the pile of frames immediately.

'You're not throwing all those out are you?'

'Well I was going to. I mean some of them are in a terrible state.'

'Ah now,' he said, squatting own and picking one up, 'you need to hold fire there and let me have a look through them. I can see a few crackers.' I watched him expertly examine each frame, succinctly putting them into two distinct piles. 'There,' he said, 'you're right, this lot are for the bin but,' he pointed at the smaller pile, 'I have plucked some diamonds from the rough. Look at this wee beauty,' he said, holding up a blackened frame that to me looked like it was burnt and ready to be binned. 'Under all this dirt and grease lurks a Georgian silver frame.'

Grabbing a soft cloth from the kitchen, he rubbed hard on the edge and slowly he cleared the sooty blackness, shifting enough layers of grim to reveal the unmistakable glint of what, if he said so, must be silver.

I smiled.

'And more to the point, how are you getting on with the pictures?'

I gulped. I was finding it very difficult to look at them at all, which I confessed to Noel.

'OK, some will be easier to look at than others – just flick through them quickly, let your gut tell guide you as to which ones you want to put back on the walls. Just keep doing that until they're whittled down. Then we can get them back into the frames and once they're grouped together the right way, I reckon it will look fab. We can repaint the chipped ones and source some nice news ones and they'll look great. Trust me, I'm an antique dealer,' he said as he gathered all the frames up into a pile and stuffed them under his arm. 'I'll head back to the shop and start sorting these out and leave you to it.'

He was right: contemplation was the way of madness so I didn't dilly-dally. I followed instructions until I had a pile of photos to rehang in the restaurant and a pile for myself.

Mid-afternoon, Frank came to life and was stomping around the arms of the couch looking bored. Clipping on his lead, I decided to take a wander round to Noel's shop, say hi and maybe have a look at the bothy.

It was literally two minutes' walk from the cottage. I knocked and opened the door to find Noel sitting behind a desk, on the phone. Seeing me, he smiled, waved me in, put his hand over the receiver and whispered, 'Have a look round. I'll be with you in a minute.' And so as he chatted on, I took in my surroundings. The walls were covered in paintings, sketches; polished wooden surfaces held any number of objets d'art, a bust, magnifying glass, a ship's bell, a violin, carved wooden implements, beautiful vases and china cups so thin they were almost translucent. A collector indeed. He finished his call.

'Hi, Mads,' he said, 'sorry about that.'

'No, don't be daft, this is your business! I thought I'd pop in and say hi and if it's convenient, maybe have a wee look at the bothy?'

'Oh yes, great,' he said, lifting a key from a hook near the French windows at the back, which led out into the garden.

'This is so cute,' I said, seeing what looked like a mini cottage in the corner of the garden, with a peeling green door, which Noel opened with a huge key and pushed open with a thud of his shoulder. 'As you can see it's not the Ritz,' he said, flicking on a light.

Shuffling in behind him, I saw a plain square room with one window to the right of the door. Stone walls, floors and a wooden ceiling covered in cobwebs and dust. My heart sank. 'Maybe this isn't such a good idea,' he said when he saw my expression.

'No, no, it just needs a bit of a spruce-up and it will be great,' I said, more to convince myself than anyone else. 'Honestly it's just what I need, somewhere to escape,' I said, sounding more optimistic than I felt. 'I'll get on my marigolds and give it a good clean – it will be transformed!'

'But not today,' he said. 'Come on, it'll be getting dark soon. Why don't we head back to the cottage – we've plenty to do there. You carry on with your photos and I'll get the tea on.'

I wasn't going to argue. So as I sat curled up on the couch, Frank in the crook of my knees, I went through everything in more detail.

There were about a dozen black and white photos – all genuine from the fifties and sixties. Some of Dad growing up, some with his friends, others with golf stars of the day who had been to St Andrews, many of whom came to The Birdie & Bramble to eat. We moved then to the faded colour ones of the late seventies, some small and barely discernible as to who or what was in them; ones of special significance had been blown up to A4 size. There was a fair number of chunky knit cardigans and awful mullet hair.

'These are great,' said Noel, grinning at the fashion victims in front of him. Plucking one out of the pile he asked, 'And who is he?'

'That's me!' I snorted. It was Noel's turn to look surprised. 'I looked like a wee boy until I was about fifteen. Dad used to send me round to the post office to get stamps and I would queue up and the wifie in there would say, "Right you're next, laddie," and I used to shout "I'm nae a laddie, I'm a lassie."'

Noel laughed companionably. 'Well happily you grew into your looks,' he said, putting the photo into the usable side.

'What on earth are you going to use that for?' I asked.

'Scaring the locals,' he said, plucking the next one from the top.

With Noel's help we went through them all fairly quickly. Folding up the bags to put them away, he suddenly exclaimed and pulled from the bottom of the bag the chain I had spent ages earlier untangling from the antlers.

'What's this?' he asked.

'I have no idea; it was hanging on the wall under all those hats – it must have been there forever.'

He fished out his eyeglass from his pocket and examined it more closely. 'This is a nice chain … it's real gold.'

'Really?'

'Yes, eighteen-carat and—' he weighed it up in his hand '—quite heavy. Probably worth a few hundred quid.'

'Oh,' I said, thinking it was typical of Dad to have no idea of the value of such a thing, twisted, abandoned and out of sight.

'Resale value isn't much but it's a nice piece of jewellery,' he said, peering at the charm that hung on the end of it. 'I have no idea what this is.'

I scrutinised it. 'Me neither.'

'It's a bit grotty. I'll clean it up for you,' he said as the door flew open and William careered in, collapsing onto the sofa with a WHUMP!

'Another day, another squalor.'

'Is it that bad?'

'No I'm joking. It's looking so much better! Really. Torbeck has finished the dining room.'

'Wow!'

'I know! That man is fast. He's already moved into the kitchen and he reckons he will get that finished by midnight. So it should be dry by tomorrow afternoon when the deep-clean people are coming to give the kitchen an absolute boiling from top to toe.'

'I can't believe it but we're almost there,' I said, impressed at the speed the transformation was taking place.

William grinned. 'I know,' he said, putting his feet up on the coffee table.

Timeously Noel appeared with three glasses of red wine. 'Feet!' he ordered, disappearing back into the kitchen. William immediately took them off the table and put them back onto the floor.

After a long sip I asked, 'So when do you think we'll be ready to open our doors to the general public?'

'We need to be open as soon as possible,' he said. 'How about Thursday next week?'

My stomach did a somersault. 'Shit! Really?'

'Yes!'

'Oh my God, it's so soon.'

He smiled as I continued, 'What about an opening do?'

'Well, we don't have any money to throw a proper party but I do think we need to have a small opening do for locals, suppliers and friends but we can't let it get it out of hand because we need to open for business as soon as possible and start making some money!' He rubbed his hands together.

'Well, if there's one thing I can do,' I said, 'it's organise a piss-up in a brewery. Let's do a guest list now.' I rootled around in my bottomless pit of a handbag.

Ten minutes later and a worrying number of names were already on the list when Noel announced dinner.

The red wine had done its job and gratefully I let William haul me by my hands out of the chair and followed him through to the kitchen to eat. Comfort food, well named. We ate silently, eyelids drooping, before settling on the couch with Frank to watch *MasterChef* and fell instantly asleep.

Chapter 15

Next morning William left me to sleep. When I opened my eyes, I saw Frank was watching me. How could I resist that face?

'OK, cheeky chops, give me five minutes,' I said as the wee face lit up.

I had a quick shower and despite the dog managed to get dressed, hopping about on one leg as Frank made his presence felt. It was all I could do to stop laughing long enough to wrestle my jacket, jumper, hat and then each glove off the dancing joyful wee dog.

Within moments we were on the north sands striding along apace. The clouds were high, the sky a washed-out blue and the wind a refreshing blast, which made me throw my head back and inhale the glorious air to my boots. A great night's sleep had energised me. I felt stronger and the fizz of anticipation in my belly as to what lay ahead spurred me on.

As is often the case the beach was virtually deserted, with only a few fellow dog walkers in the distance. The tide was far far out, leaving a vast sweep of pristine sand as far as the eye could see.

Kitesurfers whipped along the waves. The brusque wind on this exposed coast was perfect for any number of water sports. Running towards the water's edge with Frank in hot pursuit, I laughed out loud as I came to a stop and he continued into the fizz of life-affirming spray, the cold causing his eyes to pop out in surprise. Then he did his usual trick of producing an impressive stick, seemingly from nowhere, and bounded around, desperate for me to throw it for him. Watching him gambol in the waves waiting for the tide to roll his stick back to him, rather than the fruitless plouter of plunging into the waves, which would knock him over in an instant, suddenly it hit me this was the first time I'd been on the beach on my own since...

Since before Dad died.

In fact since Christmas. Hard to believe it was only five months ago, I thought, with what felt like a kick in my chest, when the two of us, wrapped up and rosy-cheeked on Christmas morning, had walked arm in arm laughing and kicking up sand, taking it in turns to throw a stick for Frank. The desolate miles of sand that stretched in front of me suddenly seemed like a metaphor for life. Alone in an unchartered world, no Dad, no home, no roots, no idea what on earth was supposed to happen now.

A moment of panic. Insurmountable. A vast blank canvas where I stood alone and suddenly very unsure, with the thumping in my chest. What on earth was I doing? What was I thinking? Back in St Andrews, the restaurant – had I taken leave of my senses? Fighting the panic and burning sensation behind my eyes, I upped my pace, ignoring the dancing dog at my feet and marched on purposefully. I felt like I was losing my mind. I needed to get out of here. This wasn't my place; this was my father's place. I let out a sob. Coorying deep into my scarf, I stomped on.

'Excuse me but are you OK?'

'Em...' I glanced up into a pair of the darkest blue eyes, lined with the longest darkest lashes imaginable, which rather put me off my stride.

'Why?' I blurted, sounding like I thought he was going to mug me.

'Sorry, I just thought you might need this,' he said, offering me a huge white hanky.

'Sorry?' I said, a little confused and putting my hand up to my face. I had been so lost in my own wee world I hadn't even noticed I'd been laughing and, as the tears proved, crying. Mortified.

'Gosh I hadn't realised, thanks,' I said, sounding like a halfwit and taking his hanky to wipe my wet face and blow my nose.

Surprisingly he didn't run off but smiled. 'We've met before, at Fraser's shop,' he said. Of course. Those eyes. I knew I'd seen them before.

I nodded, still dabbing my eyes, not trusting myself to speak.

'I didn't realise he was your uncle,' he added. 'Such a lovely man ... and condolences – he told me about your father ...'

I was shocked that he was so direct; most people thus far had been chatty enough but avoided saying the words out loud. I didn't quite know what to say so I just stared at him, mouth open.

'Well,' he said awkwardly, 'as long as you're OK, I'll leave you in peace.' Silently I watched as he turned to walk away.

'Oh, do you want this?' I shouted, suddenly realising I was still grasping his sodden hanky.

'Em ... tempting though it is, no thanks, you can hang onto that.'

And off he strode. Just like that. I watched him go. The collar of his Barbour flipped up to protect his neck from the chill, snapping wind and then I heard him whistle and watched as two huge dogs ran out from the sand dunes, loping elegantly over the white deserted beach toward him at such speed I fully expected them to send him flying, but just at the right moment they slowed down, seamlessly falling into step beside him. Beautiful dogs. The three walked off into the distance.

'Well well well,' I said out loud.

Stuffing the wet hanky into my pocket, I bent down, picked up a stick up and threw it with renewed gusto for Frank before turning back towards the town. 'Come on, Frankie Frankie Jimmy Spankie,' I shouted – a name only Dad used for him. 'We've got work to do!' And sensing a change in the air, the wee dog yipped with delight and went roaring off ahead.

On my back from the beach I nipped into The Birdie & Bramble and collected a measuring tape before heading off to the bothy to measure and make sure I could squash all my bits and pieces in. The shop was already open and Noel was sitting behind his desk when I arrived. His face broke into a smile when he saw me.

'Hi!' I said, breezing in, bringing a cold whip of air with me, which rustled the papers on his desk.

'Hello you,' he said, standing up and coming round to give me a hug.

'Do you mind if I go back and look at the bothy? I was so excited last time, I didn't really take it in.'

'Of course – but hang on a moment,' he said, going back over to his desk. Scooping something up, he turned and held out his hand. On his palm was the chain we had found twisted and dull, tied round the antlers. It looked completely different.

'God is that the same chain?'

'Yes, it's cleaned up very nicely.' He dangled it in front of me. 'This charm on the end seems to be a kitsch piece of Victoriana. An elaborate key of some sort.'

'Oh,' I said, looking at it properly for the first time. 'And what's that?'

'I think it's initials – NCB.'

'NCB? I wonder who that was?'

'No idea. I thought you might be able to hazard a guess.'

'Nora Claverton Bonnet,' I joked. 'Neil Chopstick Bunion.'

He picked up the theme quickly. 'Nincompoop Clavichord Binswanger.'

We became quite hysterical – then my eyes filled with tears. 'If only Dad was here he would know, or if he didn't he would make up some outrageous story,' I burbled.

Noel could see what was happening and so took control. 'It's pretty though, whatever it is. You should wear it.'

I nodded, blew my nose and turned round so Noel could fasten it round my neck.

I ran my hands up and down the chain. A little piece of my history to be worn close to my heart. Whatever reason Dad had kept it, I would do the same.

As I stroked it, Noel held out his hand.

'And this is yours too. I had another key cut for the bothy,' he explained. 'And, my dear girl, it is yours, for as long as you like.'

'Thank you,' I said, hugging him tight, before heading outside to acquaint myself with the tiny stone house. What had looked like peeling green paint the other day in the dullness of dusk looked quite different now. It looked brighter and much to my relief more shiny and inviting. My previous misgivings quelled, I took in the ivy-covered roof and approaching it, noticed the door was slightly ajar. Surprised to find it unlocked, I pushed it open further and was startled to find lights on and, blow me, Torbeck the painter halfway up a ladder just finishing off giving the whole place a lick of paint.

'Torbeck!' I exclaimed. 'What you are doing?'

'Well we had some paint left over from the restaurant and we think good to give it a quick suck of paint.'

'Lick,' Noel corrected him.

'Oh yes lick, lick,' he said, shaking his head.

'Thank you so much, it looks wonderful,' I said, tears welling. 'What a lovely, lovely thing to do.'

'What a difference a day makes!' Noel grinned.

'Noel, I can't believe it really, I am so touched.'

'Och away you go, now come on, let's get this place measured up and we can move your bits and bobs in over the next few days.'

Measuring confirmed it was a titchy space. I had just enough space for a single bed along one wall so decided my bed from Dad's flat was coming with me. This meant I really had to go back and start clearing it. It was looming large in my mind, and now I had a place to call home, I was running out of excuses to put it off. But not today; today William and I were meeting the suppliers and deciding on the menu – so I was off again.

The original plan of meeting in The Birdie & Bramble had been scuppered by the smell of paint, which was lingering, so we had agreed to meet potential suppliers at William's cottage.

Davy the Fish was first in, midday on the dot, staggering under the weight of two huge iceboxes.

'Morning!' he shouted, hefting them up onto the table.

'Morning, Davy,' we said in unison.

The first container held an eye-popping array of seafood sitting on a bed of ice. This was going to be fun. Oysters, crab, lobster langoustine, cockles, winkles, mussels. The second container held haddock, cod, plaice, halibut and sea bream.

'All local, all caught right here,' he said, clocking the open mouths and raised eyebrows of his audience. 'But you know all that.'

Over the next half hour the three of us talked fish and he agreed to honour Dad's wholesale rate.

'Thanks, that's brilliant,' I said, giving him a particularly cheesy, head-tilting grin before asking outright to give us a twenty-eight-day line of credit.

He rolled his eyes and reddened, standing up and tucking away all his goods. As he closed his cool box, he stopped and looked at me. 'Maddy, your dad was a lovely bloke. It will be a pleasure to do business with you and if you're anything like him, you won't be half bad.' His face verging on purple and throat tightening, he coughed. 'Twenty-eight days' credit it is,' he said as he picked up his cool box, shook our hands and left.

'Tear to a glass eye,' said William.

'I know,' I said, my voice shaking.

'Och don't you start!' he said, changing the mood before we all broke down and howled.

My mobile pinged. I glanced at it. Marcus. *'Hey, babe, really need to hear your voice.'*

Ignoring it, I put it facedown on the table.

'OK what's next?' I asked.

'Wine supplier, cheese man, fruit and veg man and Rory the baker,' said William efficiently. 'And Uncle Fraser of course.'

'You haven't asked him to come over and show us his stuff have you?'

'Yes! Why?'

'He's Uncle Fraser!'

'I know, but business is business.'

'You're right of course but there's no way I would ever use anyone other than him. I'll nip round and see him and ask him round for a drink about six – and we can talk turkey then.'

And so we did. Fraser didn't need to be asked twice and being Fraser arrived ten minutes early with a huge bin liner groaning with food. He saw William's expression.

'I know I know it's no' very PC but I just walked round from the shop so no-one will see my chill cabinet,' he chuckled, heaving the bag up onto the kitchen table where it landed with a WHUMP! 'Now,' he said, peering into the bag, reminding himself. 'What have we got here?'

'Well, before you do that, Fraser, what would you like to drink?'

My mobile buzzed. It was Marcus again. A twinge of guilt prickled. I really needed to speak to him – it had been nearly three days.

'Listen, I just need to take this call. I'll be back in five minutes,' I said, stepping outside onto the pavement for a decent signal and some privacy.

I rang him back. It rang twice before he picked up.

'Hi, it's me!' I said.

There was a muffled noise, and then the unmistakable sound of a busy bar in the background. 'A pint please, mate, yeh back in a mo,' and it sounded like he too moved outside to speak to me.

'Maddy. Are you all right? It's been ages. How you doing?'

'OK,' I said and then on second thoughts, 'Actually, better than OK – really well.'

'Thanks, mate,' I heard him say before giving me his

attention. 'Great, great, good.' He sounded like I did when I used to humour my father by pretending to listen to him.

'How's work?' I asked.

'Oh fine,' he said. 'The usual.'

'Marcus!' I heard a familiar voice call.

'Is that Felicity?'

'Oh what – that? Yeh, you know it's Friday so we all hit the pub straight after work.' He guffawed and I heard her horsey laugh join in.

'Well, have fun. I'm up to my neck in it,' I said, straining not to sound like I was really pissed off, which I was.

'OK, babe – can we talk in the morning then?'

'Yeh fine,' I said and hung up.

Bloody Felicity. No sooner was I out of the picture and there she was, trappers hat on in the pub on a Friday afternoon. She never went to the pub any night let alone a Friday, disapproving of fraternising between colleagues, claiming it was very unprofessional. Gggggr.

Still, in all fairness, it sounded like there were loads of people there. I was just being paranoid, far away and so disconnected just now; it was natural to feel a bit … insecure.

Standing up tall, I rubbed my hands over my face to wake myself up again, and stepped back into the room. Fraser and William were settled by the fire sipping glasses of red.

'So by the look of things, business is over for the day,' I said, closing the door behind me.

They smiled at me.

'Not quite, we thought we'd better wait for the boss.'

I almost looked behind me, until I realised that I was now the boss. Gulp.

I coughed. 'OK then, what did Dad get from you? That's as good a starting point as any …'

'Steak, the good stuff. Twenty-eight-day hung rib-eye,

sirloin and fillet. Though I don't know why cos he just clarted it in sauce.'

Dad's Steak Diane was renowned, for all the wrong reasons. The meat was delicious but the emphasis on the pint of creamy mushroom boozy sauce drowned out whatever lurked beneath.

'Aye a' that good beef,' Fraser harrumphed. 'Might as well have been carpet, but,' he conceded, 'his sauces were a triumph. Aye. I told him for years just serve a cheaper cut if you're going to drown it anyway, but you know your father – he wouldn't listen to a word anyone said.'

'So why didn't he buy the cheaper stuff?'

'*Only the best* was his motto. Huh. I told him it was like giving a violin to an ape, cremating this lovely stuff then slopping a funcy sauce all over it.'

I knew my dad and this was typical.

'Well his heart was in the right place,' I said, defending him.

'Oh God knows I wish he was here now to have a good argy-bargy about it,' said Fraser. 'I mean, I just can't believe he's gone.'

William detected another emotional outburst was imminent so did what was rapidly becoming his party trick of changing the subject. Fraser produced a gnarled-up hanky out of his jacket pocket and emptied his hooter into it before coughing and looking a little lost for a moment.

'Just try a wee doad of this,' he said to William, who flipped up the Aga hood, and flung it directly onto the hotplate.

'Just a second now,' Fraser bossed.

William followed instructions and put it down in front of us.

After it was cut in three we tasted it. It was unbelievably good. We were both in raptures, much to Fraser's amusement.

'Och, Madeline Campbell, you didn't think I was a crap butcher, did you? Cheeky besom!' he snorted, his now empty hooter trumpeting with mirth.

William was moved to agree in his most serious tone. 'Where does all your stuff come from?'

'St Andrews and hereabouts – none of my stuff ever travels more than ten miles from cradle to grave.'

'God.' My creative synapses fired again. 'The whole traceable thing – Dad's been doing for years! He just hasn't bothered telling anyone about it!'

'Aye right enough, I never thought about it like that,' said Fraser, swirling the last bite of meat through the last of the juices and popping it into his mouth.

'Right, so will you send us a note with all the prices on it?' William requested.

'Why? Are you shopping around?' Fraser snapped, his eyes bulging.

'No we are not!' I said, giving William the evil eye. 'You are as much part of The Birdie & Bramble as I am. Just let us know how much things will be so William can do his whizz-kid accounting.' I turned back to Fraser. 'You know we could not or would not ever use anyone else, OK?'

Fraser visibly relaxed. 'Aye, OK then.'

'So,' William interjected with the tone of a children's TV presenter, 'we're getting there. Now let's decide what else we're after.'

'Aye okey-doke,' said Fraser, licking the end of his pencil and writing a list on a wee pad of paper. Lamb, pork, haggis, black pudding, chicken, guinea fowl game and venison.

'Could you source organic if we wanted it?'

'Oh it is?'

'What?'

'Organic.'

'Is it?'

'Och yes, but we don't like to bump our gums about it – folk are suspicious you're going to charge through the nose. So we don't mention it.'

William and I looked at each other again.

'So Dad has been serving organic lamb, free-range pork, haggis, black pudding and venison.'

'Oh no, no venison.' He shook his head.

'Why not?'

'Oh Joe didn't like venison.'

'Why ever not?'

'He had it once, said it tasted like overripe cheese so he wouldn't entertain the thought of it.'

'Well I say we've got to have venison – everyone loves venison!'

'I agree,' said Fraser and William in unison.

'Well good, I have a guy – The Merchant of Venison we call him – who has a great supply of wild deer, supplies the shop and I can't get enough of it. Folk love it. Lovely stuff.' He reached into this bag and took out a slab of red meat, handing it to William who heated up the pan, shadowed by Fraser giving instructions.

'Now,' he shouted in his ear, 'just add some butter. Melt the butter and sauté that for a minute or two each side. Serve it rare.'

William followed instructions and within minutes the meat was served onto a plate. 'Now try that!' said Fraser, putting the plate on the table with a flourish.

It was as meltingly tender as the beef fillet before.

'I can't believe this is venison,' I admitted, dreamily cutting another piece to eat as the first bit had evaporated so quickly.

'Aye there is a myth,' said Fraser, 'that venison is hard gamey meat that needs to be casseroled for hours. And right

179

enough that is true if you get a hoary old stag who's been running aboot the hills for years; but if you get a hind, which we do at this time of year, then they are as tender as the night. You treat them like you would the best fillet steak and that's what you get.'

'And,' I added, 'it's low fat and protein-rich!'

'Brought to you in association with the venison marketing board,' said William.

'Yes!' I squealed. 'We'll be health freaks! What other bits can you eat?'

'Well the whole lot! You can casserole it, smoke it, make a terrine from it, mince it for pies, use the bones for stock. It really is brilliant stuff and when The Merchant takes them off the hill, we do the butchery across there,' he said, pointing at this shop.

'OK, let's dig a bit deeper and see what we have,' I said.

'Pigs from Porkham Farm – free-range beauties, black pud, haggis and sausages we'll make for you. Of course your father wouldn't have haggis on the menu.'

'Why not?'

'He didn't want to come across like a wee hairy Scotsman.' We all laughed.

'That's exactly what he was!' I guffawed. 'A wee hairy Scotsman.'

'I know. Maybe he thought it would be like cannibalism. Well I love haggis and if there is one thing I would want to eat if I came to Scotland, that's it,' said William.

'It's back on the menu,' I announced.

So we agreed, as if there was any doubt, that Fraser would handle all our butchery including, whenever possible, a good knucklebone for Frank.

After hugs and handshakes and words of encouragement and commitment, Fraser announced he was off home for tea.

'For tea? You've just stuffed your face!' I laughed.

'I ken,' he said, patting his belly, 'but Margaret's a great cook and I don't want to get on the wrong side of her!' He laughed and, after a protracted farewell, left.

Noel as ever timed his arrival perfectly. 'Drink?'

'Oh yes please!' we said in unison.

'Come on then,' said Noel, reaching for my jacket.

'What, not here?' I asked, feeling panicky.

'No, not here.' His tone changed to cajoling and gentle. 'Come on, Maddy, it's about time you ventured out of the Bermuda triangle of the beach, our house and this place,' Noel laughed as he handed me my coat. 'William and I are taking you to the pub.'

My stomach lurched. Going out amongst normal humans in another place altogether frightened the hell out of me. Before I could think of an excuse, William was helping me on with my coat, wrapping my scarf round my neck and even plopping his knitted bonnet on my head. 'Yes,' he said, holding me at arm's length, 'it's definitely a look.'

'But not a good one!' Noel chipped in as the two of them, laughing, manhandled me out of the door. William kept me talking as Noel locked up behind us and before I realised, the three of us were walking along the road three abreast, me in the middle, arm in arm between these two lovely men. Despite my reservations I was amazed how good it felt to be part of this tight band.

Marching along the street chatting excitedly, our hot breath puffed out into the cold night air around us. Within minutes we arrived at The Hoozier. Swinging the door open and heading right up to the bar, Noel asked, 'OK, madam, what are you having?'

'A pint of Snakebite for the lady,' boomed a voice.

'Hamish!'

'Hi, Cuz.' He grinned. 'You're back!'

'Well...' I hesitated, about to go into the usual spiel about sabbaticals and London but I hadn't the energy. 'Yes! I suppose I am!' I said, grinning. 'And you're still here! That's a record for you, isn't it?' I teased.

'Ah yes, the pull of the homestead is too hard to resist,' he added. The pull of the homestead indeed, I mused, raising an eyebrow at him. 'So what's it to be then – a Snakebite?'

'Good God no!' I laughed.

'What's a Snakebite?' asked Noel.

'Half a pint of lager and half a cider in a pint glass,' I said.

'Commonly known as rocket fuel,' added Hamish, 'and something Ms Madeline Campbell used to drink on a regular basis.'

'From a jam jar in my handbag,' I guffawed. 'It was bloody lethal!'

'Which is why it was banned about ten years ago!'

'Really?"

'Oh yes. So what would you like?'

'A half pint of cider and a half pint of lager and an empty pint glass,' the minxy side of me piped up.

'Certainly.' Hamish grinned. 'Gentlemen?'

'A pint of cider,' Noel said.

'Thistly Cross?'

'I beg your pardon?' Noel retorted, sounding as camp as Christmas.

'That's the kind of cider made in East Lothian, very popular in these parts.'

'I know,' Noel grinned back.

'And a pint of 80 shilling,' said William.

Perching on a high stool I turned to face the boys as they excitedly talked over the day's events, leaving Hamish to attend to the hordes of students streaming through the door.

Periodically I watched his easy way with customers and heard the laughter and chatter as the place filled up, creating a lovely warm atmosphere, which explained why one drink turned into several and then a few more besides.

Then someone pressed Fast Forward and the next thing I remember was Jack coming in. Oh God. Cringe. I must have been speaking utter shite by then. He was at the other side of the bar ordering a drink and I stood up on the footrest of the stool and waved like a loon from our side of the bar, beckoning. He smiled and made his way over, and then rather than pipe down I told a shocking joke and then became quite hysterical laughing at it. My own joke. Bloody hell and then the last thing I recall was William helping me off my high bar stool, plonking my hat back on my overmangled hairy head and steering me out of the door as I shouted and waved goodbye to Jack and Hamish.

Chapter 16

When I awoke the following morning my tongue was glued to the roof of my mouth and my head felt like a bag of bolts. I lay stock-still. I had no choice; my head felt like it might explode. Now I understood the reason Snakebite was banished. It *was* rocket fuel.

I pieced together the early part of the evening and then put my hands over my face. 'Oh God,' I moaned, having a flashback to the bar cacophony during which it was coming back to me. I think I offered Jack a job?

There was a knock at the door. Aaargh. The pain! The pain!

'Hello?' I murmured into the mattress.

'Cup of hot tea and some jammy toast? The only way to start the morning after the night before,' chirruped William. 'Noel was not much better when he woke up so don't worry – you're not alone.'

As I shuffled into an upright position, William plumped up the pillows and presented me with the toast and judged correctly that my shaky hand wasn't the ideal place to put a mug of boiling tea, so he placed it on the chest next to the bed.

'Where is he?' I pointed at Frank's vacant spot on the bed.

'He's taken Noel for a walk.' He opened the curtains. 'To be honest, Frank wasn't that bothered but I thought Noel might pass out if he didn't get into the fresh air – it's the best hangover cure in the world, that beach.' William laughed and sat down on the edge of the bed. 'Good night?'

'Great,' I said, looking him in the eye. 'I think.'

He laughed. 'OK you. I'll leave you in peace. I just wanted to check you were still in the land of the living.'

'Just. Thanks, William, you are an angel,' I said, picking up a huge buttery piece of toast and taking a bite. 'Mmmmm, this is amazing bread.' I shouted after him.

'Thank you, they don't call me the Mr Kipling for nothing!' he laughed as he padded downstairs.

Once I came round a bit I realised I was buzzing. Absolutely buzzing. I felt – well, alive! Running over everything that happened yesterday – Uncle Fraser's stuff, Davy the Fish, the menu, the closing and tarting up of The Birdie & Bramble – there was so much to think about. But before I could do anything there was a sudden gust of cold air and a whirling noise then silence as Frank arrived home, whizzed up the stairs and took off from the other end of the bedroom. He literally flew through the air and landed on me, wagging, wet, wriggling and determined to lick my face.

'Frank!' I laughed, admonishing him but finding it impossible not to embrace the wee thing as his stumpy tail thudded furiously against the bed and his muddy wet paws tramped the duvet cover.

When I released him he stood there and looked right into my eyes with an expression of utter joy. Walked, happy, with his beloved mistress and now what?

'Dinner!' came the shout from downstairs and without so much as a glance he was off again, flying through the air and rat-tatting downstairs at Noel's cry.

Even after a shower I was a shaky mess, the dehydrated wreck of the *Hesperus*. It was time to march it off. I was going to the beach. One night on the lash and I was a gargoyle. My skin dry and flaky, my hair was so out of control it repeatedly sprung the beanie hat off my head. It was a cold, windy day, the sort of chill that infiltrated through every fibre of your clothing and then your skin and bones, and with so much to do I'd decided to turn back and cut the walk short when I saw him.

Two elegant loping dogs by his side, smooth confident gait, head down, hands deep in his pockets, long legs striding ahead, marching into the wind. He was coming my way. Jack.

My first instinct was obvious.

Hide.

We walked slowly towards each other, his head down, protecting his face from the wind; mine pretending to be down too whilst keeping a beady eye on him.

Then Frank took the lead, rushing over bark-bark-barking as if he was out to kill the poor guy.

'Frank!' I shouted. 'Stop it!' Mortified, I walked towards him and tried to clip his lead on, but the wee bugger was too fast for me and ran round in circles evading capture. I felt the blood run to my face. As I mumbled an apology for his appalling behaviour, Jack raised his head and our eyes met.

'Oh hello,' he said, his expression registering amusement.

'Hi,' I stammered. 'I'm so sorry about him.' I pointed at the dog. 'He is just an embarrassment really. All talk and no action. All mouth and no ...' I hesitated as my mouth seized up then said slowly '...trousers.'

Why did I have to talk about trousers? And why did it feel wrong to mention trousers? Everyone had trousers. I was wearing trousers for God's sake and yet the word suddenly felt like sexual harassment. My tongue now stuck to the roof of my mouth, which was precisely the moment my hair chose to rebel again and, SPROING, broke free from its elastic band. Off flew my beanie hat and as it broke free, my bloody rat-tail hair tumbled wildly round my head, snapping left and right in a great knot of wildness in the wind. It could take someone's eye out, I thought, as my hat went rolling off along the sand at speed. In three deft steps Jack had caught up with it, seamlessly lifting it up. He held it out to me.

'Here you are.'

'Thanks.' I was mortified.

Red eyes, no make-up, flaky skin, hair with a mind of its own currently blinding me and swirling round my head like the Tasmanian Devil.

My tongue was thick. 'Sorry about last night. I now understand why they banned Snakebite.'

He laughed. 'Yeh, I have to say my head's a bit thick this morning too. I don't know why I let you talk me into drinking one.'

'Did I? Oh God, sorry.' I willed a sinkhole to appear below me and swallow me up.

He grinned again. 'Oh and I was delighted to hear venison is back on the menu at The Birdie & Bramble.'

How on earth did he know that? And why on earth would he give a monkey's? I knew St Andrews was small but really? Does that count as good gossip in these parts?

'Yes ...' I said. 'Dad wasn't keen on it. But personally I love it!'

'So you said last night.' His face lit up, an ear-to-ear grin, which made his eyes even more sparkly, and if it were possible, his eyelashes even longer. That couldn't be possible could it, I wondered, boldly looking back at him and grinning.

'Did I – I really shouldn't be allowed out ... So why does that delight you?' I batted back.

'Well I'm the guy who supplies Fraser!'

'Oh!' The penny dropped. 'So you're The Merchant of Venison?'

'Yes.' He nodded. 'God knows who coined that phrase but it seems to have stuck.'

'Well it's nice doing business with you,' I blurted in a flirtatious way – unlike me at the best of times but in this fragile state unheard of.

'And you too,' he said, meeting my eyes.

There followed an achingly long silence. It felt like about a year and a half. It seemed I was in anaphylactic shock; my tongue seemed to swell up. I was unable to speak. I looked at my wrist – where there was no watch.

'What time is it?' I barked.

He looked at his wrist where there was a watch. 'It's nearly nine.'

'Oh gosh, right, I'm off then ... bye,' I said rather abruptly.

'Oh, OK, bye then – see you around,' he said, stepping back and giving me a slow smile, shielding his eyes from the sun and watching me go, before setting off and calling, 'Duke! Gaston! Here!' I turned and peeked back, watching as the two elegant hounds turned and ran towards him, following his lead and heading down the beach.

Duke and Gaston – big hairy dogs. The penny dropped again – of course they were deer hounds! It was all falling into place now. The Merchant of Venison. Well well well.

Back at The Birdie & Bramble, I sat and snorkelled about three mugs of hot sweet tea, reliving my encounter with The Merchant of Venison whilst pretending to read the paper as William busied himself clattering about doing cheffy things in the kitchen.

Eventually he came bounding through. 'Hey, Maddy, I honestly think we are just about good to go,' he said cheerily. 'There are a couple of bits and pieces I want to get before we open so I'm going to drive down to Edinburgh and get them this afternoon. I was wondering if you might do me a favour?'

'Of course,' I said.

'Well we're still short about twelve chairs as well as two or three tables and Noel told me there's an auction on the outskirts of St Andrews tomorrow. Would you go?'

'Yes sure. I love an auction.'

'Great. Noel is working and I'll be in the kitchen, but he said he would happy for you to take his car.' He hesitated. 'You have got a driving licence?'

I laughed. 'Yes, William.'

He went on, visibly relieved. 'Good. Right, the tables need to be the same height so we can join them together if we need to and preferably the chairs should stack. I don't know about you but I would rather have real vintage stuff than go down the shiny new flatpack route if we can.'

I agreed.

'OK, can you go online and have a look to see if there's anything that might do us?'

So off he went as I set about my task. It didn't take me long to identify there were quite a few potential bits and pieces that would fit the bill, so efficiency personified, I wrote down the item numbers and then job done sat back feeling rather pleased with myself.

A glance at the clock told me it was just after midday. Jeez. A hangover, an early morning and a walk all before nine certainly slowed down the passage of time, I thought, wishing I'd gone to Edinburgh with William for a change of scene.

It was the first time in a long time I didn't have a hundred things to do at the same time. Anxiety bubbled up. If I stopped for too long, my head and my heart would return to default setting. Aching for Dad, anger at Marcus, guilt at not phoning Sarah, confusion as to how I feel about London and St Andrews and, for the hundredth time that day, the eyelashes and trousers of The Merchant of Venison.

Over and above all these pressing things, I realised the elephant in the room was Dad's flat. Hard as I tried to pretend I wasn't thinking about it, it was just below the surface at every waking moment. There was no avoiding it. I had to go back. I had to clear it, especially now I had the bothy lined up. The twenty-eight days' notice period was slipping away. Fuelled by two flat whites, I made up my mind to get on with it. I had contemplated it every day and managed to find some excuse or other to put it off, but time was marching on. I had to get my head out of the sand and sort it out.

So I got as far as stepping outside The Birdie & Bramble and was standing on the pavement, looking up at the outside of the flat, dithering, when Mouse came round the corner and clocked me.

'You OK?' she asked.

'No. I'm just trying to get it together to go up to Dad's flat to start clearing it out.'

'Oh God,' she said with the gravitas of someone who understood what a trial it was going to be. 'Do you want a hand?'

Well I didn't expect that. In London I had become quite self-sufficient. I was unused to relying on people and unused to people having the time of day to stop what they were doing just to help me. London Maddy would have said, 'No, no I'm fine' and battled on but this new overemotional rollercoaster version of myself said, 'Really?'

'Yes of course. I've got nothing on just now. I was just nipping in to collect my tips from the wedding.'

I looked at her, I looked at the end of the road, I looked back at her. Despite myself, I still felt like running off.

'There's no time like the present,' Mouse declared, eyebrow piercings aloft, almost putting her foot out to stop my one-hundred-metre sprint in the opposite direction.

And so I handed her the key to the door. The black shiny door with battered copper numbers and the name 'Campbell' on the first of four small plastic doorbell boxes. As she turned the key, opening the door felt like opening a can of worms, a Pandora's box.

As I trudged slowly up to the first landing, dread sat heavy in my heart. Nothing could have prepared me for it.

Day one or year three. I slipped the worn key into the lock and in we went.

It was as if Dad had just left a minute ago.

The coat rack in the hall was overwhelmed with jackets, hats, scarves. The hall stand held an old ashtray full of golf tees. A pen lay beside a Post-it note on which were hastily written notes: dog food, beer, loo roll. Day-to-day stuff.

I found myself fidgeting until I had the chain, which I now wore night and day, between my fingers. I twisted it round my fingers and took a deep breath. A tight band secured itself round my head and squeezed as the familiar smells filled my nose. Every place has a unique smell, a mix of everything and everyone in it, and Dad's was no exception. The wisps of carpet, dog, Old Spice, waterproofs were all apparent as I walked through to the living area. The *Press and Journal*, the local newspaper, lay open on the couch next to a Dad-shaped dent. The remote controls lay on the coffee table in front of it. Evidence he'd enjoyed a relaxed evening in front of the telly the night before it happened.

There was nothing else out of place. He lived a low-key

life. Everything else was as it ever was. Comfortable, homely and familiar.

Mouse came up and put her arm round me. 'You sure you're up to this, Maddy?'

'No,' I said in a tiny whisper, 'but let's do it.'

'OK,' she said, walking into the kitchen, putting the kettle on and doing her magical trick of whipping up a hot sweet cup of tea in an instant.

'Milk's off I'm afraid. I'll run down and get some – back in a sec,' she said before I could stop her.

The silence was deafening, as tentatively I opened my bedroom door and walked in. There it was, just the way I had left it. Single bed, brass bedstead, bedside table, My Little Pony lampshade and a wall covered with pictures, posters, remnants of Blu Tack as I'd chopped and changed posters over the years from My Little Pony to Zac Efron, Beyoncé and latterly Gustav Klimt. The one constant was the oversized world map covering most of the wall. Stepping towards it I began to shake, eyes brimming with tears, seeing the series of pins sticking out all over it.

When Mum died, Dad became the bedtime story teller. Mum could create fantastical stories as we lay there in the dark together, whereas Dad was more of a practical man and after some complaints from his audience one day, he came in, unrolled a vast world map, which we plastered to the wall together. Lying there at night, he would tell me about the world: different countries, continents, people, food, the oceans, the fish, just everything… It was wonderful. Every night, teeth done, jammies on I'd shout 'Ready!' and we'd be off on another adventure.

How I loved lying there, curled up under my blankets, snug as a bug, watching him talk, imagining these faraway worlds, drifting off into sweet dreams, secure, warm, excited for the future and the adventures we would share. As I dozed off every night it was to Dad, kissing the top of my head, turning off my bedside light and whispering, 'One day we will visit every single continent in the whole wide world… and boy what a day that will be …'

The memory felt like a punch in the gut. I slumped onto my bed. He was gone. We had missed the chance, we would never visit the continents, we would never visit anywhere again.

Whilst I was inconsolable, Mouse chose this moment to tiptoe in with a hot mug of tea. Silently she sat down beside me, patting my back until the tears slowed a little.

'Sorry,' I blubbed. 'It's the map …' And bless her, calmly she sat there as I told her everything, about our plans, about my realisation it would never happen, and she waited until I was all cried out, offering me a tissue when the worst was over. After a major blow of my hooter I felt lighter … and stronger.

'OK,' I said, 'you're the boss – let's get on with this.'

Mouse had a system.

It was simple and effective.

She held things up at random; I nodded or shook my head, or gave a brief yes or no.

It was so very hard to discard anything to do with my beloved dad but strangely it became apparent as we went through his belongings how little we need in life. All material goods were meaningless; all I wanted was the one thing I could never have, the person who owned all of it, my lovely dad. After another existential crisis Mouse flipped on some lively music and we began to make good headway by applying the same system as we had downstairs in The Birdie & Bramble for the bigger items.

Pink Post-its for things to keep – the rest to take away.

About 4 p.m. Mouse went down to help William unpack his haul from Edinburgh and I kept plodding through things. I called Laurel and Hardy, the auction guys, to beg them to come and take the furnishings. The next auction was early tomorrow and it was very late in the day but much to my delight they agreed to include Dads, stuff, a decision undoubtedly helped by the fact I promised them an invitation to the opening of the restaurant.

'We'll be there within the hour.'

And they were. Watching the pair of them stumbling about kept things light and giggly for a while. With most things boxed, binned and collected, Mouse said she would have a last tidy-round and let me escape. She could see I needed to get out and have a break.

I popped in to see William. He was happy and playing with his new super-duper mixer. 'You OK?' he asked, putting away the various whisks and paddles it came with.

'Yes, we got through a helluva lot but I just can't face any more.' My shoulders slumped.

'OK, that's the goons away with the stuff for the auction,' said Mouse. 'It's just the clothes and bits and bobs now, Maddy.'

'What do you say we crack on for another hour and then we can call it a day – we can finish off another time?'

It was a long hour. The problem was I could see him wearing every item she held up. There were certain items that were too hard to look at. His kilt, which he had proudly worn since he was a twenty-four-year-old rugby player and still fit him, lay on the bed. The MacKenzie tartan. I could see him in it, singing, dancing, wrapped up for rugby internationals, going to weddings, my mum's funeral, my graduation – it was too sad.

In the end the only things I really wanted to hang onto

were the kilt and his dark blue bobble hat, ubiquitous on his head in winter days since I was a wee girl. I stuffed it into my pocket.

My phone rang. Brad Pitt's face popped up. Marcus. I let it ring and texted: *'Clearing Dad's flat – not a good time. Will try you later,'* and then turned to Mouse. 'That's enough for one day. Come on, let me buy you a drink.'

She grinned. So we retired to The Hoozier for a pint of cider and a pint of lager, which we mixed.

'This is illegal apparently,' she said.

'Good,' I said. 'Cheers!'

Chapter 17

'You were late last night,' said William.

'I wanted to buy Mouse a drink to thank her for helping me with Dad's flat.' Tears sprang up.

'Of course,' he said sympathetically, 'emotionally draining to say the least... Listen, if you can't face the auction I can go instead.'

Shit, I had completely forgotten.

'No. No. I'm off to have a shower and I'll get going,' I said, necking my orange juice and rushing off to have a shower, as ever pleased to have something to do.

I showed William my list. 'There are a couple of medium-size tables. Similar size and height so hopefully they can be joined together for big parties and twelve chairs – mostly in twos, though there is a set of six from the golf club, which look nice and chunky. They won't stack but they will look fab – and even though the rest don't match at least there will be no stained velour.'

'You do know our stuff's up for sale today too – the stuff from here?' he warned.

'Yes, and Dad's flat too. Laurel and Hardy swooped in last thing yesterday. I promised them an invite to the opening.'

He smiled. 'Ha! Good call. Well as long as you're sure you're OK? I can always ask Noel to step in.'

'No, he's got his business to run. Honestly I'm fine and

anyway I want to make sure all our stuff goes to a good home,' I said with a high-pitched fake laugh.

'OK,' he said, walking me outside and giving me a brief talk round how to drive Noel's car, issuing last-minute instructions not to get too carried away.

'I am not a child,' I said indignantly, waving goodbye before coming back when I realised I'd left the car keys on the table.

It was still blowing a hoolie and I was very glad to have Noel's car complete with satnav to guide me to the farm where the auction was taking place. On the other side of St Andrews, it was in the middle of nowhere. As I drove up the rough track road, my head began throbbing, a combo of dehydration and the lurching of the four-wheel drive. There were about two dozen cars parked up behind the house, which I inched in beside before marching up to the rather austere-looking farmhouse for shelter. Inside, the auction was in full swing. There was a lot of stuff to get through, from books to random boxes stuffed with single forks, plastic flowers and old wooden spoons, cutlery, ornaments, furniture, bric-a-brac, art on the walls, the whole jingbang.

The auctioneer stood on a small platform with his gavel raised, talking with such speed I couldn't understand a word he was saying. Everyone was holding a card with their own number on it, which they raised and twitched periodically indicating their bid.

First things first, I had to register. Padding around, I soon found a couple of people hovering round a card table in the large room off the hall. 'I'd like to register please,' I said.

'OK. We started about twenty minutes ago. Just put your name and address here. We need a credit card and then I can issue you with a number.'

'Thanks,' I said, taking the board in my clammy hand and

retreating to the back of the room to perch on a chair and fill it in.

On returning the form I was handed a white card with the number eighty-three on it. Having a quick scan round where the lots were laid out, I estimated it would be another half hour before my first lot of four chairs came up. The auctioneer was getting through things fast so I inched my way to the front of the room, perching on the corner of an old lumpy sofa, waiting for the lot to come up. Intermittently the gavel hit the desk and he shouted 'Sold!' before moving quickly to the next lot, so I had to concentrate hard. Some lots were left unsold and others went for way above their expected amount, others for a pittance.

I was poised and ready when my first lot of two Bentwood dining chairs was announced and the bidding started. I kept my head down and didn't start bidding until the initial frenzy had died down. They were up at £15 each, extremely good value and I tried not to look too excited. The auctioneer announced they were all going at £30, going, going, and just as he raised his gavel I waved my card. The auctioneer accepted my bid of £35, nodding in my direction. Another bidder jumped in and then they were going up in increments of £10 each time. It was between me and one other.

Craning my neck I couldn't see who I was up against. They were determined. But then so was I. The auctioneer was on the ball, winding one up against the other. Until it was £85 – well over my maximum if I was going to be led by William. Which I promised I would. But a little more wouldn't do any harm. My hand was up again and then the other bidder as quick as lightning upped it again. This could go on forever, I thought, and decided to let it go at £115. I sat back as the bidding reached £160 and accepted defeat. There were another few lots of chairs so all was far from lost.

I was so confused at the speed of what was happening that I actually bid for a collection of hideous velour chairs from The Birdie & Bramble but happily was outbid on those too, though who on earth would want them!

On the upside I secured two lovely Victorian oak tables, square, which pulled out to about twice the size, accommodating about six or eight people, which I was chuffed about; but before I could relax it was time for the next batch of chairs. Not nearly as nice as the Bentwoods and yet still they went way above my limit. Damn.

The theme of being outbid continued until there was only one lot left that I was interested in and that was the six chairs from the golf club. My heart was ruling my head – I realised that – and although they were battered and bruised they would look great in The Birdie & Bramble. Crucially Dad must have sat in them many a time, and would have loved them too.

The bidding gathered momentum and then it was down to me and one other person, inching it up and up. It must be the same person who was bidding against me earlier. I looked in the direction the auctioneer was accepting the other bids from. As my hand shot up, so did theirs and then finally as I was over double my budget, I capitulated. William would kill me.

Simmering with frustration when the next lot came up, my hand flew up spontaneously and I put in an unplanned bid for a couple of vintage wall lights. I bid £35 and when the gavel came down and the auctioneer pointed in my direction shouting sold, I felt a flutter of excitement. Apart from the tables and the wall lights I also got a china tea service for £5 – not complete but it was a really sweet white bone china with muted delicate irises painted over it. Perfect for the bothy.

I was just about to leave when I realised the next lot was the dresser from The Birdie & Bramble.

My heart contracted seeing it there.

It was not a thing of beauty by any stretch of the imagination; in fact it was downright ugly. Chunky, chipped and far too big for the place it had occupied in the restaurant for as long as I could remember. The auctioneer was looking around touting desperately for bids; he started at £100 and no-one bit, so it was down to £50, £20, £10. My God, no-one wanted it. Not one bid. I wanted to howl.

My hand shot up.

'That's £10,' said the auctioneer instantly on seeing my paddle. 'Any advance on £10?' He looked round the room and tried to noise the crowd up. They weren't having any of it.

And so on the count of going, going, gone it was mine.

Still mine.

For God's sake, I thought, I had better leave before I ended up buying all my stuff back. Emotion, anger and auctions were not a good combination.

Pushing through the crowd, I made my way back to the registration desk to pay.

I dug about in my pockets looking for some Extra Strong Mints. Now all the excitement was over, my hangover was back. The person in front of me turned.

'Hello again.'

Looking up I found myself face-to-face with Jack.

'Are you stalking me?' he teased.

I felt my whole body go beetroot and my heart rate elevated fast.

'I thought you were the stalker,' I smiled quite pleased at my response. It was, I thought later, the first intelligent thing I had said to him. Ever.

'Next,' blurted the women behind the desk, indicating to Jack. He didn't seem to notice.

'NEXT!' she shouted impatiently.

'I think that's you,' I laughed, nodding in the woman's direction.

'Oops. Excuse me.' He grinned and stepped forward.

I nodded and smiled, feeling relieved he had moved away as breathing seemed impossible when in close proximity to those eyes.

'Lot number,' demanded the plump wee lady behind the desk.

'Fifty-six,' he said, turning to smile at me again.

'Ah yes,' the woman said, flicking through the cards, 'here we are. Fifty-six … two Bentwood chairs.'

'You got the Bentwoods!' I said out loud.

'Yes. Why?'

'Well I was after them too.'

'Oh were you? Sorry, I didn't realise,' he said as the women read out the other lots. Digging out my scrap of paper from my pocket, I checked them all off and without exception they were all the bloody chairs I had been after – including the broken ones from The Birdie & Bramble. What on earth did he want those for? What the?

'You got all the chairs!' I blustered.

'Yes, were you after those too?' he asked, fishing about in his pocket for his wallet, which he withdrew and counted and handed over a great roll of notes to the woman.

'Would you like a receipt?'

'Yes please, if you can make it out to The Chairman of the Board.'

'Please yourself,' she said, looking bemused as she scribbled it down and handed it over.

I couldn't believe it! He was there buying furniture from

right under my nose. The bloody cheeky of it. I was livid and about to give him a piece of my mind when his mobile rang and he took the call. 'Hi, yes it's just finished and yeh I got them all!' he said triumphantly, as he nodded in my direction, mouthed goodbye and wandered off, deep in conversation.

That, I thought reasonably, is a declaration of war. 'Are you next?' asked the woman.

I shuffled forward.

'Well, chop chop!'

'Bloody charming,' I said under my booze-soaked breath as I handed over my registration number card. My heart was thumping as I asked quite casually, 'So have you any idea what The Chairman of The Board is all about then?' to the top of the snippy woman's head.

'Me? No. Never heard of it. Cash or credit card?'

Bloody Merchant of Venison. Coming over all nicey-nicey. He is clearly a snake in the grass. A low-down dirty dawg, I thought in my best Texas brawl. A snakebite in the grass. Well I would have to find out exactly what was going on and make damn sure there was no other opportunity for him to get one over on me, I thought as I heard the woman's piercing bark enter my consciousness.

'Hello? Are you with us, dear? Come on, I don't have all day – now is it cash or credit card?'

Transaction complete, I collected the cardboard box with the light fittings wrapped in newspaper as a big man in a long brown overcoat retrieved it for me and humped the box up onto a table. Then I headed over to see Laurel and Hardy to arrange delivery of the tables to The Birdie & Bramble and of course the dresser to the bothy.

'This looks quite like the one we took here,' said Hardy.

Laurel scratched the top of his head. 'Yes it does.'

'It is,' I snapped.

'Oh OK, you're the boss.' They grinned and then stopped when they saw the expression on my face had changed. I'd just clocked Jack wrestling a pile of bloody chairs into the back of a big pick-up truck.

I turned back to my box of wall lights and china.

'Are you going to manage that?' asked Laurel.

'Yes I am,' I said as I hoicked the box up higher and tottered off under the weight towards Noel's car.

Despite adrenalin, I ran out of steam and rested the box on the ground as I opened the boot. Just as I was about to launch it back up, it levitated into mid-air. 'Here, let me give you a hand with that,' said a disembodied voice. Guess who: the bloody Merchant of Venison.

'No thanks,' I said, wrenching the box out of his firm grasp and back into mine. 'I can manage.'

Clearly taken aback, he did as instructed and stood back and released the full weight of the box back to me.

'Be my guest.'

'Thank you,' I puffed as I virtually threw it into the back of the car. The juddering thud was accompanied by a tinkling, which sounded suspiciously like broken china.

'Maddy,' he said, 'I had no idea you were after those chairs – really.' At least he sounded somewhat genuine, I conceded.

'Oh well, them's the breaks,' I said through gritted teeth. 'Now I have to get going if you'll excuse me.' And with that I brushed past him, lunging into the driver's seat. Such was my haste my handbag slipped off my shoulder, and onto the ground spewing the contents out. Instinctively Jack bent down to retrieve all the embarrassing crap that had just fallen out. I could have died there and then as he picked up mangled tissues, a tampon, an ancient grotty make-up bag, a dog lead and my phone, which chose that second to ring. A cursory look at the screen showed Brad Pitt. It was Marcus, as ever with impeccable timing.

Jack looked at it, his eyebrows raised, smiling as he handed it over.

'That's my boyfriend,' I said like a petulant seven-year-old, grabbing it.

'Oh I thought it was Brad Pitt.' He smiled.

'Well no, well yes, well ... whatever ...' I flustered as I wrestled the door handle and slammed the door shut. I didn't hear another word as his voice was muffled through the car door.

Intent on starting the engine and getting away as quickly as possible, I threw my bag on the passenger seat, wrenching Noel's car into reverse amidst a cacophony of metallic grinding. 'Whoa,' he shouted, 'watch your gear box,' sounding like Jeremy Bloody Clarkson.

I wound down my window quickly in short bursts as I turned the handle round and round. For God's sake, how old was this bloody car anyway? 'Thank you, Jack,' I said in perfect Miss Jean Brodie dialect. 'I will watch my gear box – and you!' I blundered on. 'Well you can ... you can jolly well watch your own,' I said, even angrier that such a meaningless stream of words had just barked out of my mouth. 'Pah!'

'OK will do,' he said, stepping back. I swear he was stifling the urge to laugh. Adding insult to injury, I ground the gears back into first and put my foot on the accelerator with such force the wheels threw up mud and splatters as I sped off along the road. Once out of sight I slowed right down to about five mph as I knew Noel would kill me if I came back without the chairs, with a box of broken china and the bottom ripped out of his car. What a bloody day.

Driving back I was angrier than was good for me. What

on earth did that man want with all those chairs? My chairs! I thought, putting my foot down again. Ggggrrrrr.

When I skidded to a halt outside the restaurant, William came rushing out, his eyes on stalks.

'Jesus, Lewis Hamilton – slow down,' he said as I got out and slammed the door.

'Bloody Merchant of Venison.'

'What?'

'He bought all the chairs in the place. Even the crappy broken ones from here!'

'I know.'

'What do you mean "I know"?'

'He's just phoned.'

'What?'

'He was buying them for Hamish.'

'What?'

'Yes, you know Hamish – always the one for a mad idea. Well he'd decided on a whim he would buy all the chairs he could get his hands on before the Open and rent them out to all and sundry. There is always a chair shortage during the Open; everyone underestimates the thousands of folk that arrive. Every single place is mobbed – restaurants, golf clubs, pubs, hotels, cafes, pavement eateries, B&Bs, even the bakery – so it was just his latest scheme to try and make a few bob. He had no idea we were after the chairs for The Birdie & Bramble or he would never have bought them.'

'Oh,' I said, feeling hideously guilty that I had been so awful to Jack.

But William wasn't finished. 'So anyway he's coming round in about twenty minutes and you get the pick of the bunch.'

'Who, Hamish?'

'No. Jack.'

Oh God. There was no way I could face him. I wanted to die. Now I felt like a complete shit.

'Hamish says he just wants what he paid for them and not a penny more.' Oh God now I felt even worse. Jack was the messenger, who I had metaphorically shot, and even Hamish was coming out of this like a knight in shining armour. I had gone from wanting to kill him to wanting to canonise him.

'Gosh that's good of him,' I said, knees weakening under the strain of the day.

'What a lovely guy,' said Mouse, practically swooning.

'Who, Jack?' I snarked.

'No,' she giggled, 'Hamish.'

Indirectly it seemed Cupid was hitting the mark after all with this unlikely pair.

'Oh God, I wish I hadn't been so harsh on him,' I said as a flash of heat crawled up my neck and I thought about the tirade of meaningless bluster I had directed at him. Cringe.

Trying to work out how best to make it up to him for being such a grumpy besom, I unpacked the car. I was not overimpressed with my purchases. A now broken tea service and two lights that had looked rather funky amongst all the vintage gear at the auction and now in the cold light of day back at The Birdie & Bramble, they just looked – well shit.

'The good news is I bought two cracking tables which Laurel and Hardy promise they will deliver first thing in the morning.' And I couldn't avoid it and added as nonchalantly as I could, 'Oh and I bought the dresser back.'

William looked at me smiling. 'You didn't?'

'I did – well there was no-one was bidding on it and I couldn't bear the thought of it going to the dump so I decided I'll use it as a dressing table, for displaying photos and it will double as a bedside table in the bothy. The cupboards underneath will do for my clothes and other stuff and I can put a wee light on it – mark my words I'll be snug as a bug in a rug.' William grinned as I continued. 'And Stan and Ollie are also going to collect my old brass bed from upstairs so all I need now is a kettle, a lifetime's supply of Pot Noodle and I'm good to go.'

As the twenty minutes ticked down, I pleaded with William to do the chair transaction with Jack. William tried to talk me round but tears were never far from the surface and so he agreed. I would have to canonise him too.

I was wrung out and I couldn't face Jack again, not after my appalling behaviour. And so I disappeared back to the boys' place to hide, run a bath and pack my bits and pieces as I was off to the bothy in the morning. I had no choice really. The dreaded dresser had to go somewhere and there was no time like the present.

Chapter 18

The move to the bothy was painless. By painting it the wonderful Torbeck had transformed the room. For starters it looked twice the size. The stone floor was completely covered with a brightly striped IKEA rug. By dismantling and rebuilding the dresser we managed to squish it in – just. It was a tight fit with no space at all between it and the roof, taking up most of the back wall, leaving just enough space on the right-hand side to squash in the single brass bedstead from the flat. Torbeck and William also retrieved my mattress and a small bedside lamp, which sat neatly on the edge of the dresser with its My Little Pony lilac shade.

Mouse arrived with a jam jar full of cut flowers, some fairy lights and a scented candle, which she insisted on lighting to get rid of the smell of paint. Literally thirty seconds after she arrived, Hamish ambled in too with a six-pack of beer. 'Cheers, Cuz,' he said, smiling at Mouse.

William's room-warming present was a mini kettle and two mugs with cartoon golfers on them and a pint of milk, which just fit in the tiny promotional Budweiser fridge we had commandeered from the restaurant. Noel and William sat on the blanket box under the tiny south-facing window to the garden; Mouse on the end of the bed with Hamish squished next to her. Frank was on my knee as I sat cross-legged on the pillows at the top of the bed beaming. Home sweet home.

'OK that's you!' said William.

'Yes it is,' I smiled. 'And thank you.'

'Noel and I have decided you will eat with us every night until we open and then we will both be on staff meals,' said William.

'Are you sure? I do a mean Pot Noodle you know!' I felt I could never repay their extraordinary hospitality as it was.

'That's what we're worried about. We need you alive for the opening of The Birdie & Bramble so please come to us!' joked Noel.

I felt a warm glow for these lovely people, giving their time, energy and thought to me, a virtual stranger.

'It's perfect,' I said. 'Just perfect.'

After hugs and thanks and in my case tears, they left.

I walked the three steps back and forth a few times, drinking in my new home. Small and bijou was an oft-used expression but never had it been quite so accurate, I thought, as I boiled my mini kettle and enjoyed a cup of tea from my new mug. Despite being so busy, Jack had been on my mind constantly.

I desperately wanted to apologise for my appalling be-haviour at the auction but where on earth to start? William reported as promised that Jack had driven the chairs round to the restaurant and given William free rein.

'He was completely covered in mud,' he said, bemused. Oh God it was getting worse. My dramatic exit must have splattered the poor man.

William had cherry-picked the golf club chairs and the Bentwoods – the pick of the bunch and they looked perfect. Face value was all he wanted and all William paid. A fair deal well done. A gentleman's agreement.

The problem was I didn't even have a phone number for Jack. Uncle Fraser might have his number but I didn't want to involve him. I could leave a message for him via Hamish, though I preferred to keep it between the two of us. So I made the decision to get up early in the morning, head to the beach with Frank and make peace with him face-to-face. The mature thing to do. Having made my mind up, I felt lighter as I unpacked my two boxes, fed Frank and put my feet up for twenty minutes before heading round the corner for supper with the boys.

After we ate I was keen to get back to my new pad. I made my way round, let myself into the shop and then out the back. Closing the door behind me, the first thing that struck me was the silence. Padding about, with my slippers and dressing gown on, I turned off the overhead light, put on the fairy lights, sidelight and electric blanket, then lay on the bed. It was like my own magical fairyland. I had no Wi-Fi but if I extended my hand out towards the window I had an intermittent one bar of mobile signal so I was not completely out of touch.

I had been so busy I hadn't even looked at my phone. As I extended my arm it pinged a few times.

A text from Keira: *'Hope you're settling, can't wait to hear all about it. I am back from US tomorrow will call.'*

A text from Sarah: *'You know I'd love to see you anytime. I'll leave it up to you. I know you're up to your neck in it. LOVE XXXX'*

Three texts from Marcus.

First one: *'Hey babe. Called earlier no reply.'*

Guilt. I had forgotten to phone him back after the hang-over and auction debacle.

Second one: *'Tried calling again tonight – no reply. Think you might be having dinner? Night. Love you xxx'*

Third one: *'Great news, babe – got Friday off so I will be up on Thursday for the opening party and I can stay for the weekend if you'll have me!'*

Oh. That took the wind out of my sails. I wasn't sure how I felt about that. I had so much to do and would have virtually no time to spend with him. I knew only too well if he was not the centre of my attention then he would seek it elsewhere. My gut reaction was to put him off but I couldn't. He was my boyfriend. He was making an effort to come all the way to St Andrews for the second time, to support me relaunching my father's restaurant. It was a lovely gesture and I would read it as such.

I texted him back: *'Great news! Let's talk tomorrow and make a plan. Love Mx'* and I stood in the garden with my arm in the air until it sent.

What a day, I thought, as I snuggled down into my child-hood bed. Frank kangarooed up and down beside me until I lifted him up, then with a focused expression he tramped up to the top of the blankets and, after nosing them up, shot down into the cosy cave and spooned into the back of my knees. Despite myself I couldn't help giggling as he squirmed around making himself comfy. I turned off the lights.

I'll call Marcus back in the morning, was the last thing I thought before my eyes shut.

Chapter 19

Early the next morning I left the bothy to walk Frank when a text pinged in from Gerald.

'Have had the Laird's lawyer in touch, just a wee reminder, today is the day you need to hand the keys back to Joe's flat.'

I groaned. God. I had completely lost track of the days. Was it really twenty-eight days I had been on this planet without my father? The pace of life since I got back was such I had not had a moment to dwell on it. I'd not been near the place since Mouse helped me do the initial clear. I'd better drag myself round there now. I could avoid it no more.

It was unchanged from outside. My stomach twisted on entering the hall downstairs, empty of all Dad's things. I trudged upstairs and turned the Yale key, prepared for piles of homeless stour, and couldn't believe my eyes. The place was immaculate. I did a double take. It was as clean as I had ever seen it. Actually? Cleaner. Someone had hoovered, polished, scrubbed and transformed it. I walked through to the kitchen, my jaw hanging open ... What the ... Who on earth ... A cursory look in the bathroom proved someone had broken their back to make the place look like this. It was ready to be handed over, but who on earth ...?

The buzzer went. Automatically I picked up the handset. 'It's 10 a.m. Time to vacate,' said the odious bark of the Laird. I slammed the handset down. The interruption prevented a protracted goodbye to the property. I stomped downstairs and dropped the key into his grasping pudgy hand.

'It's all yours,' I said, refusing to let him see what an indescribable wrench this process was for me.

After watching his waddling form bump and wheeze through the door, I turned and walked straight into The Birdie & Bramble.

Mouse and Hamish were sitting down, next to each other, sipping coffee and whispering. They had gone from shy strangers to inseparable in a matter of days. They jumped apart and Mouse stood up.

'Fancy a coffee?'

'Yes please and make it a super-strong one please, I need it,' I growled.

'Did you get the keys back on time?' Hamish butted in.

I looked at him. He would have had no idea what day of the week it was, let alone what date I was due to vacate the flat. I looked at Mouse, who was pink. Mystery solved.

'It was you!' I said.

She went from pink to purple.

'It was you wasn't it? You did a full-on Fairy Godmother spick-and-span flat clean didn't you?'

Hamish grinned proudly, watching this exchange.

Mouse looked extremely uncomfortable, taking a step back. 'I'm sorry I didn't ask or say but … well I knew you had such a lot on … and … God I hope you're not too angry.'

'Angry? Angry! Oh my God thank you,' I said, lunging over and embracing her. She cringed as if she had been expecting a clout round the ear not a hug. 'You've saved my bacon, Mouse. Thank you so so much. Barclay was shuffling about like an expectant father, waiting for the bells to toll at 10 a.m. and oh God,' I said and burst into tears, 'I don't know what I would have done if you hadn't… It was such a shambles and I just couldn't face it…All that stuff…'

'You're so welcome,' said Mouse, stroking my back as I regained control. 'Like I said before, your dad was like a dad to me too and I meant it – he really really was. I didn't have a real dad, at least not one I wanted anything to do with, and when I met Joe and started working here in my first year at art school, I felt like I had found a real family. He took me under his wing and it was just after you'd moved to London and he said he had a girl-shaped hole in his life so it suited us both perfectly.'

A girl-shaped hole. Me.

Now she started crying and embraced me, as I snottered on her shoulder.

'All that stuff…' I sobbed.

'I know, I know.' She patted my back again. 'I scooped up all the personal bits and pieces and put them in a box. Noel's put it in the shop so it's there when you can face going through it.'

'Thanks, Mouse, so so much…'

We were having a full-on snotathon by now.

'OK you two,' said Hamish in a bossy voice, 'let's break it up here…The coffee is getting cold and we have the small matter of relaunching a restaurant. So—' he handed us a napkin each '—blow your noses and let's get cracking.'

Mouse and I broke apart, smiled at each other, did as we were told and made as if to embrace him.

'Oh no you don't,' he said, stepping out of the way. 'Someone's got to stay in control.'

Chapter 20

The next couple of days flew by, filled with preparations, invitations, walking along the beach and settling into the bothy.

Hamish had cleared his diary and true to his word was there helping. A lot. I watched from the wings as he continued to woo Mouse.

Mouse in turn was head down, beavering away behind the scenes. Her role had evolved. She was becoming William's wing woman and she certainly had a spring in her step, her rare smiles developed into giggles, which became a familiar sound. I didn't think Hamish would need my help in winning over his gothic maiden. He was doing a great job winning the heart of fair Mouse without it.

The restaurant itself was looking fresh, clean, warm and welcoming. All clutter gone with the exception of Dad's rogues gallery. Most of the photographs had been rehung but rather than looking like a ragtag collection with no coherence, Noel had elevated the collection to a work of art. All frames the same Farrow & Ball off-white colour, all photographs carefully labelled.

'Noel, I can't believe you've done all this,' I beamed at him as I reacquainted myself with the photos, admiring his handiwork. They even seemed to be more in focus, I observed, almost blinded by the garish plaid of a golfer's trousers in a photo labelled *1980 Greg Norman* and suddenly

I squawked. There was the one of me looking like a boy, labelled *Madeline Campbell – Proprietor*.

'You wee horror! I can't believe you put that one up!' I laughed.

Suddenly the kitchen door flew open and in came Hamish, togged up in his new Birdie & Bramble apron, looking the part.

'Roll up, roll up, ladies and gentlemen, the tasting is about to begin!'

William followed, balancing two huge platters on which were a selection of canapés. Some cold, some hot. Some meaty, some fishy, some veggie and some vegan. Without exception they tasted divine.

'Basically they're our menu in miniature,' he explained, 'so people will get a real idea of what we are about now.'

Tiny cups of Cullen skink, mini prawn cocktails, venison carpaccio. Smoked haddock mousse, smoky jackfruit burger, tiny hazelnut cakes, banoffee pies, shot glasses of boozy chocolate mousse.

They were exquisite.

We ate in silence, punctuated by oohing and ahhing, giving the food the reverence it deserved.

'Wow,' I finally managed to say after scooping up and swallowing the tiniest, lightest millefeuille pastry with a fresh raspberry and dot of crème anglaise on top.

'If we're not careful we'll have a Michelin star by the time we open!' said Mouse.

We all laughed, and started chattering on excitedly as it collectively dawned on us that this was real and with food like William's we might even stand a shot at success.

'So canapés and Prosecco?'

'Champagne,' said William.

'What about the expense?'

'I know, but we must start the way we mean to go on. This is the new Birdie & Bramble – we want people to talk about it, be surprised and we only have five weeks so we must attract the right clientele.'

'OK, champagne it is,' I said, a sudden rush of excitement ticking that box. Next we ran over the guest list. What had started as small gathering of family and friends had by now turned into quite an event. Hamish had drawn up an impressive guest list including friends, relatives, suppliers, the great and the good of St Andrews and the unavoidable too.

Included were journalists from *Press and Journal*, presenters from the local radio station, and the concierges from the hotels in St Andrews. Noel invited his best (and nicest) clients from the antique shop, William got in touch with all existing customers, Mouse with the student reps. As far as we could work out, we had all ages and stages covered.

Invitations had been sent out online with a few hard copies for the old guard. We had RSVPs of fifty, which could mean anything between thirty or seventy, so we were nervous as hell as the big night approached.

The night before the launch I tore off to collect Marcus from Edinburgh Airport in Noel's car, screeching to a halt outside Arrivals just as he emerged into the dark Edinburgh night. I saw him straight away, well-cut suit, tie askew, hair slicked back, shaking someone's hand he likely met on the flight. He had come straight from work. It was easy to see how I had fallen for him. He was a very good-looking guy. I tooted the horn and waved. A slow grin spread across his face as he walked over and jumped into the car. As he leant over and kissed me, there a waft of booze and his ubiquitous Armani aftershave. God he always smelled great.

'Hi, Mads. I've missed you,' he whispered in my ear, sliding his hand up my thigh.

'Marcus, I'm driving,' I said, pulling out as the next car slid into the congested pick-up zone.

'OK, babe.' He sat back and put his belt on.

It took just over an hour to get to St Andrews. Marcus talked about business and I did my best to look interested. It felt like a million miles away: London, office politics, Felicity, the general cut and thrust of daily life in the South. It felt like years, not a few days, since I'd been an integral part of the world he was describing. Hard as I tried to pay attention to his chatter, my mind kept returning to the launch party, which was less than twenty-four hours away and there was still so much to do.

'Maddy? Maddy?' His voice cut through my thoughts.

'Oh sorry, yes?' I said, back in the room – or the car to be more accurate.

'Did you hear me?'

I had been completely immersed in the world of lobsters, champagne and guest lists.

'Sorry … I was miles away.'

He sat back, turned his head to look out the window and harrumphed. We arrived in St Andrews, not speaking.

The next issue was he laughed when he saw the bothy.

'Bothy, Mads! This is the outside loo!'

Anger gripped my belly. William and Noel had put so much thought and effort into finding somewhere I could stay, somewhere private, and Marcus obviously didn't get it at all.

'And it's only got a single bed …' he mumped.

I looked at his petulant expression, irritation growing.

'There's a B&B round the corner you can stay in,' I said.

Then seeing his chance of a leg over receding, his face changed.

'Aw, babe, I didn't mean that.' He stroked my arm and

moved in for a kiss. As our lips met he reached for the top of my jeans, deftly undoing them, and his hand reached further down. I stepped back. We had not connected on any level and he had misjudged the situation badly – thinking, just like that, I would be up for it.

'Would you like a drink?' I asked, knowing the answer.

'Yeh, that would be great. What have you got?'

'A nice bottle of red,' I said, using it as an excuse to extricate myself from his grasp. I wasn't in the mood for drinking, the last thing I needed was a hangover for the launch party, but it would give me time to regroup, so I poured him a generous glass and myself barely a mouthful. Naturally he didn't notice.

We managed to sit companionably on the bed next to each other and caught up in a more measured way. He continued to talk about his work and the only question he asked me was, 'So what time does the party kick off tomorrow night?'

Despite doing all the talking, it took him no time to neck the first glass and so I topped him up continually until within forty minutes he had drunk the whole bottle with the exception of the mouthful I had in my glass. I recognised his lairy snoozy look as I stood up.

'Give me ten minutes. I'll be back,' I said, leaving the bothy and heading into the shop to the loo.

I took fifteen minutes intentionally and by the time I got back he was sprawled over the bed asleep.

I looked at him. I had a choice.

Scramble in beside him for an uncomfortable night of red-wine-fuelled snoring or text the boys and ask if I could stay at theirs. It was a no-brainer.

I left him a note.

'Sleep well. I didn't want to disturb you – have a long lie-in and

call me in the morning.' And I tiptoed out with a huge sense of relief and almost giggled as I ran round to the boys where I received my usual warm welcome. The three of us talked logistics for the following day and then I made my upstairs to my second home and fell asleep.

Chapter 21

It was another early start; by 8 a.m. the next day we were all in The Birdie & Bramble. Noel even took the next day off to help us. William was in the kitchen with Mouse. Hamish was stacking away endless cases of wine and humping furniture around, rearranging it to accommodate the ever-increasing number of guests we hoped were coming. There was a lot of work to do and only a few hours to do it.

A disgruntled Marcus texted me about 9.30 a.m. asking where I was before coming round to The Birdie & Bramble and thankfully offering to help.

It was hard to know what to ask him to do. He was a fish out of water but I wanted him to feel involved so he was charged with washing and polishing the champagne flutes and laying them all out on the table by the door. Noel showed him how to get a glass so bright and shiny you could see your reflection in it. Watching his face of intense concentration, I felt a wave of affection for him. He was doing his best to contribute but his ham-fisted attempts ended in a few glasses hitting the deck, which proved too much for William's nerves; in typically Kofi Annan style he sent him off to collect the flowers from the florist's with a map, an envelope of cash and instructions.

The whole day went by in a flash; a whirlwind of preparation and suddenly our guests were due in less than an hour.

Mouse dashed home to change, Hamish changed out

the back, William slipped into fresh whites and for the first moment that day I stopped, wiggled my skirt on top of my jeans in the middle of the restaurant and stepped out of my jeans, rolling them up and putting them in my bag. It dawned on me I hadn't seen Marcus for hours.

Where the hell was he? Just as I searched for my phone to text him, in he came, clearly the worse for wear.

'Lavender blue dilly dilly,' he sang as he staggered in with the ordered flowers in his arms. Seeing my expression he stopped singing. I took them off to the kitchen to plop them into their planned vases for Mouse to primp.

And then it was time, and with minutes to spare, I assessed. Bar Marcus we had all scrubbed up very well indeed, as had The Birdie & Bramble, which looked sharp, warm, inviting and dare I say it – ready?

I felt for the chain round my neck, and ran my fingers down it to the charm, picking it up and kissing it, closing my eyes and wishing Dad was here to see this and hoping he would approve of what we were about to do. Then I tucked it away, taking a deep breath and standing as tall as I could. We were on.

First in was Stevie the Slab. He had a Zoot suit on and a fedora hat perched jauntily on his head. The sweet soul handed me a good luck card, before settling down to play the piano. Hamish, clean-shaven and in what looked suspiciously like new trousers and white shirt, and I stood rigid, staring at the door, hoping to God someone would arrive soon. A huge ice bucket held chilled bottles of champagne next to which Hamish stood with a tray of champagne flutes ready for the first guests. William came out of the kitchen with Mouse close behind him, both hovering with trays of canapés that would have looked quite at home in the new V&A in Dundee. He quickly described each one to

Hamish and I to share with our guests, before changing from his whites into a beautiful linen suit, leaving Mouse in the kitchen where she was intent on staying in the background. Her challenge was keeping everything moving, clean and organised.

Uncle Fraser and Auntie Margaret were first in with Uncle Ted and Auntie Faye – a collective exhalation could be heard as the first cork was popped and flutes filled. We toasted The Birdie & Bramble. One swig down and the door opened and there began a constant stream of the great and good of St Andrews, flooding in the door.

Crossing names off the list as they came in, I realised we must have had about seventy people at one point. The volume of laughter, talking, and oohs and aahs as the canapés disappeared was high, when having had two glasses of fizz I felt the urge to speak. I had no idea what I was going to say, I just knew I had to say something. As I was about launch onto a chair, I clocked a loud checked suit bumping through the crowd – bloody Barclay MacPherson, clasping a glass of champagne. He was heading my way.

William clocked him and whispered, 'Rise above it.'

And I did. Literally. I climbed onto a chair as William, taking my cue, hit his glass and asked for silence.

'Ladies and gentlemen. Welcome to The Birdie & Bramble,' was all I managed before applause and a raucous cheer went up. I raised my glass. 'Thank you so much for coming to help us celebrate a new era at The Birdie & Bramble ... It's so lovely to see so many of you here tonight and without further ado I'd like to invite you to raise your glass to absent friends, to my beloved dad, Joe—' my voice warbled '—and to The Birdie & Bramble.'

An even louder cheer went up and everyone clinked glasses shouting, 'The Birdie & Bramble!' as I retreated off the chair with wobbly legs. William, by my side, grabbed my arm to steady me.

'Perfect,' he whispered.

'A bit short?'

'No. Perfect.'

'Thanks, Will.'

I was happy to see Barclay had disappeared back into the throng and as the volume went up, Stevie played the piano, William and Hamish passed round the canapés, Mouse kept replenishing the platters and sending them out, and everyone topped up champagne glasses constantly and I suppose I sort of played mine host.

Amidst the bustle I kept an eye on Barclay MacPherson, fighting the urge to confront him, realising it was neither the time nor the place. Naturally he stayed long enough to scoff more than his fair share of food. He also managed to swig a few too many glasses before pushing his way through the crowd and out of the door. Relieved he was off the premises, I made my way over to the door and poked my head out, checking he was on his way – I didn't trust him one iota.

He was already talking to a couple of people and they seemed to be having a heated exchange, during which the Laird turned round pointed at The Birdie & Bramble, threw up his hands in exasperation and stomped off. I turned away in case I was seen, my heart rattling. The other party was none other than The Merchant of Venison and an elderly lady. Of course Barclay and Jack knew each other – after all, St Andrews was a village – but it hadn't looked like a friendly exchange and I couldn't help but wonder what they had been talking about. None of my business, I said to myself unconvincingly, wondering how I could find out.

The one good thing about Marcus is I could really take him anywhere. He knew he would be left to his own devices so I didn't feel I had to check on him every five minutes. By now the party was going like a fair, his natural habitat at the centre of it and running on adrenalin. I mingled and introduced myself. I noted with irritation his inability to let a tray of champagne go by without deftly grabbing a glass and necking it. And my blood was boiling, as each time I caught him out of the corner of my eye, his volume had gone up further as he went lurching outside to have a fag with one of the local journos. He only smoked when he was really drunk, which confirmed what I had suspected. I could have strangled him.

Hard as it was, I knew I had to rise above it. If I let him get to me, it would ruin the night, and the purpose of this event in the first place. But by God he knew how to push my buttons, I thought, as he and the journo went bobbling outside for a second fag no more than fifteen minutes later. I could not contain myself a moment longer and marched towards the door, opening it ready to storm out and give him what for, only to come face-to-face with The Merchant of Venison. Flustered, I stammered some unintelligible gibber at him.

'Wow,' he grinned, stepping inside and scanning the room. 'You've done a wonderful job.'

I felt my face heat up. 'Thanks,' I said, grabbing a flute of champagne and handing it to him.

Just as he took it, Hamish whizzed up behind us.

'Jack! Good to see you! And Flora! What a treat.' He embraced the elderly lady on Jack's arm who I had seen outside earlier.

Jack stood back. 'And this,' he said proudly, 'is my grand-mother Flora.' I held out my hand and shook her delicate one gently.

'It's lovely to meet you, Flora,' I said. 'Welcome to The Birdie & Bramble.'

'Oh, Flora knows The Birdie & Bramble well,' Jack interjected.

She smiled beatifically and nodded. 'The Birdie & Bramble,' she said happily.

'Well, welcome back. I hope you like what we've done to it,' I said, beaming at her. 'What do you think?' I enquired, watching her eyes sparkle as she took in her surroundings.

'Magical. Just magical,' she said, keeping her grip of Jack's arm.

'It looks so amazing, Maddy. Really.' Jack took two glasses off Hamish's tray, handing one to me and the other to Flora.

'So I'd like to make a toast,' he said, lifting his glass, as Flora and I followed suit. 'Here's to you, your team and all your hard work.' Our eyes met. Gulp. 'We wish you every success!' We clinked glasses. I held his gaze as the delicious chilled fizz slipped down my throat. My stomach lurched. Those eyes.

Before I regained my power of speech, the door flew open followed by a ham-fisted grab round my waist. 'Hey, babe,' slurred Marcus. 'How are you doing?'

'Fine.' I stood rigid and much as I hated to do it, I had no choice. I stood back. 'Marcus, this is ...'

And The Merchant of Venison stuck out his hand. 'Jack.'

'Hey, Jack,' he slurred, not releasing me to return the gesture but slinging his arm over my shoulder. 'She's a star is my Mads – hasn't she done a cracking job?' he said, looking at me with a soppy stupid drunken face.

A flicker crossed Jack's eyes as he retrieved his outstretched hand. 'Indeed she has. Now if you'll excuse us,' he said gently, taking Flora's glass and his own and putting them down on a nearby table. 'We just popped in to wish you well and must be off. Good to meet you, Marcus, and—' turning to me, those eyes '—best of luck with it all, Maddy.'

And with that he was off, carefully guiding Flora through the door, ensuring she wasn't jostled or caught up in the increasingly lively party. How sweet, I thought, as my teeth gnashed with irritation, the polar opposite to the proprietorial arm Marcus had draped over me. Then, his point made and distracted by the near-empty platters that were still being passed around, he released me and concentrated on scooping up the remnants. As I moved away I could hear him making a weak joke and laughing too loudly. I just felt empty.

Disappointed, alone and empty.

We kept to our policy of herding everyone out, hard as it was, by 10 p.m. We were open for business proper the following evening. Most people took the cue until there was a little group of three people left, one of whom was Marcus.

I closed the door as the final hint that they would be locked in for the night if they didn't move on. I was on my knees with tiredness.

'Right, where are we off to now?' Marcus asked, red spots on his cheeks, high on champagne.

'Well I'm going to bed,' I said, fixed grin in place. 'It's a big day tomorrow and I need to be bright-eyed and bushy-tailed.'

William caught my eye. He understood exactly what was happening.

'OK, please yourself,' said my erstwhile boyfriend turning to the two girls hovering round the door. 'Anyone else up for another one?'

One of the girls, recognised as his smoking friend from earlier, a little wobbly on her heels, mumbled something into her friend's ear and they both said, 'Yeh, we're going to head to The Hoozier,' and tottered out the door.

Marcus dragged his eyes away from the door. 'I'm only up for the weekend – you don't mind if I go for a nightcap, do you, babe?' he asked.

Speechless, I shrugged. Taking that as a yes, he pecked me on the cheek and waved at William in a cack-handed way. He went off out the door at speed in case he lost his new friends.

I felt like I might burst.

'All the way to Scotland to humiliate me. He could have done that without wasting £150 on a ticket,' I said, furious and on the verge of tears as the door closed behind them.

William held me close. 'Come on. You're tired, Maddy, it will all feel better in the morning. We've got a big day – Marcus is just in the mood for a party.' He squeezed me round the shoulder. 'Come on, we've all done that.'

The voice of reason. He was right. Of course we had. I had. It was just… timing, I thought an hour later, lying in bed, alone and livid with just two thoughts running through my head.

Marcus had come up to support me, help me, be there for me, but it was becoming more and more apparent his lord master came in the shape of a bottle. Increasingly I had a feeling he was not the man I had once believed him to be. Then a flashback to the moment my eyes met those of The Merchant of Venison. An electric charge. And now Jack knew I had a boyfriend, a blustering drunken ass but a boyfriend nonetheless, and that, I noted with surprise, seemed to upset me more than anything.

Chapter 22

My heart was physically aching when I woke after a fitful night in the bothy. Alone. Shoulders round my ears, having looked at my phone every five minutes for the whole night, I was surprised when I opened my eyes, as I hadn't thought I had slept a wink. I was also surprised it was to an empty bed.

'Oh shit, where the hell is he?' I said out loud to the hugely disinterested dog.

I had visions of Marcus sleeping on the beach, freezing to death overnight – such things happened in this part of the world. It looked balmy and lovely and yet overnight the temperature could plummet to freezing and a boozer with slumped sugar levels could easily die of hypothermia. Grabbing my phone, I ran out into the garden to see if there were any messages. None.

My heart was in my throat. I shouldn't have left him. I should have gone with him. I called William.

'I can't find Marcus,' I said.

'He's here,' he said, sounding unamused.

'Oh.' I wasn't quite sure what to say. 'Is he OK?'

'You better come round.'

I made my way round to the cottage. There, curled up on the couch under his coat, was Marcus, sound asleep and snoring unbelievably. The room smelled overwhelmingly of stale booze.

I felt sick.

Frank ambled over and sniffed him, and then turned his back and walked away with a look of disgust.

'How did he get here?'

'The police brought him round about 2 a.m. this morning,' said Noel. 'He didn't know where he was. All he knew was the name of the restaurant and of course your name. They tried your dad's flat, but of course that's empty, so they came here.'

'Shit I am so sorry,' I said, fuming that this drunken oaf had crashed into their lives and buggered up their night as well.

A rustle from the couch indicated he was awake.

'Eeeeugh. Where am I?' he asked, craning his neck, lifting his crumpled, puffy face up. On seeing me he had the audacity to grin, revealing he had a tooth missing. 'Hey, babe,' he said.

The boys were brilliant with him, polite, hospitable, giving him a towel, letting him shower and change and then cooking him a huge breakfast, which he wolfed down seemingly none the worse for his skinful the night before.

'Great party,' he enthused, slugging another mouthful of orange juice. 'So what are we doing today then, babe?' he asked.

'I have no idea what you're doing. But we are opening the restaurant to the public at 6 p.m.,' I snapped in a strangled sort of voice.

He looked confused.

The boys subtly made excuses and left us to it.

Marcus topped up his tea and crunched into his third piece of buttered toast like he didn't have a care in the world.

'OK then, I'll just find somewhere to watch the football,' he said. 'They show it up here in scotty land do they?' he asked, thinking he was being funny.

I cringed, maybe seeing this man properly for the first time. A selfish drunken football fanatic who up here, in my neck of the woods, was like a fish out of water.

Hugely confused, I couldn't think clearly. My head was full of a million things.

Was it stupid of me to think he was going to come up and support me? He had done the polar opposite. He had drunk himself into a stupor, pissing everyone off and the worst thing about it was he had no idea.

I looked at him, standing up and tucking in his shirt, trying to sort himself out, running his hands through his hair and offering a sheepish grin.

'Listen, Marcus, I can't do this just now. I need to focus on my business.' My business! Get me? 'So I think it's best if you just go.'

He stared at me.

'I'm serious.'

'But…'

'Why did you come up here, Marcus?'

'To see you, babe, to come to the party.'

He blinked, stuck for words, so I helped him.

'To come to the party? Not to support me after the recent passing of my father?'

'Well yeh of course that too.' His face dropped.

'To stand at my side and help as we work our arses off to rebuild his business so it's worth more than tuppence ha'pny when I sell it?'

He nodded slowly, reality seeping into his thick head that this was not foreplay but something altogether less fun. 'Yeh.'

'So getting drunk, leaving with another girl, and then being brought home by the police to the manager of the restaurant's house in the middle of the night is what you call supporting me, is it?'

He had the good grace to look a bit shifty. 'Well when you put it like that.'

I had so much to say, but stopping short I realised it was pointless. Looking at the dishevelled, rumpled idiot with crumbs all over his chin, red eyes, in the cold light of day.

'So get your stuff together and I'll drive you to the station.'

'The station?' He sounded genuinely surprised.

'Yes. I'm going to have a coffee. Be ready to leave in five minutes,' I ordered.

I was shaking when I went into the kitchen and burst into tears. William handed me a coffee instantly – of course being in such close proximity they had heard every word.

'You OK?' William asked.

'No.' I blew my nose. 'I mean yes. Yes I am,' I said, fooling no-one, including myself.

William and Noel drove him to the station, made sure he got on the train, returning to dispense hugs, tea and a vast French pastry they had bought at Rory's Bakery.

Despite this awful start to the day it was impossible not to be buoyed up by the feedback. It was amazing.

Messages of support, texts, emails, pinged in. Even The Birdie & Bramble's long-dormant TripAdvisor page sprang into action with some lovely comments, *'Canapés were divine, the atmosphere positively fizzy,'* and the feedback from friends old and new was without exception great.

We were exhausted of course but this was just the start so we had better get used to it. In less than eight hours we were opening to the public for real so there was no time for licking wounds – onwards and upwards.

Running on adrenalin only, we made our way to the restaurant.

Apprehensive to open the door, we needn't have been. Mouse, bless her cotton socks (black), had stayed on and the kitchen was immaculate. The tables were all set, the glasses sparkling, so William headed off into the kitchen to check his supplies and began to cook.

We had decided to open for dinner, needing every second to prepare the restaurant for the big moment, and I was the only one working the floor as we had very low expectations for night one. At 6 p.m. after a group hug and some out-of-character fist-pumping, the menu was put in the window, the Closed sign flipped over to Open, the door opened wide. Now all we had to do was wait.

Forty-five minutes later there was still no-one. After an hour and a half William called Noel and I called Hamish to come round and sit in the table at the window to make it look busy. God love them they were there within fifteen minutes. Hamish was headed straight for the kitchen when I got him by the sleeve. 'Ahem, visiting the kitchen can be arranged later.' He grinned and coloured slightly. So Noel and himself sat, lit candle between them, nursing a glass of wine each, as William and I chatted nervously glancing intermittently outside to see if there were any likely customers. Daylight was fading, the fairy lights were twinkling round the window when at last a group of three people ambled past and glanced in.

William grinned at them, they smiled back, slowed up and examined the handwritten menu, which we had hastily stuck in the window just an hour earlier.

They chatted and then hallelujah, they turned and walked back to the door of the restaurant.

By the time they had opened the door, we were on the other side of it grinning.

William shook their hands and introduced himself and rushed off into the kitchen whilst I nodded to Hamish and Noel, the agreed sign to vacate the prime spot. I straightened up the table before introducing myself and leading them over to the table the boys had just vacated.

They looked a little confused so I confessed, 'You are our first customers and we'd like to buy you a drink!'

'You'll not make much money like that,' they laughed and as I insisted, they ordered a glass of wine each as William whizzed back to the table holding menus.

'I'll leave you to peruse the menu,' I said.

'Would you like a jug of iced water and some bread whilst you wait?' piped up an adrenalin-fuelled William.

Their heads turned from me to him. 'Yes please.'

Seeing their slightly alarmed expressions as we both ran round after them, I took control.

'William,' I said, 'I think we're scaring our guests,' and everyone laughed again as we backed off and left them to settle in. Smiling, they realised that tonight was a very special night indeed for us.

Five minutes later the order was in. William was hyper-ventilating in the kitchen. On returning to the dining room, I saw the door open and two more actual people came in on spec. The window table was the lure. The only tablecloth we had – white linen – it looked so inviting, candle lit, sparkly glasses and happy people. Time flew, orders were taken, wine was opened, tasted, decanted, more people wandered in and soon there was a low hum of conversation as The Birdie & Bramble gently came back to life.

The music was kept at a low tinkle, the smells coming from the kitchen amazing. The first table had our three-course menu and two bottles of wine and when they asked for the bill I managed to produce it accurately and without drama. Their bill was £124 and they left £20 tip – it might as well have been the crown jewels. A tip! There and then we decided to frame it – it was a moment we would never forget.

If I'd had a red carpet I would have rolled it out for them. I opened the door for them, thanking them profusely for being our first and thus best customers ever as they left looking very happy and after two bottles of wine half cut to boot.

There was no time to waste; as I waved goodbye, another four people meandered in and so without a moment's rest I cleared, cleaned and reset the table. And so it went on.

William's head was down all night. My heart sank when someone waved me over, pointing at their plate. 'I have a problem with my steak.' Boggle-eyed, I looked at it, as he continued, 'It's a little too rare. Could you ask Chef to pop it under the grill for another minutes each side?' he said amiably. Relief flooded over me and William took care of it instantly. Everyone was happy. And so, all in all, clenched from the hair on our heads down with anticipation and fear, we survived our first night of real service at The Birdie & Bramble.

Our system for ordering was a little haphazard, and I kept forgetting the table numbers so a few dishes were delivered to the wrong places, and I did ask an elderly couple if they were ready to order sweet when they hadn't actually seen the menu as they had just sat down, but all things considered everything went remarkably well. By close of play we had served seventeen people, the kitchen was mayhem, I was a gibbering wreck and the restaurant itself looked as if it had just enjoyed an end-of-tour party with The Who. But we did it.

After the guests left, William cleaned down the kitchen, put the food away, completed a speedy stock check before emailing his order to suppliers for the morning delivery.

After sweeping and washing the floor, Mouse and I reset the restaurant for the next day. We left it pristine two hours later and we were still buzzing as we traipsed along the road.

After lying awake for a couple of hours reliving an extra-ordinary day, I finally dropped off.

Four hours later I woke up feeling as if I had been crushed by an all-in wrestler. Whoa, and that was just one dinner service. Groaning, I rolled out of bed shadowed by Frank who, like myself, was getting used to our early morning routine. I had a lot to do before opening the doors for our first full day at 10 a.m.

Putting a sweatshirt over my nightie, I wiggled into my scruffy jeans and splashed cold water on my face. A quick brush of the teeth and we were off to the beach. I'd shower and change later. Physically exhausted, my head was buzzing with what had to be done today. The second I was within range, the phone in my pocket buzzed with a text.

'Maddy I am so so sorry. What an arse. I hope you can forgive me. Can I make it up to you? M xx'

One of the upsides of being so engaged in what I was doing was I had not had a minute to think about Marcus. Pressing delete I upped the pace. I had to be walked, washed, and presentable within the hour – it would take a small miracle, a pint of Beauty Flash and four inches of make-up, I thought, bursting into a run to keep up with Frank who rollicked ahead.

We had three for lunch.

'Better than nothing,' I said two hours later to Mouse, exhausted and disappointed.

'Yes and we already have eight booked for tonight and we should get a few walk-ins,' William said, analysing the book-ings book. 'Hamish said he'd be in later if we needed him.'

'Great,' said Mouse, perking up immediately.

My phone rang. I looked down. It was Marcus. I pressed silent and put it away.

'I think I'll manage on my own tonight,' I said as Mouse's perk left the building. The busier the better to block out thoughts of Marcus, thoughts of Dad, thoughts about what I was going to do with the rest of my life and the small matter of cash flow, which was non-existent.

William agreed. 'OK I'll see you back here for six.'

By midnight we were ecstatic, exhausted and in need of a thirty-six-hour sleep. We ended up with eleven for dinner – not busy but good for William, who handled the food perfectly. I coped out front on my own and I had not a second to think about anything so the second my head hit the pillow I was asleep. Until the alarm went off the next morning.

Chapter 23

I was getting into the habit of seeing the same people every morning on the beach. Serge the beagle's dad, Hector the Scottie's mum, Gabby the dog walker who always had a phalanx of dog leads twisting and tangling round her as she deftly moved them in her hands like an Orkney weaver miraculously preventing a snarl-up. We all shared a cheery wave on a colder day and on warmer mornings took a moment to pass the time of day as the dogs snuffled round one another, enjoying their own social interactions.

The sun was now high in the sky, the ground a silvery sheen, light catching the millions of pearlescent shells all ground to make the soft sugary sand. I bent to take off my shoes. I couldn't resist. Today the sea was a translucent green, the crest of the waves all the more white against it as they crashed onto the beach, reaching as far as the tide allowed before being dragged back over the shale and revealing bubbling wet sand and slick stones beneath.

Relishing the cool fizzy water between my toes, I stood eyes closed, facing the sea, just breathing in and out, in time with the waves. In and out. In and out. My lips felt tight and salty as they stretched into an enormous smile. Feeling a nudge from Frank on my leg, I turned round and broke into a trot, splashing along the edge of the sea, kicking up the spray as he yip-yipped around me.

Out of breath, my jeans now soaked to the knees, I spotted

Hamish in the distance waving. Waving wildly back at him I noticed he was with Duke and Gaston as they careered over the hill behind him and then I realised The Merchant of Venison was coming over the dunes too. Gulp.

Marcus had behaved like such a buffoon the other night at the party. The last time I had seen Jack, Marcus was manhandling me like a piece of meat. Jack, being perfectly polite, had quickly bowed out of The Birdie & Bramble, the thought of which made me cringe. I was horrified to think he thought Marcus was my boyfriend even though he was. Or had been and well, might still be, but it seemed unlikely. God even my thoughts were making no sense.

Why I should tie myself in knots about the opinion of a man I barely knew, I had no idea. I put it down to tiredness, stress and Marcus being a pillock. But there was no ignoring the torsion in my gut telling me something was afoot, something I was fairly sure was not going to make this already complicated life any easier.

My instinct was to turn and run. I hadn't even washed my face and it resembled an accordion, squished and tired, and as for the hair! I had only just wrestled that into a topknot, which had earned me the nickname Po from the Teletubbies in the past – in other words I was not looking my best. Rising above it, I decided to be brief and businesslike and get on with things so I marched along the beach to meet them.

'Well?' said Hamish. 'How did your first official day go?'

'We only had three for lunch but last night we fed and watered eleven real customers,' I said with a triumphant grin. 'And I didn't know any of them!'

Hamish grinned. 'Wow.'

I could feel those deep blue eyes boring into me as I heard Jack say, 'Well done.' I glanced briefly in his direction and smiled but thankfully Hamish was his usual self and butted in.

'So you didn't poison anyone?'

'No, luckily I wasn't cooking but if you pop in later I can rectify that,' I said, whapping his arm. The Merchant smiled. Our eyes met briefly, a charge went through me. What on earth was going on? I hardly knew the man. Flustered, I focused on Hamish, adding, 'Much as I would love to stand here chatting all day I have a restaurant to open – and Hamish?'

'Yes.'

'If we get busy are you around to come in and help?'

'Yeh of course ... is Mouse on?' he asked, looking shifty.

Aha I thought so! He really fancied her. Great.

'That's for me to know and you to find out!' I said, teasing him, and turning on my heels and running back in the direction I had come from, 'Byeeeee.'

I arrived back at the bothy refreshed, energised and ready for the day ahead. People sometimes purported negative ions came from the sea. I had pooh-poohed that before but there was no denying something was fizzing in my belly and bubbling lemonade-like up into my chest. Negative ions or an empty stomach – whatever it was, it felt good.

And so my life took on a new rhythm. Up, walk, shower, go to The Birdie & Bramble, go to the bank and deposit the last evening's takings, get a coffee, back to the restaurant and work the lunch service. The moment the last customer left we would sit down and have a bite to eat, then I would walk the dog, sit down for ten minutes, shower, get ready for evening service. Work. Collapse. And so it went on.

Our dinner numbers were building gradually but our lunches were absolutely dead and despite his forced optimism, I could see William struggling to be positive as our food costs and outgoings were far more than the pitiful amount we were bringing in. If things didn't change soon we would have to take a long hard look at our rash and ill-thought-out plan.

Noel, the most supportive man in Europe, came in most days for a bowl of soup at lunchtime and sat in the window table as I hovered, waiting for an imaginary rush of customers. Momentum was flagging. Then one day William marched out of the kitchen, scribbled out on a bit of A4:

'Three-course lunch. Starter, main course and sweet, £10.95 includes a drink, bread and coffee.
Soused herring and potato salad
Venison sausage and mash with a red wine jus *veggie sausage alternative
Thelma's Hazelnut cake.'

He sellotaped it to the window. Just like that.

'That's bloody cheap,' I said.

'Yes but if we don't get more people in here, Mads, we're goosed. At least if people go for this menu we can cut down on our stock of other stuff. I'm throwing out more food than anyone's eating,' he said, rubbing his nose, looking horribly anxious.

That lunchtime we had five. Hardly a thundering of hooves but we were buoyed up nonetheless so the following morning we printed one hundred copies of the menu and Hamish and I hit the streets, smiling, engaging with people and handing them out. People were charming, interested and lots of them didn't even know we existed so after handing out the last one, we returned to the restaurant and waited.

At 12.05 the door opened and they started to trickle in …

by 1 p.m. we were half full and by 1.30 bursting at the seams. Even Noel grabbed an apron and started pouring drinks. We were ecstatic. As each happy customer paid, they got a potted history of the Birdie and we blatantly asked if they would review us on TripAdvisor and tell their friends.

William stumbled out of the kitchen, run ragged after the last table cleared and Noel gave him a huge hug. 'You played an absolute blinder there, Will. Well done.'

This development meant I was in The Birdie & Bramble all day, every day, from early morning 'til closing, bar a quick shower and change late afternoon, which made it easy to avoid Marcus's calls. I understood the pressures of his day, and the nine-to-five madness meant when I was quiet he was working and then when he was home I was running about like a lunatic but he was relentless with his messages and texts and one day a stunning bouquet of flowers arrived in the middle of lunch service which I hastily grabbed. I read the card later. It simply said, *'Forgive me I'm an arse. Love Marcus.'*

I was softening slightly and sooner rather than later I would have to make time to talk to him. I just wasn't sure what on earth to say. A sabbatical from work was a no-brainer to concentrate on the restaurant but I was beginning to think Marcus and I should have a sabbatical too, give each other some space, time to think things through, work out how we really felt. After all in a few weeks this sojourn to Scotland would be over and I'd be back to my real life in London.

On that note, Felicity sent me an email the other day, surprisingly chatty, hoping I was getting on well and wondering if I had a date when I was coming back.

I replied saying things were hard but enjoyable and I

aimed to be back at the beginning of August, exact date to be confirmed. Maybe it was true that absence makes the heart grow fonder – there was no denying she and Marcus weren't nearly as irritating 600 miles away.

Other than the restaurant customers and suppliers, the only people I talked to were on my morning stomps. As the days went by we all got to know each other by name. But the one I always looked out for was Duke and Gaston's dad, Jack.

Quite often Hamish was with him, which took the pressure off as I could talk to Hamish without looking into those hypnotic deep blue eyes. But when I did, for some reason I had difficulty breathing. Jack always wore the same battered, patched old Barbour, de rigueur in this part of the world. His trousers were well-worn soft khaki moleskin, though why I had to even notice the texture of his trousers I didn't know. For God's sake I did wonder about my mental health. The muscles of his legs were evident as he strode the beach and his hands. Oh my God. His hands were huge and capable.

STOP, Maddy! I was far too interested in everything about him and despite giving myself a good talking-to, I could not help myself.

Chapter 24

The following days passed in a whirl. Every day was different, every day was long, the customers came and went and told their friends and so they came and went and so it went on. The place was getting busier every day. Be careful what you wish for, I thought, as we were all on our knees, but we were not going to let up, not for a second. We had our designated few weeks to make a difference and every penny counted.

One afternoon after lunch I went home to put my feet up and slept right through 'til six – my supposed start time – rushing about, it was closer to seven by the time I tore round the corner to work. Approaching the restaurant I did a double take. It was packed. Not only that, but there was a group of three or four people hovering round the door waiting to get in. Not quite sure if I was dreaming or not, I eased my way back to the other side of the road, stood back and watched.

Hamish was twirling round the tables, delivering plates, glasses, removing plates, glasses, talking and smiling all the while. Mouse, who had been coaxed out front, looked confident and happy clearing tables and pouring wine and with a white shirt on in place of her goth T-shirt, her whole face lit up. The tinkle of glasses, the ooohs and aaahs as delicious plates of food were placed in front of them – it was like one big happy family party.

The sun was setting outside, the light dimming emphasised

the tea lights, fairy lights and candles twinkling from within, giving an almost ethereal glow reflecting off the mirrors and glasses. Tables of two, four and one table of ten along the far wall were deep in conversation. It truly felt like The Birdie & Bramble's heart was no longer broken.

Entering the fray, squeezing past a table of customers deep in conversation, I slipped behind the bar and through to the kitchen. William was wiping his forehead with a cloth, his eyes ablaze.

'Holy shit!' I said maturely.

'What the hell happened?' he grinned.

'I slept in.' I added, 'Sorry.'

'No, not that!' he said smiling. 'That!' He nodded at the dining room, the throng of laughter and clink and fizz of the busy restaurant.

'I have absolutely no idea,' I laughed. 'What can I do?'

'Take these, Table 6,' he said, pointing to the pass where two plates of Cullen skink were waiting.

'Back in a flash,' I said, picking up two plates, balancing them on my forearms and then lifting the others.

'You never lose it,' I said, nearly losing it as I pushed through the door. 'Of course I never had it!'

'Table 6!' he shouted after me.

I gave the diners a grin as I delivered their plates, followed up with a jolly, 'Bon appétit!' and was a little nonplussed when they barely acknowledged me. Oh well it takes all sorts, I thought, wondering who they were, and why they were clearly not entering into the spirit of the evening; after all, the place was buzzing.

Wine bottles were opened, champagne corks popped, litres of Highland Spring, jugs of iced tap water, St Clements, cocktails. Hamish was a whirling dervish behind that bar. I danced my way between tables; it was relentless.

245

The assembled throng's appetite for food and drink was impressive.

The torn-faced woman and her equally serious partner at Table 6 ate slowly, methodically and did not engage in conversation at all.

As I cleared her plate I prompted, 'I hope you enjoyed your starter.'

She looked at me, her tight lips giving nothing away, a barely perceptible nod.

Oh well please yourself, I thought.

She ate two more courses, had a couple of glasses of wine, which were ordered on my recommendation and when it came to pay the bill, paid cash. Oh well it takes all sorts, I thought, as I realised she had left no tip but had left her business card.

Odd, I thought, and plopped it in my pocket to examine later.

As one table finished, another party arrived, we turned the tables as fast we could and by midnight the last few stragglers were sitting enjoying a restorative whisky when we finally drew breath.

'If I hadn't seen that with my own eyes, I wouldn't have believed it possible,' I said, flumping onto a chair next to William.

'We were like a finely tuned military operation,' said William, eyes wide.

I guffawed. 'I know! How did that happen?'

'Well it's nothing to do with me. I don't know my arse from my elbow,' joked Hamish. 'It was a real buzz though!'

'Oh yes,' said Mouse. 'And the number of compliments to the chefs I passed on was – well it was loads.'

William glowed as we grinned at each other. Day by day, little by little, Mouse's various piercing adornments were becoming less, two small nose rings were still in place, but the lip rings were a thing of the past, the tunnels in her ears gone and underneath all the make-up and folderol a rather beautiful Mouse was emerging. Although William and I had discussed it, we decided not to mention our observations; like a crab being coaxed out of its shell, it would be too easy to scare it away. Someone else who had noticed was the increasingly smitten Hamish.

'Yeh, there were people from all over tonight.'

'Where from?'

'A real mix, a few locals, Americans, Spanish, Japanese – I tell you, those concierges are worth their weight in gold, sending everyone here.'

We stopped to hungrily devour the fish pie William had prepared for staff supper.

Hamish stopped and jumped to his feet, wiping his mouth with his napkin, as the last few stragglers made their way over.

'Don't jump up – we don't want to disturb you. We just wanted to say that was superb! Just superb! And to ask if you've got a table for tomorrow night?' said the bill payer as she bumped between tables towards us with the relaxed gait of someone who had thoroughly enjoyed their evening.

'Em … yes I think so – let me check,' said Hamish, grabbing the bookings book off the bar top and examining it.

'We have one early table for two at 6 p.m. but we need it back by 8,' he said apologetically.

'We'll take it,' said the woman, handing him a £20 note. 'Name's Purdy.'

'Thanks but we don't need a deposit.'

'That's a tip, honey,' she laughed as she waved an arm. 'See you tomorrow at six.'

The door closed behind her and Hamish nipped deftly

over and put the snib down making sure we wouldn't be disturbed, and then turned and grinned widely. 'What a night.'

Sated with delicious food ourselves, we sat each lost in our own thoughts as Mouse punched numbers into the calculator, the digits showing the cash mounting up from the evening's takings. Mouse wrote down various figures in various columns as I suddenly remembered the quiet woman from earlier and plucked her business card out of my pocket, handing it to William, explaining what had happened. He looked at the card. The blood drained from his face; he was stricken.

'What is it?'

'Oh my God.'

'WHAT?'

'BB McGill – the toughest food critic in the land.'

'She was here?' said Hamish.

'That was her?' asked Mouse, calculator forgotten.

'Oh God I'm sorry, I had no idea who she was,' I confessed. 'What does that mean?'

'Well, we'll have to wait until Sunday when *The Sunday Telegraph* is printed to find out,' said Hamish.

'This could make or break us.' William sounded like the harbinger of doom.

'God she can't be that bad,' I said, trying to bring some perspective back. On the rear side of the card she had written '*photographer will be in touch*' and that was that.

We relived the interactions I had with her, what she'd ordered and every nuance in her body language. Of course she had given nothing away whatsoever.

'I'll call the photographer in the morning,' I said as we got up, put our plates into the sink, cleared up, reset the tables. Mouse tackled the pots and William cleaned down the kitchen. It was after 1.30 a.m. when we finally left for the night and we were going to do it all again tomorrow … and the next day … ad infinitum. This was the hardest work I had ever done in my life and I loved it.

William and I walked barefoot along the road, feet throbbing, arm in arm. 'Guess how much?' he said.

'How much what? You mean how much did we turn over?'

'Guess.'

'Oh £200?'

'More …'

'£400?'

'More.'

'£500?'

'More!'

'For God's sake just tell me!' I said, exasperated with this game.

'£986.23.'

I stopped dead in my tracks.

'Oh. My. God.'

After jumping up and down and hugging one another, William stopped and looked at me.

'Maddy, will you do me a favour?'

'What?' I said, the tone suddenly changed.

'Take tomorrow off?'

'What?'

'You heard me.'

'But I can't. I've to call the photographer and …'

'OK, you can do that but then you're off.'

I looked at him.

'Why not?'

'Well …' I couldn't tell him the thought of doing nothing was too much to bear. The moments of stillness I had experienced recently were sheer torture. I had to keep moving, keep busy, keep the voices in my head quiet.

'Exactly, there's no reason you can't take a day out. Relax. Do nothing. Have a long lie-in. Chill out.'

'OK, but I'll be in tomorrow night,' I said, my legs watery at the thought of some time away from the frenzy of the business. And by the time I crawled between the sheets, I had come round to the idea that a long long lie-in was in order and a day of doing very little at all might be what I needed after all.

The adrenalin was not going to let me sleep. My head was like a toyshop going over and over those extraordinary figures in my head. God if we weren't careful we'd have a successful business on our hands. I lay there in the dark with Frank's head in the crook of my arm, concentrating on my breathing.

Then I panicked. BB McGill – what did she think about The Birdie & Bramble? Shit, what a day. Highs, lows and me loving every second of it; a tear rolled down my face at the thought of Dad missing this extraordinary time and then remembering his joie de vivre, his lust for life, his insistence that life was for living. I smiled in the dark, eyes flooding with tears until finally I nodded off.

Chapter 25

With full permission for a long languorous lie-in, I rolled over to look at my phone. Thanks to my bloody body clock, I was wide awake by 7.30 a.m.

Frank, sensing a stirring, was standing on the end of the bed with his lead in his mouth. How could I resist?

'Come on then,' I said, rolling out of bed reluctantly. Gosh I had aches and pains in places I didn't even know I had. This life of a working waitress was not for the faint-hearted, I thought, as I lumbered into the shower.

It was a beautiful morning; the world had never looked so good. High white clouds skipped along as if in a spectacularly good humour. The sun was not shy, blasting down on the spiky green grasses of the sand dunes. Taking one of the wooden ramps, Frank and I walked down towards the beach. The tide was in this morning, restricting the width of sand for the dog walkers already out.

Marcus would be up, showered and on his way to work, so parking my bum on a bench, I gave him a call. It rang once.

'Maddy. Thank God. How are you?'

'I'm good.'

'Good, good. God it's so good to hear your voice ...' He sounded like he really meant it.

'Thanks for the flowers.'

'You're welcome ... You know I meant what I said. I am sorry ... and I am an arse.'

I smiled. 'Yes, I know you're an arse.'

He relaxed and laughed, my answer indicating banter was back on the cards.

'I really miss you,' he said, unexpectedly staying serious – most disquieting.

'Yeh.' I gazed down at the sweep of sand ahead and my determined little dog forging ahead onto the beach alone. 'I miss you too but it's only for a few more weeks and I'm literally working sixteen hours a day and a complete wreck.'

'I'm sure I could help with that...' he said, putting on a deep sexy tone.

I laughed. 'I'm sure you could... but listen I've been thinking.'

'Oh God, that sounds ominous.'

'No, no it's not. I don't want to fight or make any big decisions about anything just now. I can't, I just need to focus on The Birdie & Bramble... and do the best I can.'

'Yeh I know. I get it.'

There was a lull. I could here the cacophony of London rush hour behind him. The signal coming and going.

'OK.' I broke the silence. 'So let's keep in touch as often as we can and...'

He took over cheerily. 'We'll just keep on keeping on...?'

'Yeh.' The dog, the wee bugger, had disappeared. I had to cut him short. 'OK listen, I've lost sight of Frank. I have to go... Take care, Marcus, let's speak soon, OK?'

'I love you,' he said, just as I clicked off my phone.

Bloody hell, I don't think he's ever said that sober, I thought before leaping up. 'Frank!' I shouted, running off to find him.

It seemed the weather had put everyone in a similar mood. Waving and good mornings from every one who walked past.

'He went that way,' shouted Serge, the beagle's dad.

I spotted him thundering along as fast as his little legs would carry him. I was gaining on him but suddenly he changed tack and started galloping towards the dunes – I assumed to chase a rabbit – when two elegant long-legged deer hounds came into view, stopping and sitting down obediently to wait as The Merchant of Venison appeared behind them. The dogs watched Jack intently as he raised his arm, giving the signal to run, and they did. Side by side, noses together, they were off – fast, lolloping, along the sand, getting smaller and smaller the further they ran.

Frank's fat little bottom didn't stand a chance of catching up with them but he was determined nonetheless. Frank arrived at Jack's feet and skidded to a halt. Jack patted Frank's head and turned, waving to me. My heart lurched. He was coming my way.

Walking towards him, I felt my throat constrict and could think of not a thing in the world to say. Breathe in, and out, in and out.

'Morning,' he said, stepping into time with me. 'Mind if we walk along with you?'

'Great,' I squeaked.

'How are things at the restaurant?' he asked.

'Great.' Oh my God, I was officially monosyllabic.

'Roe deer selling well?'

'Great.' My brain was in Groundhog Day whilst the rest of me walked alongside this man. Staring at his scuffed leather boots. 'They look like they've seen a lot of action,' I said.

'What? The roe deer?' he asked.

'No. Those,' I said, pointing at his feet.

'Oh yes, I've had them for years ... they are a bit ...'

'Big,' I suddenly blurted out.

Laughter erupted from him. 'I was going to say old but well I suppose they are.'

'What size are they?' I said, incredulous I had asked such a ridiculous, personal and irrelevant question.

'Twelve and a half.'

'Wow,' I said as if I was the world expert on foot sizing when in point of fact I had never ever in my life up until this moment noticed, thought about or commented on anyone's feet – nor would I ever again. Cringe. And then my lifelong need to fill any silence didn't let me down as to my horror I continued, 'You know what they say about men with big feet?'

'No?' he asked, genuinely sounding interested.

'They need big shoes,' I said and then burst into a ribald guffaw straight out of *Carry On Up the Khyber*.

He smiled and continued walking. My face felt flash-fried. What a stupid bloody woman. I felt like the silence went on for about three days in my head. In reality it was more like five seconds when thank God he broke it.

'So, Madeline, how are you settling back in St Andrews?'

Hardly anyone ever called me Madeline. I hated it. Well I did until now. From the mouth of this man I loved it. Just hearing my name in his low Scottish brogue was a thing of joy. Oh God what was the question?

'Sorry, what was the question?' I asked like the halfwit I am.

'How are you settling?'

Oh for God's sake, of course.

'It's been a complete whirlwind. I haven't really had time to think about it but one thing I do know is I just love being here, on the beach every day.' I waved my hand about a bit. 'It really clears the cobwebs and sets me up for the day.'

Clears the head – I thought given my recent conversational prowess, surely he would think my head was full of mince.

He grinned. 'Yes, St Andrews is a very special place.'

We walked on.

'Have you lived here all your life?' I asked, sounding sane.

A shadow passed over his face. 'Mostly.'

'Your folks?'

'Divorced.' He didn't elaborate.

Something in his demeanour stopped me from asking any more.

He smiled sadly, turned to me. 'And what about your mum?'

'Oh my mum died when I was four. Dad brought me up on his own,' I said matter-of-factly. I had told this story so many times the words no longer stung the way they had a long long time ago.

'Do you remember her?' Jack asked. Usually people changed the subject quickly. A shift in my chest confirmed that despite time and denial, the loss was still keen. 'Yes I think so ... I remember her ... brushing my hair, I remember her laughing and I think I remember her smell ... but I think it's more from the stories Dad tells—' I corrected myself '—em ... told ...'

'What happened?'

'Well she was out in the garden, always out in the garden, and she cut herself. Just a small cut, nothing dramatic. She didn't even put a plaster on it. The next day she felt a bit fluey and went to bed and then that night when Dad popped up from the restaurant to see how she was doing, she was unconscious. By the time they got her to hospital she was in a coma and she died later that night.'

He looked shocked.

'It was blood poisoning. Sepsis,' I added. 'There was nothing anyone could have done.' The wobble in my voice gave it away. I hadn't spoken about it for years, but the hurt was still there, visceral, unexpurgated.

'Gosh, what a shock for your poor father and you.'

'Yes, but I was so young, they protected me the best they could, but there was a sadness. I don't think Dad ever really got over it, never moved on, never married again.'

'That's hard,' he said, putting his hand on my arm.

His hand felt like a branding iron, the heat through my jacket radiated up my arm. It was an electric shock.

Eyes brimming with tears again, I went on, 'Yes, all the things they planned to do and never did, all the things I planned to do with Dad – we never got round to doing…' I slowed down, bottom lip quivering. 'It makes you think.'

'Carpe diem,' he said.

'Seize the day.' I picked up the cue.

'Come on then,' he said, stopping dead in his tracks, turning to face me.

'What are you doing right now?'

'Walking the dog?'

'After that!' he said.

'Well nothing actually – I've been banished from the restaurant until tonight.'

'Excellent.'

'Why?'

'Well after these goons have run themselves ragged, I'm going foraging. Why don't you come with me?'

'Foraging?

'Yes, foraging.'

'Gosh I don't know if I remember what to do – I've not been since I was about ten when I went off with Dad to find mushrooms.'

'Well why don't you seize the day?'

Looking up into his smiling face, I saw the crinkles round his eyes, and maybe it was just me but I thought there was a hint of expectation in those dark blue eyes.

My heart threatened to jump from my throat. 'Why not!' I said.

And so we parted after arranging he would swing by and pick me up outside Noel's shop in an hour.

An hour.

I walked as fast as my legs could carry me, Frank pinned to my heel sensing something was going on. Shit. So was this a date? No, no of course not. Jack thought I had a boyfriend. Which I do. Though less than an hour ago that was up for debate, but that was then and this is now, and for now we agreed to keep on keepin' on. So I wondered what the hell I was doing.

I looked at my watch. I had less than forty minutes to get ready. I should call Jack and cancel. All of a sudden it felt wrong. What was I thinking agreeing to go off into the hills with a virtual stranger? A hugely attractive one but a virtual stranger. The last thing I needed was more complications in my life. Marcus and I had put ten months into our relation-ship and more or less just made up. So I made up my mind to cancel but by then it was just twenty minutes until he was picking me up.

On the other hand, I countered, what harm would a day out of St Andrews do? In fact it would do me nothing but good. I hadn't been anywhere but the Bermuda Triangle, as William called it, since coming back. OK, I would make it clear to Jack that this was purely platonic and then there would be no awkwardness. Despite that, of course I wanted to look reasonable, not like I'd been dragged round the town by a herd of buffalo. I wanted to put my make-up on so it looked as though I was wearing none. There was no time to pluck my eyebrows; plus if I did I'd have the red throbbing upper eye look.

No, in reality there was just enough time to get to grips with the corkscrew bush standing perpendicular from my head. By the time I had slapped on tinted moisturiser, waterproof mascara and slick of lip gloss I had a natural flush to my cheeks which made me look a little mad, I thought, flicking shut my handheld mirror and grabbing my mac. He may have noticed that already.

I said a hasty farewell to Noel as I whizzed past his desk.

'Where are you off to?' he asked.

'Foraging,' I answered, spotting a muddy Land Rover parked outside. 'With Jack.'

'Oooh,' he said as I exited the shop. I smiled at Jack who approached and we shared an awkward non-hug, head-clash, cringe moment before I headed round to the left-hand side of the car. To my surprise Jack followed on behind me, I assumed to get in and drive.

'Oh left-hand drive – very posh,' I bantered, backing off to go round to the other side.

'No,' he said. 'I was just opening the door for you.'

Beetroot-faced, I giggled. Never had I been in the company of a man who would open a car door for me. And as a result I was, as usual, making a show of myself.

'Oh thanks,' I mumbled, digging about in my handbag, trying to get myself together as he ran round and jumped deftly into the driver's seat and started the engine.

'So where are we going?' I asked.

'Perth.'

'Perth!'

'Yes, it's not far, it's beautiful at this time of year and we have a mission.'

'Oh, what?' I asked.

'Picking elderflowers. My elderflower cordial is a thing of beauty and even better...' I looked at him. 'Elderflower champagne.'

'Mmm, that sounds amazing.'

'It is – it has to be the most delicious thing I have ever tasted.'

'Yum,' I said as Duke or Gaston's head came lolling from the back of the Land Rover and rested on my shoulder. Frank responded with a low proprietorial growl.

Jack laughed. 'He's obviously not going to share his mistress with anyone.'

I swallowed with difficulty, stroking Frank's soft pointy ears 'til he took his eyes off Duke or Gaston, and then curled up on my lap and fell asleep.

I had forgotten how beautiful Perthshire was, green rolling hills, ancient pine trees reaching high into the sky, vast sturdy oaks – even the grass seemed greener, foliage abundant, lush plants, trees, ferns, licking the side of the car as we twisted and turned following the road as it became narrower and narrower. Purple heather covered the hills all around, the raspberry farms of Blairgowrie advertising their wares at the side of the road.

We stopped at an honesty box where we took a punnet of plump berries and left more than the suggested amount in the box. The contrast between the rugged sandy windy beaches and the lush, rippling mounds of highland Perthshire was equally as beautiful. Why I had never noticed before, I had no idea.

Swinging off the road onto a track, Jack announced, 'This part's a bit rough – hang on!' We lurched and plummeted over rocks and stones on a deserted-looking farm track, laughing with the undulations and discomfort, until we ground to a halt.

'How do you know about this place? It really is the back of beyond.'

He tapped his nose and grinned. 'I'm an international man of mystery. Now come on,' he said, opening the back to let the dogs out. Duke and Gaston jumped down and stretched as Frank bounced between their long legs, waiting for someone to take the lead.

Jack guddled about in the back a little longer and then handed me a large basket and after taking one of his own, we were off. Walking behind him, through thick bracken and overhead branches, I tried not to focus on the muscles of his legs evident as he strode on through the undergrowth.

'Watch out,' he would say as a large branch swung back and swooshed by my head. The smell was of damp, lush, growth – musty, mossy. The acoustics were dampened by all the living, breathing vegetation round us. It was magical. Spores. Wisps. Spiders' webs. Mossy banks. Stones seemingly dropped from nowhere nestled in the middle of this heavenly place. Pine trees so high they almost blocked the light. It was intoxicating.

After walking for no more than fifteen minutes, we came to a clearing. In which was a vast frill of white flowers.

'Elderflowers!' he announced. 'This is what we're after.'

He issued instructions and we got to work until we had cut, folded, and pressed into the baskets as many elderflowers as we possibly could – they were full to bursting, brimming over.

Pollen everywhere, sticky leaves, sticks, a twig tangled in my hair – typical.

'I think we deserve a break,' Jack announced as we stood back and admired our handiwork.

'Yes, Boss,' I said, grinning up at him.

His face was flushed with exertion and his long black eyelashes seemed to have gathered pollen on their tips. Our eyes met. I felt the shape of my heart; a charge went through me.

'Come on,' he said, taking his jacket off and putting it on the ground. 'Have a seat here. I'll just be a minute.'

Opening car doors, putting his jacket down for me to sit on – I felt like I had been beamed into a Jane Austin novel, a swoon imminent.

Channelling Emma, I inhaled the scents and sounds of the forest as Jack trudged off with the baskets. Hearing the footsteps fading, I lay down for a second and the next thing I heard was: 'Wake up, lazybones.' Opening my eyes, I saw him standing there in front of me, another basket in his hand.

'Oh God not more picking,' I groaned.

'Have a look,' he said, putting it down next to me.

Peering in I saw something tartan: a rug. I peeked under and found the most delicious-looking picnic.

'Ooooh wow,' I said, beaming.

'Fair pay for a fair day's work,' he said, throwing the rug down on the ground and digging out the goodies.

A bottle of wine in a sleeve that had kept it chilled – he plopped it into the stream, shoring it up with rocks so it didn't slip away. Sandwiches wrapped in silver paper.

'Smoked salmon in these ones,' he said, 'and venison carpaccio in those ... and a packet of salt and vinegar crisps.'

I laughed.

'What?'

'Everything is so sophisticated and yet here we have ye good olde salt and vinegar crisps – I love them!'

He grinned. 'Me too. I'm no Gordon Ramsay but hopefully this lot will do you, madam,' he said revealing two hard-boiled eggs, two Royal Gala apples and a paper bag that held two huge lemon meringue tarts.

'Rory's,' I said. 'Delicious.'

And so with everything unravelled and unpacked, we sat in companionable silence, munching and laughing as the dogs crept closer and closer until we shooed them away, as they were in intent inhaling our picnic. We shared the wine. After a large glass on an empty stomach, I plucked up the courage to ask him about his family.

'Mum and Dad had an acrimonious divorce. Years ago. A nightmare all round.'

'Oh I'm sorry.'

His demeanour shifted as he continued, 'My grandmother Flora, on Dad's side, is still going strong.'

'Oh of course, that lovely lady you brought to the opening. You're lucky. I haven't got any grandparents left.'

'Yes, Flora is an angel. She moved into a residential home on the outskirts of St Andrews a couple of years ago. That's one of the reasons I'm here, to keep an eye on her, make sure she's OK.'

'Is that your mum's mum or your dad's mum?'

'Dad's. And she's a great old bird, diagnosed with dementia four years ago. We knew something wasn't right for a while before that but, well, when she was unable to live independently I found this great place just on the outskirts of town for her … which she loves. She has her network of friends who pop in. She recognises them but no longer recalls their names. She knows the area like the back of her hand and I just want to spend as much quality time with her as I can whilst she still remembers me.'

Tears filled my eyes. 'Gosh I'm sorry. That's hard.'

'Yes, in some ways it is, but you know she still enjoys life, loves walking, loves these two—' he gestured to Duke and

Gaston '—and she still has a great sense of fun.' His words were light but the deep hurt on his face was hard to disguise.

'You must bring her in for lunch one day. I would love to meet her properly. She sounds wonderful.'

'She is.' He smiled softly.

'Well she's lucky to have you,' I said, daring to glance up at his face. The silence was deafening.

He turned to me. Time stood still. I fell into those deep limpid eyes. My chest constricted. I watched him clench his jaw as he looked away from me, reaching for the bottle of wine bottle only to find it was empty.

'Gosh, have we scoffed the lot?' I said, under no illusion – I had enjoyed the majority of it as Jack was driving.

'Yes, you have!' He grinned at me.

I felt quite giggly as Frank came shambling over and dug in between us. 'As I thought, he is quite protective isn't he?' said Jack, as Frank nuzzled closer and closer until he was virtually in my oxter.

'My wee hairy wingman.' I scruffed his hair. 'I don't know what I would have done without him over the past few weeks.'

Jack, propped on one elbow, reached over and stroked Frank's ears. Frank watched him carefully and despite himself closed his eyes and plopped his head down onto the rug.

I smiled. 'God that picnic was just … perfect. I don't want to move. In fact I can't!' I said, eyelids heavy as the warmth of the day and the wine washed over me. Lying warm on the rug with only the sound of bees buzzing and the leaves rustling in the wind, I felt so at home, so relaxed, so content, and half cut, so on I warbled. 'When I was a wee girl picnics were my absolute favourite, usually down at the beach with sandy sandwiches and little twists of salt for our boiled eggs, nothing as posh as this.'

263

'Well, I had to make an effort; after all, you're a restaurateur,' Jack smiled gently.

I smiled back. 'When I was about four, Dad and I went off to the beach with buckets and spades, Mum was following on with the picnic, and when we got there he dug a huge hole and then lay right down in it and buried himself with my help, up to his neck in the sand until the only bit of him showing was his head. "When you see your mother coming this way," he said, "put your bucket on my head and don't say a word."'

I laughed at the memory and heard Jack gently chuckling at my silly story too, giving me the momentum to continue.

'It's one of the most vivid memories I have of Mum, her shiny dark bob, her flowery summer dress, walking towards us, and when she thought I was alone she dropped the picnic and came tearing over. "For goodness' sake, Maddy, where's Dad? What on earth? You're on your own, lassie." Such concern on her face, and just as she bowled over to scoop me up to give me a hug, I grabbed my bucket revealing Dad's head grinning from ear to ear. We all had absolute hysterics. Then when we'd calmed down, she grabbed the rug, rolling it out right beside him, and sat down. "Right, Joe," she said, "you can stay right where you are whilst Maddy and I enjoy our egg mayonnaise sandwiches and red lemonade."

'His face was a picture as we started to scoff the food; of course after about thirty seconds I took pity on him and fed him half my sandwiches as he chatted away, quite the thing, much to the amusement of passers-by. When we eventually dug him out, we all lay on the rug, full of delicious food, holding hands, watching the clouds skidding past, when Mum asked, "So, Joe, what's the moral of the story?"

'We both shrugged.

'"Quit while you're a head," she said, bursting out laughing again. Dad rolled over and tickled her and me until we were all screeching with laughter.'

As I told the story I felt tears rolling down my face at the memory of that carefree laughter coupled with such overwhelming sadness because those two wonderful people, the two who were pre-programmed to love me more than anything else in the world, were both gone.

I opened my wet eyes to apologise for yet another out-pouring of grief but before I could say another word, Jack's lips brushed mine. My watery eyes met his and I felt that insane connection again as his face brushed against mine. It was unlike anything I had ever experienced before. I blinked, breathless and wanting the world to stop.

'Come on, you, much as I would like to stay here for the rest of the day, it's nearly 4 p.m. so I think we had better make a move. You're due back soon.'

He stood up. My head was spun, and it wasn't just the wine.

'I'll give you a hand up,' he said, holding out his hands. I lifted my arms and our fingers entwined, electricity snapping between us. Good Lord, even my fingers loved him.

'One … two … three … hup!' he said, launching me into a vertical position.

Suddenly on my feet, I felt quite dizzy and held on tight. My light-headedness should have passed but strangely it seemed to be getting worse. My breath was quite ragged and my heart banged inside my chest.

'Are you OK, Madeline?' he said, bending his head to-wards me, a look of concern in his now flint-grey eyes.

Before I knew what happening, I moved towards him.

I stood there for a second. Our eyes locked. I felt as if an electric charge had surged through me. Time stood still.

I struggled to breathe. Every fibre of my body willed me

to submit to this beautiful big man. My head was full of Jack. The Birdie & Bramble. Dad. Marcus. Wine. Confusion. Timing. London. I was in suspended animation. I wanted to kiss him so badly and as he moved towards me, my phone, lying on the rug, rang, breaking the moment.

We both looked down. Brad Pitt's face came up on the screen.

It was Marcus.

'You better get that,' he said, stepping back.

'I'm sorry,' I said. 'I ... just ...'

'No ... I'm sorry,' he said, turning away.

'Jack ...' I said, but it was too late. The formality was back, the phone still ringing, he brushing himself down, coughing. 'You better get that ... I'll get all our stuff together. It's time we went.'

I didn't know what to say. I was struck dumb. I felt like such an idiot, as he gathered all our stuff up and put it roughly in the basket.

The moment had gone. I had wanted to respond. God had I wanted to respond. It had felt like the most natural thing in the world but it was completely left field. I had no idea he had any feelings for me. I was delirious with joy and yet at the same time completely shocked.

Suddenly sober. Embarrassed. Confused. I had no idea he even liked me like that. Maybe he didn't, maybe he felt sorry for me; after all, I had given him the full life story, which tended to make people feel very sorry for me. That was why I never told anyone. And then waffling on about that bloody picnic too ... But what a surprise! The kiss – it was so out the blue. Was it out of the blue? Was I being naive? I'd handled it so so badly. My body had responded like we were one half of a whole. All I had wanted was to sink into his lips, his arms, his embrace and then Marcus. Oh God what a mess. I hadn't answered his call.

'OK, that's us ready to roll,' he barked and off he walked, flanked as ever by Duke and Gaston.

Rubbing my face with my hands to wake myself up and check it wasn't all a terrible nightmare, I trudged down the path behind him feeling distinctly wobbly. By the time I got to the Land Rover he was in the driver's seat, the dogs were in the back, the passenger door open, the engine idling. Sheepishly I climbed in. He politely waited until I put my belt on and pulled away wordlessly.

The set of his jaw made it clear there was no discussion to be had. I felt panicky. At sea. At a loss. We trundled back in silence. When he pulled up outside the shop I turned and – he was still looking straight ahead – I thanked him pointedly for a lovely day and as I opened the door, tears threatened to pour down my face. I tucked Frank under my arm and climbed out.

'Goodbye, Madeline,' he said as I closed the door. He was off in a shot. Relieved Noel was on the phone when I rushed past, I took refuge in the bothy and tried to work out what had just happened. I was in knots. I had a boyfriend in London. Or did I? Well sort of. Yes, Jack was the most delicious gorgeous handsome thing I had ever seen but it hadn't even crossed my mind he liked me like that. He was so cool and distant. I genuinely thought he felt sorry for me, alone on my day off and just took me along for the ride.

Getting ready to go to work, I could not settle as I relived the moment we kissed again and again. Flashes of heat surged through my body. God what was wrong with me? Why hadn't I grabbed him and wrestled him to the ground – it was a mystery. Carpe diem. I hadn't even dared to imagine him fancying me as a possibility, which is why it had come

267

as such a shock. The last man to kiss me was Marcus and I was rather shocked at the response one kiss from Jack had elicited from my senses. Marcus and I had enjoyed a very physical relationship but this felt so very different. When it came to men I had no faith in my judgement and at this point the last thing I needed was the added complication of another man in my life.

I made up my mind to clear the air the next time we met and then we could get back to normal and put it down to experience, but it would have to wait until tomorrow as I was late for work ... again.

Chapter 26

I didn't have time to give it another thought as the restaurant was hoaching by the time I arrived. Our tight team worked its magic and another happy band of customers came and went amidst promises to return soon. The figures were great and as William pointed out to Mouse and I, with all the rushing around, the weight was dropping off us.

'You two better watch it, you're not a very good advert for my cooking,' he joshed as my skirt seemed to whirl round my waist with no effort. I hadn't really thought about it but it had been tight as hell a couple of weeks ago, and at this rate it would need taking in. A look at Mouse confirmed she was the incredible shrinking woman too – her black maxi dress hung from her shoulders in swathes so it was hard to see how much weight she had lost but if the spare material in that dress was anything to go by, it was a lot.

There were a few familiar faces in that evening. Locals who had been before, a couple of my old school friends and some tourists, which was most gratifying. One face in particular I recognised but couldn't yet put a name to was a bottle blonde. She was memorable for all the wrong reasons, as William had said: 'With teeth like those, she could eat an apple through a tennis racquet.' Smiling at the memory of our bitchy conversation, I racked my brain. I was fairly sure she'd been at the opening, and maybe once in-between times so I reckoned this was her third visit. I welcomed her back with a smile, which she ignored as I took her coat and she sashayed past me into the window seat sitting down like she owned the place. I must remember to ask someone who Harry the Horse is, I thought, as I approached the table with the menu.

'Nice to see you again,' I said. 'Would you to see the wine list?'

'No, a large gin and tonic – ice and lemon,' she barked.

Charming, I thought, as I made my way to the bar to mix it up.

The door opened and the dreaded Barclay MacPherson bumbled in. Craning his fat neck round until he clocked Harry the Horse, he walked over and sat down roughly in the chair opposite.

Of course! She was Tooty MacPherson. The Laird's wife.

Infuriated, I stomped into the kitchen. 'What the hell is he doing here?'

'Who?'

'Barclay MacPherson, he just came in – Harry the Horse is his wife!!'

'Really? Shit!'

'What do you think he's doing here?'

'Probably hungry,' he said.

'But what will I do?'

'Rise above it, serve him. This is your business and he's a customer. End of.'

'God, easier said than done,' I said, emotions rising. Could I serve this horrible individual – the one who had ousted me from my father's flat a matter of days after his demise. It was going to take all my strength.

William was watching me carefully. Mind-reading as usual. 'Maddy?'

I took a very deep breath. 'Of course you're right,' I said, smoothing down my whirling skirt, pinching my cheeks to get some colour into them, fixing a smile in place and re-entering the fray. 'Fuck him,' I said, grin in place, marching confidently over to their table.

'Good evening, Mr MacPherson, can I get you a drink?' I grimaced, trying to hide the clenched teeth.

'Large gin,' he said.

'And the menu?' I said, holding it out for him to take.

'Steak. Rare,' he barked and turned back to the blonde.

'And you, madam?' I enquired, fixed smile in place.

'Salad.'

'And ...'

'No "ands", just a salad,' she said, effectively dismissing me.

'Certainly,' I said, backing away. Obnoxious swine. I left them to it, retaining my professional exterior whilst inside wanting to lamp the pair of them.

The room was busy so I had no time to ruminate on them and their appalling manners. I efficiently delivered their drinks and in due course their meals. Moments later I was summoned again.

'I hope everything was OK?' I asked, clocking the virtually untouched steak in front of him. They looked at each other and said nothing so I persevered. 'Can I get you something else?'

'The bill,' the blonde snapped.

Rather taken aback, I did as they asked. They paid the exact amount, cash, no tip, and off they went.

At the end of service William and I always analysed the evening. Tonight everything was very positive apart from the bizarre behaviour of Barclay and the blonde.

'He was probably just trying to upset you – he's such a balloon,' said Mouse.

'Yeh,' said William, 'and he's bound to have heard on the grapevine that The Birdie & Bramble is going like a fair.'

I nodded. I was too tired to second-guess what their latest shenanigans might entail and I had no doubt if there was a reason for visiting The Birdie & Bramble, we would find out what it was soon enough.

Chapter 27

The following morning I was up even earlier than usual making an extra effort to battle my hair. I dug out the petrol-blue scarf that Dad always said made my eyes look greener than the sea. I was taking the high ground and was off to walk along the beach, find Jack and clear the air. After all there was no point in ruining a perfectly good friendship over one silly kiss, I thought, putting on my lip gloss and checking my teeth to make sure they were clean as a whistle, feeling sick.

The beach had been busier than ever; summer had really arrived. The usual dogs and their owners were in evidence with a few more besides. There were clumps of people in golf gear. The bucket and spade brigade were out in force too. This meant I had to keep Frank on the lead, as he had decided many years before that his mission in life was to try and invade any sandcastle built on his beach. Believing they were ripe for demolition he would barrel up, shouldering the soft malleable structure flat down before lifting his leg as a final insult and galloping off, leaving the upset child and his bucket behind.

But this morning the beach was deserted. The tourists and golf fans, and anyone with any sense, would be in bed or eating a full cooked Scottish breakfast.

I stood inhaling the cool salty air and saw Jack in the distance. He raised his arm and waved.

273

A flutter of excitement passed through me as a smile broke through and I walked toward him.

Mature woman tackling embarrassing moment head on, I thought.

Frank galloped ahead. Jack was walking alongside someone at a considerably slower pace. I hesitated when I noticed, but he waved me over.

Approaching the pair of them, I could see his companion was Flora.

'Granny, this is Maddy,' he said tentatively, I suspected to test if she remembered meeting me before.

'Lovely to meet you,' I said, smiling into her twinkly dark blue eyes.

'Let's have a look at you,' she said, peering at me right up close. 'Macular degeneration – it's a bugger. Lovely freckles.' She released my arm.

'Thank you,' I said, looking at Jack who smiled at her and then turned his gaze on me.

She wrinkled up her nose. 'Have we met?'

I smiled. 'Yes, we have. We met at The Birdie & Bramble – the opening party – you popped in with Jack for a glass of champagne.'

'Oh The Birdie & Bramble! I love The Birdie & Bramble!' she said, leading Jack further along the beach with gusto. 'What a glorious day!' she said, tilting her head up towards the sun, smiling, tottering slightly. Jack noticed and held out his arm, which she grabbed.

'Indeed it is.' Jack paused.

Then stopping, she turned round and observing me with a look of suspicion added, 'Yes, The Birdie & Bramble! Ha! I'm cuckoo!'

Not sure what she meant, I looked at Jack who shrugged.

'A cuckoo is a mad person,' she said, fully aware of our

exchange of glances. 'I'm a bit dotty, I think – Jack! Am I dotty?'

'Not dotty—' he paused '—eccentric,' he said gently.

She smiled, rather pleased with that.

'You knew Maddy's dad Joe – he had The Birdie & Bramble for years. Joe Campbell,' he said slowly.

Her eyes shifted, focused on something in the distance and then her face broke into a smile. 'Joe,' she said.

We both waited.

Nothing was forthcoming. She was lost in thought for a moment and she exhaled. There was no more to be said.

I took up the mantle, keen to stimulate any memory she may have. 'Yes, Dad loved the restaurant, The Birdie & Bramble. And now, after all this time, I'm beginning to love it too.'

This was as big a surprise to me as anyone. As far as I was aware, I had never even thought those words in that order, but there they were, and they had just come tumbling out of my mouth with a degree of certainty, which I found rather shocking. 'Oh!' I said, sounding unhinged and then apropos of nothing, 'Did I just say that?' I exclaimed.

Guffaw. 'You're dotty!' said Flora as I caught her eye.

We both burst out laughing.

'You mean eccentric,' I retorted and we graduated to snorting. She asked a few pertinent questions.

'Who are you?'

'Madeline Campbell.'

She looked at me again and smiled.

I smiled back. She looked a little lost again.

'It's a beautiful day,' I offered.

Turning to the blue blue sky, she smiled. 'It is that.'

We walked on a little further. Frank was getting antsy.

'I was hoping to bump into you,' I said in a low voice to Jack. 'I wanted to say sorry...'

He shrugged. 'Forget it,' he said. 'I just misread the situation... I was out of order.'

'No...' But before I could continue, my infernal phone alarm went.

Damn. 'I'm sorry but you'll have to excuse me. I have to get back to the restaurant to sign for the deliveries. William's having a well-earned long lie-in.'

'Restaurant,' said Flora.

'Yes,' I confirmed. As we all stopped to say goodbye, Flora bent forward to look at me again. Her gaze dropped from my freckly hooter to the chain round my neck.

Gently she picked it up and ran her fingers over the charm. 'It's pretty isn't it?' I said.

She smiled.

'I wear it every day cos it reminds me of my dad.'

She held it in her hand gently.

I looked at Jack.

'Come on, Gran, let's let Maddy get back to work – we are due at Rufflets for coffee in twenty minutes.'

She released my necklace and looking at me said 'Cuckoo' again.

'OK, shall we go to The Birdie & Bramble for lunch one day? Would you like that?' offered Jack as a distraction. She smiled.

'Oh yes!' she said and with a renewed sense of purpose turned to Jack.

'Righty-ho off we go!' she said, leading him away back the way they came. He gave me such a sweet smile, a head-tilting gentle smile acknowledging this lovely old lady meant the world to him. My heart melted.

★

Deliveries arrived on time and I have to confess I was getting more than twitchy as it was nearly midday when William finally burst into the restaurant.

'Sorry I'm late,' he shouted. 'I slept in. I have never slept in. God!'

'No problem,' I shouted from the kitchen as the door flew open and our first table arrived.

I kept them talking, got them drinks, bread, butter and some olives and by the time they ordered, William was vaguely under control.

Forty-five minutes later we were packed. It was fast and furious and we had only one table left when a very soberly dressed woman marched in.

'Afternoon,' I said, smiling at her. 'Table for one?'

'No thank you. I am looking for Madeline Campbell.'

'That's me!' I said, breezily trying to counteract her dour expression.

'Environmental Health,' she said, producing an ID badge from the inside pocket of her blue jacket. 'We have a report of a rat infestation on your premises. I am here to do a spot check.'

Appalled she did not lower her voice to impart this devastating news, I gently ushered her over to the bar area as it was clear the table nearest us had heard exactly what she said and they understandably looked more than a little concerned.

I could have strangled her.

I'd deal with them later. 'Follow me,' I said and led the woman into the kitchen where I blurted the devastating news to William. He took off his apron and came rushing out from behind the stove ... Thinking on his feet as ever, he offered to show the woman everything she wanted to see as I tried to work out what on earth to say to the customers.

It was obvious that someone had been spreading rumours that we had vermin. True or not, the attitude of 'there is no smoke without fire' would always prevail, so I had to come up with a story for the customers and fast.

By the time I re-entered the dining room, the best I could come up with was we had a suspected gas leak. So one by one I explained to the customers, we had a problem and for their safety we had to clear the area.

No-one argued. They looked concerned, gathered themselves and their belongings together as I waived their bills and apologised profusely, opening the door and watching them go.

After putting the snib down on the door, I entered the kitchen. The woman from Environmental Health, torn-faced, was now clad in a white plastic suit flashing her torch and poking about in the underbelly of the kitchen, determined to find a rat.

'I don't know who has said what, but you could eat your dinner off that floor,' I said to the woman's back.

Ignoring me, she prodded, scribbled, got her thermometer out, took the temperatures in the fridges and asked a few pertinent and impertinent questions. William was calm and answered in a level manner. I on the other hand wanted to punch her. Livid. I mean did she have to turn up in the middle of a lunchtime service? Had she no idea how hard it was to run your own business? Who had reported it? Actually rephrase that, there was nothing to report. So who had made up such a heinous lie?

I asked the last of those questions out loud to her directly.

'I'm not at liberty to say,' she said.

'No-one is ever in the kitchen apart from us – even if we did have a rat, none of our customers would have seen it,' I said, catching William's eye. He was drawing his hand across his throat – meaning 'shut the hell up or I will kill you.'

She noted something on her pad.

'That sort of attitude is not going to help. Vermin are a very serious matter,' she said. 'However, from the investigation I have just made, it does seems everything is in order.'

From hate to love in a heartbeat.

William and I looked at each other. I took a deep breath.

'We have a pest control book and a Rentokill certificate saying we are up to date,' said William, handing the relevant paperwork over calmly.

She scrutinised it quietly as Hamish came in and on hearing what was going on, he set about her with a charm offensive that would have had turned Genghis Khan into a pussy cat.

'How does he do that?' I said to William as the woman capitulated and told Hamish that her report was 'clean bill of health'.

Mouse's face glowed. 'Isn't he wonderful?' she gasped.

I rolled my eyes.

'OK, William, what needs to be done?'

'She has highlighted two small areas for improvement, neither of which would have had any bearing on anything. 1) The extractor fan cover was loose. 2) There wasn't sufficient signage up for the recycling bins.'

'And that's it?'

'Yes.'

'So it's business as usual. Apart from that table who overheard the rat conversation.' I cringed. Whoever they were, I hoped to goodness they hadn't left running through the street screeching about a rat in the kitchen.

It was difficult not to speculate as to who was behind such a low blow. 'The obvious candidate is Barclay MacPherson trying to undermine what we're building and keeping the value of the business low. But would he stoop to that level?' I said.

'And she did say the complainant was a she,' added Hamish.

We sat and threw around a few ideas, none of which sounded plausible. A competitor?

'All the other businesses round here support each another as there are plenty of customers to go round,' said William.

'Well, my only worry is that table who were sitting beside the door – I'm pretty sure they heard what the Environmental Health woman said.'

'Had they booked a table or were they a walk-in?' I checked the bookings book. 'Walk-in.'

'So we have no way of contacting them.'

We fell into silence again.

'Well with a bit of luck they were passing through and will leave it at that.'

Waking up the next morning, it appeared I had been rather optimistic. 'Fuck,' was all William said when I answered my phone at 8.30 a.m.

'What?'

'Those people who were there when the rat woman was in – they've written about it on TripAdvisor.'

'What?'

'Listen. "Newly opened and highly recommended, we went to The Birdie & Bramble today. The staff were friendly, the atmosphere lively and we had just settled down to our langoustine starter when a woman arrived in the restaurant to investigate reports of a rat in the kitchen. We left quickly and will not return."'

William and I talked it through before I got online and responded.

'From time to time Environmental Health do spot checks on all establishments that handle and prepare food. Our systems are strict and our hygiene and customer satisfaction paramount. Unfounded reports cannot be foreseen and whether a competitor or someone who bears a grudge has tried to ruin us, we are not sure. However, we are delighted to report we were not found to be lacking in any of the systems and levels expected. We were reopened immediately.'

'That's the best we can do,' I said.

The other reviews up there were brilliant.

I hadn't even read TripAdvisor since we'd reopened. I hadn't had a moment.

'It is an unfortunate part of business these days,' said William. 'If you engage with it you have to do so just about every day and if you don't, people think you're arrogant. Either way you're damned. I hate it.'

'Me too,' I said. 'So what do we do?'

'Rise above it. We have no option.'

We sat in silence on the phone for a moment, then William had a brainstorm.

'Hey, what about Ewan, the editor of the local rag? He made a great speech at your dad's wake – he might help us set the record straight.'

'Ewan Blair,' I said. 'Great idea, I'll give him a call.' So I did.

I arranged to meet him for lunch the following day. He was a journalist and a bon viveur and, true to form, the lure of a free lunch proved too much to resist. It just so happened it was the day designated for the photographer from the *Daily Telegraph* was due to come too.

BB the food critic had told the photographer the dishes she would be writing about and needed specific images to go with the copy. Gulp.

Cullen skink, venison in any guise and Thelma's Hazelnut

Cake. William made plans to stay on after service to make the dishes fresh so they looked their utter best – no matter what the accompanying review said.

Hamish was working the lunch shift and when Ewan arrived I joined him and we sat at the window table to eat and catch up. Niceties over, I came to the rub.

'Someone reported us to Environmental Health saying they a saw a rat in the kitchen.'

'For God's sake.'

'I know the inspector who came round gave us a clean bill of health but someone who overhead the conversation wrote about it on TripAdvisor. It's a nightmare.'

'Yes, I can see it's one of these things that can grow arms and legs,' said Ewan, shaking his head and squeezing fresh lime on the hot tempura fried squid that had just been placed in front of him. 'Mmmm. This is so good!'

'Thanks,' I said.

'So who do you think would do such a thing?' he asked, sporking another twirl of squid.

'Well I don't know for sure, but Barclay MacPherson owns this building and is desperate to buy the lease.'

With a substantial mouthful of food and unable to speak, Ewan rolled his eyes and nodded so I continued. 'He's already given us an offer, which I turned down flat.'

Ewan bent forward, lowering his voice to a whisper, 'Well confidentially—' he tapped the side of his nose '—I have contacts in the planning department and know for a fact Barclay has asked them on the QT about the feasibility of turning this whole building into a boutique hotel.'

'There you are!' I shouted. 'It must be him!'

'Sssssssh,' said Ewan. 'That has to stay between us.'

'Sorry,' I said, back down to whispering.

'But he is such a well-known figure round these parts, I'm not sure if even he would stoop to such tactics,' Ewan said.

'Well he was in here the other night with that leather handbag he calls his wife and I can't think of anyone else who would have it in for us. And if what you've just told me is true, that is quite an incentive for him to do his best to get us out.'

'Yes quite,' Ewan said, taking a swig of the Albariño I had chosen for him. 'Mmmm, this wine's delicious and it goes perfectly with the squid,' he mooned.

As I digested this new information, we changed the subject for a while just catching up on all the St Andrews gossip. The Open being imminent had changed the rhythm of the place already. It was busying up; the stand had been erected on the eighteenth green for the spectators, which gave it that iconic look, renowned worldwide. There was a palpable excitement and the streets were thronging with tourists.

Our main courses arrived. For Ewan, haunch of venison with mash, steamed asparagus and a red currant jus, and for myself fresh-caught mackerel and new potatoes.

His eyes sparkled as he tasted the meat. 'Melt in the mouth,' he said, smiling and staring at the plate in front of him.

'Try a glass of this,' I said, pouring the Rioja I had put aside for him earlier. He did.

By this time we had at least seven tables in. He looked around.

'Your father would so proud of you, Maddy. You've done a remarkable job with this place. Really, you are credit to him.' He raised his glass to a well-kept face on the other side of the room and smiled.

'Who's that?' I asked.

'George Farquharson, Secretary at the golf club,' he said. 'A great pal of your dad's.'

I smiled at him. The past few days and weeks had sped past and sometimes it even slipped my mind that Dad was no longer here. This was his place, his world, his friends. I had difficulty swallowing. 'Thanks, Ewan, that means a lot.'

At this point Hamish came over to the table and said discreetly, 'That guy hovering by the door is the photographer from the *Telegraph*.' He pointed.

'OK, let William know he's here and I'll be there in a minute.'

Ewan looked intrigued so I told him BB McGill had been in.

'Oh my God, that woman has a tongue that can wound at a hundred metres.'

'So I believe and as a result William is seriously wetting himself.'

He nodded. 'I'm not surprised. Well, no publicity is bad publicity – isn't that what they say?'

'Hmm.' I looked over.

Ewan sensed I wanted to go and speak to the photographer. 'Listen, Mads, you better go, and thank you so much for a cracking lunch,' he said. 'I'll be back and often.' We hugged and as I left him, he stood up to join George Farquharson at his table.

William was getting on famously with the photographer, who was already enjoying a cappuccino and a slice of freshly baked shortbread.

'As soon as the restaurant is clear we'll set a table and Lewis here will take the photos.'

'OK,' I said, helping myself to a piece of shortbread – the stuff was irresistible even on a full stomach.

'So ...?' I smiled.

'There's no point, Maddy, I've already tried. Lewis is a freelance photographer and has never even met BB McGill.'

'Oh,' I said, impressed at William's investigative powers. 'Do you at least know when it will be in the paper?'

'Yes,' he said.

I stopped shortbread eating mid chew and stared at him.

'Friday.'

'This Friday?'

'Yes.' He grinned.

For better or worse, it was going to be a hell of a weekend.

Chapter 28

Amidst all this madness, Hamish came up with a brilliant idea to take the pressure off the numbers streaming through the doors. Courtesy of a double espresso.

'Why don't we expand out onto the street? The weather is on our side and the pavement's wide enough, and of course we have enough chairs – well I do!'

I laughed. 'Of course!'

'Yeh, all those bloody chairs I bought at the auction are sitting in storage. I've not had a second to even think about renting them to anyone.'

I thought it was genius and after a brief chat, William, despite being under the cosh with the numbers already, agreed if it worked it would up our turnover considerably, so we decided to crack on with it there and then.

Hamish phoned Jack, who obligingly retrieved them from the store, piled them into his Land Rover and brought them straight round. Hamish called in some favours and borrowed a few bistro tables from round and about and William asked Noel to contact the local council and check the red tape side of things.

We set it all up, being mindful to avoid causing any obstructions and hey presto! We added another sixteen covers to our total. Almost half our capacity again.

It was an instant hit! Good weather was a godsend at this

time of year and everyone loves to sit outside and bask in the sun whilst being fed and watered.

William adjusted his orders and supplies accordingly and stripped the menu down for the outside tables to wine and tapas.

Noel reported the council were a bit iffy but eventually he talked them into granting us retrospective permission on the condition he filled out the necessary forms today and bless him, he did exactly that.

Hamish and Mouse committed to working full time, my theory being they would have committed to running naked round St Andrews as long as they could be in the same room at the same time, and so we expanded overnight just like that. Now we really were running at full tilt.

By now we were practically living at The Birdie & Bramble. Our eyes were on the end game and it was whizzing by with only a few days before the Open so we didn't have to sustain it for much longer – well we couldn't.

Amidst all this I kept my sanity by walking. Walking early in the morning and walking home at the end of a busy service during the warm, balmy summer nights was a tonic; my ears ringing from the constant chatter and clatter, my feet throbbing after walking miles and miles back and forth across the floor of the restaurant until the door closed at the end of the day. I would walk home barefoot, the coolness of the pavement a blessed relief to the hot soles of my feet.

Hamish and Mouse were stars. They worked every day and every night, keen to help and even keener to be together. They were virtually inseparable these days. Mouse was emerging as a confident young woman now, happy helping out front if required, her facial piercings removed, her white goth make-up scrubbed clean, her long curtain-like hair tied back – all this for purely practical reasons, and health and safety, but in the process it revealed her flawless skin and the most startling green eyes. She also came up with some wonderful ideas to enhance the look of our rather utilitarian menu, egged on and encouraged by an adoring Hamish.

And Hamish! Well his ratty beaded pigtail disappeared overnight, and his frayed wristbands were down to single figures. It was William I worried about most. He was irreplaceable. We had no sous chef, no back-up. Mouse helped prep as much as she could but without that indefinable magic that was William, the whole place would come to a juddering halt. Every night he would go straight home, soak in a bath, sleep like the dead, arriving back fresh and fired up for the next hectic day.

With literally days to go, even he was looking a little jaded.

'Are you sure you can keep this up?' I asked.

'It's not for much longer,' he said – not an answer, I noted, but I didn't press him. We were all at the end of our tether living on adrenalin, the finish line in sight.

I hugged him. 'The show must go on!' we said in unison.

Most mornings on the beach I met Jack. The awkward tongue-swelling, stuttering moments were becoming less intense as we had so much to say to one another. Too much. The après-kiss awkwardness long forgotten. Well when I say forgotten I could not imagine ever forgetting the feel of his mouth on mine, the lust that beat through my body like a drum was countered by the feeling I had known him forever. He talked, I butted in; I talked, he did the same. We swapped stories of everything that was going on. I banged on about The Birdie & Bramble, the customers, the ups and down, Hamish and Mouse, the fun and the general exhaustion, the perceived vendetta, the evil Laird, whilst Jack defused the madness with a different rhythm of life, one that involved the red deer coming off the Southern Perthshire estates, the fishing season now in full swing.

I would stomp along the beach quickly to keep up with his leisurely long-legged gait. I would rush along rapt as he regaled me with tales of his rambles up the Perthshire lochs catching wild trout, which he would periodically deliver to The Birdie & Bramble with a flourish. He described the making of the elderflower champagne, which was now bottled, the seasonal mushrooms now pushing up through the mossy hills. The great thing was thanks to the Open, all the businesses in the area were doing a rip-snorting trade. Halcyon days indeed.

And then it was here. The Open. All the build-up, pressure and associated stramash were basically all for this one week of golf. A good walk spoiled.

The final furlong. The home strait. The light at the end of the tunnel.

And if we thought it was busy before? We had no concept of what busy was, as the world and his wife arrived in St Andrews on the back of the entourage of golfers, their wives, their security. It was a tornado that transformed our sleepy, coastal idyll into another planet. The weather helped; it was glorious. The beach looked like California. The shorts and bikini brigade were out in force. The knotted hankies and red rotund bellies were there too, tucked behind striped windbreaks dotted along the beach and enjoying sandy sandwiches and being sprinkled by wet dogs rushing to and fro from the sea to the picnic rug. Children dashed everywhere, free of school and clocks, rock pooling, paddling, building sandcastles, playing frisbee.

During this time I had no time to speak to Marcus and when I got a rare moment to myself, I felt guilty that I had barely thought about him. Thursday after lunch I was outside having a breather when I saw a missed call from him and I picked up his message.

'Hi, Mads. Short notice but I'm coming up for the last day's play – we are doing some corporate hostility. Felicity is heading up and has given me a pass to come. I'm arriving on Saturday for two nights. They're putting us up at the Old Course?' Typical Marcus – the poshest hotel in town and tickets for the last day's play, which real golf fans would kill to attend. Marcus would undoubtedly spend his time schmoozing and boozing with an occasional look at the golf. Analysing his message, I wondered about the hotel – was he staying there because he was being thoughtful and didn't want to take anything for granted or maybe he just couldn't face staying in the 'outside toilet' as he had charmingly called the bothy. One way or the other I would find out soon.

I sent a one-word text back: *'Fab'*

'Will text when have my timings. Can't wait to see you. M x'

My stomach lurched. I sat down on one of the chairs and took stock. How was that going to play out?

It was a salutary reminder the Open would be over in a matter of days, my initial commitment to the business over.

My challenge fulfilled for better or for worse.

A revaluation would be the next thing on our list – a sobering truth.

Then I would return to my life, job and flat, my relationship, London. It was too much to think about as there was too much still to do.

I blocked it out of my thoughts and focused on the now. Breathe in. Breathe out.

As I sat outside gathering my strength to get up and get on with it, Hamish crashed through the doors.

'You're not going to believe this!'

'What?'

'The bloody council have just phoned and told us to get all the chairs and tables off the pavement.'

'What? Why?'

'We've been reported for not having a licence.'

'But they know we've applied retrospectively. It was all agreed – they said it was just a formality.'

'Yeh, I know, but apparently someone phoned and complained and insisted until we had the licence, we had no business clogging up the pavement.'

'Who was it?'

'Well obviously they wouldn't say.'

'I bloody bet I know who it was.' My blood boiled.

William joined us, concerned about the raised voices and the thunderous look on my face.

'You don't know for sure, Maddy,' he said, forever the gentleman.

'Come on, William, who else would go out of their way to try and make life difficult?' said Hamish, firmly in my corner.

'Well what's done is done – we will have to do as we are told or they could revoke our licence to serve at all.'

'Shit, I hadn't thought about that…'

'So it's all hands to the pump,' he said, picking up a chair and stacking it onto another one.

William as ever was talking sense but my blood pressure was at an all-time high. I felt like driving straight out to the Laird's house to have it out with him face-to-face. I was incandescent. William saw my contorted chops and suspected I was considering an assassination…

'Don't rise to the bait, Maddy, we have too much going on as it is. *Plus*, we don't know for sure it is him and—' he held his hand up as my mouth was open and ready to rant

'—if it is him, he will just revel in the fact he has managed to get to you – to us. So I vote we ignore him.'

'For what it's worth so do I,' added Mouse, handing me a camomile tea.

And then Hamish slipped his arm round Mouse's shoulders and chipped in the winning shot. 'Yes, and despite my chair business going into liquidation before it gets off the ground – I also agree wholeheartedly.'

So a democrat at heart. I allowed myself to be talked down.

Mouse and I began unsetting the outside tables, the boys stacked the chairs whilst assuring passers-by we were very much open for business – it was just our temporary terrace that was shut. Hamish called the cavalry, aka Jack, who obliging as ever said he could pick up the tables and chairs within the hour. True to form he appeared with the Land Rover well within time.

Still smarting, I canvassed him too.

'Can you believe someone has done this?' I said, hands on hips watching as he silently picked up the chairs one by one, stacking them carefully in the back of the four-wheel drive. I continued, 'I mean we're just a small local business. Who would do such a petty thing? I'm telling you, it's a bloody vendetta,' I ranted, waiting for a reaction.

A non-committal 'Yeh' was all he managed.

Gathering strength, I was off again. 'I can feel it in my water it's that bloody Barclay MacPherson,' I growled. 'He's had it in for us since day one. He owns this whole building you know – and would like nothing better than to shut us down and get us out,' I said, waving my pointy finger about. 'Well I can tell you it will be over my dead prone body that he ever gets a sniff of The Birdie & Bramble.'

During this diatribe Jack remained stoic, his jaw set, not uttering a word, until the pavement was clear.

'Is that all of them?' he asked, making no comment whilst looking positively thunderous.

'Yes it is,' I said, looking at him, willing him to get on his high horse on my behalf after venting my spleen.

By the look on his face it was obvious he didn't agree with my take on the matter. He didn't say one word! WTF? 'Some bloody friend,' I grumbled under my breath as he secured the back of the truck, said a gruff goodbye, ground his gears and was off.

Watching the Land Rover lurch along the road, I couldn't help but be deeply disappointed in Jack's reaction or lack of it. I naively thought we had become allies over the past few weeks but clearly I was wrong. He was so grumpy! I expected him to be furious at the thought of someone being so underhanded and petty. I expected him to say something supportive. Well I'd called this one wrong. Maybe all he cared about was shifting enormous amounts of his venison, which would explain why his face was tripping him. After all, sixteen covers down meant our turnover was going to go down significantly. I was frustrated at his lack of reaction. I thought he had more gumption. Well bugger him.

With that ruminating in my mind, customers began arriving for lunch and we were off again, so you can imagine my surprise when a couple of hours later Jack arrived at The Birdie & Bramble for lunch with Flora.

The man was an anathema.

Putting aside my earlier consternation, I decided to rally for Flora's sake. She didn't deserve to be inveigled in any of our ongoing shenanigans.

Her eyes twinkled as she stepped in, looking around.

'Oh I love this place,' she said, holding Jack's arms as I led them to the window table, the best seat in the house.

I stayed with them for a minute or two, to say hello, to take their drinks order. She peered closely at me and smiled gently, reaching out and touching my hand.

'Mary,' she said.

Startled, I stood up, but not wanting to alarm her, I gathered myself and sat down again.

'Mary was my mother,' I said, gently smiling. It was such a long time since I had heard her name I was rather taken aback. As was Jack.

'Mary,' Jack repeated, looking at her, his eyebrows aloft.

Flora smiled. 'Oh yes, Mary loved The Birdie & Bramble.'

She paused, distracted by the door flying open and four rather loud American guests ambling in, all talking at the same time. 'Bloody Americans,' she said. Jack rolled his eyes. You never quite knew what she was going to say.

The moment gone, I excused myself to get them menus. The throng of people was endless, and though I delivered iced water and some fresh warm bread straight from the oven it was a good ten minutes until I swooped back to their table to take their orders.

She looked up at me as I bent down to let her see me properly, taking into account her failing eyesight. As I did so, my chain fell forward from where it usually sat securely round my neck, and she took it gently in her hand. 'Pretty.'

'Yes, isn't it?' I agreed as she held onto it.

Jack gently coaxed her to let it go. 'Maddy is working, Gran, we can't keep her captive. Let it go,' he laughed. 'Would you like a glass of sherry?'

Dropping the gold charm, she answered in the affirmative so I went about my business.

That was the second time she had remarked on my

necklace. I couldn't help but wonder if she could tell me a little more about it.

Once Jack and Flora finished eating, there was a lull in service. As I delivered their coffees, I joined them again. I took my chain off and handed it to her.

'You like this, Flora?'

She focused on it for a third time. 'Cuckoo,' she said.

I looked at Jack, which was always difficult, in case he could read my mind, which was saying the most unspeakable things about him, his hands, and those eyes, and me and … I shrugged my shoulders at him and focused back on Flora.

'Gran, give Maddy her necklace back.'

Rather than relinquish it, she balled it up into her hand and closed her frail fingers around it with a look of determination and shook her head.

Jack looked alarmed. 'Granny?' he said as her face shut down and her hand remained tightly closed around it.

I could see she was becoming upset.

I shook my head at Jack and whispered, 'It's fine. It's fine …'

He smiled gratefully.

I stood up and finished the last few tables as Jack asked for his bill.

Helping Flora on with her coat, I noticed her hand was still firmly clasping the chain. Jack pulled me aside.

'I'm so sorry. I have no idea why she's taken such a shine to your necklace. It's not like her at all. She's usually so easy,' he said.

'Honestly don't worry. Just drop it off when you get the chance. She won't hang on to it forever,' I said, thinking this twist in fate meant I would be seeing him sooner rather than later, which gave me a lovely warm glow despite still smarting about the fact he didn't stick up for me earlier.

'That's very kind of you,' he said, slipping on his jacket. 'I don't quite know what to say.'

'Nothing to say,' I said as coolly as I could before asking Flora, 'Did you enjoy your lunch?'

'I'm hungry,' she said, turning to Jack who gently ushered her out despite her protestations she hadn't eaten in days.

I felt heartsore for Flora that her memory was slipping away. I wondered if she knew what a wonderful grandson she had. Despite his inability to stick up for me, I couldn't think of many people who would spend so much time with an elderly grandparent and exude such patience and understanding. Earlier in the day I had doubted his ability to be a supportive friend and now I was considering if he was officially perfect? I was clearly losing it.

Chapter 29

I had little time to ruminate on such things as it was officially mayhem.

From the second we arrived early in the morning, the phone didn't stop. People arrived looking for coffee from 8 a.m. and realising the demand was there, Hamish had slotted in an early dash to Rory's to buy a dozen or so croissants on his way to work. 'Every pound is a prisoner.' He laughed when I complimented him on his enthusiasm.

The Birdie & Bramble was packed all day and all night. Every table booked once, twice, thrice.

There was no denying William's original suggestion had seemed like an insurmountable climb, but to look back and see how far we had come in just five weeks was phenomenal.

It had been such a long shot – the whole ridiculous scheme – and not one of us in our wildest dreams imagined it would result in this.

Adrenalin was the only thing that kept us going; with eighteen-hour days, little sleep, minimal food, we were flagging but it wasn't forever.

Sunday was the last day of play at the Open. It was already Friday morning; we were nearly there.

Friday started the way it always did: walking, running, me arriving a few minutes later than I should and when Frank and I burst in, the others were huddled round the table reading the paper.

'Gosh, Hamish, I didn't know you could read,' I said, taking my jacket off to prepare for the day ahead, smirking at my hilarious joke. He raised his head, beaming.

'It's the review!' he announced. I felt sick. 'And it's a fucking triumph!' He stood up, kissing Mouse square on the lips, and punched the air as William, also beaming, slid the article under my nose as he rushed off to phone Noel.

It was the Restaurant Review Column by BB McGill in the national *Telegraph*. My heart was in my mouth.

I scanned through it.

'*A veritable institution in the seaside town of St Andrews, The Birdie & Bramble was recently reopened by the daughter of the original owner Joe Campbell. I had the dubious experience of eating here some eight years ago and chose not to file my copy for fear of being accused of being an assassin. It was of such a low standard. But this time, in the charmingly rustic restaurant, I was greeted warmly and within moments of being seated, a jug of iced water and fresh warm bread arrived with the menu. The menu lacks pretension of any sort. The Birdie & Bramble's set price menu (12.95 for 2-course lunch, 19.99 for 3) harks back to the days before foams, veloutés and liquid nitrogen became de rigueur in restaurant dining rooms up and down the country. Daily specials of locally caught lobster, haunch of venison and langoustines were displayed on the ubiquitous chalkboard. All dishes on the charmingly designed handwritten menu sounded equally appealing, all unnecessary words cleverly omitted from the menu. Smoked haddock pate and Melba Toast – a retro favourite from my childhood – was first choice. A ramekin of creamy, smoky fish pâté – generous fibres of fish evident amongst the fresh herbs, lemony tangs. A set butter topping with a shoogle of paprika. Simple but perfect. The Melba Toast transparently thin yet crunchy, warm and perfect for salty butter to smear over. My, how things have changed.*

'*Licking my lips, it was with trepidation I awaited my venison main, cynically thinking I had already met the star of the show. I was so wide of the mark as the melt-in-the-mouth, medium rare rich haunch of venison was without a doubt – smelling salts for regular readers – the best roe deer I have tasted. The texture, the flavour, the right amount of resting, the richness, I could go on – just imagine the most wonderful thing you have ever eaten and times it by ten. The art of the food critic is to remain neutral, give nothing away, and as I seeped up the last meaty juices from this plate, my face puckered as I fought to keep the grin off my face.*

'The dessert, a simple chocolate pot, was far from simple. Depth, intensity and creaminess the perfect finish to – dare I say – the perfect meal. Rumours abound The Birdie & Bramble is closing at the end of the summer, so I urge you to go. Go as soon as you can. Go now! And when you do, I will be the grinning lone diner in the corner. Simply superb.'

I jumped on a chair and punched the air too.

'Her face was puckering not grumping! I thought she hated it but she loved it!'

Mouse burst into tears and William returned grinning from the kitchen. 'It is a knicker-wettingly fabulous review,' I blurted.

'I couldn't have written it better myself,' William conceded.

'Is BB McGill on the payroll?' Hamish chirped.

'She is now,' I laughed.

'I love her,' said William, tears filling his tired eyes.

'I want her children,' Hamish said, then seeing Mouse's face changed that to: 'I will name our firstborn after her – even if it's a boy!'

It was just what we needed to give us that extra oomph to push this last weekend over the line. We ripped it out, scanned it, put it in the window. Hamish copied it again and again until the whole front window was filled with copies of the review and there was one on every table.

Nine out of ten. The only reason we had lost a point was because nothing was perfect, though she couldn't pinpoint exactly what.

Without missing a beat we were back up and at it, as despite BB McGill, encouraging the hordes to head to The Birdie & Bramble we could not be any busier. We physically had no more seats, there were no more hours in the day, but there was no doubt such wonderful words would add extra clout for our imminent revaluation.

As the day progressed everyone congratulated us. Customers and suppliers and tourists got caught up in the excitement, popping in to say well done. Sarah dropped in just to give me a hug and insisted on coming into the kitchen and shaking William's hand, declaring she and her entire family were lifelong customers forever, which they were anyway but it was still lovely to hear. Late afternoon we closed the door for an hour, to regroup and draw breath. I had just scoffed a bowl of soup when the front door opened.

'Sorry we don't open for another fifteen minutes,' I said, my mouth full of bread, turning round, and coming face-to-face with The Merchant of Venison, who was grinning from ear to ear.

'Sorry I didn't come in earlier – I just heard. Maddy.' He looked deeply into my eyes; my knees predictably wobbled. 'Well done you ... you're an absolute star.'

I swallowed my bread, jumping up, but still felt like I had a boulder in my throat. I was so happy he had come in, I just stood facing him, eye to eye, grinning like a loon, recognising this unfamiliar feeling as unadulterated joy. He was supportive. I had been wrong; he was in my corner. I had no words.

Hamish came bowling out of the kitchen. 'Oh it's you,' he said to Jack somewhat coolly.

'Hi, Hamish. I just wanted to say congratulations,' he said.

'Is that all?' he asked mysteriously, holding Jack's gaze.

Bloody Hamish was still harping on about Jack's lack of support over the snake who'd reported us to the council.

'Would you like a cup of tea?' I asked, trying to break the deadlock and hopefully encourage Jack to stay around for at least another few minutes. I hadn't seen him for a day or so and everything about me felt better when he was in the room.

Jack looked at Hamish, who responded by saying, 'Actually, mate, we're really up the wall ...' quite rudely.

Jack took the hint. 'Right, OK, thought as much. I'll take a rain check on the tea, Maddy. I'd better be off.'

And he was gone. I rounded on Hamish. 'What the hell was that about?'

But before he could answer, the front door opened again and in wandered a familiar-looking face. I scrutinised it, grabbed my soup plate and rushed into the kitchen.

'William! I think Jack Nicklaus has just come in.'

William was round the other side of the stove in a flash, piling through to the restaurant, his face beaming as he sashayed towards Mr Nicklaus and his guests.

'Mr Nicklaus, it's a privilege,' he said to the smiling blonde American man, who retorted, 'The privilege is all mine. I come to The Birdie & Bramble every time I'm in town.' His face fell. 'I was so sorry to hear about Joe.'

'This is his daughter, Maddy,' William said, ushering me in front of him. 'She's responsible for keeping it all going.'

His booming voice filled the air. 'I've told these guys all about The Birdie & Bramble.' He turned to his guests, an entourage of twelve, some golfers and some officials from the

R&A. Their booking was under the name Nicklaus, which should have been a clue but we were so rushed off our feet none of us had noticed. Well my goodness we did now. Oh my God! No sooner had we settled them down and taken their drinks order than the door flew open again and three women came tottering in, amidst snorts of laughter and over-whelming clouds of perfume. All mutton dressed as mutton, wearing unfashionably high heels and short skirts revealing crepey knees, Chanel jackets and a variety of different chest shapes jutting out and up, defying gravity. They plonked themselves at the table right next to the golfers without checking in with any of the staff, scraped their chairs along the floor noisily as they hung their vast expensive handbags on the backs of their chairs.

'Can I take the name of the booking please?' I asked, trying not to bear my teeth.

'Sharp,' barked one of them. By name and by nature, I thought, as I scored the name off the bookings list.

'Girl!' one of the other women shouted at me. 'Drinks!'

'Oh here she is,' screeched another of the harridans as a fourth clashing cloud of perfume whooshed through the door. It was Tooty MacPherson. No show without Punch, I thought bristling.

I walked over to hand them the wine list and one of them whispered something behind her hand and they all stopped what they were saying and just stared at me. I had just come on shift and was looking fairly tidy and organised or so I thought until the eyes of this lot settled on me. I feared my skirt was tucked into my pants or I had a smear of chocolate pud, which I had recently scoffed in the kitchen, down my face, but they carried on.

Ignoring the wine list, Tooty barked, 'Four large Hendrick's gin and Fever-Tree tonics.'

Hamish mixed them super fast, adding the requisite slice of cucumber, not wanting to give this table of trouble the slightest opportunity to criticise.

I heard the clink and 'Chin chin!' as they slugged it down. It was the only silence to be heard from the table all night.

The evening moved on, every table busy. The golfers and their entourage were utterly charming. They happily signed autographs for those brave or pissed enough to ask. They were patient when their food took ages to come out, understanding we were rushed off our feet. They selected the most expensive wines on our list, which as far as I was concerned meant they could move in permanently. They also left a stoating tip. William had played a blinder, his penultimate night in the kitchen. It wasn't until 10.30 p.m. that Tooty and the witches demanded their bill.

Handing it over to the ringleader, Tooty took her cue. 'So, daaaahling, you must be Madeline?' she said, curling her lip up to reveal smudged fatty lipstick on her tombstone teeth, reminding me why I hated the full version of my moniker.

'Yes,' I smiled.

'Well well well. I thought so,' she said.

I smiled politely, simmering as she played her game.

'I'm sorry ...' I stammered, 'but ...'

'Oh of course, he's such a dark horse ... I hear you've been seeing quite a lot of James?'

The others swivelled their boozed-up eyes and over-made-up faces in my direction.

'I'm sorry?' I said. 'Forgive me but I'm a little confused ... James?'

'James,' said one of the others through the gap in her nicotine-stained teeth.

'I don't mean to be rude but I honestly don't know what

303

you're talking about,' I said, a twirl of anxiety warning me this was not going to be good.

'Her stepson,' said one of the harridans, pointing her orange talon at Tooty.

'I'm sorry, I'm not quite with you. I'm not sure I know a James.'

The ringleader butted in again impatiently. 'Oh sorry, of course ... I mean Jack! Darling Jack!' She turned to her coven. 'That's what he calls himself these days.'

I must have reddened.

'Barclay mentioned the two of you are thick as thieves and I thought I simply *must* introduce myself – after all, at this rate I could be your mother-in-law,' she crowed, throwing her head back with a parrot-like screech of laughter.

A strange pickling sensation crawled up my neck. I stared back at her.

'We are talking about the same man here aren't we, sweetie? James, or as you might know him ... Jack MacPherson?'

As if this wasn't hard enough, one of the others added, 'Yah, you know ... The Merchant of Venison?'

My mouth hung open. I was in shock.

'MACPHERSON darling,' she said slowly, as if I had donated my brain to science, 'as in Barclay.'

Barclay MacPherson. The Laird. My father's nemesis. The man who had evicted me from the only home I had ever known and was in the process of trying to ruin my already fairly ruined business. I felt physically sick. I held tightly onto the back of the nearest chair. My pasty face and sick expression must have made her next question rhetorical.

'Oh – didn't you know?' she drawled, vaping wildly and blowing a cloud of droplets in my face.

I felt like I might pass out.

'Excuse me,' I mumbled, hanging onto the backs of the other chairs to make my way to the kitchen.

I practically fell in the door.

'Good God, Maddy, what's wrong with you?' William clocked I was in distress straight away.

'Did you know?'

'What?'

'Did you know about Jack?'

'What?'

'He's Barclay MacPherson's son.'

William stopped what he was doing, eyes popped and his jaw hanging.

'WHAT?'

I glanced at Hamish. He was puce. He knew. 'You knew,' I accused. 'How could you?' I hissed, shaking as I scrabbled about trying to find my coat in the overpopulated hook on the back of the door.

Mouse was already untying her apron, and taking out her few remaining piercings. 'Listen, Maddy, you go – I can handle this.' She looked at Hamish with venom. 'We will cope. You – just go …'

I had never loved anyone more.

My entire body was trembling. Livid. Angry. Speechless. Shocked. Jack MacPherson. The snake in the grass. The low-down dirty double-crossing swine. How could he? Why would he? All the inside info he could have been giving his red-faced buffoon of a father. He knew every single thing that had been going on. I had used him as a sounding board, admittedly a very silent one, which all of a sudden made perfect sense. No wonder he didn't join in my diatribe when I pilloried Barclay – it was his father. Feeling physically sick, I walked out of the front door of The Birdie & Bramble, ignoring Tooty who was waving me over. I stomped on past the bothy, heading on the road out of town, the opposite road to the one I walked every morning to meet Jack. Enraged. I was never going near the beach again.

As I walked I shook with anger; I couldn't believe I had been completely hoodwinked. That sweet-faced man with his bloody eyes was a bloody Oscar-winning actor, advising me on how to do this and that, when all along it was in his best interests to get me to sign over the lease and give his dad and thus him presumably exactly what they wanted.

The furious sky matched my mood, rolling dark clouds, a deep violet blue-black and distant rumbles of thunder as I stomped, head up, hands rammed in pockets, until my breath was ragged and I realised I was quite a long way from where I wanted to be.

Stopping and turning, I saw the lights of St Andrews in the distance. How far had I come? I wondered. The breeze had picked up, bending the trees, whistling through the copse and chilling me to the bone, which brought me to my senses. I was the first one to caution people against getting stuck out in the middle of nowhere, believing summer in Scotland was a balmy affair when in reality the temperature could drop like a stone with no warning whatsoever. I needed to get back.

Catching my breath I looked back over the wild east coast and wondered what the hell I was doing here anyway. Counting the hours was over and I was ready to go right now. Fuming. My phone went. Brad Pitt appeared.

'Hey, babe,' he said.

'Hi, how are you? Where are you?' I asked, panicking.

'Flight was delayed, we're just waiting for a taxi from Glasgow now.'

Oh God, yes of course – today was the day he was coming up. How awful was I – I had completely forgotten.

'Oh ... so ...'

I couldn't tell if he was expecting to come over or not but as far as I was concerned it was a not. Not after the day I'd just had.

Picking up on my hesitation he said, 'So I think I'll just check in to the hotel as I don't want to disturb you. We won't get there 'til about 2 a.m.'

Relief flooded through me. Followed by guilt.

'Can we see each other tomorrow? I've corporate hospit-ality all day, so any time that suits you?'

'I am up to my neck in it. Tomorrow's the last day, but text me later tomorrow night and I'll do my best to get away,' I said as the wind blew into the receiver and our connection was lost.

Maybe I had been hasty about Marcus, assuming he was incapable of growing up, of changing. He did sound more on it, more thoughtful, not just crashing into my bed in the middle of the night, the night before our last day at the restaurant. Well I would see him tomorrow and keep an open mind; after all, this trip was the ideal opportunity to prove his excessive partying was a thing of the past and to redeem himself. Walking back to the bothy, I concluded the sooner I got out of St Andrews and back to my life in London, the better. I was fooling myself that I could ever live in this tiny little place where everyone knew your business and, as I had just been reminded, knew it better than you did yourself. I was finished with St Andrews. The party was literally over.

By the time I got home, I was cold, unhappy and just wanted to go to bed.

Frank was waiting for me, wagging and happy. I picked up the loyal little subject and snuffled him as I lay down on the bed and, fully clothed, crawled under the covers and fell asleep.

Chapter 30

Morning came too soon but this morning, despite Frank's eager face, I was not going to the beach and I was not going to meet Jack or James or whatever his bloody name was. I had plans to make and he was not, nor would he ever be, part of those. I was onto him and he could bugger off.

I showered, changed, slapped loads of moisturiser on my wind-burnt face and headed out the door. Without thinking, I opened the door and without waiting for me to clip his lead on, Frank was off. Of course he had no idea we were on a different route today and so he was off at a lick towards the beach.

'Frank!' I shouted.

He turned briefly and looked at me, his stumpy wee tail wagging madly. He thought we were playing the game we played most mornings. Chase. Only this time it was for real. I needed to catch him before he got to the beach. Those little legs moved fast and as my shouting became more desperate, his speed seemed to increase. By the time I fell against the railings above the beach, my lungs screaming, I could see the hairy white dot was so far ahead of me I didn't stand a chance of catching him.

As I gulped air, my rib cage felt like it might crack and my heart might burst. And then there they were, like two elegant scribbles in the distance, loping over the dunes and running along to meet their vertically challenged friend. I felt like I might be sick as just behind them the now familiar gait of The Merchant of Venison strode on down to the flat of the beach. He was looking round for me having spotted Frank. I stood back, watching. A minute or two later he spotted me and began waving wildly and gesturing for me to come on down to the beach. I looked at him with a deep sense of sadness as those longed-for moments of seeing him, talking to him, confiding in him, I realised were all a lie. Fury filled me. How could he? A sob escaped as a text pinged in.

'Hey, slowcoach, are you coming down or what?' It was from him. I looked up. He stood with his arms out in a questioning way.

Twenty-four hours ago I dreamt of running towards his open arms, wrapping myself round his rangy body and kissing him so deeply we were utterly lost in the moment. But right now, if I had an air rifle, I would have used it. The bastard. I texted back.

'No, JAMES. Not today, not tomorrow and not until hell freezes over.' SEND.

I saw him looking down at his phone, step back as if he had been slapped and look up. I couldn't read his expression from there but he was most definitely surprised. Wondering how I'd found out, no doubt.

'Frank!' I shouted. 'FRANK!' But he was lost to the game of cat and mouse he was playing with Duke and Gaston and could no longer hear me.

I had a choice.

Tear along the beach and try to gather Frank up, which would end up in an embarrassing scene of upset and blustering, or text Jack or James or whoever the hell he was and ask him to look after Frank 'til later. I chose the latter.

'James. I have to go to work. Please take Frank back with you

and drop him at The Birdie & Bramble on your way through town. Thank you. M.'

Succinct and to the point and fuck him.

Turning on my heels, I made my way back to the bothy for a super-quick shower and change and then The Birdie & Bramble. Unable to eat anything, I downed a coffee and, shaky as hell, got ready for work.

The restaurant was saving my life.

It had suppressed my grief, my anger, my disappointment, kept me occupied. With every hour that passed, the pressure rose, reality receded and I had the unsettling feeling I was on some sort of runaway train.

Of all days for this to kick off, the final day of play was the worst. We were overwrought and exhausted as it was and this latest development threatened to push me over the edge, I thought, as I dithered about trying to find a clean shirt, clamping my hair into a ponytail, which like the rest of me was even more out of control than usual. I'd had virtually no sleep and I looked like I'd been in a wrestling match. I ran in.

'You just missed Jack,' said William, watching my reaction. 'He wanted to drop Frank but we're just about to open so he said he would hang onto him and drop him in to you later.'

'Thanks,' I said, giving nothing away and not taking on the quizzical expression on William's face.

He knew not to probe by my demeanour. And as ever, we had not a second to spare so the stream of people began and the next time I drew breath we had just finished serving lunch. It was busy. It was more than busy. Mouse and William in the kitchen. Hamish and I out front.

Hamish. The moment I saw him he put his hands up.

'Maddy, I am sorry, I …'

I held my hand up. 'Please don't,' I said, feeling wobbly and tearful. All I said to him as I pushed past towards the door to welcome some customers was: 'I thought blood was thicker than water …' in a low tone.

He looked like a skelped arse.

Good.

For the next few hours my new-found professionalism took over. The four of us worked as a team the way we always did. But there was a coolness between Hamish and I. No banter. Just an arch politeness born from the fact that one word out of place and the hairline splinter that was evident would crack wide open and the whole hellish story would come spewing out in front of everyone.

As soon as one table emptied another arrived. We turned the tables one after the other. We took breaks at different times – there was not a moment to have a conversation, which suited me fine. At 6 p.m. I grabbed a mug of soup and went back to the bothy to shower and change. As I rushed round the corner I clocked Jack's Land Rover sitting outside and staring out the passenger window was Frank.

Frank yipped with excitement when he spotted me. Jack opened the door and the stumpy wee dog came barrelling towards me and jumped up, defying gravity, into my arms.

'Hello, little man,' I said into his fur, holding him close, wanting to make him realise none of this bizarre day was his fault.

'Thank you,' I said coldly, turning to go inside.

Jack, ignoring the obvious snub, followed me. 'Can I talk to you, Maddy?'

I said nothing.

'Please?'

I wanted to have it out with him. Now wasn't the right time but I could see by his determined face I wasn't going to be able to deflect him.

'OK,' I said, 'but not here.'

He followed me in through the shop past a silent Noel who was with a client, but whose eyes widened as he caught my eye. Opening the bothy, we entered.

This was the first time Jack had been into my Lilliputian home and he dwarfed the place. He made it seem so tiny. I felt I was in the presence of a giant.

The air was sucked out of the room.

We were standing millimetres apart.

Surely he could hear my heart moving and swelling in my chest, breaking. 'You ignored my texts,' he stated simply.

My eyes filled with tears.

'You wouldn't return my calls.'

'The Birdie & Bramble is so busy I couldn't see you there,' I squeaked in a strangulated whisper.

Frank was joyous and twirling round his legs yipping. I could have strangled him.

I had run out of words.

'So I thought I had better come here and have it out, once and for all.'

'OK,' I said, backing away the whole metre and a half until I half fell, half sat down on the bed.

'Let's hear it,' I said, struggling to my feet to give some semblance of control.

'OK. First and foremost I would like to know what I have been accused of?'

'Identify fraud.'

'Sorry?'

'You told me you were called Jack. Apparently you are called James.'

'Christened James. Always Jack. Next?'

'Well that's identify fraud isn't it?'

'That's not identify fraud – that's what I've been called

since I was four. My grandfather was called James so to save confusion I became Jack.'

I swallowed hard. I cut to the chase. 'Why didn't you tell me Barclay is your dad? I just can't take it in, I mean …' My bloody chin started wobbling as I went on, 'I told you everything that was going on, from the insulting awful offer he made for the business – repossessing Dad's flat – I mean for God's sake, he evicted my dad!' I said as it dawned on me again, anger flaring. 'Your dad has a vendetta against me! In fact not just me – my family.' My chin stopped wobbling, hands on hips now, in high dudgeon. 'I told you I thought it was the Laird who reported the imaginary rat, cancelled our food orders, wrote the fake TripAdvisor reviews and caused the stramash about the bloody chairs on the pavement! I stood there like a daftie ranting and raving to you about them and you said not a word.'

Before he could utter a word I was off again, changing tack, on a roll. 'And what about Hamish? He's *my* cousin,' I said, sounding like a four-year-old having a tantrum. 'Mine! And he obviously knew all along. Why didn't he tell me? You two must have had a really good laugh at my expense.' I was running out of steam. I felt quite weak and wobbly again.

'No, no,' he interjected. 'Hamish felt so bad about it – he really did. The only reason he kept schtum was because I begged him not to say a word until I had time to tell you everything, the right way. And anyway, Hamish's not speaking to me now.'

I said out loud to myself more than him, 'What is the right way to tell me your dad is the man who has been trying to ruin me and—' fat tears spilled from my eyes '—my dad.'

'God I can't tell you how I wish he wasn't,' he said, clearly exasperated.

'Well he bloody well is and you should have told me that on day one.'

'I know I should have but it didn't seem relevant and then when I realised what was going on – well the opportunity never presented itself.'

'Well the opportunity presented itself last night,' I snottered, 'when Tooty your lovely stepmother told me – in front of everyone in the packed restaurant.'

'Told you what?'

'Told me your real name is James and that your father is Barclay MacPherson!'

He had the good grace to look stricken as I continued.

'And that we've been seeing a lot of each other.'

'Well we have.'

'Yes, well, if I'd known who you are, were … em … I wouldn't have.'

'Really?' He took a step towards me.

'Yes really.' I stood my ground, my resolve disintegrating like water.

His voice dropped another octave, his fists clenched. 'That woman is not my stepmother – she is nothing but a crass opportunist who married my fool of a father for his money.'

'So how does she know about me?'

'Maddy, everyone knows about you – about me – about us. Think about it. Why would we hide it? She was just stirring it and trying to upset you – and it's worked.' His anger was now palpable.

'Don't pass the buck – you should have told me who your father is.'

'I know, I know, but you made it perfectly clear how you felt about him and by the time I began to …' he reddened '…well anyway, the moment never seemed right to tell you.

I tried, Maddy, I did ... but the more I ... the harder it was ... and ...' He seemed to deflate. 'Well, I'm glad you know now.'

'Really?' I said, standing up to my full height, which next to Jack was just below shoulder height, which was most irritating when trying to be authoritative.

'Yes really. I have been estranged from my father since I was old enough to recognise him as a dishonest bully. I was brought up by my mum and we had nothing to do with him. The only reason I don't shout and scream about what sort of man he is, is because of Flora. No matter what a buffoon he is – he is her son and she loves him.'

God I hadn't even thought about Flora. I blurted, 'How could that lovely lovely woman have given birth to that beast?'

'Well they say you marry your mother and my mother Patricia is a sweetheart. A lovely, lovely woman. Flora and she got along famously from day one and whatever flaws my father displayed as a young man, Mum fell for him, and you know all bets are off where love is involved. Love is blind.'

'You can say that again,' I said out loud, wishing I hadn't as my entire body stung.

Ignoring my discomfort, he was intent and continued, 'Tooty appeared about ten years ago and married Dad for the title and the money and then found out he was virtually penniless. So now Tooty, aka Lady Barclay MacPherson, hasn't got a pot to piss in. When she saw the big house she thought she was set for life – then when it was too late she found out the house was falling to bits and is mortgaged up to the hilt. All she has is the title and the potential development of 125 North Street into a boutique hotel – the only possible compensation for having hitched her wagon to Dad.'

'Gosh,' I said rather unimaginatively.

'It is also in her best interests that my father and I stay

estranged because if the two of us were ever to rebuild a father–son relationship – which will never happen – all his assets and the title would naturally fall to me and my heir, was I ever to have one. That—' he struggled to find the right word '—trollop and I—' he erred on the side of generous '—have exchanged no more than twenty words in my life. She knows nothing about me.' He growled in a way that I'd never heard before. It made me quiver. I stood up even straighter. This was a new Jack. James or whoever the hell he was.

It was my turn. 'Well I feel like a bloody idiot. I have ranted and raved about the Laird this, the Laird that; the least you could have done was to tell me he was your bloody father!' I blurted, thinking stick that in your pipe and smoke it. 'And you didn't say a word … not a word …' Bloody tears were off again, rolling down my cheeks.

Jack handed me a handkerchief. Pavlov's dog almost took it but I shook my head, choosing instead to wipe my nose on my sleeve. Classy.

'Maddy … I was so …' he said, his eyes aflame.

Suddenly the door to the bothy swung open and there stood Marcus.

'Marcus!' I shouted.

'Oh! I do hope I'm not interrupting,' he said, his face twisting with sarcasm.

'You're not,' I said as Jack swapped places with him and barked, 'I've got things to do. I was just leaving.'

Things to do! He couldn't justify himself. He gave up just like that. He was off like a whipped dog. I wanted him to stop. See this through. I wanted Jack to turn round and say whatever he was going to say. Bloody Marcus.

'Are you OK?' he said, showing genuine concern that I was standing there in broad daylight blubbing. Which caused an immediate cessation of waterworks. Christ this was all I needed.

'What are you doing here?' I blurted in a not entirely friendly fashion.

'I wanted to surprise you,' he said.

'Well you certainly managed that,' I snapped, as Jack's back disappeared through the door into the shop, storming past Noel and away.

'I wanted to see you, Maddy, before tonight,' he said, moving in to kiss me. 'I want you to know how much I've missed you.' We kissed briefly. It did not feel good; he felt like a stranger.

I looked at him. The poor man did look upset and for a change sincere and what had just happened had nothing to do with him. I softened slightly.

'Come on, Marcus, sit down,' I said, moving to one end of the bed. He sat down next to me, shuffling closer. He didn't meet my eye, choosing to stare at the floor instead. 'I have thought a lot about the way I've behaved and it was wrong. On every level wrong. I didn't know how to handle it ... the whole death thing.'

I cringed. He was doing his best to make amends.

'So I have decided to cut down on my drinking and I'm not in Valencia,' he added dramatically.

'Valencia?' I blurted, having forgotten all about his sodding football trip.

'Yes, that was this weekend. I'm here!' he said triumphantly, insinuating I had won the big prize and a round of applause and a blow job might be in order.

He was on another planet. I had been so busy I had completely forgotten the whole Valencia thing, which seemed so inconsequential in comparison to the life-changing events

317

that I'd been dealing with. I felt a kernel of irritation in my belly; as usual it was all about him.

I had to deal with this but not now, not here. I just couldn't take any more bullshit.

'I'm sorry, Marcus, I really can't talk now. I need to get back to work. It's madness in the restaurant – it's the last day and we are stowed out. Tell me where you will be later. I'll come and meet you for a drink after we shut and we can sort things out. OK?'

Chapter 31

Our last shift. The final day of the Open went by in a flash. There was a constant queue of customers from the moment we opened until the moment, after waving our final customers off, I closed the heavy wooden door of The Birdie & Bramble for the last time.

I leant against it and sighed.

We had done it.

We had fulfilled our obligation to one another.

We were exhausted, elated and emotional.

The journey we had been on together was one none of us would ever forget.

I scrawled 'Closed for a well-earned rest' on the blackboard and put it in the window of The Birdie & Bramble before turning and indulging in a group hug with William, and Mouse, during which we were giddy with tiredness. Hamish was clattering around in the kitchen and that was fine. The less I saw of him when in the vicinity of a sharp knife, the better. Energy expended, it was with a sense of sadness everyone said their goodnights and trudged off to their respective homes apart from me. Exhausted though I was, I was off to meet Marcus. My one concession to going out was swapping my trainers for a pair of ridiculous heels, which I changed into at the entrance of the hospitality marquee Marcus had arranged to meet me in. I was well over an hour and half later than our planned meeting time so I wasn't even sure he would be there.

The pass Marcus had given me got me straight into the golfers' enclosure and over to the Bollinger Tent, corporate entertainment heaven. Not the ideal place to meet someone who had claimed to have stopped drinking, I thought, as I tiptoed over the grass trying to avoid my heels sinking into the marshy ground below to the entrance. It was rammed with people, all dressed to the nines, drinking, roaring with laughter and shouting at the same time. The golf had been over for some time and the party was in full swing. A couple of the professional golfers were in there too, surrounded by hangers-on, glassy-eyed and snapping photos.

Craning my neck, trying to see Marcus, I did the rounds for a couple of minutes being jostled and pushed between huddles of boozy party animals. I was just about to throw in the towel when I spotted a couple of familiar-looking faces from the office towards the bar so began to make my way over to say hi when something caught my eye further along the bar. I recognised him instantly. Marcus with his back to me in one of his devastating suits, hair slicked back, with a strikingly thin blonde clutching his arm, hanging off him like a string of snot. Felicity.

Taken aback I stopped and watched as Marcus's arm, casually thrown round her waist, moved lower and squeezed her bony bum and held her closer. Squirming, she threw her head back and laughed, before suddenly stopping, looking him in the eye and moving towards him for a kiss. Watching the way their lips met and their comfortable body language it was very obvious this was not the first time they had been in such close physical proximity. Drinking and snogging, periodically coming up for air, for a swig of wine before getting stuck in again, they had cleared quite a space round themselves at the bar. This explained why Felicity had been so keen to find out when I was coming back and encouraging me not to rush. What a bitch.

I was shocked. Not at their behaviour, nor their blatant lies, or her hypocrisy allegedly disapproving of interoffice relationships, but shocked that my reaction was relief. Relief that this ongoing non-event was officially over. That he could play tonsil hockey in public with another woman and I couldn't give a monkey's. Relief and freedom that at last we could move on. Well I could move on. He clearly already had.

I walked up behind them and tapped Marcus on the shoulder.

Dropping Felicity like a hot potato, he turned. 'Maddy!' He stepped away from her.

'Hi,' I said, smiling though my heart was yammering.

Felicity was drunk, her mascara halfway down her face, a complete mess. I smiled at her and looked her straight in the road-map eye.

'Welcome to St Andrews, Felicity.'

She was so pissed she just leered, revealing lipstick-stained teeth, grasping for Marcus to shore her up. She was steaming.

'I didn't think you were coming,' slurred Marcus.

'Clearly,' I said, looking at the bag of bones hanging off his arm.

'So anyway, I just popped in to let you know I've decided I'm not coming back.'

Stunned, they both looked at me. I turned my attention to the bottle blonde.

'And, Felicity, just a wee heads-up for you. When I upload the footage I just took of you two snogging, groping and ignoring your clients at the biggest corporate event of the year onto YouTube,' I said, waving my iPhone at them, 'given company policy about not shagging your colleagues, you'd better get into the office early Monday morning and resign before you're both sacked.'

Felicity started spluttering something at me, so for old times' sake, I held my hand up in front of her face, indicating she should shut up until I was good and ready to hear what she had to say. Which in this case was never.

Their jaws hung open. I bent down, took off one shoe, then the other, dropped four inches in height and with my head held high, stomped straight out of the marquee without a backward glance.

My gut was telling me to take time out, think long and hard where I wanted to be, what I wanted to do. The faster life was whizzing by, the more I wanted it to slow down so I could draw breath, think clearly, breathe. So I assumed it was my gut that had just resigned as it was as much of a shock to me as them.

Wandering back to the bothy barefooted, it was well after midnight. The streets were still populated with stragglers. Laughing, loving life, arm in arm, happy, and the reality of what I had just done hit home. The contrast between them and me. Here I was, single, unemployed and looking round my temporary lodging, virtually homeless. Peeling off my clothes and falling into bed, I was fully expecting a sleepless night and was hugely relieved when the next moment I knew, I was waking up with Frank snuggled into me. I had slept like a log.

Chapter 32

Jumping out of bed the following morning, it was a few moments before I remembered I didn't have to. It was all over. As I lay there reliving the previous night's extraordinary events, my phone beeped. A text from William. 'Fancy breakfast?'

'Yes!' I said straight back to him and we met thirty minutes later in Northpoint.

We were like two lost souls. Every waking moment had been spent in The Birdie & Bramble and now here we were, cast adrift with no idea what to do with ourselves.

I regaled him of the story of the previous night.

'Oh my God,' he said, his eyes on stalks. 'I wish I had been there.' He roared with laughter.

'Their faces were a picture.' I mopped up the tears of mirth seeping from my eyes.

'Are you going to upload it?'

'No. I didn't record it!' I grinned. 'But they don't know that.'

'And your resignation?' he said.

'God yes, I'm not quite sure where that came from, but in the cold light of day, despite the fact I am officially wetting myself, I have no regrets.' William squeezed my hand smiling as I confessed, 'Thing is, Will, I'm not sure where on earth I belong anymore.'

We sat in companionable silence, William feeding bits of

his croissant to Frank. Me sipping a cup of hot sweet tea. I couldn't eat a thing; my gut was knotted tight. 'I have Paul Sandiman the surveyor guy booked to do the revaluation tomorrow,' I said.

'Oh God how exciting!'

'I know but bloody terrifying – then what?'

'Well, Maddy, that is up to you.'

'That's the problem. Do I sell? And if so, to who? What if Barclay bloody MacPherson still wants to buy the lease?'

'Well he will but that's your call.'

I grimaced. He was right of course.

'The problem with The Birdie & Bramble is, no matter what, Barclay will always be the evil landlord and – most upsetting of all – he will always be Jack's dad and I never want to have anything to do with either of them again. So on that basis I think the best thing is if I move on and sell to the highest bidder, whoever that turns out to be.'

William understood and so we paid our bill and walked back to the cottage to put our feet up and do nothing. Bliss.

It was sad to think of all that hard work, the fun, our small but perfectly formed team, the goodwill, the customers, the feedback, the review, the column, the whole life-changing six weeks of madness all leading to this one moment.

William and I went along to let Sandiman the commercial property valuer in early the next morning. The place was immaculate and the guy was cautious, of course, but hugely positive and he had really done his homework.

'The upturn in turnover is incredible,' he observed, countering it with: 'Of course the Open is once in a blue moon, so they are exceptional circumstances,' before scribbling in his book.

Paul had a good look round the building. 'I have to say the place looks great, very sharp, and I have been doing a bit of background – your social media presence is strong.' He flicked through our cuttings and stats, which Noel had collated for us. 'And that review in the *Telegraph*. Well that is liquid gold,' he said, pointing to the window where the copies of the BB McGill review were still proudly displayed.

As we talked through everything in detail, we were constantly interrupted by people popping in to try and book tables who had to be told, 'Sorry we are closed.'

'For today?'

'No, full stop.'

The exclamations of disappointment, shock and in one case anger were overwhelming. The agent noted everything down.

As well as human interruption, the phone rang constantly as William tried to take the messages off the answerphone.

'We have over thirty-five requested bookings and we have only been closed two days – that must be worth a few bob,' he said as he rejoined us, with fresh coffee and the last of the home-made shortbread.

The valuer's poker face receded, failing to hide the fact he was impressed as he jotted it down in his notebook – either that or he was in love with the shortbread like every other human I had encountered.

'Well it's such a shame but we will have to phone them all back and let them know we are closed,' William said.

'Well if you want my advice,' said Paul, 'you should take the bookings. It would add to the potential value and show that there is ongoing support for the business – the message being it is not just about the Open.'

'True,' said William, 'but that's a major change of tack. We thought we were closed. End of. So what do you think?' he asked me.

'I don't know,' I shrugged.

The valuer added his tuppence worth. 'I would suggest you stay open or things will cool off very quickly. And ...'

'What?' I said, stunned at his advice having just mentally shut down on my life as a restaurateur.

'Well the second the doors close on any business, the momentum is lost. Most buyers will be looking for a business with potential, a healthy future, and are likely to be far more impressed with a busy bookings book and as for that goodwill? Well that is priceless to be honest.'

'Oh.' William and I looked at each other. His eyes sparkled. I grinned back.

'Well that was the shortest retirement in history,' I laughed.

'I'd better phone Mouse and Hamish as we can't do it with them,' he added and as an afterthought: 'And Noel!' He shot up out of his chair. 'And I'd better call Fraser, and all our suppliers too.' He disappeared through the twin door into the kitchen as I turned back to Paul.

'That was unofficial advice, not an order.' He smiled.

'To be honest, one day of doing nothing has just about killed me and by the look of that—' I gesticulated at the place William had recently vacated '—my partner in crime too. And what you said makes perfect sense. So thank you ... and what now?'

'Well you have options.'

'OK ... like what?'

'As soon as I give you a valuation, we can upload it onto our website and wait to see what happens.'

I nodded. This was what I had assumed. 'What are our other options?'

'Sell it at auction.'

'Auction?'

'Yes, traditionally a property auction was more of an Australian or American way of doing things but it has gathered momentum in the UK now too. The good thing about an auction is, it is a fast way to attract a lot of people as it is marketed far and wide. We only have two or three a year and we have one coming up – though it may be too soon.'

'Why, when is it?'

'Next week!'

'Shit! Is that enough time?' I turned towards the kitchen. 'William!' I shouted before he could answer. 'You need to hear this!' I turned back to Paul, who was rubbing the ear I had inadvertently hollered into. 'Oops, sorry about that.'

William came running back into the room already back in his apron with the bookings book in his outstretched hand.

Once William was up to speed, the valuer continued, 'So … yes … it is short notice but because of the Open, St Andrews is on the world map just now. It's been all over the TV, radio, newspapers and it's been looking idyllic. The weather has been good to us these past few days and you would be amazed at the number of people who dream of upping sticks and starting a new life somewhere like this.'

'Yes, it has been channelling *Brigadoon* with this weather,' William conceded.

The reality of living in Scotland in the winter months was a dramatically different experience, less than five hours of daylight, rain, snow, fog, sleet, and a biting wind that could render you numb from the nose down. Were we to highlight that side of life in the North, it would certainly result in a different offer and outcome.

Paul went on, 'Of course we also have a list of clients who are registered for commercial opportunities, people who already run food operations here or elsewhere and some of them are big hitters like Costa and Pizza Express,' he added.

I bristled at the thought of seeing the beloved Birdie &

Bramble subsumed by some faceless multinational. It was not appealing but I kept my mouth shut as he continued. 'So although it is late in the day if you two want to discuss it and let me know, I am fairly sure we can add The Birdie & Bramble onto the auction listings as a late lot.' My head was spinning. 'Of course it's your decision but my advice is, if you want to strike whilst the iron is hot, it's not going to get any hotter than this. I would go for it! But as I said before, this is just my advice not an order.'

I looked at William who, despite his grimace at the mention of Costa Coffee, as ever had my best interests at heart. He nodded sagely. 'Well, Maddy, I have to say, I think it makes perfect sense.'

I hadn't spent much time considering the timings or machinations of this bit of our plan. We had been so darn busy, but the feeling of getting everything finalised and done sooner rather than later was very appealing indeed. I could move on and if there was enough money after all the expenses, go and have a break, a real holiday. I had the small of matter of what I was going to do with the rest of my life to sort out, I thought drastically, and then my gut let its presence be known again as it blurted out via my mouth.

'OK, let's do it.'

William clapped his hands. 'That a girl!'

Paul sat down. 'OK. Let's get cracking.'

One phone call later he confirmed The Birdie & Bramble was being added onto the existing auction lots. We were on.

After several coffees and phone calls it was all set and Paul left saying he would call us later in the day to confirm it was all systems go.

William and I set about getting the restaurant ready to reopen the next day.

Thank goodness Mouse and Hamish didn't hesitate. They

were back on board. Hamish would have served customers butt naked if I had asked him, he was so keen to make up for not telling me about Barclay being Jack's dad. He was very keen to talk it through but I wasn't there yet. I needed distance, the wound was too raw, but at least I didn't want to kill him anymore.

Chapter 33

The following morning we reopened for business. It was as if we had never shut. The rapturous response we received from our customers was so encouraging and of course Ewan Blair put a piece in the St Andrews paper and Facebook page, which gave us an enormous lift reading the positive and supportive comments from so many people.

With just seven days exactly until the auction, we caned it. Our exhaustion was replaced by adrenalin for this last push as our banter and working rhythm kicked in. Although the Open was over, the throng of tourists that flocked to the east coast of Scotland in midsummer didn't seem to decrease at all.

Working hours numbed my ability to think about anything other than seeing our plan through to its conclusion. During the occasional moments of peace between waking and sleeping, my mind would turn to Jack.

Since his rapid departure from the bothy, I hadn't seen or heard one word. I was desperate to ask Hamish where he was but I didn't want it being reported that I was interested in his whereabouts. I had some self-respect. I was the one who said I didn't want to discuss it. Which I didn't. But the whereabouts of those eyes, that man, those long rangy limbs, was the only thing I could think about during those brief moments of rest. Of course life went on and Frank needed his morning walk so after a few days I decided to take the high ground and return to my beach routine. I knew by the skittish feeling as I approached the beach that despite the pretence, I didn't really care – every cell of my body protested and willed The Merchant of Venison to be there. Of course my plan was, if I did see him, to ignore him. This being the best way to show him my routine had not been disrupted by his shenanigans. Despite this bravado, my heart ached for him – and guttingly he was nowhere to be seen.

Walking to and from work I looked for him. Depositing the takings, collecting fresh bread, nipping back and forward to the bothy between shifts, at all times I kept my eyes peeled. Casually meandering into Uncle Fraser's, I gazed at the cold counter aimlessly, focusing on the venison. He had clearly been here.

Fraser was on it. 'You aright, Maddy? You look like you've lost a pound and found a penny.'

I hoisted the corners of my mouth into a smiling formation. 'No I'm fine ...' Desperate to ask if he had seen Jack ... I started, 'I just wondered ...' Oh God. How to ask without sounding like a lovesick, annoyed, confused idiot.

'Wondered what, dear?' he said, trying to guide me to the end of a sentence, which was proving difficult as I mooned about.

'I was wondering ... if ...'

'Aye, Maddy, spit it out will you?'

'Oh yes, sorry, I was wondering if I could have half a dozen of your St Andrews sausages, please.'

'Sure,' he said, scooping up a link of six stalwart sausages, wrapping them in greaseproof paper and handing them over.

'Please put them on the slate,' I said.

'Okey-doke,' he said, watching me carefully, aware I was behaving strangely. 'Anything else I can help you with?' Meaning anything other than butchery.

'No, I best be off. Thanks, Fraser, see you soon.'

So all my attempts to find Jack failed. He was still supplying Fraser and as a result, the restaurant with his venison, but he seemed to have disappeared off the face of the earth. I thought I saw his big old four-wheel drive a couple of times but on the off-chance it was him, I had dived into a doorway or turned away pretending to be looking for something in my handbag. So I couldn't be sure if it was him; although I was looking for him, I was hiding from him at the same time. It was manoeuvre of monumental proportions but I had no option. I was upset he was who he was, upset who his dad was, upset he had hoodwinked me and upset I was as upset as this, as I was fairly sure by this stage I was in love with him. So all in all it was a lose-lose situation; the sooner I was off, the better.

Six days of mayhem later, auction day arrived. The Birdie & Bramble was closed for the day. We had made an executive decision that we would all be there. After all, no-one wanted to miss out on this, the culmination of our hard work and months of planning. The level of excitement was high as William, Hamish, Mouse and I gathered outside Russacks Hotel, the venue for the auction, watching as bidders gathered.

We filed in and sat at the back of the room to get an overview of proceedings. There were a good few people on phones round the room dealing with the online bidders. There was a real buzz as the auctioneer took to the temporary podium, which had been erected in the now-packed conference room.

As a late entry we had been given the number 37A – right at the end of the auction. We had a good while to wait but

I wanted to see the process in action and get a feeling for who was bidding for what.

The lots were a real mixed bag. Quite a few residential flats, a few repossessions, a hotel in Pitlochry, a cafe in Pittenweem, a commercial block in Sighthill, Edinburgh, some forestry lots and a ski chalet in Glenshee. The only other restaurants were in the Central belt, one in the heart of Dundee and the other at the side of the A90. So The Birdie & Bramble was unique in that we were the only restaurant for sale in St Andrews. We were all wedged onto a bench as the sale kicked off. It was going to be a long wait but the whole process was fascinating – my fate was in the auctioneer's hands and I wanted to see if he knew his onions.

I was a nervous wreck.

What if no-one bid?

What if it was less than I was offered all those weeks ago?

How much was enough?

Was the bar open?

Paul, the commercial estate agent and valuer, waved and came over, smiling broadly.

'Well it's looking good; we have had over sixty information packs requested – now that doesn't guarantee sixty bidders but it does indicate a very high level of interest.'

I grinned at him. 'Sixty! Wow.'

'Yes quite.' He smiled and looked at his watch. 'You realise you've quite a wait?'

'I know but we couldn't be anywhere else today. We're too excited.' I indicated to the others squashed alongside me on the bench. William stood up and shook his hand, Hamish joined in too and Mouse waved shyly.

He laughed. 'Quite the day out!'

'How long do you think it will be until it's us?' I blurted.

'Well we are the late and last entry so I hope you've got

333

your sandwiches with you.' William nodded and held up the cool box containing an array of snacks and drinks, indicating they were prepared for all eventualities. Paul laughed. 'Of course you do.' He returned to his lift. 'Well on average a lot takes between five and ten minutes so ... about three hours.'

If he had said twenty-four we would have stayed put.

I wasn't going anywhere. Neither were the others by the look of things. Hamish and Mouse, hands clamped together, William scanning the room for familiar faces.

After the initial excitement had died down, we were all getting restless and taking it in turns to stretch our legs whilst the others held firm on our bench. It was my turn and after checking for messages I was satisfied there was nothing of any importance going on and was ready to return to the others when I saw him. Jack. He just strode in and the second I spotted him I felt physically sick. I hadn't seen him since that day in the bothy and here he was.

Brazen as you like, I thought, he's here to do his father's bidding ... to buy The Birdie & Bramble right under my nose. How I could have fallen for his obvious charms? Eliciting all that information from me, finding out how I ticked, how I would react ... What an idiot I was, as now in the cold light of day it all seemed so obvious.

Anger flooded through me. I turned away, annoyed at how he made me feel, which is when I felt his touch on my shoulder.

'Maddy,' he said.

'Jack,' I croaked.

'What lot are we on?'

'Fourteen. Don't worry, you've plenty of time 'til The Birdie & Bramble comes up,' I said coldly.

'Maddy. You have to come with me now.'

334

I looked at him. 'Now? Are you mad?'

'Maddy, I'm serious – you have to come with me.' He pulled my arm with some force.

'Get your hands off me,' I wheezed in a stage whisper, pulling my arm out of his grasp.

'Please,' he said, holding my shoulders, forcing me to look at him. To avoid a scene and because I had forgotten how to breathe, I nodded and followed him outside.

'Thank you,' he said gently.

'Never mind the niceties,' I said. 'What on earth are you talking about? You can't just burst in here after…'

'We need to go and see Flora.'

'Flora?' I felt my stomach drop. 'Is she ill?'

'No. But it's something to do with The Birdie & Bramble, Maddy.' He stopped and looked seriously into my eyes. 'Trust me.'

'Trust you?' I snorted bitterly.

'OK then, never mind me, trust Flora,' he said, turning to face me and looking straight into my soul again. I do wish he wouldn't do that. I was putty in his hands. Bloody man.

'Well… I…' My body response was to turn to jelly. My gut told me to go. My heart was in my throat. Logic warned me it might be a trick. I looked round. William, Hamish and Mouse were all in the room. We still had a good hour and a half before our lot came up. If it was really that important then…

'OK,' I capitulated. 'But this better not be another trick… and we have to be quick.'

I knew when it came to his grandmother he would never do anything other than honour her, which was why I allowed myself to be ushered into his Land Rover, double parked outside.

'Come on!' he said again, opening the door. 'They are expecting us.'

'Who?' I asked, but we were off at speed. I had no time to get my seatbelt on as he ripped into first and tore off along the road, screeching to a halt not a minute later outside the bank. Hazard lights flashing, he abandoned it right outside on the pavement, much to the incredulous stare of passers-by, and we went skidding into the bank.

Marching up to the front of the queue apologising to the assembled customers, he announced, 'This is a matter of urgency. Gordon Ferguson is expecting me—' he looked at me ... gulp '—us.'

My eyes were out on stalks as I dashed over to stand behind him, as confused as the bemused onlookers.

'Come this way, Mr MacPherson,' said a neat little man, in a surprisingly gruff Scottish voice. Wordlessly we did as ordered, following him to a door leading us downstairs to a long dimly lit corridor. What on earth was going on?

'Mr Ferguson is waiting for you,' he said, opening a vaulted door at the end of the corridor.

In we went, to a room where the walls were lined with small numbered boxes and to my astonishment sitting at a small table in the middle of it all were Gordon Ferguson and Flora.

'Maddy, take your necklace off,' Jack commanded. Melting at his authoritative tone, dumbstruck, I did as he asked.

He laid it on the table. Flora smiled, uncurled her hand and plopped something down next to it. 'Thanks, Gran,' he said as he unfurled it and much to my amazement, it was a chain, with a charm on it, the exact mirror image of my necklace.

'Snap!' said Flora, laughing.

'There's two of them? I'm sorry I don't understand,' I said, blinking to see if I was imagining things or seeing double.

'Gosh, would you look at that. It's been a long long time since we've seen one of these,' said the bank manager, holding the two chains aloft.

'What's going on?' I demanded.

'Well this is a key, to be exact two halves of a key, which meant in the old days, the two key holders had to be present in order to open the safety deposit box. Sort of insurance if you like.'

My eyes were boggling now. 'So you're saying my charm isn't a charm at all but half of a key and Flora's is the other.' My voice was at least three octaves higher as the penny dropped. 'So who is NCB? Do they own the box?'

'National Commercial Bank,' said Ferguson, 'that was what the Royal Bank was called in the early days. Now as I said to Mr MacPherson earlier, don't get your hopes up. More often than not, the safety deposit boxes these keys are made to open are empty, but because they are rather attractive in their own right, a piece of kitsch, Victoriana if you like, they were kept as pieces of jewellery.'

Sounds about right, I thought. Still holding the two keys, one in each hand, I saw they were almost identical. I could have screamed I was so excited.

'So ... this key ...' He examined them closely. 'I would estimate is from about ...'

Jack, on a knife-edge of anticipation like myself, butted in. 'I don't mean to be rude, Mr Ferguson, but we are very tight for time,' he said.

'Oh of course, I'm sorry,' said the whiskery wee man who happily halted his infomercial on the quirks of the Victorian banking world and, looking at the number on the keys, slid a ladder over and examined the myriad of boxes in front of him, until he saw our one, No. 286. Stopping, he slid the long rectangular box out of its slot, lifting it down carefully and putting it on the table.

'Right, one key should fit in that end, the other one here,' he said, pointing to the elaborate locks at each end.

I couldn't breathe.

'Right, I will leave you to it,' he said, his eyes twinkling. 'Good luck.'

They were almost mirror images of one another. I picked up my one. 'After you,' said Jack, pointing at the box.

'Let's do it together,' I said.

My hands were shaking as I placed my key in the lock at one end. He placed his in the other.

'After three.'

'One, two, three.' There was a click.

'Maddy?'

'No, you do it,' I said, my heart beating in my throat.

Another slight turn and the lightly sprung lid was free. The air in the room was stifling. From knowing nothing about this thirty minutes ago, I was all of a sudden imagining rubies, diamonds, cash, but rather disappointingly, all that it held was a buff envelope fixed with a wax seal. As I had suspected not very exciting, I thought, slightly irritated I was missing the auction for this melodramatic nonsense as Jack took the paper out and read it.

Screaming back to Russacks Hotel, we made it just in time. 'God, Maddy, where have you been? The Birdie & Bramble is the next lot! I've been phoning and texting – we thought you'd been kidnapped,' squealed William.

'We thought you were going to miss it!' said Hamish. 'We're up!' squealed Mouse as the auctioneer confirmed.

'Next up, ladies and gentlemen. Lot 37A.'

There was a frisson round the room.

Jack caught my eye from the other side of the room. I nodded. And so the bidding started.

Barclay's big red fist went up straight away. Hardly a poker face, I thought.

Another man in an awful pair of pink trousers in the corner stuck his arm up too.

'He's one of Dad's stooges,' whispered Jack.

An online bidder put in a bid indicated by the hand of the guy in the corner holding the phone.

The bids were coming in thick and fast.

'For God's sake, are they all after the lease?' exclaimed William.

'It's your fault,' I said, 'you're a brilliant chef!'

He grinned.

Mouse and Hamish were rapt.

Watching Barclay stretch and preen and bluster was very satisfying and he got himself into quite a lather.

No matter how much over the odds the bids went, we knew how much it meant to him. The determination on his fat face was evident, Tooty by his side egging him on. One by one the other parties dropped out until Barclay was the highest bidder.

I was on tenterhooks.

'Going. Going...'

My nerves couldn't take it and just as the gavel was about to come down on the lease at just over £123,000...

'STOP!' shouted Jack, holding his arm up.

The auctioneer looked nonplussed.

'Stop,' I repeated, standing up, pushing my hand in the air in a far less confident manner.

William, Hamish and Mouse stared at me, then Jack, then me again, their mouths open, incredulous.

All heads rotated between the two of us. 'This is most irregular,' said the auctioneer.

And then, in front of the crowd, in front of everyone, Jack made his way to the lectern, stood up at the front and read out the content of the letter from the safety deposit box.

'This legally binding letter dated 1969 states the Campbell family, represented today by Ms Madeline Campbell...' He pointed in my direction.

All eyes were on me as I waved and confirmed, 'Yes, that's me!'

Instantly they turned back as Jack continued, 'The Campbell family are leaseholders of The Birdie & Bramble until such time as the business ceases trading. And I quote: "Until that day Joseph Campbell and his descendants retain the right, in accordance with an agreement between Sir James B MacPherson" – my grandfather,' he stated clearly, '"and Joseph Campbell – to buy the building in which The Birdie & Bramble operates, outright, freehold for the princely sum of £1."'

Barclays face went from its usual purple to deeper undulating crimson as he sat down with a clatter on a chair that looked like it would give way any second. He uttered not one word of objection; he looked stricken.

Jack nodded to me, and William, Hamish and Mouse, gawping, stood up to let me out from our bench. I walked from the back of the room up the central aisle to the front where I stopped right in front of Barclay, the sputtering buffoon.

He looked at me.

I held out my trembling hand.

His fat fist unclenched and he held out his palm. I dropped a coin onto it. 'There's £1 as agreed,' I said.

'The building and The Birdie & Bramble is yours!'

declared Jack, jumping up. And suddenly the room was in an uproar.

The auctioneer ruffled his papers, and marched towards us.

The other bidders and the assembled throng of nosy locals looked on. Tooty, whose face despite excessive Botox scrunched up into a grotesque shape, was holding onto Barclay's arm, thumping it, trying to galvanise him into action. But his livid face told us, without any doubt, he had known about it all along.

He was counting on the fact the keys would never be found, the letter left undiscovered, the truth never discovered. But now it was over.

The Birdie & Bramble, the business and the premises were mine forever.

The aftermath was not pretty.

Barclay, speechless, was led out by his lawyer.

Tooty, tottering behind in her inappropriate shoes, demanded answers, 'Barclay? Barclay? For fuck's sake, Barclay! What the hell have you done now?'

Jack, William, Noel, Hamish, Mouse, Frank and I?

We went to the pub.

Chapter 34

Our initial euphoria was quenched after a few drinks yet I was still reeling that The Birdie & Bramble was officially mine – bricks and mortar, the whole jingbang. As the initial hysterical chat calmed, we sat down to listen as Jack explained where he had been for the past few days.

Jack was frank and succinct without dressing it up.

Determined to prove he was not in cahoots with his estranged father and to make amends for the way he had handled things, he made it his mission to prove as best he could that Barclay was behind the various ham-fisted attempts to defame us and to collate all necessary evidence for us to take appropriate action.

And he had done a sterling job.

It took time, cooperation and some underhanded methodology to gather the proof but he did it. Barclay was no technical genius and had failed to cover his tracks so once Jack got into the system he simply printed out copies of emails Barclay had sent to Environmental Health reporting the sighting of a rat under an assumed name. Carly Brose Chapman.

He placed the relevant emails on the table for us all to read.

'Jeez that's a name and a half – who's that?' I asked.

'It took me a while to work it out but if you put Barclay MacPherson into Anagram Generator, it spews out all sorts of answers and that was one of them. Which is of course in itself another way of confirming it was him.'

'Pratt,' said Hamish and then seeing Jack, 'Sorry, mate, I know he's your dad.'

'Don't apologise,' said Jack, 'he is my father in name only – Carly Brose Chapman or otherwise.'

I stifled a smile. And he went on.

This new moniker Barclay had put to good use, using it to complain to the Planning Department and insist we remove our outside seating area.

Carly had a TripAdvisor account too, which Jack had been able to prove quite easily was a sham account as he had only ever reviewed one restaurant – The Birdie & Bramble and it was brutal.

'Not exactly a criminal mastermind is he?' said William, rocking back on his chair with mirth.

'Exactly, so his account was shut down immediately when they realised he was not a genuine diner and clearly had a vendetta against us.'

And the review that must have galled him the most. Taking it upon himself as a 'fellow foodie' to email BB McGill at the *Telegraph* to tell her that The Birdie & Bramble had just reopened and would be ripe for review, thinking that would really finish us off. This explained how she ended up eating in The Birdie & Bramble just three days after we reopened, and of course that backfired spectacularly when she loved it.

'Wow, Hercule,' I said, leafing through the papers he had read out. 'I can't believe you managed to find this all out – how did you do it?'

'Basically I needed access to his email account, it's an AOL account, and he's had it forever. In fact I set it up for him when I was just a kid – the password was his birthdate and the name of my dog at the time. It was a long shot but

I tried that first and couldn't believe it when I got straight in. So I could get into all the stuff if I needed to, actually so could you now.' He grinned. 'He really has no idea what happens in the real world.'

'Poor Carly,' said Hamish and we all burst out laughing.

'So what will happen to him?' I asked, being vaguely sensitive of the fact he was still Jack's father, and more pointedly Flora's son.

'Well he's in trouble for setting up a stooge to bid for him at the auction so his credibility is shot and of course he's got all these debtors who've been hanging about for years waiting for his elusive hotel project to come off. I hear they are after him like a pack of wolves.'

'What will he do now?'

'Who cares?' blurted Hamish.

'Well, Flora?' I said more to Jack than any of the others.

'The big house is on the market, which may make him a few thousand, if anyone is mad enough to buy it – it's falling to bits. That should give him enough time to either pay off some of his scarier debtors or disappear.'

'What about Tooty?' I asked.

'She knew what he was the day she married him – a pillock. Admittedly she thought he was a rich pillock but it seems she's standing by him, so who knows, maybe she did love him after all.'

'Birds of a feather and all that,' said Hamish.

'Better the devil you know,' added Mouse.

'Well one thing, by the sound of it, he won't be bothering us again,' said William.

'I think that deserves another round,' said Mouse as she and Hamish approached the bar with our drinks order for a canoodle.

William, Noel, Jack and I sat silent for a moment, just letting it all sink in.

'So do you think Barclay knew The Birdie & Bramble should be Maddy's all along?' William probed.

Jack nodded. 'No doubt about it. You saw his face at the auction, resigned to what was happening when you gave him that coin. He knew damn well. Apparently there were two copies of that letter, both signed by Sir James and your Joe. Joe got one copy and the other one was kept by my grandfather, which, with all his papers, fell to my grandmother Flora when he passed away. Barclay insisted he handled all the paperwork in Grandpa's estate, as she knew he would. But Flora is a bright woman and nobody's fool and she knew her idiot son well enough to realise he would liquidate everything into ready cash; so to protect herself and the rest of the family, she had the foresight to make copies of everything, which she handed over to him. Of course he was none the wiser. But Flora kept the originals.'

'Do you think Barclay destroyed his copy?'

'Yes, I'm sure of it. Losing The Birdie & Bramble was the only thing stopping him turning 125 North Street into a hotel and the only hope he had of getting out of the shitstorm of debt he's created. Flora knew your dad would never take advantage of Sir James's offer to buy the building for a pound, so she popped the original document into that safety deposit box, gave one key to Joe and kept the other for herself. Out of Barclay's hands and in the safest place of all.'

Wow. We all sat staring at our drinks. Jack sat back, understandably quiet after declaring in public that his father was a liar and a cheat.

'So what do we do from here?' I asked.

'You're the boss,' said William.

'Mine's a pint,' I said, as leaping to his feet Noel made his way to the bar.

Drink was taken; fun was had. I still kept a distance from Jack. There was nothing about him I didn't adore but things were in such a state of flux I had no idea if what I was feeling was real or it was just the extraordinary circumstances that had brought me to this point. I was so confused. My priority was to work out what the hell I was doing.

Living in London?

St Andrews?

Somewhere completely different?

And what to do.

The Birdie & Bramble belonged to me now but did I really want to be a restaurateur? Having watched my father live and breathe the business, was it truly my destiny to live and work here too?

It was a huge responsibility and one I couldn't quite see myself taking on, not now, not on my own.

My head was like a toyshop as I tossed and turned all night.

Frank watched me punching pillows and checking my mobile every half an hour from under his hairy wee eyebrows sensing change was coming.

By 5 a.m. I was up, hauling the box Mouse had filled with Dad's stuff, from Noel's storeroom into the bothy. It was bursting with pictures, knick-knacks, all sorts of things that meant nothing to anyone yet everything to me. Having sorted through it by 7 a.m. I needed air so headed off to the beach with Frank, throwing a stick, laughing as he skipped through the waves and the further I walked, the clearer my thoughts became. By the time we turned for home some time later, I was lighter of step and suddenly like a slap in the chops, I stopped dead in my tracks and I knew what I had to do.

Chapter 35

By nine I was knocking on the boys' door. A bleary-eyed William opened up and leaving the door ajar mumbled, 'I'll put the kettle on. I'm never drinking again,' as Frank shot past him like an exocet into the kitchen and plonked himself next to the Aga, a place he always received snacks and cuddles.

Closing the door behind me, I followed them through as William shakily poured boiling water into the teapot and shuffled about slicing some bread to make toast. His hair was on end looking, for the first time since I had met him, dishevelled.

'Are you OK?' I asked.

'Yeh,' he said, flumping into a chair and raking this hands through his hair leaving him looking rather Ken Dodd, I thought. 'It's just ... well ... I'm just sad it's all over ... I barely slept last night ... It's been hard as hell but ... well I've loved every minute.' He looked at me.

'I know exactly what you mean,' I smiled back.

He poured the tea as we contemplated what he had said.

The toaster pinged as he reached over, plopping it onto our respective plates.

'Thanks,' I said, smearing a thick buttery layer on to it.

'You're welcome.'

A couple of sweet jammy mouthfuls later, I took a long

swig of my tea, cleared my throat and started, without really knowing how I was going to tell him.

'So ...' I said.

'So what?' he said smiling and brushing crumbs off his dressing gown.

'So I have made a decision.'

'Oh? Really?' His eyebrows indicated interest.

'Yes.'

'So what is it?'

'Well one thing I know in my heart of hearts is I do not want to run the restaurant and then wake up one day and find thirty years have sped by and I am still here – just letting time pass, letting the wheels go round ... you know?'

William nodded. 'He did love it though.'

'Yes he did. And I do too but if I stay here now I will end up resenting it, and him and even you and I have a lot of places to see and things to do before I settle down, if I settle down ... and even then ... well I don't know where I want to settle ... the whole restaurant world, well it was Dad's thing, not necessarily mine.'

'Oh right,' said William, his shoulders drooping, failing to hide his disappointment and stirring another teaspoon of sugar into his tea.

I continued. 'The thing is you and I have come so far and achieved so much ... it is really has been phenomenal ... and you know I couldn't have done any of it without you.'

William stopped staring at his tea and met my gaze. 'Nor me without you – you have helped me realise what I want to do, and mad as it is being in a hot kitchen working un-sociable hours at the beck and call of the general public—' he laughed '—I can honestly say I have never loved anything more.'

'But, William, you have a rare and remarkable talent,' I added.

'Thanks, Maddy.' He blushed. 'I suppose what's for you doesn't go past you,' he added.

'Well put, which brings me to my decision.' He looked at me directly. 'If it's OK with you, I would like to make you my business partner. Fifty-fifty. Straight down the middle.'

'What?' he said, all semblance of droopiness gone in a second. 'But I don't have the ...'

I held my hand up. 'Let me clarify – in case there is any doubt – I am giving you half of the business.'

'Maddy, you can't do that.'

'I can and I am. I have already sent an email to Gerald asking him to draw up the necessary documents.'

'But I can't accept that,' he objected.

'Why not? Anyway you can and I sincerely hope you will, William. Regard it as a gift.' He was about to object when I raised my hand. 'Please let me finish. You know we are a great team and in addition you have Noel in your corner and he loves the very bones of you. We are at a different stage in life – you are settled, you know what you want, which is great, but I am all over the place and I have a lot to sort out. I know St Andrews is in my blood and The Birdie & Bramble is very much part of that so if you accept my gift, you will be my business partner and caretaker of The Birdie & Bramble. All I ask is that you keep the door open for me if and when I ever want to come back.'

William was speechless at first, but as he nodded, his eyes filled with tears as he spread his arms wide and I stepped into his dressing-gowned embrace.

Chapter 36

A couple of days later, all necessary documentation signed, witnessed and registered, a very excited William and supportive Noel and I left Gerald's office. It was almost lunchtime.

'Hungry?'

'Does a fish have a waterproof head?' I was off early the next day and having spent the last couple of days packing up the bothy I'd been surviving on crisps and pot noodles... old habits and all that.

'OK, you nip round and get Frank and we'll meet you outside the Birdie. We can grab something there,' said William.

Minutes later with Frank strutting along by my side I turned the corner and saw a clump of people standing outside the restaurant. As I got nearer I realised it was William, Noel, Sarah, Hamish and Mouse ... What on earth was going on, I wondered, when the familiar muddy old Landy crunched to a halt and a pair of long, khaki-clad legs swung out onto the pavement. My heart stopped as he turned and waved at me, The Merchant of Venison.

'Come on, you lot!' he said. 'Everybody in ...' And opening the back of his Landy, everyone started talking at the same time, all carrying baskets and rugs, overemotional with tears teetering. I was absolutely thrilled as I scooped Frank up and clambered in beside them.

Rollicking over the dunes, we drove to the furthermost part of the beach. Rugs were rolled out, a windbreak put up for effect. Jack even produced some plastic buckets and spades and dug a huge hole before asking if I wanted to be buried up to my neck for old times' sake. I could have wrestled him into that hole and kissed him until the world ended but there was food to be eaten.

There were posh sandwiches, salt and vinegar crisps, hard-boiled eggs, smoked salmon blinis, Perthshire berries and a lemon tart from Rory's. We were about to get stuck in when Jack held his hand up and said, 'Wait!' He handed round some champagne flutes and produced a bottle. Clearing his throat he announced, 'As you know today is a very special occasion. It's our little send-off for you, Madeline Campbell, and I think it would be fair to say one way or another since you came back to St Andrews you have turned all of our lives upside down. So I, sorry *we*, wanted you to know, we will miss you and hope you come this way again soon and what more fitting way to mark the occasion than with this?' he said, popping the cork. 'It's the elderflower champagne, made with the elderflowers you picked with your own fair hand.'

My throat closed, as the bubbles gurgled up out of the bottle and into my glass. I couldn't see a thing, my eyes so full of tears, as we gathered together and chinked glasses.

'To Maddy,' said Jack, laughing at me now as I was heading into a full snottery sob.

'To The Birdie & Bramble and to the best friends in the world,' I warbled, necking it in a oner.

We stayed on the beach until the sun went down and we were wearing all the beach towels, and the windbreak was being used to tuck in our legs to keep us warm. At some point we built a bonfire and then settled down again, singing songs, telling stories. Then the night was over, it was sunrise, and gathering our stuff we trailed back, dropping off our stuff at the Landy before walking along the beach back to St Andrews.

Mouse and Hamish arm in arm, Noel and William throwing sticks for Frank, Jack and I dragging behind, paddling at the edge of the tide, savouring every moment.

'Thank you for this,' I said. 'I loved every minute of it.'

'Me too.' He grinned, slipping his arm round my shoulders. I shivered as we walked on in silence. The thought of leaving this man, this place, this moment was too much.

'What happens now, Maddy?'

'I need to remember what it feels like to be me again, to work out what I want out of life, where I want to be and...'

'With who?' he asked, stopping and turning me round to face him.

I looked up at him, into those eyes, today dark liquid, as they burned into mine. I held my breath, then as if attached by an invisible thread, my heart winding it in, I parted my lips and gently he kissed me and this time I kissed him back.

Our timing was impeccable. I was leaving St Andrews in less than an hour. We walked back to the bothy hand in hand, with an unspoken feeling something extraordinary had happened. I had no words. I had committed to go, and go I must. Stopping outside the bothy, he held my face gently in his hands, and we kissed again.

'Madeline Campbell...' he sighed in a voice that made my insides liquefy, memorising the sensation of his lips on mine when a taxi pulled up, window down, elbow poking out, a cheeky face above it.

'Aye aye, you two get a room,' he laughed.

'Taxi for Campbell?' said William, bustling out with my luggage.

Between William and Noel hovering, Hamish and Mouse dashing out behind them, Frank twirling in between everyone's legs, getting in the way and Jack standing there looking a little lost, there was just enough time for some hurried hugs and promises to stay in touch before I was off.

Chapter 37

First step: London.

I had arranged to see my old boss to thank him in person for sanctioning my sabbatical and more awkwardly to explain my sudden resignation. I was candid, as was he, admitting his generous offer of time off had been less to do with my grief and more to do with the not so 'secret' relationship I had been conducting with Marcus. He had known about it all along, in fact he described it as 'Marcus's modus operandi'. So it seemed I was neither the first nor the last. The little shit.

He also told me on the Monday after the Open he arrived at work to find Felicity in his office in a terrible state. When he asked what on earth was going on, she blurted out the whole sorry story of their trip north culminating in the confession that she was living in fear of a threatened YouTube upload of herself and Marcus groping each other in the Go Radio hospitality tent going viral. The footage that didn't exist – a fact I chose not to mention.

Incandescent Marcus was at it with yet another member of staff, Adam sacked him the same day and put Felicity on a final warning.

As I thanked him for filling me in, he reiterated if I had a change of heart his door would always be open, which was lovely to hear.

Coming out of his room I saw Felicity at the other side of the office gesticulating wildly, bouncing up and down out of her chair, practising for the Horse of the Year Show. I waved sweetly, turning my back on her, said my final farewells and slipped out, smirking.

That night, as my old flatmate Keira cooked us a spag bol, I unfolded the huge map of the world, crinkled and worn, rescued by Mouse from my childhood bedroom wall. All pins were now replaced by yellow stickers and numbers, which corresponded to the itinerary I now held in my hand.

'All seven continents?' she exclaimed.

'Yes.' I grinned nervously. 'I made a promise to Dad—' I gently stroked a rumple on the map '—and I'm going to keep it.'

'How long will you be away for…'

'I don't know … It's a one-way ticket, in one direction round the world…'

A flashback to Jack and I, our kiss on the beach, gave me a shiver. I had never felt a connection like that with another living being, and yet, I had to go. Half to Keira and half to the memory of Jack, I whispered, 'I'll be back one day.'

As the jumbo taxied along the runway, I imagined Felicity reading the email I'd sent late last night finally putting her out of her misery, admitting there never was a recording of her and Marcus groping each other at the Open. Wishing her well and suggesting in future she would be best advised to follow company policy and refrain from shitting on her own doorstep or anyone else's, specifically mine, again.

Soaring higher and higher, further and further away from London, St Andrews, my friends, family, my life, my heart squeezed. Jack. Cheeks wet with tears, I closed my eyes and, taking a deep breath, I whispered, 'One day we will visit every single continent in the whole wide world … and boy what a day that will be.'

Acknowledgements

Thanks to my husband David Howie Scott for starting his restaurant Howies all those years ago, which gave me the setting and a whole lot more for The Birdie and Bramble.

Thanks also to the men and women I am proud to call friends who have been with me all the way.

Thanks to Allan Rennie, who took a leap of faith and gave me a column in the *Sunday Mail* many years ago. Without that, this would never have happened.

Thanks to Professor Simon Johnson, the expert on LAM, the rare lung condition I live with, whose knowledge and expertise fill me with the optimism and belief I can do anything.

To Jenny Brown, my extraordinary agent and the most patient woman in Europe, who had faith that one day after many false starts I would finish and I have!

And to Victoria Oundijan at Orion, whose infectious enthusiasm and belief in this book has made my dream come true.